Praise for *The Helios Conspiracy*

"A terrific tale with a whirlwind plot. Jim DeFelice has all the tools of a masterful storyteller. *The Helios Conspiracy* is a world-class adventure."
—Clive Cussler,
New York Times bestselling coauthor of
Crescent Dawn

"Jim DeFelice has an extraordinary imagination and a delightfully readable style; his stories sizzle."
—Stephen Coonts,
New York Times bestselling author of
The Disciple

"*The Helios Conspiracy* grabs you with a great story and intriguing characters. Even the bad guys are well done. It's fast paced and thoroughly enjoyable."
—Larry Bond,
New York Times bestselling author of
Cold Choices

"This book is a complete success with its appealing investigator, rapid-fire dialogue, and convincing storytelling, which exposes the overlap between science and politics. The climax, played out on New Mexico's Indian ruins in the dead of night, could hardly be more satisfying."
—*Kirkus Reviews* (starred review)

THE
HELIOS
CONSPIRACY

JIM DeFELICE

A TOM DOHERTY ASSOCIATES BOOK
NEW YORK

This is a work of fiction. All of the characters, organizations, and events portrayed in this novel are either products of the author's imagination or are used fictitiously.

THE HELIOS CONSPIRACY

Copyright © 2012 by Jim DeFelice

All rights reserved.

A Forge Book
Published by Tom Doherty Associates, LLC
175 Fifth Avenue
New York, NY 10010

www.tor-forge.com

Forge® is a registered trademark of Tom Doherty Associates, LLC.

ISBN 978-0-7653-6301-5

First Edition: February 2012
First Mass Market Edition: February 2013

Printed in the United States of America

0 9 8 7 6 5 4 3 2 1

AUTHOR'S NOTE

Because some of the events described in this book might be used by terrorists or other criminals as blueprints, in some instances critical technical details or other facts that might assist them have been purposely omitted, changed, or otherwise disguised. However, the general technology, as well as the vulnerabilities and possibilities outlined here, exist.

While this book is fiction and intended as entertainment, the idea of a satellite solar energy system is very real. It is also achievable. I believe it could solve America's energy needs for the foreseeable future. For more information, please see the page at my Web site: www.jimdefelice.com/helios.

ACKNOWLEDGMENTS

Books are always the products of many influences, most of which are only partly known to the writer. It's hard to know where ideas germinate.

In this case, however, I can state that *The Helios Conspiracy* was inspired by conversations with my publisher, Tom Doherty, and my editor, Bob Gleason. Tom urged me to write about something that had the potential for changing the world; Bob helped supply some ideas and contacts that made this a better book.

Thanks, guys.

THE NEAR PRESENT

ONE

A Heart, Battered and Scarred

1

NEW YORK CITY

Most people who met Andy Fisher on the job would never believe he'd been in love. They wouldn't even think it was a possibility—past, present, and certainly not to come.

This was not to say that Fisher wasn't good-looking, or attractive. He had an athletic build and a pleasing face, even if work often caused it to prune up into a scowl. He was generally quick-witted and occasionally funny, and on closer inspection proved to have few outstanding debts and a full set of straightened teeth.

There were *some* flaws: Anyone trying to gaze into his azure blue eyes generally had to do so through a haze of cigarette smoke. And to kiss his lips, they would generally have to pry a coffee cup away. But these were likely to be seen as eminently fixable, if they were viewed as flaws at all.

The more one knew of Andy Fisher, however, the higher the caution flags flew. For one thing, he was an FBI special agent. And special in his case meant special.

All field agents for the Bureau were, literally, "special," but in Fisher's case the adjective was not merely a product of union negotiations or civil service posting requirements. Fisher held a unique position within the Bureau. Officially, he headed an agency subunit in charge of investigating high-tech crimes; unofficially, he was a one-man problem-solver for the head of the Bureau, who though he liked Fisher's results was sufficiently horrified by his methods to keep him at least one supervisor removed at all times.

Fisher's job meant that he traveled often, kept ungodly hours, and bulged in unlikely places even when wearing a custom-tailored suit.

Or would have, had he owned such a suit.

But it was the aforementioned scowl that was the real problem for any potential lover. For Fisher, despite his excellence as an FBI agent—and his track record indicated that he really was excellent, despite his unorthodox methods and the litany of complaints from those who tried to supervise him—was a full-blown cynic. And a sarcastic one, to boot.

True, cynicism was a common trait in twenty-first-century America, where anyone over the age of five could not only artfully debunk the latest statement from the White House but identify at least three private interest groups who would increase their donations in the next election cycle because of it. But Fisher was a particularly hard case, even for the FBI, which had investigated Santa Claus for Communist affiliations during the reign of J. Edgar Hoover. (The file remains sealed.)

This did not hinder his work product. Fisher was not a vitriolic cynic, fortunately, and his habit of look-

ing at a thing five or six times before drawing a conclusion was an asset to an investigator. He could even
cite philosophical underpinnings for his approach,
mentioning Aristotle or Descartes or Heidegger when
appropriate, which fortunately it rarely was.

But his general distrust of all information—
authority, too—hampered him in social settings. As
for human relationships, it was alleged by some
supervisors who knew and loathed him that he had
not been born, but rather sprang directly into being
full-formed. They held that no mother could have
raised such a child.

Those of a more religious and philosophical bent
swore that while he was in fact human, he suffered
from a soul blackened by skepticism and disrespect.
They believed the cigarettes he pretended to smoke
were actually a cover for the fires of hell smoldering
within his chest.

Fisher would have objected immediately to such
a theory: What proof was there that he *had* a soul?
No one in the Bureau could offer any such proof, not
even the chaplain, who on more than one occasion
had been reduced to muttering "Even God makes
mistakes" after an exchange with the Bureau's most
special special agent.

But Fisher *had* once been in love. And as great a
mystery as this might seem, it would be easily explained by meeting Katherine Feder. For if there was
one person in the world capable of loving someone as
skeptical as Andy Fisher, Kathy was that person.

She was not gorgeous. In a certain light, with
certain clothes, she could easily be called pretty,
but Kathy was not a model. In photos she tended to
look awkward, a little too skinny or a few pounds

overweight, her hair just slightly off or too perfectly arranged.

Meeting her in person was a different matter entirely. In person, her essence shone through. Five minutes with Kathy was enough to liquefy any heart, even one made of igneous rock like Fisher's. Ten minutes might be enough to make the devil leave hell and follow Mother Teresa.

Describing why this was, however, was difficult. Fisher, with all his gifts, could not have done it. The things that made her personality shine—her generosity, her good humor, her easy laugh—when examined separately seemed common enough. Her honesty, tact, and goodwill were somewhat rarer, yet certainly not unknown. Her respect for others, her genuine concern for strangers as well as friends, her ability to make whomever she was talking to feel as if he or she was the center of the universe were rarer still, but not extinct.

The fact that she was tremendous in bed—again, an extremely admirable quality, one certainly appreciated by Fisher, but one that was not completely without peer, even in Fisher's experience.

It was the combination of all these things and more that made Kathy special. Yet at the same time she was not a Hallmark card; there was a toughness about her, and a touch of skepticism, without which a character like Fisher would never have been attracted to her. She was, in many ways, the perfect match for him—sweet where he was sour, soft where he was hard, yet unlikely to wilt under the brunt of his glare.

The relationship had begun, as many things do, in college. It had extended on afterward, even as Fisher became an FBI agent. And then it had failed, suddenly and ingloriously. It was an implosion rather than an explosion, but it was violent and tortuous nonetheless, with multiple attempts at reignition, until finally a pale of darkness settled in, and there was nothing left but ashes.

The failure of their relationship still hurt, though it was by now several years past. And so when Fisher checked his e-mail queue that night and spotted the familiar address, he felt a pang under his ribs.

Indigestion, he would have sworn.

He looked at the address a moment, wondering if his memory or eyes were playing tricks—if perhaps he had misremembered the address or if his eyes were confusing a letter. But the address was her name, with the middle initial, at AOL, and there was no mistake.

His finger hovered over his BlackBerry, poised to delete. Then it backed off.

He moved the cursor up and down the screen, uncharacteristically indecisive.

Maybe it was the fact that he was in New York on Bureau business as a representative at a security conference. He'd always had a complicated relationship with the city.

In the end, he did what many men would do: He left the message unread, and went down to the hotel bar to have a drink.

It was a decision he would regret for the rest of his life.

2

NEW YORK CITY

About the time the bartender tipped a bottle of Jack Daniel's toward Fisher's glass, Katherine Feder was sitting at a table at a hotel bar across town. She had no idea that her old lover was in New York; in fact, she would have been surprised to find him here, as neither chance nor fate had pushed their paths together since they broke up. While she thought of him often—very much so in the past few weeks—her feelings toward him were no longer romantic. She had in every sense moved on, even if the fact that she had no boyfriend at present might belie that.

Her availability floated over the table tonight, subtly. She'd nursed two chardonnays over the past hour and a half, listening politely as a pair of men from one of her firm's subcontractors bemoaned the decline of the American education system, as evidenced by the lousy job their children's teachers were doing. Feder had spent most of the time listening, or at least pretending to; their firm's contribution to the project was crucial, and with Icarus's cash tight its goodwill was critical.

But goodwill was only worth so much, and finally Feder decided she had stayed long enough.

"Thank you both for a lovely evening," she said, rising from the thickly padded armless chair. "I'm going to turn in."

Both men looked a little more disappointed than they should have, Feder thought; undoubtedly they had been hoping for something beyond conversation.

Separately, she hoped. Not that she would have considered *anything* beyond business with either one of them. But together would have been just too comical. And sickening.

Kathy got up and began making her way out of the hotel lounge. The room was crowded with people from the alternative energy convention she was attending. She nodded as she moved through the room, first to Martin Styson from the Northeast Powergrid Association, then to Thomas Maleen from Wind-Central, Janeen Ryder of Martin Lypp, William Ryder of BlueAtom.

Competitors, most of them, in one way or another. But she regarded them benignly. Unlike the group of men huddled around backless chairs near the entrance of the bar, holding court with loud guffaws.

Dressed in casual but expensive clothes, they leaned back in the sofas and easy chairs they'd commandeered, sprawling as if they were in their own living rooms. They acted as if they owned the place, and though that wasn't technically true, they did own a sizable portion of the firms at the conference Feder was attending. They were "the money"—representatives of venture capital firms and hedge funds that invested in or loaned money to businesses involved in energy production.

And, not coincidentally, manipulated the system to make money on energy futures, directly and indirectly, with little regard for the practical effects.

The man at the far end of the table took an unlit cigar out of his mouth and smiled at Feder. She smiled back.

His smile was closer to a leer. Hers, had it been anything other than a smile, would have been a sword plunging into his heart, then chopping off his head.

The man was Jonathon Loup, and he was not only the richest trader there, he was by common agreement one of the most powerful men in the alternative energy business—the original big swinging dick, in the phrase made popular by Tom Wolfe.

He could have easily stepped out of Wolfe's novel, with a slight wardrobe change to bring him into modern times: He wore casual though pricey jeans, an Italian wool sports coat, and a thousand-watt smile. Kathy hated him for many reasons, not the least of which was that phony smile.

Loup's fund owned pieces of energy plants and firms around the country. It traded energy-related commodities in conjunction with them. Using small firms it had bought or otherwise preempted, Loup was a serious player in the sale of electricity, mostly in the west and south where the regulations were generally weaker than in the rest of the country.

Loup—and a whole host of others—speculated in the market, buying and selling futures and other contracts tied to energy production. These financial instruments were priced without real regard to the underlying value of the fuel or energy. As a practical matter, they tended to add artificially to the price, sometimes wildly.

That was bad enough. But Kathy believed Loup went far beyond speculation, actively manipulating the price of his electricity by holding it back at different times and aggressively seeking to put rivals out of business.

As far as anyone could tell, he never broke the patchwork of laws governing energy and its sale. But no one would ever say his tactics were fair.

Kathy Feder thought of the speculators as pirates; Loup was the devil himself. But he was a rich devil, and one she had to deal with, by necessity.

Two years before, Loup had loaned $10 million to her company, Icarus Sun Works. In the world of energy generation, $10 million was a relatively small sum—it took billions to build a power plant, and $10 million would not buy enough fuel to keep many plants going for a year.

The terms of the loan were not particularly onerous. Icarus paid a nominal interest-only fee each year until it reached certain milestones. At that point, it would have five years to repay the loan, or allow it to be converted to equity according to a complicated formula. The final interest rate was hefty—23 percent—but the deal was unarguably better than Icarus or its founder, T. Parker Terhoussen, could have gotten from anyone else.

At the time of the loan, Icarus was a fledgling company with an interesting idea: to generate electricity in Earth orbit, then beam it down for consumption on Earth. Now Icarus was just a few days from launching its first satellite, proving the concept, and altering the nature of energy generation forever.

Not coincidentally, it was right before Kathy Feder had joined the company. Her work, as much as anyone's, even Terhoussen's, had made the satellite possible. But there was one thing that hadn't changed in two years: Icarus was still deeply in need of cash.

Terhoussen had refused any number of offers, including several from Loup, to sell part of the company. Loup was now offering a new loan in exchange for a series of warrants that would give him a nonvoting seat on the company board—a seemingly benign offer, but one Terhoussen and Feder viewed as the proverbial camel's nose in the tent. So far, Terhoussen had resisted, but Feder wondered how long he would be able to continue doing so.

Not very long, if something went wrong with the launch. But if Loup ever got any real say over Icarus, she would resign. Quickly.

It would kill her, because it would mean walking away not just from the company but from a dream she had nurtured long before she even decided to become an engineer and scientist. But she would not allow herself to be associated with someone so evil.

Smiling now was a way of saying *fuck off.*

He smiled back. Probably not thinking *exactly* the same thing.

Feder hadn't realized how attractive she was until she was in her senior year of high school. Until that point, her face had been dominated by glasses and thick braces. Her body had been skinny rather than lean, gawky rather than long-legged. But her real problem was that she was smart, good in math, good with words. Most of the boys were threatened by that.

And still were.

Feder left the bar and walked down the hall to the lobby elevators. The walls were made of polished marble, and the chair rail that ran along the wall gleamed of gold inlay. It was as if the place were a palace—a phony one, Kathy thought, where the guests could pretend that they were kings and queens, in charge of their own destinies.

Inside the elevator, the long day seemed to close in on her. She leaned against the wall of the car, tired, longing for sleep.

Images flitted through her mind. The satellite they'd built. The rocket to launch it—unexpectedly one of the biggest problems. The transmission network.

Computer diagrams of the systems she'd been working on . . . The company financials.

Then fantasies: She and Terhoussen were accepting the Nobel Prize for their work. It was a special prize, for contributions to mankind—solving energy and pollution problems, lowering the cost of power, eliminating the root evil of many wars.

It was a great fantasy, one she'd played over in her mind in various forms since childhood. And now it was going to become a reality.

Almost. As long as they got through the other troubles. And got the launch off. And found money to keep going.

The elevator door opened on her floor. Kathy paused, unable to get her bearings. Was her room left or right?

Left, she decided.

She found it about halfway down the hall. She flipped on the television absentmindedly as she went in, the drone of a CNN anchor vaguely reassuring in the background. Feder kicked off her shoes and sat on the bed.

Maybe she should have more wine, she thought—have room service send up a glass. Or maybe a bottle.

What she'd really like was a bath, and a chocolate truffle.

Two chocolate truffles . . . and a massage.

Her fantasy was interrupted by a knock at the door.

"Room service," said the voice outside.

"I didn't order room service."

"Chocolate and champagne—compliments of the gentlemen in the bar."

Good God—they'd read her mind.

"Just a minute," she said, slipping off the bed.

She cracked open the door just enough to see the cart with its white folded cloth at the top. Feder pushed the door back closed and pulled off the safety latch that kept it from opening too far. Realizing she needed money for a tip, she turned and walked to the dresser where she'd put down her pocketbook.

"Who sent this?" she asked, her back turned.

The attendant, wheeling in the cart, didn't answer. Feder picked up her purse. She saw a five-dollar bill and pulled it out.

"Do you know who sent it?" she asked, turning.

Katherine Feder saw many things in the instant that she turned—the cart, a bottle of champagne, candy, a pair of glasses, a gun, and her murderer. Before her brain could process any of the images, she was dead, killed by a bullet through her forehead.

3

NEW YORK CITY

Fisher woke with the taste of stale corn mash in his mouth. As morning breath went, Tennessee whiskey ranked somewhere above year-old Listerine but below rancid ratatouille. He decided he could have done worse.

Fisher pulled on his pants, then walked to the door of his hotel room to retrieve the carafe of coffee that room service had delivered precisely sixty seconds before his alarm sounded. The Tuscarora Hotel was a small establishment, but it was highly efficient where it counted most—caffeine delivery.

The coffee was black, bitter, and burnt: just the way he liked it. Restored to full vigor, he picked up his BlackBerry and went through his messages.

Yesterday's e-mail from Kathy was deep in the queue, sandwiched between an advertisement for something called "prostate helper" and an autogenerated notice from FBI accounting asking for last month's expense voucher. He forwarded the prostate ad to accounting, then opened Kathy's note.

Andy:

I know this is coming out of left field. It's been a long time.

I'm working at a company called Icarus Sun Works. I'm the vp for finance. We have a project called Helios that has some federal funding and stands to get a good bit more. Because of that, I thought maybe you could help me. There's something terrible going on and I need to talk to someone.

I have to come east for a conference this week. I'll be in New York Tuesday through Friday. I could easily take the shuttle to D.C. to see you one of those days/nights. Call me at 515-679-8707.

Surprised that she was in New York, Fisher started to dial the number, then realized it was only a quarter to seven, far too early for her to be up.

"A project called Helios."

Fisher looked up "Helios" on his Internet connection while he drank the rest of his coffee. As the name implied, it was a solar energy project, but unlike most, it was space based. Large collectors were to be placed in geosynchronous orbit and the energy then beamed down to the Earth.

That sounded like her. In school Kath had double majored in physical engineering and accounting. But she was also, more important, a dreamer. She hadn't taken all that training to get rich. She wanted to change the world.

"There's a lot we can do with technology," she'd often said during their many long evening walks. "Getting the right money to the right project—that's going to determine mankind's future."

Mostly, she'd talked about medicine and ecology,

things that were obvious do-gooder areas, as he called them.

Energy?

Sure. Stop pollution and power the world at the same time. Kathy was a real multitasker.

According to what he read on the Web, the project had a number of technical difficulties, from getting the panels into orbit safely and cheaply, to getting the energy down to Earth. Still, even the critics admitted it was extremely promising—and in fact relatively inexpensive, especially as the cost of oil continued to skyrocket. It was estimated that the entire country's needs could be met at a cost to the consumer near twelve cents a kilowatt hour—about half of what Con Ed customers were paying in New York City, and even lower than the roughly eighteen cents an hour they had been paying before the escalation of the energy crisis.

Fisher finished getting dressed, then headed downstairs, emerging from the elevator fully armed with a Camel smoldering in his fist.

"I beg your pardon, sir," said a desk clerk from across the lobby. Her tone was more demanding than begging, but Fisher wasn't one to offer pardons anyway. "Is that a cigarette?"

Fisher looked down at his hand.

"Looks like it," he said, pausing.

"You can't smoke in the elevator."

"I'm not in the elevator."

"It is against the law in New York to smoke inside public places."

Fisher looked around the lobby. He and the woman were the only public around.

"Pissy law," said Fisher.

The desk clerk's glare intensified. Fisher sighed, and reached to his pocket.

"They're unfiltered," he told her, holding out the Camels.

"They'll do."

Fisher lit the smoke off his.

"Fresh," said the woman, referring to the cigarette, not him. "Indian reservation?"

"I have my sources," he said. "There's a conference on alternative energy somewhere in the city. Where do you think it would be?"

"You don't look the green type to me."

"You don't look like someone who prefers filters."

"Touché." The woman walked over to the registration desk and began playing with her computer. "I see a conference on aromatherapy."

"Close," allowed Fisher. "But this would be something that someone who worked for a company that made solar energy plants would go to."

"You mean like solar panels?"

"Kinda. Except they're in space."

"Solar energy in space?"

"Weird, huh? The sun in outer space."

The woman shook her head. "The things people come up with."

"Boggles the mind," agreed Fisher.

The conference was entitled "Alternative Energy Pathways: Beyond Green," and was being held at the Hyatt, right next to Grand Central Terminal, the large train station in Midtown east of Times Square. It was only a few blocks away, and Fisher decided to walk over, see if he could find out Kathy's room, then ask her out for breakfast. She'd have a hard time saying no if he was in the lobby.

Assuming he wanted her to say yes. But he could use the walk to decide.

It was relatively early, but already the city was on its second or third wave of commuters. The vendors selling coffee and donuts and pastries were well through their stocks. Fisher stopped at a cart that featured danishes wrapped tightly in waxed paper; they appeared to have been sat on during transit.

"Got any jelly?" Fisher asked, pausing.

"Sold the last one five minutes ago."

Fisher grimaced.

"Two for a dollar," said the man, holding up what looked like a crushed chocolate cruller. "Good chocolate. Just like Krispy Kreme makes."

Had the man said Dunkin' Donuts, Fisher might have been tempted. He was a Dunky partisan from way back.

Fisher ducked into the train station from Vanderbilt Avenue, walking across the large waiting room to the hallway leading to the back of the hotel lobby. Inside, a sign said the convention was on the second floor; a note added that the "early riser" sessions began at seven.

The scent of coffee drew Fisher upstairs. He turned the corner of the stairwell and came out in front of the meeting halls, where a pair of large tables had been set up with coffee urns and pastries. The choice left something to be desired; once more all the jellies had been taken.

The coffee had a metallic taste to it—tin, with just

enough of a steel hint to ward off an iron deficiency. Fisher double-cupped and took a pass around the hall, looking for Kathy.

A small crowd of bleary-eyed conventioneers clutching netbooks and laptops circulated in and out of the rooms, looking for their next session or their misplaced coffee cups. Kathy didn't seem to be among them. Fisher wandered back to the elevator and rode back down to the lobby level. There he took out his BlackBerry and thumbed up the number she had left.

The phone rang once, then again, then a third time.

Fisher was puzzled. Kathy was a compulsive two-ringer—always answering before the third bell.

A fourth ring. A fifth. Fisher waited.

A sixth ring. Fisher prepared for voice mail.

"Hello?" said a gruff male voice, answering.

Somehow, Fisher hadn't considered that possibility. He hesitated for just a second.

"This is Andy Fisher. I was looking for Katherine Feder."

"Why?"

"I wanted to talk to her. I'm in the lobby."

"Which lobby?"

"The gun lobby," snapped Fisher, figuring he'd stumbled onto a particularly jealous boyfriend. "Look, I'm not trying to sleep with her. She sent me an e-mail yesterday about wanting to talk to me. It was strictly business."

Fisher turned toward the front doors, which were down a level from the lobby. There were several police cars outside, lining the bus lane.

All of a sudden he had a very bad feeling in his gut.

"Tell her to call me," said Fisher, clicking to end the call.

He turned toward the elevators and saw a pair of plainclothes officers exiting. They practically sprinted toward him.

"You Fisher?" said one of them.

"I'm afraid I am," he said, putting away his Black-Berry.

"You want to come with us."

"Actually, no I don't," Fisher answered. "But unfortunately I'm going to have to."

4

NEW YORK CITY

Tommy Dolan had joined the New York Police Department roughly thirty years before. He had worked his way up from patrolman to detective to lieutenant, a climb complicated by departmental politics and a wound he received while serving in Iraq for the National Guard. The politics were several times much more treacherous than the war had been.

"So you're the famous Andy Fisher, huh?" said Dolan, after Fisher had been brought upstairs. "I understand you're a pill."

"I'm an oversized enema," said Fisher. He took out a cigarette.

"You can't smoke here."

"I'm not paying for the room."

Fisher sat down on the edge of the bed.

"You're a piece of work, Fisher. What does the FBI want?"

"Everything you got," said Fisher. "What happened to Kathy Feder."

"Why'd she call you?" asked Dolan.

Fisher shrugged. Dolan wasn't exactly sure how to take it—Fisher was not from the local FBI office, several of whose members he numbered as friends, and a few of whom he regarded as close cousins to equine posteriors. But the agent was well known in the city, since he had helped foil a terrorist attack on Madison Square Garden during last year's NCAA basketball tournament. He was regarded as aloof, arrogant, a chain smoker, and exactly the guy you wanted behind you in a crisis.

Or in front, which was where he could usually be found.

"You know she's dead, right?" said Dolan.

Fisher flinched, ever so slightly.

"I had a suspicion that's why the people in the white suits were next door," said the FBI agent. "What happened?"

"I don't know. We'll see what the forensics people come up with. I don't know."

"Body still there?"

"Yeah."

"Mind if I take a look?"

"I'm not letting you in there with a cigarette. You'll contaminate the goddamn place."

Fisher took a long pull from his Camel, then got up slowly. He pretended that he was reluctant to lose a good smoke—not unreasonable at the price, even from his friends on the rez. But the truth was he really didn't want to see the body.

Though he had to. Absolutely had to.

Fisher picked up a nearby water glass and dropped the cigarette inside.

"You'll have to wear booties," added Dolan. "And don't touch anything."

Fisher had seen more than a few dead bodies in his career, but never one belonging to the woman he had once loved.

They had her under a white sheet.

Kathy had sprawled on her back between the bed and the dresser as she died. Her right arm was up, lodged awkwardly against the foot of the bed and her body as she fell.

Fisher knelt next to her.

"For christsakes, don't touch," said Dolan, practically screeching. "And don't step in the blood. Crap. Jeez. I thought you knew what the hell you were doing."

Fisher had no intention of touching. He needed to see what he didn't want to see.

The bullet had gone straight through her forehead. It left a small hole; the really noticeable damage would be at the back.

She was still as pretty as he remembered.

He stared at her eyes, frozen open.

If I had read that e-mail last night, she'd still be alive.

Fisher rose and stepped back, quiet, forcing himself to remain professional—to remain Fisher. He studied the scene. The gun lay a few inches from Kathy's hand, positioned in a way that suggested she had dropped it.

"You think it's suicide?" asked Dolan.

That was the *last* thing Fisher thought. Even if he hadn't known her, the entry angle of the bullet looked too level for that—not impossible, of course, but unlikely.

But he had to keep an open mind. Neutral. Questioning. Even when questions were inappropriate.

"I don't do a lot of murders," he told Dolan. "What do you think?"

"I think the murderer dropped the gun there. We need the autopsy, though. I can't automatically rule it out."

Fisher could, but his arguments were mostly personal.

"Check for residue on the bed," he said. "Besides her hand. To have fallen like this—"

"I know my job, Fisher," said Dolan, annoyed. "What's the FBI's interest?"

"None," said Fisher.

"None?"

"I can't really say."

If I had read that e-mail last night, she'd still be alive.

"Come on, Fisher. I'm cooperating here. I just gave you a big favor. Payback time."

"I didn't shoot any of your guys in the lobby, right?"

Dolan's face reddened. "That's the way it's gonna be, Fish?"

"Did I say you could call me 'Fish'?"

Dolan's face turned even redder.

"Let's get a cigarette," offered Fisher. "Outside."

"I don't smoke."

"Now's a good time to start. Come on."

5

NEW YORK CITY

Cooperating with NYPD—or any local police force for that matter—was official FBI policy.

Unofficially, cooperation was considered a desperation move to be employed only when all else failed.

Sucking every bit of usable information out of the locals under the guise of cooperation, on the other hand, was standard operating procedure.

"I knew her, a few years ago," said Fisher. "We were friends. I haven't seen her in years, though. She sent me an e-mail yesterday telling me that she wanted to talk to me about something."

"You have that e-mail?"

"Erased it."

"I can send somebody over to check your computer. I'm sure we can fetch it out."

"Bureau's got guys that can do that," said Fisher. He hadn't actually erased the e-mail, but didn't see any point in giving it to Dolan. It wouldn't help him.

"Why'd she want to see you?" asked Dolan.

"Good question."

"Personal?"

Fisher shrugged.

No, it hadn't been personal. It was the company, obviously.

"If it's personal, Fish, you ought to tell me right now."

"It's not."

Fisher really didn't like being called "Fish" by people without his permission, unless they'd grown up in the neighborhood or taken a bullet for him. He took a slow drag from his Camel.

"What's her company do?" Dolan asked.

"It has to do with solar power," answered Fisher.

"Well that's obvious. What is the Bureau's interest? What aren't you telling me? Is this national security? I know you don't handle chickenshit murders."

"You think this is a chickenshit murder?"

"Hey, relax. Don't twist my words around. Is this a personal deal or not?"

"Everything's personal, Lieutenant. On some level."

Dolan waved his hand and started back into the hotel. Fisher followed.

"Where are you going?" demanded Dolan.

"You're going to talk to the people who were staying here with her, right?"

"One person. Her boss."

"Great."

"You're not talking to him," said Dolan. "I don't need you contaminating witnesses."

"He saw what happened?"

"No."

"Then how is he a witness?"

"You're not talking to him until my people are done."

"I thought you were cooperating."

"Cooperation is a two-way street."

Fisher was a great admirer of pithy clichés, but he chose to ignore this one. They got into the elevator and started up. The lights dimmed after the second floor. The car slowed and finally stopped. A faint emergency light replaced the overhead fluorescents.

Fisher looked toward the ceiling, wondering if there was an escape hatch.

"Somebody forget to pay their electric bill?" he asked.

"It's just the daily brownout," muttered Dolan derisively. "Damn city has less electricity than Des Moines."

The lights came back on and the car jerked upward, then stopped. The door opened. They were between floors.

"Climb or jump?" asked Fisher.

"Neither. We wait until someone comes and fixes it. It could start at any second. Fisher—what the hell are you doing?"

Fisher had decided climbing was a better option. He put his hands on the floor of the hallway visible above them and pushed himself forward, rolling across the carpet. His chin scraped against a lollipop stick stuck to the floor.

"Damn it—you could have been crushed if it started moving," said Dolan.

"You getting out?" asked Fisher, brushing himself off.

"No. Where do you think you're going? I told you—I don't want you contaminating witnesses."

"What I have isn't catching."

By the time Fisher found the room where T. Parker Terhoussen was being questioned, Dolan had managed to call his detectives and tell them not to let the "cowboy FBI agent" interfere with their interrogation.

Told this at the door, Fisher smiled. He'd never been called a cowboy before.

"Makes me almost want to switch to Marlboros," he said.

"I heard what you did at Madison Square Garden, and I know you're okay," the detective told him. "But I got to be careful with my boss."

Fisher shrugged. Dolan actually didn't seem like a bad sort—the kind of cop who pretended to be a hard-ass at a crime scene, then kicked a C-note to get the victim's family home in a cab when everyone's back was turned.

"You're not going to say anything, right?" the detective asked Fisher. His name was Frank. A size 48 belly flowed over his size 36 pants.

Fisher shrugged again. Frank took this as a yes and let him in.

Terhoussen was talking to the other detective, Jackson, telling him about his company. Tall and thin, he had an austere look about him—except for his eyes. These seemed glassy and far away, much more youthful than the rest of his face, whose nooks and crannies put him well into his fifties, if not his sixties.

"This is an important project," said Terhoussen. "Once the satellites are launched, the entire energy industry will be revolutionized—"

"No offense, Doc, but I'd like to get back to this morning," said Jackson. "What happened when you knocked on the door?"

Terhoussen's eyes widened a bit. He looked as if he'd been punched in the stomach. Then he frowned.

"No one answered."

"Yes."

"Then what?"

"Then I went downstairs."

"Even though the newspaper was there."

"If it was there I didn't notice. I don't have time for newspapers. I looked for her in the lobby where we were to meet. She wasn't there."

"You had the desk call up to her room."

"Yes, I did."

"Why?"

"I didn't know where she was."

"You didn't use your cell phone?" asked Jackson.

"Yes, I did. There was no answer. As I said before. I did tell you this." There was more than a hint of annoyance in Terhoussen's voice. "I've told you everything already."

"And you were expecting to meet her downstairs," said Jackson.

"No, I expected her to have met me at my room. Knocking on the door. As we had arranged. As was usual when we traveled."

"She was an early riser?" asked Fisher.

"Not particularly." Terhoussen turned and tried fixing him with his eyes. Fisher returned his gaze with a blank stare. Kathy was, absolutely, an early riser. Either she'd changed her biorhythms, or Terhoussen didn't know her all that well.

"And you got up at what time?" said Fisher.

"Six."

"What time did you go to bed?" asked Jackson, trying to reassert control over the interview.

Fisher leaned back in the chair, ignoring Frank's apocalyptic death stare. The scientist's suite was Midtown plush—not overly stuffed, but each piece of furniture cost the equivalent of a small country's GDP. The suite room, where they were sitting, was twice the size of the average Manhattan studio—only fair, since Fisher guessed the nightly fee was probably twice the equivalent monthly rent.

As the detective led Terhoussen back over the events of the morning, looking for inconsistencies, Fisher got up and walked into the bedroom. One side of the bed was undone. He went to the side that was still made up, leaning over and examining the spread.

"Excuse me. What are you doing?" said Terhoussen, coming in.

"Looking for the restroom," said Fisher.

The scientist walked over to the desk, where a laptop was open and running.

"I have proprietary information on this," said Terhoussen. He closed the top.

"There's a bathroom off the suite room," said Jackson.

"What sort of proprietary information?" Fisher asked Terhoussen.

"Things relating to our company. None of your business."

"Fisher? What the hell are you doing?" said Lieutenant Dolan, entering the suite room.

"Just looking to take a leak," said Fisher.

Before Dolan could say anything else, a woman dressed in a black jacket and skirt came through the open door behind him. The suit jacket clung to her hips like the skin on a ripe grape; it was cut long, perhaps to compensate for the skirt, which ended several inches above her knees. A faint scent of gardenias in heavy rain competed with the thick scent of fresh leather as she swung her briefcase by her side.

"Excuse me." A business card appeared in her hand, almost like a coin in a magic act. "I'm looking for Dr. Terhoussen."

Dolan took the card, but the woman wasn't fooled. Her face brightened as soon as she saw Terhoussen near the desk.

"Dr. Terhoussen? I'm Amanda Ross, from Lupkend, Bolt, and Speer."

"Very good," said Terhoussen.

"Are you his lawyer?" asked Frank.

"Public relations," said Ross. Her tone expressed credulity that she could be mistaken for such a low form of life. "I'd like to prepare for the press conference."

"What press conference?" said Dolan.

Ross asked who Dolan was. He introduced himself with a frown, then told her they were at the very early stages of the investigation, and the inadvertent release of information—he stressed the word "inadvertent" to the point of turning it into six syllables—might complicate things.

"So I'd truly strongly urge you not to say anything," added Dolan. "I know this is a tragic loss. If you could give us a few days—"

"I'm afraid that's impossible," said Ross. "Icarus has a critical profile in the alternative energy community. Attempting to sweep this under the rug will only increase scrutiny and engender rumors."

Fisher thought her skirt already did that very well, but he kept his mouth shut.

"We're not a public company," said Terhoussen. "I don't have to worry about the SEC, at least."

"Please, Doctor. Let me do my job," said Ross curtly. "There are certain realities attached to a high-profile firm, Lieutenant. And one of them is the fact that they are news no matter what happens. Dr. Terhoussen has a responsibility to his board of directors, and to his stockholders."

"And the country," said Terhoussen.

Fisher took the patriotic note as his cue to leave.

Fisher was going to blow off the press conference until he spotted Gavril Konovalav in the lobby, sitting in one of the oversized chairs behind a large newspaper, trying to look inconspicuous. Konovalav was a spy, "covered," in the lingo of the art, as a member of the Russian Federation's trade delegation. He showed up at conferences like this pushing wares from obscure Russian companies while actually gathering information on American high-tech projects. Most of that information could have been easily gleaned from the Internet, but every so often Konovalav managed a scoop or two, generally by bribing an underpaid or unemployed freelancer to violate his nondisclosure.

Konovalav's presence piqued Fisher's interest; generally the Russian couldn't be bothered to get out of bed before noon.

"So what does FASPI want to know about alternative energy?" said Fisher, plopping himself down in the chair next to Konovalav. FASPI—pronounced as if it were a real word—was an acronym for the Russian equivalent of "Federal Agency on Government Communications and Information," the small but ridiculously efficient arm of the Russian spy service that employed Konovalav. "Or are you working for Gazprom now? Oh wait," added Fisher in mock haste. "Gazprom owns GRU. You would never go to work for military intelligence, right? Too much of a contradiction in terms."

The Russian dipped his newspaper slowly. A look of distress crossed his face. Then he closed his eyes.

"Andy Fisher," he said softly.

"Konovalav, nice to see you again."

"Agent Fisher."

"ЗДравствУЙте!"

"You've been studying Russian," said the spy.

"In my spare time."

"Charming."

"How are the lasers coming?" Fisher asked. The last time they had met, Konovalav was working on a project to steal miniaturized laser technology.

Konovalav shook his head. "Children's toys. Not ready for prime time, as you Americans say."

"So what are you stealing today? Or are you just here for the free coffee?"

"I paid my money to attend the conference, just as everyone else. I have a right to be here."

"The sessions are canceled."

"So I heard. A tragedy."

"You're not going back to bed? I thought you didn't get up until noon."

"Now that I'm up, why not enjoy the day?"

"Inside?"

"It's too chilly for golf. And why are you here?"

"I'm looking to invest."

"On your salary? Or have you finally succumbed to the Chinese bribes?"

"If I was going over the wall I'd come to you first."

"I'm flattered."

There was a sudden buzz in the room—the press conference was about to begin. Konovalav got up. So did Fisher.

"American crime intrigues me," said the Russian spy as they walked toward the meeting room. "You're such a violent culture."

Terhoussen and Lieutenant Dolan shared the podium in a room that under better circumstances and for a much higher price was a ballroom, complete with a stage and mirror-covered balls suspended from wires on the ceiling. Terhoussen looked as if he'd stopped into a beauty salon on the way downstairs. Dolan looked as if he'd run up and down the steps to the roof a few hundred times.

"First, let me say unequivocally that tomorrow's launch will go ahead as scheduled," declared Terhoussen when he took the microphone. "America's energy situation is too severe to be derailed by something like this."

The scientist then began reading a prepared statement about how much Kathy Feder had meant to the company, how they were all "family," and how she could never be replaced.

He got about two sentences in before a reporter for the *Post* interrupted him.

"Was it a terrorist act?" demanded the reporter, standing in the second row.

"At this time we're not prepared to make any statement beyond the fact that we're conducting an investigation," said Dolan.

"Is it true that OPEC has vowed to stop the Helios Project from proceeding?" said the reporter.

"There have been nonsensical rumors regarding our project," said Terhoussen. "But I doubt anyone would murder anyone over it. Kathy Feder, our vice president, was a dedicated scientist, engineer—"

"What sort of rumors?" asked a reporter.

Terhoussen looked up from the paper he was holding. "Every great scientist faces jealousy when on the brink of a breakthrough."

Terhoussen was nothing if not a supreme egotist, and the scientist he was referring to was him, not Kathy. Still, the answer opened the floodgates. Questions about the project, the nuclear industry, coal, wind—every conceivable power supplier became a suspect in the reporters' minds. After all, they had their angle: *Murder at a posh New York hotel aims to stop revolutionary energy project.*

Details to be manufactured as imaginations allow.

As they pressed for background on possible threats, Terhoussen warmed to the task. He began ticking off enemies and supposed enemies with the relish of a third grade tattletale reporting on trouble in the schoolyard. The project had many natural enemies. There was OPEC, there was the nuclear power industry, there were the power conglomerates, there were gas pipeline companies and the utilities that controlled power transmission. In short, the entire world was out to get Icarus Sun Works.

Dolan looked as if he were going to sink through the floor. The PR lady didn't look too happy, either, pulling at the hem of her skirt as Terhoussen rattled on blithely.

"What about the Russians?" said Fisher in a stage whisper as he paused for air.

Konovalav shot him a dirty look.

"What about the Russians?" asked a reporter nearby. "Dr. Terhoussen? What about the Russians? They're in the energy business, too, aren't they?"

"The Russians love us," said Terhoussen sarcastically. "They have tried to steal our technology for several years. They would not stop at murder, I'm sure."

The rest of the press conference was anticlimatic. Dolan took the podium again and took a stab at tamping down hysteria, but it was a lost cause. Finally the press rose en masse and made a beeline for stronger cell phone reception.

Meanwhile, NYPD detectives began interviewing conference attendees in a pair of rooms at the other end of the hall. Fisher tried drifting through but Dolan had issued strict orders marking him as persona non grata. Figuring there was nothing more he could do here, he made his way back downstairs to the lobby. There, he spotted a man in an ill-fitting blazer nonchalantly studying the sports section of the *Daily News* while keeping an eye on the elevator.

Bureau guy. Surveillance specialist. Trained to follow people without their noticing.

Roughly forty-five, he had a potbelly and a rapidly receding hairline. His forehead beamed with the glare from the overhead lights. He was wearing stay-at-home-mom jeans, a Mets shirt, and a yellow Windbreaker-style jacket. He blended with the scenery about as well as a chartreuse elephant.

Fisher went over to him.

"You work for Rolison, right?"

The other agent glanced over the top of the paper. "Do I know you?" he asked.

"Fisher. Special projects."

"Uh-huh."

"Your boss owes me fifty bucks from a poker game two years ago."

"I'll be sure to tell him."

"You watching Konovalav?" Fisher asked.

"Wong."

"Wong? Hong Kong Wong or Beijing Wong?"

"Neither. The guy from the Taiwan UN mission."

"We're following the Taiwanese now?"

The agent shrugged.

"How many crews we got here?" Fisher asked.

"Beats me. Listen, could you do me a favor? I'm dying for a cup of coffee. I can't cover the elevator and get one at the same time."

Fisher got the coffee, and in return received what amounted to a mini-briefing on the conference. The agent didn't know exactly how many surveillance teams were there, but he guessed at least half a dozen. There were as many foreigners as Americans, and the agent estimated half the people present were spies. Every foreign government wanted to know what the industry was up to.

And satellite solar was apparently the hot ticket. Icarus's presentation, scheduled for that afternoon, was expected to draw spies from across the globe. Between the foreign agents and their FBI tails, legitimate conference-goers would be outnumbered at least two to one.

"That's been canceled," said Fisher.

"Really? Jeez. Maybe I'll get home early enough to watch my daughter's softball game."

Just as Fisher was about to ask which position she played, the elevator door opened and Taiwan Wong appeared.

"Gotta go, sorry," said the agent, dribbling coffee as he followed his man toward the door.

6

NEW YORK CITY

Jonathon Loup saw the police cars lining Forty-second Street as his limo came around the corner. He was not afraid of the police, certainly, but where there were police there were sure to be reporters, and today he preferred that his profile be as low as possible.

"Better go around, Paul," he told his driver. "Let me out on the Vanderbilt side. I'll go through the train station."

The driver complied silently, continuing down the block so he could get to the side entrance of Grand Central Terminal. Loup turned his attention back to the display screen embedded in the back of the passenger's seat in front of him.

NY1 had just finished a live broadcast of Terhoussen's press conference. He didn't seem all that broken up about Kathy Feder's demise, despite the fact that Feder had probably been more responsible for Helios's success than anyone but Terhoussen.

Completely within character, actually.

Loup flipped the channel to CNBC. Oil futures

were down another ten cents in overseas trading. If that held, Loup was going to lose nearly a million dollars by the end of the day.

A million here, a million there—it added up after a while.

"I shouldn't need you for another two hours," he told the driver as they turned the corner. "But stay close."

"Yes, sir."

Loup caught a whiff of half-burned diesel as he got out of the Lincoln. The scent reminded him of the apartment across from a bus garage in Binghamton, New York, where he'd lived until he was fourteen. His memories of his childhood were mostly unpleasant, but there was something about buses, especially old buses, that felt vaguely reassuring, even now.

He walked briskly into the terminal, came down the steps. People walked across the wide concourse with purpose; most were commuters en route to work. Loup cut a diagonal from the stairs to the far hall, where a set of doors led to the hotel.

One of his cell phones rang about halfway across.

"Talk to me, Dennis," he said, without looking at the caller ID. His rings were set so he could tell whether it was worth answering or not.

"I just got another call from the Chinese," said Dennis Van Gross. He ran Loup's trading desk and oversaw much of the rest of his operation as well; in many ways he was Loup's alter ego, the inside man to Loup's outer player. "They were pretty nasty."

"They're always nasty."

"Either they get the cash at the end of the week, or they go to court."

"That's a bluff. The *last* thing they want to do is take legal action."

Dennis didn't say anything.

"We don't have half a billion dollars, Dennis," said Loup, as if his assistant needed to be reminded.

"The actual figure—"

"Fuck the actual figure. Tell them we'll post revenue anticipation notes from the Maine—"

"They're on to that," said Dennis. "That's why they want cash."

Eighteen months before, Loup had tried to buy a controlling interest in India's private nuclear agency. The Indian firm was capitalized at over $10 billion, but was clearly worth many multiples of that; simply mortgaging the plants it owned would bring a healthy profit. More important, the deal would catapult Loup's firm to the very top ranks of international energy players, a position he had lusted after for years.

The financier had come up with a highly leveraged and unfortunately complicated deal that involved two other hedge funds and a consortium of Chinese power conglomerates. One of the hedge funds had pulled out at the last moment and the deal went south. Loup ended up with warrants that he couldn't exercise and a large debt to the Chinese consortium.

Had the affair simply ended there, Loup would have had little trouble; he could have rolled that debt into another deal and traded his way back to solvency over several years, perhaps even a decade or more. But the Chinese consortium turned out to be fronting for the government, and the government mandarins decided that the papers he had signed actually meant what they said.

Or at least they were pretending that. The Chinese were always playing several angles in any deal, and Loup wasn't entirely convinced that they hadn't scuttled the India deal themselves as part of some as-yet unrevealed master plan. In any event, he couldn't worry too much about their motives at the moment.

"You'll just have to put them off, Dennis. Tell them we're raising the cash. Tell them we're heavy into oil. Which reminds me—have you seen what's happening to the oil futures today? We're getting hammered."

"I warned you last month this might happen."

"Yeah, yeah," said Loup. He'd only meant to change the subject. "What's the situation with the Central Combine? Can you squeeze more out of Central Plains Power and Gas?"

"We have the screws in them already."

"Get them in harder."

"They're already talking to the Canadians."

"Fuck the Canadians. Kill them if you have to. Their contracts are going to squeeze them."

Dennis didn't answer. Loup had walked into the hall between the terminal and the hotel. He stopped and leaned against the wall.

"Damn it, Dennis, I have half a billion getting called at the end of the week. We need more cash. Cash is king."

"I'm doing my best," said Dennis. "I have a conference call with L.A. Dave at noon. We'll see if we can pick up a little on the California contracts. But the regulators aren't going to sleep forever."

"Yeah, yeah." The regulators. More bastards, thought Loup.

"About the Chinese, boss," said Dennis, "do you want me to try and work out a deal?"

"How?"

"Maybe they'll take some of the smaller power

companies. If we help them past the paperwork. I can try."

The power companies that Dennis was referring to produced relatively small amounts of electricity. But they were critical to Loup's operation, since they allowed him to buy and sell power in various pools across the country. Without that access, most of his profits would dry up.

Beyond that, Loup hated the idea of giving the Chinese anything that was American. He hated the idea of giving them anything, period. They had spent the 2008–09 recession buying up commodities and related companies. The damn bastards were going to own the planet soon.

"Find another way," said Loup. "Is Balak there?"

"He's busy," said Dennis.

"He better be. Punch me over to him."

Amir Balak came on the line a few seconds later. Balak handled stock trades for Loup's InvestAlt hedge fund, one of his smaller funds concentrating on public alternative energy companies.

"What's going on with SunPower?" Loup asked.

"We're looking at ten twenty-five when it opens," Balak replied.

"It'll go down. Everybody that's anybody knows about Feder's death."

"They have hardly any business with Icarus."

"I told you, Amir, it's not going to matter in the first half hour."

"All right. I'm ready."

"And be ready for the upswing, too. We have to make money both ways."

"We will, boss."

"Oh, and Black Coyote—what are we holding?"

"Twenty thousand shares. Not much."

"Dump it. I was drinking with one of the principals last night. Idiot can't hold his liquor."

"Right, boss."

Inside the hotel, Loup took a walk around the lobby, looking to see who was around before going up to the panel sessions. He was scheduled to speak at one of the panels in a half hour, and decided he would get some coffee first. Remembering that the coffee in the urns was terrible, he went to the lobby stand and bought some there. He was just adding milk and sugar when one of the conference directors, Darwina Raine, spotted him and came over.

"Jonathon, I'm sorry," she said.

"Sorry?"

"You haven't heard?"

Darwina was a big-bosomed black woman in her mid-thirties, whom Loup thought could have been a model if she had had the patience for it. Ordinarily she was relentlessly upbeat; this morning she seemed on the verge of tears.

"I heard about the death, yes," said Loup. "It's terrible."

"It is, it is."

"Which room am I in?"

"Oh no, we've canceled the sessions today. Everyone is too—too broken up to go ahead today."

"I see."

"Have you spoken to the police yet?"

"The police? Why?"

"They're interviewing everyone who knew Kathy."

"I didn't know her very well," said Loup.

But it was too late for him to slip out of the interviews. A pair of NYPD detectives had just come down, seeking Darwina's help in finding more people to be interviewed. Loup reluctantly shook hands after she introduced them.

One was named McCann, one Reynolds. They were interchangeable as far as Loup was concerned. Tweedle Dee and Tweedle Dumb. They took him up a short flight of steps to the café area, which had been cordoned off for interviews.

"So you're here for the convention," said Reynolds.

"Correct."

"You know there's been a murder?"

Loup considered saying no, but there was no percentage in that.

"I caught the news on television. Darwina was just filling me in. She didn't seem to know much."

"Did you know the deceased?"

"Sure," said Loup. "She was the vice president of Icarus. A very sharp lady. Scientist, engineer, inventor. Handled some personnel things, I think. I've had some dealings with them."

"What sort of dealings?" asked McCann.

"I loaned them money," said Loup. He smiled, as he always did when he thought of sweet deals he had pulled off.

"You're a stockholder?" asked McCann.

"Icarus is a closely held corporation," said Loup. "The only person who owns stock is T. Parker Terhoussen. Not the way I would do things, but he has his reasons."

"What are they?" asked McCann.

"Detective, you'd best ask him," said Loup.

"You don't seem very broken up," said Reynolds. "About the death."

"You're expecting tears? I'm an investor," added Loup. "None of these people are my friends."

"So you didn't really know Ms. Feder very well," suggested McCann.

"On a business level, I believe I knew her fairly well. She was very precise. A visionary. She believed in what she was doing. That's what you need in this business."

"I see."

"She was good-looking, too. I imagine that's what got her killed."

"What's that got to do with anything?"

"It was either robbery or sex, wasn't it?" said Loup. "That's what murder is all about."

"Did you see her yesterday?" McCann asked.

"Several times, yes."

"Last night?"

"Yes. In the bar."

"Was she with you?"

"You mean sitting with me?"

"Or anything," said Reynolds.

"I certainly wasn't sleeping with her," said Loup. "She stopped on her way out of the bar to say hello."

"When was that?"

Loup put his elbow on the table, making a show of remembering, though he knew precisely when it was.

"Midnight maybe. A little later. I wasn't watching a clock."

"You stayed in the bar?"

"For a while. Then I went home. I have a driver," Loup answered. "It's possible he'll know what time it was, if it's important."

"Did she seem nervous?" McCann asked.

"Nervous? No. She wasn't that kind of person."

"What kind of person is that?" asked Reynolds.

"Ms. Feder was always sure of herself," said Loup. "Like I said—she was a visionary. She and Terhoussen. Actually, she was more practical than he is. But then, he's the one that owns the company. He's no one's fool."

"How important was she to the company?" asked McCann.

"Well . . . my impression is that she was able to turn a lot of what Terhoussen imagined into practical applications. And she was able to manage people, which he couldn't. Or wasn't good at."

"Was she essential, though?"

"Everyone's replaceable if that's what you mean," said Loup.

"Was she drunk last night?" asked Reynolds.

"Drunk? Last night? I couldn't say. Maybe tipsy. She'd probably had a few drinks."

"Did she seem depressed? Like she might kill herself?"

Loup shrugged. "How can you tell?"

The detectives had come to the end of their questions, but lingered nonetheless. They were very much out of their element, Loup thought. They were used to dealing with drug dealers and thieves, not high tech. They asked if he knew about boyfriends, and who would benefit from Katherine Feder's death. Loup answered that he had no idea to both questions.

"Really, I do have other things I should be doing," he told them finally, getting up.

"I got kind of a technical question for you, Mr. Loup," said Reynolds.

"Yes?"

"The system they're working on, right? It collects power in space?"

"Something like that," answered Loup.

"How does the microwave work?"

"You'd have to ask someone from the company for the technical details," said Loup. "But basically, the energy is transmitted in microwaves, similar to what you have in cell phones."

"What I was wondering was why it doesn't burn up things," said Reynolds.

"If you were dumb enough to stand in its way," said Loup, "it would."

It was an exaggeration, but he was starting to feel ornery. While powerful, the microwaves would require sustained exposure to actually do any harm. They bounced off metal like aluminum, so there was no possibility that aircraft would be affected, even if they could somehow manage to remain stationary within the wave. And the receiving antennas were mounted high enough that no one would be able to get close to the wave before it was received. Finally, the focused nature of the wave greatly narrowed any area of potential problems, making it easy to avoid.

"This thing gonna stop our damn brownouts?" asked Reynolds.

Loup shrugged. "Eventually. Stop everyone's brownouts."

"When's eventually?" asked McCann. "When hell freezes over?"

"Not quite," said Loup.

"If it ever did freeze over, this would melt it down," said Reynolds, laughing.

Loup remained silent.

"You think maybe some people didn't like the system, and were trying to stop it?" asked McCann.

"If you're asking me to solve the murder, Detective, I'm afraid I won't be of much help," said Loup, struggling to keep his tone civil. "I don't count homicide investigation as one of my talents."

"Have a nice day, then," said Reynolds.

"I will if the price of oil turns around," he said, heading for the stairs.

7

NEW YORK CITY

Gavril Konovalav made sure his FBI shadow was right behind him as he headed for the restroom. He didn't want to lose him too soon.

Katherine Feder's death was complication enough, but what really worried the Russian agent was Fisher's appearance at the conference hotel. It was not simply that he couldn't stand the man, who used chain-smoking as a form of intimidation. The FBI only assigned Fisher to very high-priority cases. Until now, Konovalav had been operating very much under their radar.

Or at least he'd thought he had been. All of the people trailing him had been low-level, run-of-the-mill agents, the sort of men (and women) who would be first-level agents or even retreads back home. They were competent, and a few might even be excellent at what they did. But they were the local team, the people the Bureau assigned out of a standing rotation to foreign operatives who might (or in a few cases might not) be spies. They weren't the higher-ranking counterintelligence specialists who got involved when cases were being made. And they certainly weren't like Fisher, who was important enough to have his own dossier back in Moscow.

High-level industrial spying was both more rewarding and more subtle than "normal" spying. Much of it was legal; in fact, by simply attending the conference Konovalav had gathered enough information to justify his salary several times over. Quite often, companies were eager to share their secrets—or could be made so with the right investment. Spying was rife in the energy fields, where many countries, not just Russia, were trying to catch up to the West's entrepreneurs.

Konovalav wasn't just trying to gather information in this case. Acting on behalf of the Russian national space agency, he was in the beginning stages of a campaign to persuade Icarus's president to use Russian rockets to launch its satellites once they became operational. Konovalav did not expect immediate results—he understood that Terhoussen had a deal with Punchline Orbiters, an American firm, for several demonstration launches. But eventually Icarus would exceed Punchline's capacity, and it would need a more experienced launch partner.

That was his pitch, anyway. With everything going on now, it might be months if not years before he made it.

There was much business to do in the meantime.

Inside the restroom, Konovalav went to the far stall, pausing outside the door just long enough to make sure the agent hadn't come inside. Generally they didn't, since that made it easy to identify them, a violation of the unwritten protocol that one must never be too easily identified in the spy versus spy game. Sure of that, Konovalav opened the stall door and went inside. He glanced at the floor, saw the toilet paper and a large brown shoe, then tapped twice on the stall wall.

The shoe moved. Its owner tapped the side twice in answer.

Konovalav removed his coat and threw it over the top.

"Quickly," he said.

The man in the stall—a Russian agent of approximately the same height and build as Konovalav—took the coat and went out near the sinks. He waited until another man was leaving, then went through the door right behind him. The FBI agent, who could see the coat but not the man's face, followed as he walked back toward the lobby. By the time he realized he was following the wrong man, Konovalav had ducked into nearby Grand Central Terminal, where he just barely caught a New Haven Line train heading north. He bought a ticket on the train, grousing over the five-dollar surcharge.

When he was sure that his Russian accent hadn't attracted any unusual attention, he took out his cell phone. He popped open the back, replaced the SIM card with a fresh one, then quickly tapped in a number.

"I will need a cab at the train station," he told the woman who answered the line. "They must be waiting. My plane takes off in an hour."

8

NEW YORK CITY

By the time Fisher got back over to John Jay College where his own conference was being held, the session where he was supposed to speak was just breaking up.

His boss, Sidney B. Festoon, greeted him warmly as he shambled up the escalator toward the rooms—or more accurately, the large silver coffee urns outside them.

"Where the *hell* have you been?" demanded Festoon. "I had to go on the panel in your place. Why the hell don't you answer your cell phone? Or your e-mail?"

"That's a very interesting shade of red," said Fisher. He elbowed his way through the crowd and helped himself to a cup of tepid coffee.

"Drinkable," Fisher declared.

"Fisher, where have you been?" demanded Festoon.

"The question isn't where I've been. It's where I'm going."

"Don't get philosophical with me."

"I'm not. How long will it take you to book a flight for me to San Jose?"

"Jennifer books the flights."

"All right." Fisher glanced at his watch. "It takes about forty minutes to get to the airport by cab. Tell her I'll call from Grand Central to find out which airport. She's got ten minutes. Fifteen tops. And tell her not to book Newark unless you want to okay a two-hundred-dollar cab fare."

Festoon practically choked. "Why are you going to San Jose?"

"Because that's where Icarus is located."

"Icarus? What the hell is that, a rap group?"

"They make orbiting solar platforms. Their vice president was just found murdered across town."

"And why would we care about any of that?"

"Because she sent an e-mail to us saying there was a problem in the books somewhere. And they get federal funds."

"I'm missing something here."

"Glad to hear you're being honest with yourself," said Fisher. "It's the first step to recovery."

Sidney B. Festoon was, as Fisher put it, the *ass*-istant executive assistant director for Science and Technology, in theory three heartbeats removed from the *capo di capo* of the organization, DirBur himself, FBI Director Michael M. Blitz, affectionately known as Blitzhead to Fisher, who generally reserved the nickname for use on hunting trips in the Smokies and on the odd occasion when DirBur called him at 3 A.M. on some alleged national security matter, though more likely to complain about how the attorney general cheated at poker.

Though clearly marked with a rectangle and four-point line, Festoon's position on the FBI organizational chart was both nebulous and tentative. Science and Technology's responsibilities had to do generally with providing laboratory and other technical support services to the Bureau; it did not generally handle its own investigations. The ways of government were often byzantine, and Fisher's assignment there had more to do with political machinations and mood changes than logic.

Or, as Festoon liked to theorize, the rest of the Bureau had already had its fill of Special Agent Fisher.

A strong case could be made for Festoon's theory. At various times over the past two years, Fisher had been assigned to the Weapons of Mass Destruction Directorate, the Directorate of Intelligence, International Operations, Cyber, and, in one particularly perverse stretch, the Office of Public Affairs. The nature of his assignments had remained unchanged; the primary effect on Fisher was to alter the target of his sneers, and to add further delay to his expense reimbursements.

Festoon had mixed feelings toward Fisher. On the one hand, he viewed him as a standout ACHIEVE employee, a reference to the (latest) internal employee evaluation process under which "standout" had roughly the same meaning as "royal pain in the ass" did in the real world.

On the other, Fisher's track record made it clear that he was capable of truly breakthrough results, the sort that won praise from the attorney general and the president themselves—and not inconsequently raised the profile and promotion chances of his direct superiors. Festoon desperately wanted a promotion, and was willing to risk a nervous breakdown to get it.

He also had a masochistic streak, as his decision to go not just to New York but to the same conference as Fisher attested.

But his number-one personality trait was ambition. And so, with visions of promotion and empire-building dancing in his head, he took out his cell phone and had his assistant make the arrangements for Fisher's travel.

The flight to San Jose was standing room only, something Fisher couldn't do in his window seat without putting his head through the top of the airliner. Having made a specialty of airplane crashes early in his career, he was particularly mindful of how very thin the metal holding him inside the hurtling tube truly was. And so he successfully negotiated a swap for the middle seat with his seatmate, who gladly switched to take advantage of the natural light to read by.

The seatmate was an older gentleman, sixty-five or so, who had brought aboard the latest teen vampire romance, a tome so thick Fisher wondered if he had had to pay a luggage surcharge. The man moved his finger slowly across the page as he read each word, as if absorbing the ink was necessary for comprehension. The book was a real page-turner, and within a half hour the gent had turned himself to sleep. His snores were exactly one-half octave higher than the pitch of the jet engines, and by all evidence easily outmatched the noise-canceling electronics of the high-priced Bose headphones worn by the passenger to Fisher's immediate left, on the aisle. Fisher considered requisitioning the headphones in the name of national security. Instead, he decided to grab a cigarette.

The restroom at the rear was equipped with smoke detectors. Early in his career Fisher had made a study of the devices, mastering not one but half a dozen techniques to defeat them. This one bore the signs of having been jumpered out of action by a pro; there were very slight nudges on some of the wiring discernible only when the harness was shifted back and out of the way. Fisher made his own adjustments, then leaned against the sink and communed with Joe Camel.

About halfway through the cigarette, the aroma of freshly brewed airplane coffee began percolating through the air vent, wafting in on the breeze. Fisher had always wondered how airlines managed to get the just-burnt taste into their coffee, but his need for nicotine outweighed his curiosity, and by the time he emerged from the restroom the stewardesses had already begun wheeling the carts up the aisle.

The man on the aisle had fallen asleep and was spread somewhat disconcertingly over his seat. Fisher put a recent refresher course in rock climbing to good use, gripping the indentations in the overhead panel as if they were crevices as he swung himself monkey-style into his own spot.

"Coffee, sir?" asked the attendant.

"Coffee, yes," said Fisher.

The woman started to pour him a cup.

"I said coffee," said Fisher.

"I'm pouring you a cup."

"That's not coffee. It's decaf."

"Oh, all our coffee is caffeinated, sir."

"You know it's a federal offense to lie to a federal agent?"

The woman paled.

"I'll see if I can find some real coffee for you later on," she told him.

9

SAN JOSE, CALIFORNIA

The sun. Essential for all life on Earth . . .

Since the dawn of time, mankind has basked in its glorious rays, soaking in its vibrant energy.

And that energy is truly awesome. Each hour, 1.366 gigawatts of pure, environmentally safe energy strikes every square kilometer of Earth. The sun's rays striking a mile on either side of the equator could power every electrical device on Earth, with ample energy left to run all of our vehicles and heat our homes.

But no one has been able to harness that energy. Until Helios.

Fisher shifted the laptop to cut down on the glare. He was sitting in the San Jose airport lounge, such as it was, catching up on his coffee and doing background research while waiting for his rental car to be prepped. He'd found a promo video from Icarus that explained the project.

The narrator intoned the project's promise with a voice so deep the tiny speaker on Fisher's laptop vibrated the table. Meanwhile, images of the sun mixed with mechanical drawings of the different satellite parts, along with photos of the project.

Conventional ground-based solar energy solutions, as important and admirable as they are, face many complications.

At their heart, they are by definition inefficient. Not only is much of the sun's energy lost as it travels through the atmosphere, but at best ground-based solar collectors are limited to daylight hours. They are impotent half a day, every day.

How does Helios fix that?

By collecting the sun's rays closer to the source—from Earth's orbit. The satellite system will work practically around the clock 365 days per year.

Some previous attempts at solar-based collection plans have stalled when their inventors contemplated the large size and weights necessary for the satellite system to succeed. But Helios will be both lighter and smaller. Even better, the system will be able to interlock with other satellites, expanding its coverage.

Fisher sipped his coffee while the video played, giving more details about the satellite. The video was intended for a general audience, but the narrator managed to throw in just enough statistics about terawatts and geosynchronous orbits to sound authoritative. Computer-generated models mixed with video of Dr. Terhoussen explaining how mankind's energy problems could be solved by his company's work.

Terhoussen was the star of the presentation, and any viewer could be excused for believing he had worked on the project single-handedly. Sharing credit or the limelight wasn't one of his strong points.

Kathy was in one small snippet. Fisher stopped the video, replayed it on his laptop. She was with a group of other company members, looking at part of the satellite assembly. She was smiling.

God, what a smile she had.

The video was slick, but was this really real? Could a bunch of satellites answer all of Earth's energy needs?

"The Holy Grail," proclaimed Kevin Smith, a Department of Energy scientist and one of the few government employees Fisher knew could be counted on to work past five. Fisher had helped Smith a year before during an investigation into the theft of plans for a nuclear-powered satellite. All the evidence had pointed to Smith, but Fisher had proven he was innocent.

"The first person to suggest it, as far as I know, was Dr. Peter Glaser," said Smith. "It was back in the late 1960s or so. He really paved the way."

Glaser was an incredible thinker, whose interests extended to archaeology as well as outer space. Now retired and into his nineties, he was still in many ways the godfather of the space-based solar energy idea.

"But Helios's inventor doesn't really get along with him," added Smith. "He doesn't get along with nearly anyone in the field."

"What about Kathy Feder," said Fisher. "What do you know about her?"

"I don't. Who is she?"

"Vice president of the company," said Fisher. "Except she's dead."

Fisher felt the slightest hitch in his throat, but kept talking.

"It's a murder I'm looking into," he added quickly. "I'm just looking for background on the company and Terhoussen. Why doesn't he get along with anyone?"

"Personality. Scientists, you know, we're a crazy bunch. But his idea—Helios—it's potentially a good one. More than that. A game changer. A big game changer. Can you imagine, Andy, if the electricity you got didn't pollute the air? If instead of paying exorbitant amounts of money to Iran for gasoline and diesel fuel, you'd be paying less than a penny a mile to drive and taking your kids to the movies with the savings."

"I don't have any kids."

"I forgot, you're a misanthrope."

"On my better days."

"There are a lot of technical hurdles," continued Smith. "But the potential—it's real. Ten years."

"Ten years?"

"It'll be possible in ten years."

"They have a launch this year."

"That's to prove the concept," said Smith. "That's critical. But it would only be a first step. Because seriously, this could provide all of the nation's energy needs. And the world's."

"You sound like a true believer."

"Some things you can't be cynical about."

"What about Terhoussen? You trust him?"

"I don't know him."

"Isn't he working with DOE?" asked Fisher, using the abbreviation for the Department of Energy.

Smith laughed. "Andy, you really don't know the political background to this, do you? A whole slew of these projects have been proposed, but shot down for funding for various reasons. NASA says it's an energy project. DOE says it's space."

"Why aren't you guys behind it?" asked Fisher.

"Priorities. Plus, the time line's too broad. Ten years? Ten years from now I'll be somewhere else. So will most of my colleagues. So he has no champion."

"Can't take a long view?"

"Does the FBI?"

"Touché."

"A lot of people outside the agency wouldn't like to see this succeed," added Smith. "That adds . . . inertia, let's call it."

"Really?"

"Sure. If you've just spent, what, seven billion dollars on a new plant, would you want to see that investment toasted?"

"If I had seven billion dollars," said Fisher, "we wouldn't be having this conversation."

"And think of the oil companies. Think of the countries that produce oil. Think of coal, think of— heck, think of anybody in the energy field."

But the DOE and NASA had, in fact, given *some* support to various projects at various stages. And despite everything, Smith predicted that someday the government would fund a system.

And it wouldn't even take that much money.

In a relative sense.

"Think of it this way," said Smith. "An aircraft carrier costs about four point five billion dollars to build. For twice that, NASA could put enough of these satellites into orbit to answer most of our country's electrical needs. And that's where most of the costs are. Which do you think is a better investment?"

Fisher had always liked aircraft carriers, but he changed the subject.

"What about this private launch company?" he asked.

"I don't know anything about them. They're probably a lot cheaper than NASA doing it. But really, you know why this thing isn't operating yet?"

"Why?" asked Fisher.

"It's not sexy. I just mentioned aircraft carriers. Well, they're cool. They capture the imagination. The sea, flight—your imagination soars, right? These satellites are too cerebral. Electric power?" Smith shrugged. "We just take for granted that it's there. Until it's not."

NYPD had called their compadres in the small town where Kathy lived, alerting them to the murder and asking that they secure her apartment until a pair of detectives could arrive to look it over. The locals had assigned the task to one of the department's junior officers, Patrolman (sic) Rebecca Rodrequez (sic), who was standing in front of the apartment, arms folded, when Fisher arrived. She scowled at him as he approached.

"What's your business here?" she demanded.

Fisher reached for his credentials. Rodrequez put her hand on her gun.

"FBI," he told her. "Relax."

The patrolwoman squinted at his ID, her hand still on the gun.

"You know, those Glocks don't have the little external safety switches," Fisher told her. "If you were a guy, I'd warn you that you might shoot your balls off."

Rodrequez flushed.

"I know how to handle a gun," she said.

"That makes two of us, then," said Fisher. "We got that Glock outnumbered."

Rodrequez frowned, and in her best professional voice, asked why he was a day early.

"I'm on time," Fisher told her. "You're thinking about NYPD. They're a day late. Pretty much SOP for them." He took a long drag on the cigarette, finishing it, then flicked it to the sidewalk behind him. "You got a key?"

She shook her head.

Stepping to the door, Fisher slipped a small pick and spring set from his pocket and inserted the tools into the lock. He kept his body upright as he worked, making sure Rodrequez couldn't see exactly what he was doing. Police officers, especially from smaller departments, tended to discourage lock picking.

"Why did you ask me if I had a key when you have one?" Rodrequez asked.

"I tend to ask a lot of dumb questions," Fisher said, unlocking the door. He pushed it open and stood on the threshold.

"Damn," said Fisher, surveying the room.

"What's wrong?"

"I was hoping it'd be ransacked," he said. "It's always easier if it's been ransacked."

In point of fact, the condominium apartment looked as if it had been detailed and prepped for a real estate sale. The marble at the foyer was spotless; the oriental carpet that covered the nearby living room seemed to have been shampooed recently. The furniture, sleek black and dark brown, done in an Asian-American fusion style, smelled vaguely of lemon wood polish.

Fisher took two full steps into the room and stopped. He turned slowly left to right, observing. It was neat and on the austere side. Very much Kathy. Among other things, it lacked a large-screen television, practically a mandatory accessory in a condo in this price class.

Kathy rarely if ever watched TV, though. Even the music system was bare bones, with only a hard drive attached to the amplifier, though the speakers were expensive panels.

Fisher took out his cell phone and took pictures of the room, more for form's sake than anything else.

"Are you going into the rooms?" Rodrequez asked behind him.

"In a minute."

"Aren't you worried about messing things up for the crime scene people?"

Fisher ignored her. He had gathered something useful from a crime scene investigator exactly once in his career. It concerned an obscure blood chemical that indicated poisoning. It hadn't actually come from his case, though—it was on *CSI*.

He walked through to the hallway, slowly absorbing the details of the room. He had a good view of the kitchen to the right. The stove was a large, six-burner Viking, a high-powered restaurant-style model made for serious cooking. He didn't remember Kathy as much of a cook. He walked slowly into the room, which if anything was even neater than the living room. Two magazines sat faceup on the table: *Traditional Home* and *Fortune*. An island with a stainless steel sink dominated the middle of the room; Calphalon pans hung from a rack above it. Fisher examined the pans without touching them. Spotlessly clean, they looked hardly touched.

"She musta liked to cook," said Rodrequez behind him.

"Yeah," said Fisher, still scanning the room. The air had a slight ammonia whiff, tainted by lemons.

Fisher went to the sink and lifted the strainer. There were a few sprinkles of cleanser caught in the metal crisscrossing the drain. He picked them out with his fingernails. They had yellow speckles, and a lemon scent.

Kneeling, he gripped the door handle with his jacket and pulled open the door. Cleansers lined the cabinet.

"Is there a lot of difference between Comet and the generics?" he asked Rodrequez.

"One's as good as the other."

"Same active ingredients, right? The advertised brand maybe has some additions around the edges, but they're not what gets the job done," added Fisher.

"I'm sure you're right."

Fisher found a can of cleanser. It was a generic store brand, about as basic as you could get.

Old-fashioned: no scent, read the can.

Which made sense: Kathy hated lemons in detergent, or any cleaning item for that matter. She wasn't too fond of them as food, either. She used to joke about it when they were together.

"I'm not a lemon puss like you."

The strange things you remembered.

Fisher put the can on the counter and looked for another. He couldn't find one. The other cleansers—a floor wash, a wood cleaner, something to help collect dust—were all unscented.

He poured out a little of the cleanser into his hand and took a whiff.

"I've never seen anyone snort that stuff before," said the policewoman. "Don't tell me it makes you high."

"This stuff is basically limestone," Fisher told Rodrequez, putting the can back. "Did you know that?"

"Can't say that I did."

"They didn't cover that in training?"

He leaned into the sink.

"What are you doing?" asked Rodrequez.

"Smelling."

"What do you smell?"

"Lemons."

He went to the refrigerator and opened it carefully from the edge. An array of condiments and juices populated the shelves. There were several Tupperware-style boxes filled with leftovers, and two open milk containers. The refrigerator was the most lived-in part of the house.

No lemons in the fruit drawer, or anywhere else.

There was the time she'd joked about making a lemon meringue pie for his birthday.

Only for you.

"See anything?" Rodrequez asked.

Fisher closed the door. "I always wonder about people who keep their coffee in the refrigerator, don't you?"

_____

One of the condo's two bedrooms had been converted into an office. There was more fusion furniture here, slightly different than in the living room but still gleaming. The lemony scent was enough to gag on.

A two-year-old Dell computer sat on the desk. Fisher turned it on, then noticed that it had been left unplugged, the UPS pulled out from the wall. He plugged it back in, then pushed the power button to let it boot up before continuing with his survey of the apartment.

The furnishings in Kathy's bedroom were as spare as the rest of the house. A long dresser dominated the wall across from a queen-sized bed. There was no television here, either; apparently she had other ways of rotting her mind. Unlike the floors in the other rooms, which were made of wood and covered with small occasional rugs, this one had wall-to-wall carpet. A set of white slippers was tucked neatly under the bed.

The master bath was as clean as the rest of the house, the floor scrubbed and the tub scoured. Kathy apparently had a thing for liquid soap; there were four different varieties on the sink, and several more in the shower. An even larger array of bath oils and washes sat in and around a basket on the tub's ledge, all neatly ordered in terms of height.

Fisher bent to the cabinet under the sink, opening it with his sleeve.

"Are you looking for anything in particular?" asked Rodrequez.

"Yeah."

"What?"

"A body would be best."

There was no body under the sink, just some unopened shampoo bottles and some cleaning items. Again, they were all unscented, despite the pseudo-lemon aroma emanating from the nearby porcelain.

"So what are you looking for?" asked Rodrequez.

Instead of answering, Fisher walked back into the hall. There was a closet between the master bedroom and the room used as an office. Fisher opened it and saw not one but two vacuums.

"Did you see any newspaper around anywhere?" he asked.

Rodrequez shook her head.

"It would help if we have some," he said.

"I have this morning's paper in the car."

"Go get it."

She hesitated.

"You want to learn the ropes, right?" said Fisher.

She nodded, then went to get it. Fisher went back to the computer, where he was greeted by a cursor flashing at the top of the screen. Puzzled, he rebooted, but except for a diagnostics screen that flashed by quickly, the system remained blank.

"What are you going to do with the newspaper?" asked Rodrequez.

"I haven't seen the sports yet," said Fisher. He put his finger against the computer's power button, held it down a few seconds, then rebooted once again. As the fan and hard drive began spinning, he began hitting the F2 button wildly.

The screen for a diagnostics program came up. He paged through, found a test sequence, and initiated it.

"This should take a while," he told Rodrequez. "Let me see that paper."

Both vacuum cleaners were about half full. Each had its own story to tell: The smaller, filled mostly with curls of loose hair and odd bits of cereal, told of a woman who trimmed her own hair and liked Cheerios and Lucky Charms. The larger told of a carpet that shed at an annoying rate.

Interesting, thought Fisher, though once again he would have preferred something far more dramatic: rare sea mud from an intruder's shoes, for example. He left the dirt piled on the newspapers, placing the vacuums next to them. Then he went back to the computer.

"What's that mean?" Rodrequez asked, pointing at the computer.

"It's an internal program that makes sure there are no errors on the drive. There aren't. But there isn't an operating system, either. The drive is clean."

"Really?"

"Just like this apartment. Maybe by the same person," he added.

"I don't get it. Did she clean the place?"

"She did. Pretty religiously, if the vacuums are any indication. But the last time it was done by somebody else, who probably had their own vacuum. And cleanser. Kathy hated lemons," added Fisher. "At least in cleaning things. The cleanser she had under her counter was plain. Whoever cleaned the apartment was just the opposite. They used lemon-scented stuff for everything."

"A cleaning lady?"

"Maybe," said Fisher. "More likely a murderer."

Fisher assumed that the hard drive had been professionally erased. While there were several ways of getting data off a professionally erased hard drive, none were very easy. The success rate depended partly on how good the erasing job was, and partly on how much time and effort—read, money—was spent on the recovery. In this case, Fisher figured that the erasing job would be top notch—he was in Silicon Valley, after all. And while the Bureau probably wouldn't devote massive resources to rebuilding the hard drive—byte-by-byte recovery in the toughest cases involved using an electronic microscope for a sector-by-sector analysis—it was an easy bet that the FBI would do more with it than the NYPD. And so he decided to take the drive.

"Are you sure that it's okay?" asked Rodrequez as Fisher unscrewed it from its rails with his pocket-knife. "It's part of a crime scene, isn't it?"

"Technically, no. This isn't a crime scene. Unless trespass with intent to clean the house is a crime."

"Someone trespassed?"

"Besides us?"

Fisher removed the drive while Rodrequez worked over the implications.

"You should sign something," she told him as he put the case back together.

"Sign what?"

"Like a requisition or something."

"Does your department have paperwork for something like this?" Fisher asked.

"I'll check." While Rodrequez took out her cell phone and called in to find out, Fisher went out to his car.

"We don't have official forms for something like that," Rodrequez told Fisher, trotting out after him. "But the chief says you should leave a business card or something, so when the NYPD people get here, they'll know you took it."

"They'll know who took it," said Fisher, handing over a card anyway. "And they have my number."

"What if they don't?"

"Won't matter anyway," said Fisher. "I hardly ever answer my phone."

Icarus Sun Works was located in an office complex on the border of San Jose and Santa Clara, not far from a Great American amusement park. The park's roller coaster loomed in the distance, a crooked, possibly obscene finger that jutted over the landscape of glass office buildings and semi-desert. The Icarus building looked like a stack of pretzels with one of the rings broken off. The exterior, a combination of glass and stone, was an off-key medley of green and brown. It had undoubtedly looked good in the architect's sketches; in real life it looked bizarre, though certainly no stranger than any of the other nearby buildings.

The plants lining the front walk had probably been watered in the architect's rendering as well. Now they were brown twists of neglect, decorated— Fisher noted approvingly—by cigarette butts.

Given the amount of glass covering the building's facade, Fisher couldn't help wondering how much of a contribution Icarus could make to the country's energy crisis by replacing half with plywood.

By now it was after eight P.M., but people were still working inside the building. The front desk was manned by a security guard, who double-blinked when Fisher showed him his Bureau ID.

"That legit?" he asked.

"So they tell me."

The guard blinked again, then directed him toward a Webcam attached to a wing lamp at the edge of the desk.

"State your name, please," said the guard. "And hold the card out for the camera. Near your face. Name."

"Harry Potter."

"Be serious."

Fisher leaned closer to the camera, furling his brow. "Harry Potter."

"Which floor are you going to, Mr. Potter?"

"What floor is Katherine Feder's office on?" Fisher asked.

The guard looked it up. "Eight."

"Eight it is."

The guard punched in some numbers and the printer near the camera began to grind. It spit out a piece of paper, which the guard slipped into a clear plastic case.

"Please wear this at all times," said the guard. "Is Ms. Feder meeting you upstairs?"

"I doubt it," said Fisher.

The guard called up and Kathy's assistant was waiting for him when he got off the elevator. This was unfortunate; Fisher would have much preferred ambling around the place himself.

The assistant's name was James P. Edmunds. He was a pudgy man who, despite being barely midway through his twenties, had already lost half of his hair. His cheeks were dimpled, and when he frowned they looked like sagging sacks of misdirected mail.

"You're with the FBI?"

"Andy Fisher. Sorry about your boss."

The assistant looked down at the floor for a moment, then back toward him.

"Do you know who killed her?" Edmunds asked.

"No. You have any theories?"

Edmunds's eyes welled up as he shook his head.

"Maybe we ought to discuss it in her office," suggested Fisher.

During his second week as a full-fledged special agent, Fisher had listened as a serial mass murderer—alleged, at that point—broke down in tears in a witness room, lamenting his terrible childhood. The killer then went on to describe in loving and enthusiastic detail how he had planted bombs that destroyed four school buses on their way home from elementary schools.

The episode set the tone for Fisher's career. There was more chance of Custer rising from the dead than Fisher betraying emotion—maybe even feeling it—while interviewing anyone. Edmunds could have slit his wrists in front of him without provoking sympathy.

Still, the interview was uncomfortable; after a half hour, Fisher felt a real need for nicotine, but knew that moving the venue outside would deprive him of access to Kathy's computer, which he was gradually working Edmunds toward. And Edmunds was just anal retentive enough to be not only against smoking—he clearly wasn't a smoker himself—but unnerved by the proposition of breaking the rules against it. So Fisher soldiered on, drawing as much information from Edmunds as possible.

Which, though voluminous in detail, ultimately didn't amount to anything useful.

Kathy had had no known enemies at work. No one did. Icarus was a dream to work for, a workers' paradise with stock options and pizza on Friday. Four weeks paid vacation and day care for tots at the other end of the complex. Marx would be turning over in his grave.

Edmunds also had a king-sized crush on his boss, and visibly stiffened when Fisher asked about her boyfriends. He might have been a decent candidate as a jealous murderer, had the circumstances been different.

Edmunds insisted she had no boyfriends.

"None?" asked Fisher.

"I would know."

"How?"

"I would just know. She told me everything."

"Everything about her love life? Or work?"

"Everything."

"She seem depressed?"

"They think it was suicide?"

"Not really," said Fisher.

"I can't imagine her killing herself."

"Neither can I," said Fisher.

"You knew her?"

Fisher brushed aside the question, which actually told him everything he needed to know about Kathy's relationship with her assistant.

"I'm just saying," Fisher told him. "She wasn't the type. What exactly did she do here?"

"What do you mean?"

"They didn't give me much information," said Fisher. That wasn't a lie, exactly—in fact, depending on who "they" was, it was even the absolute truth. He wanted to give Edmunds the widest possible space to answer, hoping something interesting would come out. "What did she do?"

"She was the vice president." Edmunds's voice fluttered. "She handled a lot. She was a scientist and engineer herself, but she was the money person. Officially. Unofficially, she was everything. Terhoussen worked with the project engineers, but she smoothed things over."

"Smoothed things over how?"

"You know. She was easy to get along with. He was . . . kind of like Ahab. In *Moby Dick*? A visionary but not that good with people. But Kathy, I mean, Ms. Feder, she would smile at somebody and they'd kind of melt. I know she convinced a lot of people to stay."

"None of the engineers would have wanted her out of the way?" asked Fisher. "Maybe to take her job?"

"Are you kidding?"

"How about Terhoussen?"

"He needs her. He'll be lost without her. Just wait."

"Does he know that?"

Edmunds shook his head. "She reconfigured a lot of what he did—little changes, mostly, but they were always important. And she was the one who watched the money. I mean, she had a handle on it."

"The money?"

"Everything. It's a small company."

"Would money be a reason to kill her?"

Edmunds's head jerked back in a slow-motion fatboy-style double take. Clearly the idea had never occurred to him. Fisher had already decided not to ask about the e-mail, or even directly mention that there might be financial irregularities. Edmunds would never be able to keep his mouth shut about it—which might make him the next victim, if that had been the motive.

"We don't have a lot of money," said Edmunds. "So I don't see how it could be. Why?"

"I keep hearing that no one would have a reason to kill her," said Fisher. "That's the thing."

"She was in New York," said Edmunds. "New York. It's a pit. Mass murderers everywhere. The people there are homicidal maniacs."

"You from New York?" Fisher asked.

"No way," said Edmunds. "I never even been there."

"Never?"

"No way. They're crazy. Sociopaths."

Fisher nodded grimly. "That's what happens when they outlaw smoking in bars."

There were no signs of obvious tampering on Kathy's work computer. None of the recently used Word or Excel files seemed unusual or hinted at what she'd been trying to alert Fisher to; all seemed to be connected to a presentation on why the company was worth Uncle Sam's beneficence. The only things in the recycle bin were some deleted interoffice memos about where employees should park.

Contrary to the company's security protocols, the temporary files folder and cache on the Internet browser hadn't been flushed for at least several weeks, allowing Fisher to stroll through her Web browsing. She'd checked the weather in New York twice a day for the past week, and had been keeping up with a blog written by a girl in Toronto. But otherwise all she did was check *The Wall Street Journal* and the local newspaper.

"I'm going to need the drive," Fisher told Edmunds, pulling the machine up to open it. "You'll get it back."

"I don't know how anyone could have killed her."

"Maybe somebody wanted her job."

Edmunds didn't take the hint. "No way. Everybody here loved her."

"Not even you?"

Fisher would have gotten less shock out of Edmunds if he had revealed that the pope was Jewish.

"I didn't want her job. I'm not qualified."

"What about Terhoussen?"

"Dr. Terhoussen? He wouldn't want Kathy's job. He hired her."

"What's he like?"

"He's a genius. A true genius."

There was a lot more of that as Fisher worked through the rest of the Icarus roster, running down the phone list helpfully taped to the side of Kathy's desk. Edmunds talked for another hour, Fisher's nicotine fit growing exponentially with each dull answer. He did manage to extract one piece of decent information from Edmunds: the fact that all of the company's important engineers and scientists would be in New Mexico the next afternoon for the launch of the company's first satellite system.

"So what's the amusement park like?" Fisher asked finally, readying his escape.

Edmunds's eyes blanked for a moment, then lit like a slot machine flashing a jackpot.

"It's a great place," he said. "The best time to go is real early, soon as it opens."

Edmunds gave him a rundown of the rides and the usual length of the lines. The change in Edmunds's manner was striking. Fisher let him ramble, unable to decide whether Edmunds was happy to be off the subject of his boss's death, or was just an amusement park fanatic. Finally his cigarette fit got the better of him. He rose to go.

"They're closed for the season," said Edmunds regretfully. "You'll have to wait until summer."

"I'll make an effort."

"The Tilt-A-Whirl should be your first choice," said Edmunds. "Just don't have anything to eat before you get on. Believe me, I speak from experience."

Of all the people Andy Fisher wanted to talk to about Kathy's death, the last was Erin Merril.

But Erin was one of Kathy's oldest friends, and because of that a friend of his as well, and of all the people he had to talk to, she was in some ways the most important, even though he was sure she had nothing to do with the case.

He didn't have to worry about breaking the news to her. She had sent a text to him while he was on the flight.

Terrible news. Must talk. Call.

He put it off as long as he could. When he finally did call, Erin picked up on the first ring. His name and number were blocked on the ID—FBI policy—but she somehow knew who it was even before he said hello.

"Oh, Andy, Kathy's dead. I'm so sorry."

"Yeah."

His throat caught. She started to cry.

"Listen, I'm in Santa Clara," he told her when her sobs subsided. "You still live in San Francisco?"

"No, I'm closer to Santa Clara. I can be there in a half hour," she told him. "I have to head in that direction anyway."

"All right. Is there a diner around somewhere we can meet at? I could use some coffee."

"The only place I can think of is the Throwback Diner. The coffee's not that good, though. It's always burnt and acidic."

"Sounds like the gods' nectar to me," said Fisher. "Tell me where it is."

10

NEW MEXICO

Sandra Chester paced back and forth down the hall of her condo apartment, trying to tamp down the adrenaline rolling around her stomach. She needed to get some sleep. Her alarm was set for four, and it was already past midnight.

Tomorrow was the biggest day of her life. Her rocket was going to carry its first payload into space. After more than a year of testing and two trial launches, tomorrow was the real thing. It was a day she had dreamed of when she was eight years old.

Literally, she had dreamed of it, and many times.

And now, all she could think of was Katherine Feder and her horrible death in New York.

And a million other things. But mostly Kathy.

She'd missed it on television, and wouldn't even have known about it if not for one of her staff members, who'd forwarded her the link from Google News. He had an alert set for news on Icarus, and forwarded it just on general principles. He didn't know they were friends.

Not great friends, but friends. They'd gone to

school together, two years apart. They hadn't spoken to each other for years, until Icarus came looking for a launch vehicle.

"What a great coincidence," said Sandra, the first day they'd spoken on the phone. "I'd be really happy to work with you."

Sandra told herself she had to sleep. There was a lot to do, a world of work before the rocket launched. She tried to turn her mind off. She thrashed around for something happy, something relaxing.

She thought about her father.

It was three weeks after her eighth birthday, on a Saturday. She had a soccer game, first thing. Her dad was the coach, and together they had breakfast before leaving the house. He made her an egg.

"I know what I'm going to do when I grow up," she told him. "I'm going to build rockets."

"Really?" he said. He turned from the stove, holding the flipper. Her father had a certain way of turning his head to look at someone when he was very serious, and he did that to her. "That sounds like a lot of fun."

The memory provoked other thoughts about her father—soccer and band meetings and softball and his death from an aneurysm while she was in high school.

Finding him dead on the floor.

Good God!

Daddy!

She berated herself: *Why can't I think good thoughts?!*

For just a second, Sandra felt exhausted from the work that had led up to the launch. The muscles in her shoulders sagged.

Then she was a little girl again, waiting on the grass as her father wired her very first rocket, a present on her eighth birthday. She suppressed a giggle of joy as it lifted off; rocket scientists didn't giggle.

Her father, though—he laughed and clapped his hands, stomped his feet and jumped up and down. He was as happy as she was.

He was going to be with her tomorrow, in spirit at least, watching and laughing with her. The greatest day of her life.

For just a second, Sandra felt happy. But her mind just wouldn't shut off. She saw her father's body laid out at the funeral. Then she thought of Kathy on the phone the other day, going over details for the launch.

She went back to pacing the hall.

11

JERSEY CITY, NEW JERSEY

Eighty years before, the two-story building at the base of the hill in Jersey City had been erected as a dress factory, part of a booming manufacturing economy that changed the world and America forever. Many people credited the boom to American ingenuity and the work ethic of newly arrived immigrants, but Jonathon Loup, the building's owner, knew the real secret was cheap energy.

Coal, followed by oil and natural gas, had fueled the massive industrial expansion of the early twentieth century. Electricity, generated in gargantuan plants such as the nearby Powerhouse, Jersey City's former coal-generating plant, powered everything from sewing machines to railroad cars. Local power companies erected wires, crisscrossing cities hodgepodge. Then came consolidation, medium-sized power firms buying the small fry, pulling them together. Private enterprise gave way to quasi-public utilities, owned (usually) by stockholders, but heavily regulated.

And then came Carter and Reagan, and the trend

toward deregulation. Bush, Clinton, and Bush—electricity became a commodity again, bought and sold and transported—notionally anyway—vast distances.

There were many ways to make money off of energy. Jonathon Loup knew and practiced them all. One was by buying stock in energy companies and firms that served them somehow. This was pretty much the same thing that anyone on Wall Street did, with the same techniques—leveraging, shorting, hedging, etc.—common to speculators and wannabes across the globe.

Commodities—oil, coal, natural gas—could also be bought and sold. Not just the physical product, of course, though occasionally Loup found it advantageous to actually buy some. Contracts to buy it, to sell it, all lumped under the heading of futures, could be traded for a profit. Or sometimes a loss. These contracts could be bundled into rather complex packages. Surprisingly, this market was less well regulated than the stock market, though in Loup's opinion, more regulations would only have enhanced his chances for profit, as his specialty was looking for loopholes in complex situations, such as those provided by regulations.

Trading commodities was so lucrative that big banks did it. Citi Group had famously gotten into trouble with the government in 2009 because its head energy trader had earned $100 million the year before. What it hadn't gotten in trouble for was its overall earnings on energy trades, which though difficult to figure was at least six and a half times what the trader made.

Or to put it another way: One bank's trading unit

had added about $1 billion to the amount of money charged to motorists and anyone who heated their home.

Then there was the buying and selling of electricity itself. This, too, could bring a hefty profit—especially after someone realized that shortages were good for business. The scandal surrounding Enron and its collapse had exposed that part of the game. But miraculously, this did little to tamp down either profits or the ability to make them. Reformers had managed to reinstate some of the regulations, but only at the state level. The resulting patchwork of laws and regulations made buying and selling power more complicated than it had ever been before—but Loup liked complications.

Controlling power plants could be lucrative as well, especially when combined with the other strategies. Assuming you could get in on the game. That meant avoiding the very big utilities, and operating in such a way that you didn't run afoul of laws prohibiting monopolies and other nasty trade arrangements. It also generally meant keeping one's profile low, something Loup admittedly had trouble with.

And, at least at the moment, it meant being behind the technology curve. Loup expected that to change—hence his interest in Icarus—but for now he was making a great deal of his money by living in the nineteenth century.

Over the past decade, the United States had come to depend greatly on natural gas for a growing percentage of its energy. There were many reasons—good reasons—for this. Gas burned somewhat cleaner than oil and coal. The generating technology was, in general, safer than nuclear power. But the more popular natural gas became, the more expensive it was.

This was partly a product of the old-fashioned law of supply and demand. In the case of natural gas, scarcity had to do with getting it to market rather than finding it. Loup's office sat less than a hundred miles from one of the biggest natural gas fields in the world; if all of that gas could have been easily extracted and transported to market, electricity prices in the region would have been quartered instantly.

But it couldn't. There were only so many gas lines, and government regulations—and neighbors' objections—added to the natural difficulty of extracting the gas, inadvertently helping to raise its price.

But it wasn't gas-fired plants that Loup was interested in. Their product was too expensive to produce.

Coal remained plentiful, easily transported, and thus relatively cheap. Measured in BTUs—all fossil and nuke plants were essentially big boilers—energy produced using coal cost roughly a third of what it cost when using natural gas. What you could charge for the electricity, however, had little to do with what it cost to produce it. In fact, it had nothing at all to do with that.

The new pollution caps complicated the business— but again, complication was a money multiplier in Loup's universe.

Loup owned parts of coal plants, or more generally parts of companies that owned coal plants. He also owned a string of hydro plants—mostly small ones, because the big boys had taken the big ones off the table long ago. None of his hydro plants were very new. While they had been updated along the way, several in fact had been operating when Loup's building was erected. In other cases, they had been built with the help of government demonstration grants, or been funded by public utilities during the late 1970s when the Arab oil embargo scared America into thinking about alternative energy for the first time.

Loup, who was three when the youngest of his plants was built, didn't remember those days personally and wasn't nostalgic for them. What he liked about the older plants was that they had no debt loads—all of the money the plant made could be plowed into his enterprises. And as with coal, the cost of generating energy at the hydro plants tended to be considerably less than it would be with natural gas.

There were profits to be made by controlling distribution as well, though even for Loup, this was difficult in practice. The nation's electric grid and gas pipeline system were overburdened, and in fact contributed greatly to the brownouts and partial blackouts that had been plaguing New York for the past eight months, even as the media blamed these on the age of most of the region's electric plants. The grid's lack of capacity made it difficult to import Canadian hydropower, and also hampered the construction of wind farms upstate, either of which could have eliminated the service reductions.

But one man's problems were another's opportunities. Even his problems would eventually turn a profit, Loup believed; it was only a matter of finding the way.

Which was why Loup had his usual bounce as he climbed the steps to the old factory in Jersey City in the predawn twilight this cold morning. He loved what he did, loved the challenge and above all the money and power he earned every day.

A pair of men in jeans and black sports coats stood at the top of the steps, just under the narrow overhang. They were armed, though discreetly—Glock 17 pistols tucked in shoulder holsters beneath their coats. The two men backing them up on the inner foyer were not nearly so subtle: they had MP5 submachine guns hanging down from their shoulders. The neighborhood was considered "transitional," which meant that there had been a mugging down the block a few months back; Loup didn't want to take chances.

The cement blocks lining the hallway beyond the small foyer helped the building retain its slightly run-down and semivacant look. Video cameras were encased in the bricks at both ends of the hall. They were small and hard to spot unless you knew to look for them. The door at the end of the hall was a thick metal fire door. It locked from the inside, with no keyhole on the hall side.

The lock buzzed open as Loup approached. He took the handle and pulled it toward him. A tall, broad-shouldered man with a thin moustache stood in the doorway.

"Good morning, Mr. Loup," he said. "You're early today."

"A lot of work to do today, Fred."

The guard returned to the security station nearby as Loup walked into the large room that was the heart of his operation. Two rows of flat tables were arranged as a pair of horseshoes around the outer edge. Computers and phones were stacked in small pyramids every few feet. Men in jeans and nylon athletic loungers worked at about half of the stations, some talking on headsets, others staring at their displays or tapping into a keyboard.

A platform sat between the open legs of the inner horseshoe. There were more tables here, more stations, more men on phones. Beyond them, roaming back and forth in a space roughly twenty feet square, was Dennis. Dennis was always here—he had an apartment on the second floor, next to Loup's office. His day was already more than two hours old.

He was speaking German as Loup walked up onto the platform. Loup walked to the displays at the back of the space, looking over the latest commodity prices from Europe. Oil was up again, threatening to break through the ceiling established in 2008.

Bad news for Loup.

"Call me back when you are ready to deal," said Dennis behind him, suddenly switching from German to English. He killed the line.

"Trouble?" asked Loup, still looking at the screen.

"He knows we are short on oil, and doesn't want to help us," said Dennis. "We're down two basis points today already."

"Mmmmm," said Loup. Two basis points translated into a loss of over half a million dollars. Not much in the scheme of things, but a bad way to start the day.

"So what do we do about the Chinese?" asked Dennis.

"Tell them to fuck themselves," mumbled Loup.

Dennis didn't reply. It was his usual method of disagreeing, and Loup knew his silence wouldn't last very long. He turned his attention to the screen to the left, which showed ask and bid prices for electricity in the Midwest. He controlled three companies that sold directly into that market, but they were too small to have an impact on the price.

"The Chinese are interested in Icarus," said Dennis.

"So is everyone."

"They would take an equity share—"

"Which we don't have."

"Or even our note in exchange for all of our debt."

"You talked to them about it?"

"They called me about it yesterday afternoon."

"I can't sell that note without getting permission from Terhoussen," said Loup. "I'm not sure I would."

"It would be an incredible deal."

"Not for us."

Dennis stared at him. In truth, it would be a very good deal, especially since there was no guarantee that Icarus's technology would work. Even if things went fantastically, it would be years before the company was in a position to start paying profits on the loan. Loup wasn't even sure they were going to make their next interest payment.

But Loup hadn't made the deal for financial reasons.

"Your problem, Dennis, is that you look at what we do as making money. I don't blame you—that's your job. But ask yourself this: Why would the Chinese be willing to trade what I owe them for a shot— just a shot, mind you—at getting a piece of Icarus? Think about it. The Chinese are very smart. Wan— incredibly smart. Why would they do this?"

"They tend to overpay," said Dennis flatly.

"Go back to bullying the Germans," said Loup

viciously. He turned abruptly and walked to the wide
steel steps at the far corner of the room, trotting
upward to the second floor. Slapping open the metal
fire door, he stalked down the hall to his office. Dennis was an excellent trader, but he had trouble seeing
beyond his numbers.

After tapping the combination code into the lock,
Loup pressed his thumb on the lock reader next to
his door frame, waiting for the buzz. Only after hearing it did he run his key card through the slot to open
the door—any error in the sequence forced the locks
to recycle.

The lights came on automatically as he strode into
the room. He pushed back his chair and rolled
into the space behind his desk.

Unlike the relatively spartan space below, Loup
had spared little in furnishing the office. Windows
and a skylight were a security risk; instead, the entire
ceiling was given over to an artificial skylight that
not only supplied natural wavelength sunlight to the
interior, but filtered it through an LCD screen that
mimicked the sky: The sun always shone in Loup's
office. The rosewood panels on the walls on the north
side of the office were punctuated by a pair of pseudo
windows; behind the curtains were video panels that
projected a view of the nearby streetscape. The east
wall was given over entirely to a fake view of the New
York skyline. The image, projected from a camera on
a mast high above the roof, was a vast improvement
over the actual view, which would have shown a clus-
ter of older buildings and only a bare scrap of the
river.

Loup touched his keyboard, bringing his computer
to life. The buzzer rang. Loup glanced at the video

screen, even though he knew it almost certainly was Dennis. He reached for the intercom button.

"What?" he snapped.

"We should talk."

Reluctantly, Loup pressed the button combination on the side of his desk to allow his lieutenant to enter.

"It's the best option," said Dennis.

"What is?"

"Giving them Icarus. There is no other choice. They take over the company otherwise."

"What are they going to take over, Dennis? What? You? Me? They can't touch the hedge funds."

"They can take the main company assets. The power companies. This."

"That's not going to happen. Even if it did, it'd be more trouble than it's worth for them. It would take them years to get everything untangled."

"The loan to Icarus is not worth very much," said Dennis.

"Yes, but Terhoussen will never agree to turn it over. And if it's lost in bankruptcy, the way it's set up, it's worthless."

"Get him to change the terms."

"Why are you so hot on this, Dennis?"

"I like my job." Dennis pressed his lips together.

Maybe he was right, Loup thought. Maybe he was the one whose focus was in the wrong place.

The present terms precluded a loan transfer. But if Terhoussen needed more money, those terms could be changed. Even better, it might allow for equity— something Loup himself desperately wanted.

Icarus had been in bad financial shape before Katherine Feder's death. There'd be a lot more pressure now. So maybe there was a chance there.

Half a billion dollars was an awful lot of money.

"Let's see what happens this afternoon," said Loup. He glanced at his watch. "I have to get to the airport. I have a launch to watch."

12

SAN JOSE

From the outside, the Throwback Diner looked exactly like a throwback, a dinosaur from an age that put a premium on chrome and celebrated old-school values like gum-cracking service and black cows thick enough to stand a straw in.

Inside, however, was a different story. It was a "RETRO" diner, with retro in quotes and capital letters. Where a real diner would have linoleum on the floor, this one had marble-look ceramic. Where a real diner would greet the arriving patron with a revolving case of baked-sometime-this-decade dessert pies, this one had a wine rack.

There was even quiche on the menu.

Fisher would have turned around and gone back to his car, but he was desperate for some joe.

"One for dinner?" asked the greeter. She was dressed in what looked like Alexa Chung's vision of a diner waitress's uniform, all silky flow from shoulders to hips to thighs, colors tastefully subdued. Even her cleavage was tactful.

"Just coffee, I think," he said carefully. "I'm meeting somebody."

"Booth or a table?"

"Maybe I'll just wait at the counter."

"The sushi counter is full tonight, sir. I'm afraid you need to reserve a spot at least a week in advance."

Fisher believed that diners serving raw fish shouldn't brag about it. But encouraged by a whiff of caffeine in the air, he followed the hostess through the dimly lit interior, down a set of steps, and past a fountain of running water. The walls were slate slabs of different sizes; the lighting tastefully hidden in ceiling recess panels.

"Adrian will be your server," said the woman.

"Tell Adrian to bring coffee," said Fisher. But the woman had already disappeared into one of the nearby ficus trees, perhaps to check on the squirrels.

Adrian was built like a football player, with shoulders so broad Fisher wondered how he fit through the front door. He had a rugged, sunburned face with a light scar across his cheek. Fisher thought he might have been hired as a guide through the brush that separated the restaurant's sections, or perhaps he had been one of the construction workers and had never been able to find his way out.

"Good evening," said Adrian, whose voice was as deep as his chest. "Welcome to da best diner in California. Would you like a menu?"

He might have said California, but he had a New Jersey accent. Despite all evidence to the contrary, Fisher thought there might still be hope for the place.

"I need a really big cup of coffee," said Fisher.

"Rain Forest, Mountain Home, or Asian Islander?"

"Surprise me," said Fisher, realizing he was doomed.

"Decaf or regular?"

"Do I look like I drink decaf?"

"High test," Adrian mumbled, writing on his pad. "Would you like a menu, sir?"

"What the hell. Why not?"

Adrian turned to one of the nearby trees and reached behind it. He retrieved a single piece of paper and slipped it in front of Fisher. Then he turned and disappeared faster than the hostess had.

Occasionally, one could find a diner that featured a breakfast menu only as long as a single sheet of paper. Of course, the menu would be typed single-space in a font nearly as small as that used on mortgage contracts, and would generally fill both sides of the page. Otherwise, thick menus were the rule. Indeed, several states had passed laws forbidding diner menus from being any less thick than a phonebook.

But this was California, a place where standards were notoriously lax, and convention continually flouted. Disneyland was invented here.

"Have we decided?" asked Adrian, returning with a coffee cup and a thermal carafe the size of a juice glass.

"We haven't," said Fisher. "What's in the spittoon?"

Adrian blinked, processing the question.

"Oh, this," he said finally, setting down the carafe. "Coffee."

"I didn't order an espresso," said Fisher.

"Mountain Home," said Adrian proudly. He plopped down the cup.

"Is that the milk?"

"I'll get you milk."

It was all Fisher could do to avoid drawing his pistol.

"Bring me a human-sized pot of coffee," he told the waiter. "You have thirty seconds."

"Sir—"

Fisher narrowed his eyes.

"Coffee, yes," said Adrian. There was fear in his voice. "Anything else?"

"Burger and fries. Well done on both," said Fisher.

"I'll have the chef burn them to a crisp."

"Now you're talking my language."

"I see you found it. But you were always good with directions."

Fisher looked up into the face of Erin Merril. It was a pretty face, even with the wear grief had brought.

"Hey." He rose and gave her a light kiss on the cheek.

"Just a peck?" She folded into him, her arms wrapping themselves around his chest. Her body shuddered, physically sharing its grief.

Erin stood about five feet tall, and while she might have gained a pound or two since college, Fisher doubted she weighed more than a hundred pounds. She had blond, shoulder-length hair, and no ring on her finger.

He couldn't help notice.

"Still the same old Andy," she said, disengaging and sitting down. "Hard on the outside, soft on the inside."

"Rotten on the inside," said Fisher.

"Oh, that doesn't work with me, Andy. I know you too well."

"You want something to eat?"

"No. I haven't been able to eat since I found out. And I can't stay too long, anyway."

"You should eat," Fisher told her.

She smiled faintly. The waiter came and Erin ordered a Diet Coke.

"It's great to see you," she said. "Why are you in California?"

"I'm a sucker for diners."

"No jokes."

Fisher nodded.

"Right before she died, Kathy sent me an e-mail," he said. "I'm trying to figure out if it was related to—if she died because something bad was going on."

"You're investigating? The FBI is involved?"

"Not officially. It's not an FBI case."

"But you won't let that stop you."

She smiled at him, her first smile. Before he'd been in love with Kathy, he'd had a crush on Erin. But that wasn't exactly unique—half the world was in love with her. The other half was just in lust.

The waiter arrived with her drink. Erin thanked him and plucked the small bit of paper off the straw that had been placed in the drink. She rolled it around in her fingers, playing with unconsciously.

A habit she'd picked up from Kathy, Fisher thought.

"Who killed her, Andy?" Erin asked. "And why? Why? Why did they kill her? She was . . . She was so . . . good."

"I was wondering if you saw her a lot, or talked."

"We're still close." Her lip trembled. "I—uh, we were close . . ."

"Hey, listen, if this is too hard, we don't have to do it at all."

"No, no, it's okay. Sit next to me, would you?"

Fisher got out of his seat and slid into the booth next to her. Erin leaned against him and sobbed for a while. Fisher found himself uncharacteristically tongue-tied.

"She didn't have a steady boyfriend. You ruined her." Erin sounded as if she was on the verge of a laugh. "It's a joke."

He knew it was a joke, but he sensed some truth behind it, and that surprised him. Kathy had left him, not the other way around. There should be no trace of regret on her part.

"She still talked about you. A lot," said Erin. "So—you were, you were always important."

Fisher nodded. Erin sobbed silently, then regained control. She told him what she knew of Kathy's life over the past two or three years. She was very committed to her work—too committed.

"You know she always wanted to change the world. This was her chance." Erin clenched her lips and nodded to herself. "She wanted to save the world. Is that why you loved her, Andy?"

"Must have been part of it," said Fisher. It was an admission he'd made to no one else, not even himself. To become a cynic, to practice that dark art, one had to be at heart an idealist, and an optimist as well.

Erin forced a smile. "She could have gotten a job anywhere else in the Valley—she was that well respected. But she stayed there because it was a mission."

"Did she talk about leaving the company?"

"No." Erin shook her head. "She really believed in the project."

"Did she mention any trouble at work? Specific problems."

"Oh, you know, long hours. She had to deal with some people that didn't really believe in the project, not the way she did. But nothing like murder."

"Did she mention anything about money?"

Erin shook her head. "I know it was tight. But she thought there'd be a big payoff. They didn't want investors—her boss was adamant, but she agreed. Investors would just try to control everything."

"What'd she think of her boss?" asked Fisher.

"I guess—uh—he was eccentric. Very smart. But full of himself. Self-possessed. Really smart. Einstein smart, she used to say. But a real jackass at times." Erin took a sip of her soda. "I think she got along with him, though. Because they shared the same goal."

Fisher prodded her some more. It was clear she didn't have any information that would be of use to the investigation, but he liked listening to her anyway. It was oddly comforting—even though he didn't realize he needed to be comforted.

"Sandra Chester works for one of their vendors," said Erin. "Remember her?"

"Sandra—skinny kid with glasses who could solve pi to ten million places," said Fisher.

Erin laughed. "No more glasses; she had that eye laser thing done years ago. She filled out a little."

Fisher did know who she was talking about: Sandra Chester, rocket scientist. She was a couple years younger than them, but she'd been in one of his physics classes.

Skewing the curve dramatically. Sandra was literally a genius. He couldn't remember seeing her since school.

"What is she doing?" asked Fisher.

"She helped design the rocket. The launch vehicle," added Erin. "She's one of their top people. I didn't really know her that well. She was behind us at school."

"Yeah," said Fisher.

"You remember that party the Blaze brothers had, I think it was junior year? Or maybe senior. First semester? Where she got really sick? She was having, like, a nervous breakdown? From that mesc that asshole Jamesy gave her? You and Kaths walked her around town to get her head straight."

"To get her sober. Vaguely. That was a long time ago, Erin."

"Not so long. Not really."

Apparently, the girl had taken a hit of mescaline without really understanding what it was going to do. It completely messed up her mind; she saw purple spiders crawling all over her.

What Fisher remembered from that night was Kathy, lying in bed with him hours later. It was the first time that they had slept together—literally slept, that is.

He woke up to her alarm clock, playing an old jazz song, something lively. David Sanborn? He didn't know that much about jazz.

"She worried about you, you know," said Erin suddenly.

"Sandra Chester?"

"No, Kathy. She worried that you'd, like, give up on the human race after you guys broke up."

Fisher smiled. "I don't know about that."

"Because you became so, you're so—hard." Erin reached down and patted his hand. Once more Fisher was transported back in time. It was a week after the start of school, and he knew her from class. They were in a bar a few blocks from campus.

She was cute. He was thinking what he might do to get her into bed. And Kathy came in. Something about the way she looked at him—it was like a harpoon striking his heart. Everything from that moment was preordained.

Except her leaving? Maybe that as well.

"I have to get going," said Erin, gathering her pocketbook. "I have to get to work. I'm on nights."

Fisher slid out of the booth.

"Stay in touch, right?" she said.

"Always."

"I'll see you at the service?"

"You can count on it," he said.

As long as he was in investigative mode, Fisher had no problem keeping himself distanced from his memory of Kathy—and from any thought that he could have prevented her death. But alone in his hotel room at three A.M.—six in the morning on Eastern time, where part of his body still resided—distance was a difficult luxury.

Unachievable, in fact.

Fisher was not a nostalgic person, and the fact that his mind kept wandering into the past was disorienting. He tried at first to distract himself, watching television—a mistake, since Kathy's death was big news in San Francisco, outplaying the latest blackout schedule and vying with the crowning of a twelve-year-old as the regional spelling bee champ. Fisher attempted a professional interest in the news report, studying it dispassionately; the slant was on the dangers of New York City, the reporter having decided that crime in New York was as common as hot dog vendors. The actual statistics rated New York considerably safer than San Francisco—or in fact most U.S. cities regardless of size—but such inconvenient facts didn't fit in the ninety seconds allotted to the story.

One thing that was interesting to Fisher: The reporter didn't mention anything about the possibility of suicide. Which was good.

Fisher switched off the television and went downstairs. Neither the bar nor coffee shop was open, and he ended up wandering into what the hotel proudly proclaimed its business center, though humans not employed in the hospitality field would have called it a broom closet with Internet.

Fisher did some more research on Icarus and the solar technology it was developing. The idea of using orbiting satellites to generate electricity dated back several decades. In the 1990s, scientists envisioned power stations "harvesting" energy with solar panels as large as forty square miles, with massive receiving stations, some as large as ten miles in diameter.

Size was a problem on both ends. The larger the satellite, the more difficult it was to construct in space. And the large ground station limited where it could be located and the system's flexibility. But these problems were not enough to kill the concept.

Several teams and companies were involved in the space enterprise. The most promising—after Terhoussen's—was the system pioneered by William Maness and the PowerSat Corporation, which he had established in 2001.

PowerSat was still on schedule, and expected to

launch within the next year. Its thin-film solar cells were considered an important breakthrough in the field. To a layman, Terhoussen's system sounded very much like PowerSat's; its satellites also had paper-thin solar cells that unfolded from the main body like sails. But according to what had been published about it, Icarus was able to use much smaller individual satellites while still generating large amounts of electricity.

The systems were very expensive—except when compared to everything else. The estimates put the cost for a 2,500 megawatt system (roughly one-fourth of New York City's consumption, and more than enough for most small- and medium-sized cities) at roughly $3 billion. A nuclear power plant could cost anywhere from $1 billion to $4 billion if all went well—regulations and delays could greatly add to the cost—while producing roughly half the energy. And the cost of orbiting solar was even better when compared to natural gas and coal-fired plants, so-called "mature" technologies—Duke Electric had recently spent in the area of $1.83 billion to build an 800-megawatt coal plant.

Fisher took the estimate on the orbiting solar operation with a grain of salt—a large one. The satellites cost millions to build and launch, and one little glitch in the construction would render the satellite useless.

The satellites converted the sun's energy to microwaves, then beamed them down to ground collector systems—called receiving antennas or rectenna. These were massive collections of dipole antennas—not too dissimilar in basic function than old-fashioned wire rabbit ears. Or so Fisher gathered from the words beneath the hieroglyphic formula that filled his computer screen.

There were fears about the process—people heard the word "microwave" and pictured themselves popping like corn—but the system was inherently safe, much more so than nuclear power or even fossil fuel plants, which relied on steam turbines. At twenty-five feet off the ground, the antennas "caught" the microwaves before they did any cooking; the beam was tightly focused on the antenna area or it was useless as well as harmless.

Somewhere between the science and nostalgia, Fisher felt himself dozing off. He went back upstairs and took a nap, waking at 6:30 to the buzzing of his cell phone, telling him he had a call. He looked at the number—it was Festoon—and decided it could wait until after room service arrived. He showered, retrieved his coffee, and began trolling through his calls.

The most recent wasn't from Festoon.

"That Rusky? He's all over your Icarus thing. And guess what—New York lost him yesterday. Call me."

Fisher would have known who the caller was even if he hadn't recognized the voice or checked the number. Ben Gatlin was the only one at the Bureau who called the Russians "Ruskies."

The second, third, and fourth messages were from Festoon, who wanted Fisher to call him "ASAP." Then there was a call from someone reminding him his car insurance was going to expire in four months, and wondering if he wanted to renew now. By Fisher's reckoning, it was at least five months too soon to think about that.

Fisher dialed room service, ordered another pot of coffee, then called Gatlin.

"Talk to me," he said when Gatlin picked up.

"And good morning to you, Andrew. How's California?"

"It's sleeping. What's up with Konovalav?"

"Good question. Our New York friends lost him at the hotel yesterday. Went to take a leak and never came out."

"Maybe the cockroaches pulled him down the drain."

"Could be. You got him pegged as the murderer?"

"Not his usual style," said Fisher. "Why would he even be a suspect?"

"Looks like he's been tracking this solar thing for the past six months."

"Personally?"

"Yeah. Two trips to San Jose. One out to the launch company in New Mexico, and a dozen to Nevada, where they have the collectors."

"Maybe he's hitting the cat houses."

"Oh he's *definitely* doing that."

"What else you got?"

"You looking at the Sveedes?"

"Sweden?"

"You think of them as peace-loving blondes, I'll bet," said Gatlin. "They had four people signed up for Terhoussen's talk, which he never gave. Then there's the Spaniards."

"What are they doing?"

"You know solar thermal? This directly competes

with them. Throw their economic model into chaos,"
added Gatlin. "They get the heat of the sun with these
mirrors, see, then they store the heat in tanks of mol-
ten salt."

"Is that like Morton salt?"

"You're a laugh a minute, Fisher."

"Tell me about the Chinese. Are they interested in
this?"

"Probably. Everybody is. Prediction: There will be
a dozen spies out in New Mexico today. All of them
should be suspects."

"Thanks for narrowing it down, buddy."

"Don't mention it. What's the federal connection
to the murder, anyway?"

"I'm not sure that there is one."

"Oh. Uh, then you might want to talk to Festoon."

"It's too early to call him and ruin my day."

"I'd talk to him sooner rather than later. He's getting a task force together. He asked me three times if
I'd be on it."

"And what'd you say?"

"I said I'd be glad to help from afar. I like that word,
'afar.' It has a nice ring to it. *Very afar.* Like several
continents away. No offense."

"None taken," said Fisher, refilling his coffee cup.

"By the way, he wants you to call him back."

"Who told him I talked to you?"

"It wasn't much of a guess, Andy. There are only a
few of us in the Bureau left who talk to you."

"You couldn't lie?"

"He's an assistant director."

"All the more reason to lie," said Fisher.

"He sees this as a big opportunity. Apparently the
director called him at home this morning. It's going

to be mentioned at a White House meeting, and the DirBur wanted to make sure he had his facts straight."

"He wanted his facts straight and he called Festoon?"

"Yeah. This place gets stranger by the minute."

Fisher was about to shave when his cell phone rang. The caller ID said it was Festoon, but he answered anyway. Why not give the boss a thrill?

"Funny farm," he said when the line connected. "Laughs are on us."

"You're a yuck a minute, Fisher. Where are you on this case? What do you have on the Russians?"

"I don't have anything on them," said Fisher.

"Did they murder your VP?"

"Got me."

"Gatlin thinks it's likely."

"Gatlin thinks the Cold War is still on. He also wears tinfoil hats."

"We shouldn't neglect old boyfriends. She wasn't married, right?"

"No."

"This international stuff could be a dodge. The killer might have gotten us off the trail. You have a list of old boyfriends?"

"There's an idea I hadn't thought of," said Fisher. It was rather quaint to be getting Investigation 101 advice from Festoon. Maybe he'd give him a seminar in fingerprint ridges next.

"I've been thinking this is too big for you," added Festoon. The tone of his voice shifted to something close to triumphant.

Fisher closed his eyes. "Too big for me?"

"I'm putting together a team. This is big, Fish. Big. National security, top priority. I'll be reporting to the White House. Through the director. Well, the assistant director. But the White House is *very* interested."

"I think we're getting ahead of ourselves," argued Fisher, though he knew it was a lost cause.

"At the very least, it's industrial espionage. High level. Big. Did I say big? If it's not the Russians, it's someone else. The French, probably. They're always lusting over our power plants."

"We don't really need a task force at this point."

"The White House wants answers. *Who is trying to sabotage our energy program?* That's our focus. That's our investigation." Festoon sounded like he was in the throes of an orgasm. "I'm sending Bernie Stendanopolis to run the task force. He'll be the senior supervisory agent—"

"You're putting Bernie Stendanopolis in charge of me?"

"No, of course not. He's in charge of the investigation. You're a team. You work in tandem. I know you're not a paperwork type. That's Bernie's specialty. He should be out there tomorrow. In the meantime, I've alerted San Francisco and L.A.—they'll provide whatever interim manpower you need. They're eager to get involved in this."

"There's nothing for them to get involved in."

"Don't be so sure, Fisher. Get to work."

The line clicked off.

In Fisher's opinion, once the Bureau established a task force, the odds against successfully completing a case rose exponentially. There was only one sensible course of action: ignore it.

Fisher got dressed, packed, then swung over to a

local lab where the erased computer disk drive he'd taken from Kathy's condo could be examined. Then he headed to the airport and caught a plane for New Mexico. With luck, he'd have this figured out before Bernie had keys made up for the task force restroom.

13

NEW MEXICO

T. Parker Terhoussen liked to say that the technology in the solar collector itself was relatively brainless; he boasted that he had sketched out most of it in his head while caddying his last summer before going to college. Figuring out how the pieces could fit themselves together without human intervention was somewhat more difficult; that he'd worked out in a postdoc seminar on robotics.

The hard part was finding a way to get everything into orbit without breaking the bank. That was where Punchline Orbiters came in.

Breaking the bank was a relative concept. It was difficult to gauge exactly how much a NASA launch truly cost; they had, after all, spent billions developing rocket technology, and it was impossible to assign those costs precisely to a launch program, let alone amortize them in any meaningful way. The agency's true specialty was with heavy satellites, where much of its capacity was taken up by the military. A Delta IV Heavy—the largest and most successful orbital launch vehicle ever built by man—cost in the area of $300 million. A smaller rocket like the Atlas V—for NASA, this was a comparative term— might cost in the area of $120 million per launch.

Foreign competitors were little better. Mitsubishi in Japan charged roughly $90 million per launch of its H-2A—with roughly half the payload capacity of the Atlas. A launch in Europe's Ariane 5 cost about $120 million, and rivaled the Atlas V in payload, though it couldn't come close to NASA's prestige.

But many people believed that satellites could be lofted for much less money, and several were actively trying to prove it. SpaceX's Falcon 9—using a unique kerosene-based fuel—cost from $27 million to $35 million, depending on its configuration. Launches of heavier satellites, such as those the Atlas V carried, cost closer to $80 million, still relatively cheap by comparison.

Punchline Orbiters used a modular system similar to SpaceX's. Like SpaceX, it reused its booster system. This was part of its innovation—after separating, the booster was literally flown back to Earth, steered back to the landing area using a parachute system, which allowed it to be recovered not only on land but on Punchline's own range. The system saved considerable money. According to the company's spec sheet, a lightweight launch from Punchline's New Mexico base would cost approximately $20 million. Launches from other centers—necessary depending on the orbit—cost more, but were still less than what NASA and the Europeans charged.

Of course, Punchline was only just starting its business. Thus far, it had not made any launches. And in a field where failure was an unfortunate part of every calculation, it had a way to go to prove itself.

The difference between government and private charges was not simply a function of the size of the rockets, though of course this was a factor. The launch infrastructure—made cheaper in Punchline's case by the use of a long-abandoned U.S. Army site—was an important element in the cost. But the biggest difference was the ability of the development team to implement technology much faster than their government competitors. The team at Punchline was much smaller than NASA would have fielded, and lacked the layers of bureaucrats that would have slowed things down.

Punchline used a special distillation of kerosene similar to that used in the Saturn rockets and refined to cut down on the tar residue that limited those engines' life. One of the company's first critical breakthroughs had been developing not just the fuel but the equipment to safely pressurize it and handle it in the rocket system. It had gone on to make similar breakthroughs with the oxidizer, which had to mix with the kerosene to actually ignite and propel the rocket.

The woman who had made those breakthroughs was Sandra Chester. Her list of important discoveries included hand-designing and building the small electric-fired rockets that helped steer the parachute recovery system. She was a renaissance woman when it came to rockets, hands-on in the best sense of the word. Punchline's AV-1, sitting on the launch pad now, was *her* rocket. And even though it had already undergone three extensive inspections since it was moved to the gantry two days ago, she took out her Bushnell field glasses to give the skin one last look before retreating to the observation bunker at the launch center.

It was *her* rocket. And she wasn't letting it go without one last look.

Sandra worked her way around the launch pad slowly, moving her gaze up and down the rocket's skin. She was about halfway through when her radio squawked.

"This is Sandra," she said, holding the radio to her ear.

"Some FBI guy is at the gate," said the event controller. "Wants to come in and observe the launch."

"Why?"

"Just said he wants to watch it. And talk to you."

"Is he on the list?"

Sandra actually knew the answer—with the exception of a reporter from *BusinessWeek*, the list of authorized observers included only Icarus and Punchline personnel. The control center was tiny, too small even for the dozen company people whose job called for them to monitor the launch.

"Negative," said the controller.

"Send him down to the plant," she snapped, using company slang for their main office, five miles away.

"He claims they sent him up here."

"And you checked that out?"

"Yes, ma'am. They, uh, looks like they did. Jeffrey says he's got a government clearance that is higher than anything he's ever seen, and, uh—"

"Is his name on the list or not?"

"No."

"Then he doesn't come in."

"He's pretty persistent."

"Daniel."

"Yes, ma'am."

Sandra slid the radio back into the pocket of her

cargo pants and resumed her inspection. Two minutes later, the radio crackled again.

"This is Sandra."

"I'm sorry, Doc, but this guy is pretty, uh, insistent. I mean, he's got a badge and stuff. He wants to talk to you. And he says he knows you."

I'll bet, she thought. "What exactly is it that he wants?"

There was a pause while the controller radioed the question to the security guards at the gate.

"He wants to talk to you about a murder."

"Murder?" He must be talking about Kathy. A lump grew in her throat. She hesitated, then forced herself to speak. "I can't talk today."

"He says he'll pull strings to have the launch stopped if you don't. And uh, he claims he knows you."

"Right," she said. "What's his name?"

"Andy Fisher."

"Andy?"

"That's what it says on the ID. Andy. Not Andrew."

"Escort him to the bunker," she told the guard.

Fisher looked at the gate, considering how much force it would take to break through it.

Not much, he decided. It was just a pair of two-by-fours bolted together. His rented Taurus would break through with a stomp on the gas. From there it was a straight jog into a pair of chain-link fences. Both would come down if you kept the Taurus at forty-five miles an hour or above. At that point, you'd be in the complex, with nothing but a single berm between you and the rocket, a half mile away.

Not that anyone interested in blowing it up would go to that much trouble. Much easier to set up with a shoulder-launched missile at the far end of the range. Guards in Jimmy SUVs were doing laps around the perimeter, but they could be easily timed.

"Park your car over there," said the guard who'd stopped him.

"Then what?" said Fisher.

"Then Luke will give you a ride to see Dr. Chester."

Fisher drove over to the spot. It wasn't particularly warm—in the mid-forties—but the sky was a brilliant blue, the sun untouched by clouds. Fisher cracked the windows and got out of the car.

A black Jimmy with a bar of flashing blue lights came up the nearby hill, trailing a low cloud of dust. Its windows were open. The driver wore a blue work shirt and khaki pants, along with a string tie. His eyes scrunched into his skull in a perpetual squint.

"So you're FBI, huh?" he asked as Fisher grabbed for the passenger-side door handle.

"Yeah." Fisher climbed in. There was a clipboard and radio on the seat, and a shotgun bolted to the dash. The man, like the guard at the gate, was otherwise unarmed.

"How long would it take you to get that gun out of the holder there?" asked Fisher as they drove toward the launch area.

"It'll come out pretty quick," said the man. He drew his words from his mouth slowly, as if retrieving them one by one from somewhere below his larynx.

"You practice a lot with it?"

"Enough."

"Paper?"

"Yeah, paper."

"You have much occasion to use it?"

"Snake or two in the five years I've been here."

"Not a lot of people trying to break in?"

The man looked at him, but didn't answer. Fisher took his cigarettes from his pocket and offered them to the man, who shook his head.

"Roll my own. Thanks."

"You hear anything about Russians watching your launches?"

"Nope."

"Bother you that they might be?"

"Not my job to be bothered."

The driver took a cigarette from his shirt pocket and put it into the corner of his mouth. Fisher flicked his lighter and lit it for him.

"Security's not a problem?" asked Fisher.

"We get some ATV people, bikes, four-wheelers, whatever, out beyond the fences on the eastern perimeter mostly. A lot on weekends." The driver took a long drag from his cigarette. "Don't understand that's our land. Or don't care, more likely. We chase them off."

"When you see them."

The driver gave him another look.

"We got cameras. Video," said the driver.

"Hooked up to a computer?"

"That's right."

"How often you have launches?" asked Fisher.

"We've had two. This is number three. First one with a real satellite. First paying customer, that means." He looked at Fisher and grinned. "We're moving up."

Fisher looked out the window, toward a row of hills that lined the south.

"A lot of people watch from out there," said the driver, nodding. "Make a day of it."

"What is it? Two miles?"

"Almost three. Use binoculars and even telescopes. We're a tourist attraction." He smiled ironically.

"I thought the launches were secret."

"They don't publicize them. But they're obvious enough. Something like that is impossible to keep totally secret. You can hear the sound of the Caterpillar bringing the rocket over to the pad. Makes a hell of a sound. Hear it for miles."

"So what's this Dr. Chester like?"

Another look, this one even longer than the others.

"No comment?" asked Fisher finally.

"Let's just say some might use a word rhymes with witch, and leave it at that."

"Andy? What are you doing here?"

"Hi, Sandra. Long time no see."

Fisher stepped awkwardly away from the SUV, his feet crunching the crusted sand. Erin was right. Sandra was more attractive than he remembered. No more glasses. Her face had filled out a bit. Her body, once very skinny, was still slim but better proportioned. She looked tired—there were bags under her eyes—but definitely pretty.

"You're with the FBI now?" Sandra asked.

"Yeah. You heard about Kathy?"

"I'm so sorry." Her lower lip began to tremble. "Were you . . . ?"

"That ended a while ago," said Fisher. "But life's funny, though. Things come around full circle. I'm investigating her murder."

"Oh." Sandra nodded. "That must be tough."

Fisher shrugged. "And some other things. Spying, maybe."

"Spying?"

"Maybe."

He studied her frown, then her eyes. They had widened ever so slightly when she said the word "spying." Watching a person's reactions generally told him a lot. There were a million ways to provoke reactions, to manipulate someone into showing themselves.

He'd mentioned spying to Sandra's boss, Sihar, and the security people. They seemed genuinely shocked. Which told him a great deal about the operation.

"When did you join the FBI?" Sandra asked.

"Right out of college, just about," said Fisher.

"I don't think I'd heard."

"No reason for you to."

"I, uh—I would have thought you'd go into, uh, science or something."

"It turned out to be something," said Fisher, trying to make a joke. He wasn't used to talking about himself. "And look at you. Rocket scientist."

She blushed slightly.

"This is great, Sandra."

She nodded shyly. Still a little too modest, he thought. But that was why no one hated her in school— she was a bona fide genius, yet didn't seem to actually know it.

"I know you're busy," he told her, snapping back into agent mode. "But I have a few questions."

"Kathy and I—we weren't all that close, you know. I mean, she was my friend but, you know."

"It's all right," said Fisher. "How often did you guys talk?"

"Oh, you know, maybe every other week? Once a month. By phone. She was the business contact, and I really didn't have much contact with that side of the company."

"She ever mention anyone bothering her?"

"No."

"She have any enemies?"

"Not that I know of."

Fisher looked around the range. "How good is your security team, you think?"

"They're fine. I really can't talk right now. I'm sorry," she said. "We have a launch."

"Can I watch?"

"The launch?"

"My security clearance is higher than any of your guests', I guarantee."

"That's not—sure, of course you can watch."

"And we can talk later," said Fisher.

Sandra nodded. "After we land the booster. It'll be a while, though. You'll have to hang out for hours."

"Hanging out for hours is one of the things I'm best at," said Fisher.

The launch facility had once been a government testing area and the control and observation bunker dated from the early 1950s. Graffiti in the form of initials and dates was visible through the white paint on the outside.

The inside was a different story. It had been completely gutted, and while relatively small—Fisher estimated it was roughly the size of a two-car garage—it looked like the interior of an expensive L.A. club that had decked itself out to look like Mission Control. Except it really was Mission Control. Anodized aluminum panels, fancy lighting, rubber carpet, and more flat-panel screens than a Best Buy showroom accessorized a look that screamed twenty-first-century moon shot. Or hip-hop dance escape.

The benches were divided roughly in half, with the people from Icarus in the back three, and the people from Punchline manning the others. The front of the bunker had an open slot, which allowed observers a direct view of the rocket. It was also used as an overflow area, with two engineers at the far end, hunched over five different laptops that were set on a cement ledge under the long, narrow open window. Next to them was a small, balding man wearing a headset who stared transfixed before a panel that looked more like the controls to a stage lighting system than a rocket launch setup.

Fisher would have liked to wander around the bunker asking if there was any fresh coffee to be had while subtly poking at the spying angle, but the place was simply too crowded for that. Instead, he shuffled over to a spot near the front, turning his eyes to watch everyone inside, though not exactly sure what he was looking for.

Jonathon Loup worked at keeping his mouth shut as the SUV made its way up the dusty road toward the bunker. Having had nearly twelve hours now to consider the Chinese deal, he had decided two things:

First, Icarus was a lot more valuable than even he thought. And, second, he needed to get part of it.

But that seemed impossible. Terhoussen strongly resisted his hints, even after admitting that the rumors were true and the company was short on cash. Apparently, that was why he had invited Loup out for the launch anyway—not merely to impress a major creditor, but to ask for better terms.

Loup would give him better terms—as long as Terhoussen gave him stock.

Better yet, the company could be formed into a partnership. A complicated partnership. That was something Terhoussen might agree to.

Once he was desperate.

"Here we are now," said Phillip Vijay Sihar, sitting in the front seat. Sihar was the company president, another scientist turned entrepreneur. In some ways he was Terhoussen's opposite—friendly, at times even garrulous, he acted as if he were leading friends through a garden on the way to a dinner party. He was much less hands-on than Terhoussen, leaving not only the supervision of the launch but most of the design of the rocket to his employees. Loup was sure Terhoussen could have blueprinted the Helios satellite right down to the screws holding the circuit boards together.

They pulled up in front of the bunker. Terhoussen opened the door even before the truck pulled to a stop and hopped out.

Fisher watched Terhoussen and the others walk into the bunker. The scientist looked a lot like he'd looked in New York—sure of himself, slightly aloof. His button-down shirt and black twill pants were wrinkled. He went to the back of the room and began looking at the screens his engineers and technicians were manning.

The scientist held his body stiffly, shoulders back, head fully erect. He looked directly at whomever he was speaking to, met their eyes. He spoke bluntly. Fisher wouldn't have been all that surprised if he hauled off and slugged someone.

The man with him, by contrast, seemed to be all smoothness.

A little hung over, maybe. Hard to tell, though. He had a tough face softened by a thousand-watt smile, which he turned on anyone whose gaze he met as he surveyed the bunker from the side. His khakis were pressed; his polo shirt had three buttons, and was made of thick material. His watch was an expensive heirloom. Fisher could smell his cologne from where he stood.

Money guy. Or something like that. Not a company employee.

"Your face looks familiar," Fisher said, stepping toward him. "I believe we've met."

"I don't recall," said Loup.

"Andy Fisher. FBI."

"Jonathon Loup."

"You're one of the engineers?" asked Fisher, knowing he wasn't.

"Just an observer."

"You're replacing Katherine Feder?"

"Hardly."

Loup frowned. More at himself than Fisher, the agent thought—he realized he'd given more away than he'd intended.

A smart guy, thought Fisher.

"I'm an investor," said Loup. "We do a lot of new technology deals."

"And who exactly are you?" said Terhoussen, coming over.

"Andy Fisher. FBI. Remember me from New York?"

Fisher extended his hand. Terhoussen looked as if it contained a trout.

An even better reaction than Fisher had hoped.

"We need to talk about your company," Fisher told him. "It has to do with Katherine Feder's murder."

"Now?"

"I'm available."

"I'm a little busy here, Mr. Fisher. And I've already given a statement of regret to the police. And the press."

"We can wait until after the launch," said Fisher.

Terhoussen drew the sort of exaggerated breath people use to stifle murderous intent. Fisher had always thought the homicide rate would be cut in half if "the breath" was taught in kindergarten.

Phillip Vijay Sihar, president and CEO of the company, was the last VIP to show up. To Fisher he seemed a nervous man, his hands in constant motion, his eyes darting back and forth. In his early fifties, he had the look of a health nut—narrow stomach, thin though muscled arms.

Pity.

"Mr. Fisher, you found it," said Sihar, coming over and shaking his hand. "You are ready?"

"Sure."

"I feel like I'm at Macy's Thanksgiving Day Parade," said Sihar. "This will be a good report, yes?"

"The best."

Fisher had hinted—broadly, but definitely in that direction—that Katherine Feder's death had encouraged a review of security procedures and necessitated a report to the federal agencies responsible for funding future projects. Sihar had obviously jumped to the conclusion that Fisher was preparing that report.

Strange, the ideas that popped into people's heads.

A siren sounded outside.

"Gentlemen, please put on your helmets and glasses," said the man with the headset.

Fisher looked at his helmet, which was made of plastic. If the roof collapsed, it would be crushed flatter than a postage stamp. But maybe the bright yellow would make it easier to find them in the rubble.

Fisher found a spot near the open window, sliding next to Loup and Sandra, who had donned her own headset and was staring intently at her creation on the pad. Occasionally she mumbled one or two syllables into her microphone; to Fisher it seemed as if she were talking to herself.

"We are commencing countdown sequence," said the launch controller.

"Sixty seconds," said the controller.

Fisher folded his arms and looked down the range. Two Jimmy SUVs, blue lights flashing, were parked about three-quarters of a half mile from the pad on either side. Otherwise, the range was empty. Even the snakes were hiding.

"Thirty seconds," said the controller.

"We're go," said Sandra Chester loudly. "Authority to launch."

"Launch authority. Thank you."

"Recovery crew prepared?" Chester said.

The answer must have come over her headset, for Fisher never heard it. Everyone leaned forward, waiting. Fisher was reminded of the films of the old atom bomb tests, where the shock wave pushed the observers' skin back in ripples against their bones.

"Twenty seconds," said the controller. "Nineteen, eighteen . . ."

The numbers came slowly.

"Three . . . two . . . one . . . ignition."

A wisp of white furled from the bottom of the rocket. It looked like the sort of puff you get from a cigarette that's a little too dry.

The noise came a second later. The rocket's engine sounded more like a vacuum cleaner on steroids than an explosion, controlled or otherwise. The large arm that had been holding a backup telemetry connection fell away as the rocket began to lift from the pad. A thick curl of clouds foamed from the bottom and the rocket seemed to pause in midair, as if undecided about testing gravity. Then it spurted upward, beginning to rotate.

"We have a launch," said the controller, his words drowned out by the roar of the engines.

The rocket began to accelerate rapidly, determined to put its payload into orbit. Fisher leaned forward, then turned around, looking at the others.

Terhoussen's mouth curled in a smile. Loup seemed in awe. The guys with the laptops looked like they were whistling. Most of the people in the back were studying their laptops.

Sandra Chester's fists were clenched.

Fisher turned back toward the rocket, which was now climbing away from the bunker. It spun slowly— the revolutions stabilized its track—a small, steady orange flame unfolding from the engine nozzle.

"Good launch!" said the controller.

The words were no sooner out of his mouth than the rocket exploded.

TWO

Off Course

TWO

1

NEW MEXICO

No one in the bunker spoke for four or five seconds. The people in the back stood and stared, trying to see through the window. The people in the front simply leaned forward, necks craned toward the sky.

Fisher glanced at the others, noting their stunned expressions.

The corners of Loup's mouth seemed to turn up, hinting at a smile. But maybe it was just indigestion.

"We have . . . an event," said the controller, his voice breaking.

"Secure the launch area," said Sandra Chester.

Terhoussen started for the door.

"No, Doctor. I'm afraid we all have to stay inside the bunker," she told him. "We have a protocol. We need to obtain—"

"The hell with your protocol," said Terhoussen.

A loop was playing at the back of Sandra Chester's brain, telling her to act professionally, to keep going despite the accident. Her career depended on it. The company depended on it.

Rockets blew up all the time. All the time.

"Protocol B," she said into her mouthpiece. "Controller, you haven't sounded the siren yet."

"I'm sorry," he said. Belatedly he started working through the procedure. The people on the range were already responding, just as they'd been trained to. Sandra walked over to the company president and touched his sleeve. "We'll figure it out, Phillip," she said.

"Mmmm," he said, nodding. His face seemed to have turned gray.

Fisher watched Sandra as she spoke to her boss. She was almost supernaturally calm, in control. It reminded him of Kathy.

God, he thought, *put that away.*

Fisher slipped back into FBI mode, watching the launch controller marshal the response teams. The people on the back benches were working furiously, muttering into headsets and to themselves. Telemetry was backed up onto secondary backup drives; one of the security people was waiting to take the regular backup off-site to make sure it was preserved.

Fisher went back to the window. All of the debris had landed. Except for one long finger of black smoke, it was impossible to tell anything untoward had happened.

Sandra was staring, hands on hips, out the window.

"Listen," Fisher told her. "I have to stick pretty close to Terhoussen for now. Can we talk later? Tonight?"

"I'm going to be very busy," she said coldly.

"I'm not asking for a date."

She frowned, but then nodded.

"My number's on the card," he said, reaching into his wallet and taking a clean one out from behind the fold. "You'll call me?"

"I suppose."

He smiled at her. "I know you're gonna."

She frowned, which only convinced him he was right.

But it was Fisher who called first. Watching Terhoussen was mostly a bust—the scientist barked at his people for a while, complained, shook his head, then headed to Santa Clara on Loup's jet. They didn't offer Fisher a ride.

Not that he would have taken it, but it was always nice to be asked.

Fisher spent the next few hours roaming around the outskirts of the launch area, checking on possible spies, doing background research on the Web, and making phone calls. The process left him knowing less than when he started.

When he called, Sandra picked up on the first ring.

"Hello?"

"Sandra, it's Andy. When can we talk?"

"Andy? How did you get this number?" she asked.

"I work for the FBI, remember?"

"Why is that?" she asked sharply.

"It's a long story," he told her, deciding the launch failure had set her on edge. "I'll tell you if you're interested. Over dinner. You hungry?"

She sighed. Fisher had actually gotten the number

from Kathy's work hard drive, which San Francisco had unencrypted for him that afternoon. As of five P.M., it was the only useful thing they had obtained.

"I'm really, really super busy," said Sandra. "I know—I feel terrible about Kathy. Just terrible. But I can't help you. I just . . ."

Fisher waited for her to fill in the blank. She didn't.

"I'd like to talk to you anyway," he said finally. "My case may dovetail with what happened today."

"What? How?"

"I don't want to jump to conclusions. But we really should talk."

She hesitated a moment longer than Fisher thought she would before saying yes.

The Sunrise '50 Diner had coffee that tasted as if it had been reheated three or four times, and the french fries had clearly been fried in lard.

You couldn't get better than that.

"You sure you don't want anything to eat?" Fisher asked, finishing the last of his dinner.

"I'm not hungry," Sandra told him. She'd ordered a tea; it sat next to her, barely touched.

"So why would someone want to sabotage your rocket?"

Sandra shook her head. "Why do you think it's sabotage?"

"I don't think it's anything," said Fisher. "I'm just saying—if it *were* sabotage, who would do it?"

"No one."

"So it was just lousy design?"

For just a moment she looked like Sigourney Weaver, about to give birth in *Alien 3*.

"I don't mean that personally," said Fisher.

"Well, how do you mean it?"

"I mean—who would want the project to fail? I know you wouldn't."

"Andy. Rocket design is very complicated." Sandra pressed her lips tightly together. "You of all people."

She stopped speaking for a moment, then shook her head before continuing. "A million things can go wrong."

"But you've tested this rocket already. And from what I understand, the concepts involved aren't really very new. You're just reapplying them."

"Are you an FBI agent, or a rocket scientist?"

"Look, I can use the telephone," said Fisher. "I talked to a guy named Yoshi at NASA. He says hi, by the way."

Sandra's frown deepened, and she turned her glare to the table.

"A rival company, maybe?" Fisher prompted. "They'd want you to fail. Your business is pretty competitive. Right?"

"Not like that." She raised her head and looked at him. She had pretty eyes.

Like Kathy.

He kicked the idea away, trying to suffocate it with work. He had to focus, and he would focus.

But she did have pretty eyes.

"There's a surplus of launch capacity, it's true," said Sandra. "I'm sure you've read stories in the business press if you did a simple Google search. Which, obviously, you did."

"Is it true?"

"To an extent. But I can't think of a single instance of sabotage."

Neither could Yoshi, who'd described the field as somewhat collegial. And in fact many of the major players knew each other as friends, or at least semi-friends.

"What about Icarus?" Fisher asked. "What about the company?"

"You think they blew up their own satellite?"

"It's insured, right?"

"Yes, but—" Sandra laughed. "Are you really an FBI agent?"

"It says so on my ID."

"You were going into aeronautics."

"Good memory."

"What happened?"

"This is more interesting."

She frowned. Ordinarily, Fisher would have ignored it, but then ordinarily he wouldn't be talking about himself.

"Out of college I had to make some money," he explained. "And long story short, I got a job investigating airplane accidents. And not-so accidents. The FBI hired me after this thing I was working on turned out to be sabotage and I was the only one who could figure it out. I did some other stuff. Next thing you know, I'm in New Mexico talking to old friends about rockets that blow up. And other friends who were murdered."

Sandra sighed and reached across the table. "You two were close. I know. I'm sorry."

"It's all right. This isn't personal."

"I remember you guys helped me." Sandra smiled awkwardly, embarrassed. "I still remember that."

"You shouldn't remember it at all," said Fisher. He longed for a cigarette.

"You're different as an FBI agent."

"How?"

She shook her head. "Just—the job changes you, I guess. It makes you more cynical."

"Nah. I was always cynical. You just didn't know me very well."

"You weren't this bad. Sardonic. Did you—are you bitter?"

"Did Kathy ever talk about boyfriends, anything like that?" asked Fisher, ignoring the question.

"No. I—we just weren't really close in that way. Not even in college. Maybe a little in college. But not now."

"How about Terhoussen. She like him?"

"Dr. Terhoussen is a difficult man to get along with," said Sandra. "But I don't think she had real problems with him. She was one of the few people he didn't talk down to."

"He talks down to you?"

"I don't have to deal with him too often."

"What kind of effect is Kathy's death going to have on Icarus?" Fisher asked. "Will it hurt the project?"

"Long term, I'm sure it hurts the company. She took care of a lot of the business and financial things. And the scientists respected her, because in a lot of ways she was one of them. The people in the control room today were all talking about her—I mean, before the accident. They didn't even know her, really. But there was respect there. Terhoussen—people are afraid of him."

"Was she?"

"Oh, I don't know. I don't think she was afraid of anything. Do you?"

"No." He shook his head. "Not at all."

"Terhoussen is pretty notorious for being a control freak, but I gather that he trusted her."

"So what happens now?"

"Their losing the satellite is a pretty big thing. I don't know. They have a backup, but—well, we have to find out what happened to the launch vehicle. I just don't know from their angle what happens. I'm worried about us."

"Does this kill your company?"

"It doesn't help us. But . . ." She stopped again. Fisher could tell she was blaming herself for the mishap, and would, no matter what turned out to be the cause. "I think we'll be all right," she said finally, her voice tentative.

He asked some more questions, pushing her to talk about Kathy. Sandra had a sharper edge than Kathy—she wasn't nasty, exactly, but she could come off as brusque, which was something Kathy never did. Still, they were kindred souls, having faced many of the same challenges breaking into their respective disciplines.

He could have sat there for hours, listening to her talk. It was a link not just to Kathy, but the past.

What a joke that was, he thought to himself. Andy Fisher, nostalgic.

"Keep in touch," Fisher said finally, taking out his wallet to pay. "If you come across anything you think would be useful, I'd appreciate knowing. Even just a rumor."

As he got up, Sandra touched his sleeve.

"You're going to find out who killed her?" she asked.

"Oh yeah," said Fisher. "Oh yeah."

2

CALIFORNIA

Jonathon Loup tilted his glass and looked inside it, as if it contained something more than Scotch. He wished it did—the secret to Terhoussen's stubborn and elusive personality.

The surface of the liquid tilted as Loup's private jet began a gentle banking turn. Loup had offered Terhoussen and two of his people a lift back to San Jose. He was surprised that Terhoussen had accepted; he thought he would want to personally oversee the inspection of the ruined satellite himself. But then again, there was little left of it to inspect.

"I'm not trying to pressure you, Doctor," Loup said, realizing he had little time left to make his argument. "I'm just letting you know—I still have faith in you. If there were circumstances—frankly, if there was an opportunity to help you, I'd be honored to be in that position."

"Yes," muttered Terhoussen.

Loup couldn't understand Terhoussen's attitude. Most businessmen in his position would be falling over themselves to turn Loup's hints into a solid deal.

Before boarding the plane on the way out to the launch, Terhoussen had fielded two calls from different subcontractors to whom he owed money. In both cases, he'd promised he'd have something for them in a few weeks. Clearly he'd been banking on the DOE demonstration grant, even if he was optimistic about the timing.

That wasn't coming now. He had nothing to demonstrate. He had his back to the wall financially, and didn't even have Katherine Feder to help him.

Any other person would be asking Loup how much of a percentage he wanted.

But Terhoussen sat in the seat stone-faced, sipping tomato juice—virgin tomato juice—and grunting every few minutes.

"We're on final approach," the steward whispered to Loup.

"Gentlemen, please put on your seat belts," Loup told the others. "We're about ready to land."

Loup called a taxi so he could get himself something to eat while the airplane was refueled. He tried to get his mind off of Terhoussen, but doing that only led him to think of a much bigger problem—the Chinese.

Borrowing cash to pay them back was impossible. It wasn't that he couldn't raise the money; it was that he couldn't raise it and keep it quiet. If anyone invested in his hedge funds suddenly heard he was trying to get that big a loan, the consequences would be catastrophic.

People would start pulling money out. The SEC—

given new powers in the wake of the Madoff scandal—would come knocking.

No, borrowing was out of the question. So he needed to raise the cash himself.

Pay off the Chinese. Then find some way to get Terhoussen to see the light.

The Chinese first. Dealing with them called for extreme measures.

And a little help.

There was a pay phone in the restaurant lobby. Loup stopped there on his way. He took a quarter from his pocket, stuck it in the phone, then dialed a number in New Jersey he hadn't needed in quite a while.

The quarter dropped through the phone to the return.

"Three dollars and fifty cents for the first three minutes," said a voice.

"Stinking thieves," he muttered, groping for the change.

3

NEW MEXICO

Traditionally, Fisher put off the bureaucratic details of the investigation as long as possible, knowing that the only way to beat the red tape was to outrun it. He also worked from the general premise that the fewer people involved in any enterprise—from making coffee to a murder case—the better. It was a corollary of Newton's law: For every action by an individual, there is an opposite and out of proportion reaction by someone else. And reactions always complicated things.

But just like gravity, bureaucracy and its entanglements were unavoidable in the end.

Bernie Stendanopolis was a complication in and of himself. The first time you met him, you thought he was a puppy dog type—easy to please, practically falling over himself to fill out paperwork and file requisitions.

But first impressions were deceptive. Stendanopolis was a yipper—he yipped at you like a rabid terrier, nipping at your heels incessantly. There wasn't a Bureau regulation that he couldn't cite.

Which did have its entertainment value.

"I would have been out here sooner," he told Fisher when he checked in by phone the morning following the rocket accident, "but the cheapest flight within the twenty-four-hour window took off exactly twenty-three and a half hours after I was notified. And according to reg, that's the one I had to take. Boss wants to talk to you," Stendanopolis added. "Wants you to call in ASAP. Have you filled out the A-40 electronic form authorizing team expenses?"

"I'm working on it," said Fisher.

"The A-40's new and a little tricky," said Stendanopolis. "I'll take care of it."

"Yeah, thanks. It had me beat," said Fisher. He'd actually never seen an A-40, and with luck never would.

Stendanopolis began running down more forms that had to be filled out. Fisher let him indulge his fetish for a few more minutes, then changed the subject.

"Kathy Feder's personal hard drive. We get that thing decoded yet?" Fisher asked.

"Decrypted, you mean."

"Yeah."

"Hold on."

Stendanopolis hunted through some papers.

"No go. It was a completely professional job. Totally erased. Blank. Wiped clean. We have to give a report to NYPD on that?"

"NYPD?"

"They're asking about it," said Stendanopolis. "Are we working with them on this?"

"You're asking me?"

"Well, yes. That part of the case precedes me."

"Have you filled out the form authorizing cooperation with NYPD?"

"Form?"

"Sure. I have no problem working with NYPD, as long as our forms jibe with their forms. Once you get that squared away, go for it," said Fisher. "In the meantime, I have a couple of people over at the NSA who might take a look at it. Tell Trevor to give Samie Markoff a call over there. Trev's clearance isn't high enough for Samie to talk to him, but if he tells her it's for me, she'll do it."

"You're going to backdoor this?"

"I'd never backdoor Samie," said Fisher. "She's front door all the way."

Fisher pictured Stendanopolis's mouth starting to drool. It was a nasty image.

"After you take care of that, there's a NASA liaison on the rocket people that I want you to run down," Fisher added. "Punchline. Find out what their track record is, the background crap. I don't understand why they don't have people at the launch."

"That's easy," said Stendanopolis. "It's not a NASA function."

"What isn't?"

"Launches. Totally private."

"Anybody can launch their own rocket?"

"Yup."

"There's no paperwork?"

"Nope. Not even a PDF form."

"You oughta get on that, Bernie. That's a hole that needs to be filled."

When he was particularly excited, Sidney Festoon's voice went totally nasal. It was a very *shrill* nasal, rising several octaves into a band ordinarily reserved for air raid sirens and kindergarten teachers. The pitch was so severe that it made Fisher's cell phone vibrate, maybe in fear.

Or helpless laughter. Hard to tell.

"You call this progress?" demanded Festoon when he called in. "Now you have rockets blowing up!"

"I'm not sure it's related to the murder."

"Bullshit, Fisher. Even I see the connection. Enemy agents were in New Mexico. I'm looking at the report from Santa Fe. I have Russian, Spanish, French, Japanese, German—any one of these people could be trying to sabotage this important technology."

More likely steal it, thought Fisher. But he couldn't see how that fit with Kathy's death.

The answer probably lay back in New York. Or San Jose. More than likely the rocket had simply malfunctioned. It was just a blind alley, an enticing coincidence that took him away from the main event.

"NYPD filed some sort of protest that you stole evidence," added Festoon. "What's that about?"

"First I heard about it. Are they complaining about her hard drives?"

"What hard drives?"

"Feder's. I got her work drive and her personal drive. Want me to hand them over?"

"Hand them over? To the NYPD?"

"Yeah. You know, full cooperation and all that?"

"Sometimes I don't understand you at all, Fisher."

"Yeah. Same here," he told his boss. "Look, I have to go. I have another call coming in."

"Fisher, wait—" said Festoon.

Fisher didn't wait. He also didn't have another call. But that was the problem with cell phones: It was so easy to lose a connection, especially when you pushed the End Talk button.

NYPD *was* upset about the hard drive.

Or as Tommy Dolan put it, "p-f'in' pissed." He didn't explain what "p-f'in'" meant, which added to the phrase's allure.

"This is the usual Bureau bullshit, right?" said Dolan, when Fisher called him to commiserate. "We do all the work and you guys steal the glory. And the fuckin' evidence."

"Is that the mouth you kiss your wife with?"

"I'm fuckin' divorced. P-f'in' divorced."

"There's a shock," said Fisher. "So you flew all the way out to San Jose? I'm impressed."

"Don't change the subject," said Dolan. "Why did you steal our evidence?"

"I didn't steal any evidence," said Fisher. "I secured the hard drive so it could be decrypted."

"It's encrypted?"

"Actually, it was erased. Professionally," said Fisher. "Very professionally. I have some people looking at it, but they don't think they can come up with anything."

"Who the hell would erase it?"

"One of your suspects, I hope."

"I have no suspects."

"That's a problem, Tom. We should talk about that."

"Yeah, we should." Dolan's tone suddenly changed. No longer belligerent, it became nice—or at least as close to nice as a voice worn hoarse by nearly twenty years of investigations in New York could be.

Fisher was immediately on his guard.

"You're right," said Dolan. "We should talk about this. You going to the memorial service?"

"What memorial service?"

"Feder's. It's tomorrow morning in San Jose, nine o'clock. We can meet for coffee at seven. There's all sorts of Starbucks out here."

Fisher remembered that he had promised Erin he'd be there.

Even if he hadn't, he had to go. It'd be easier if he went with Dolan, actually. A lot easier—he could stay in Agent mode.

"Tell you what—let's find a diner instead," he told Dolan. "Seven o'clock's too early to go over to the dark side."

"I'm sorry, sir, but you don't seem to be on this flight."

Gavril Konovalav thought he had misunderstood something, and asked the gate attendant to repeat what she had said.

"You're not on this flight."

"I have a boarding pass right here," he said, holding up the paper he had printed out at the hotel. "I confirmed this flight less than twelve hours ago."

"You're not in the computer."

"This is the flight to New York?"

"Yes. But—"

"This is my seat—12B."

"There's someone else in that seat, and they're aboard the plane."

"Aboard the plane?"

"The computer just checked them in."

Belatedly, Konovalav realized what was going on.

"The other passenger's name wouldn't be Andy Fisher, would it?"

"Now how can I be in two places at once?" asked Fisher behind him.

"Is there a good reason for this, Andy?" asked Konovalav. "Or has the FBI brought back rendition?"

"I wanted to buy you a beer," said Fisher. "And rendition was a CIA program. We just took people out and shot them behind the warehouse."

"I drink vodka."

"Vodka, then," said Fisher, sweeping his hand in the general direction of the bar.

"You think because I am here that I have something to do with the destruction of rocket," said Konovalav. "Believe me, this is furthest thing from my mind. Destroying rocket."

"Why would you destroy the rocket?" Fisher asked.

"Exactly. I do not. Wouldn't."

Konovalav's English grammar tended to break down when he was excited, but was he excited because he was being wrongly accused? Or maybe late for an important meeting at an Atlantic City craps table?

"So what are you spying on?" asked Fisher. "The rocket or the satellite?"

"I don't spy on anything."

"You just went out here for tourism?"

Fisher put his elbow down on the table, propped his head up with his hand, and then rubbed his eyes with his thumb and forefinger. He hated it when people assumed he was even dumber than he looked.

"It's a free country," said Konovalav. "I enjoy the weather."

"Disney World's nice this time of year, too. Why not go there?"

"Maybe next year."

Konovalav took a sip of his drink. True to his word, he had ordered vodka.

Finlandia.

Fisher wondered if it was meant as a clandestine signal that he intended to defect.

"I was figuring that it had to be the solar technology, until the rocket went down," said Fisher. "Now I'm not sure what to think. Maybe you saw them as competitors."

Konovalav made a face.

"You do any work for the Federal Space Agency?" asked Fisher. "My Russian's not good enough—how do you pronounce that again? FKE—*Federal'noye kosmicheskoye agentstvo Rossi,* right?"

"This vodka sat in the bottom of the boat too long," he said. "Very harsh."

Konovalav's nonanswer was itself a pretty obvious "yes." But even so, it got Fisher no real information. He tossed out a few technical terms he'd heard, and asked if he'd run into the Chinese or the French. He was looking more for a reaction than anything else, but aside from irritating Konovalav, he got nothing.

"It's a free country here, yes?" said the Russian finally.

"Far as I know," Fisher told him.

"So I am free to go?"

"If you have a reservation, sure."

Konovalav shook his head. "Wait until you are a guest in my country."

Fisher laughed.

"You may find you have a flight to Dallas in an hour. Once you get there, I believe there'll be a seat in first class on the next Delta flight to New York. Your job is to find the right gates. Excuse me. They just called my plane."

4

SAN JOSE

T. Parker Terhoussen put his elbows on the desk, then propped his chin with his hands.

It was all doable, as long as he could get the backup satellite into orbit by the end of the month. If he did that, the Department of Energy grant would come through. Combined with the insurance money from the satellite destroyed in the launch, they could move on to the next phase.

Fail to get that grant, however, and PowerSat would move in. Competition itself didn't bother Terhoussen. The problem was that there was only so much money to go around. If PowerSat or some other company got the grant—*his* grant—there'd be nothing left for him.

Borrowing money would also become considerably more difficult, maybe impossible. His competitors would be the fair-haired kids, favored by the feds. Jonathon Loup would be salivating over their project, not his.

Perhaps, thought Terhoussen, he shouldn't be so dismissive of Loup. At least Loup was willing to loan money without insisting on part of the company. He definitely wanted a piece—he never said it directly, but it was obvious. Who could blame him, though?

Lose the grant, get in bed with someone worse than Loup.

Or have to take on a partner. Sell the company.

He'd burn every trace of the design before he did that.

Terhoussen raised his head, looking at the engineers and scientists who'd crowded into his office. There were seventeen people, with twenty-three doctorates among them. Not counting his.

"We will launch before the DOE deadline," he told them. "That's all."

"The only company that can handle that quick a turnaround is Punchline," said Terhoussen's launch expert, Stephen Rae. "And I don't think—"

"Contractually, they owe us a launch," said Terhoussen, rising. "They will do it. It will be done. We will succeed."

5

SAN JOSE

There were instances where going to a memorial service made a lot of sense for a detective, especially in a murder case. Funerals were generally populated by people who knew the victim, making it easy to get background information. And they tended to be eager to talk about the deceased, even negatively, even if that conflicted with popular wisdom.

Showing up also signaled that you were serious about solving the crime, which tended to get people to cooperate. If you played it right, people might even remember who the hell you were when you called later on for real information.

Maybe.

There was also the possibility, depending on the type of case, that the murderer would show up. But this wasn't that type of case. And Fisher already knew everything he wanted to know about Kathy Feder. Except who killed her.

Fisher and Dolan stood at the back, near the wall. Erin Merril was sitting near the front. She turned, spotted Fisher, and gave him a discreet wave. He nodded back.

"She's a looker," said Dolan. "Relative?"

"Good friend."

"Yours or the deceased?"

"Both," admitted Fisher.

Dolan raised an eyebrow. "You talk to her already?"

"Yeah," said Fisher.

"Knows anything?"

"Not about this."

He and Dolan watched as Kathy's minister gave a reading from the Bible and then invited a cousin to say a few words. The cousin—actually a second cousin whom Fisher had never met—was barely twenty and remembered Kathy mostly as a child. She was the closest relative at the funeral.

That wasn't surprising. Both of Kathy's parents were dead, and if Fisher's memory was correct her two uncles were both well into their seventies.

The cousin spoke about how they played softball together. It was a lovely speech, short and emotional. Just the sort of thing to make Fisher wish he hadn't come.

Then Erin walked to the podium. Fisher stood biting his lip as she talked about her friend and his ex-lover, how she saw the good in other people. It went beyond the personal, said Erin. She wanted to help all of humanity—that's why she had been working for the company that built Helios, working 24/7 to solve the world's energy problems. Someday, the success of the project would be her greatest memorial.

"She talked about doing something like this, exactly like this, the first night I met her. That was back in college," said Erin. She sniffled a little, but her eyes remained dry and she kept talking, clearly determined to pay her friend the respects she deserved.

"When this system works," concluded Erin, "it will be her lasting legacy."

Fisher fidgeted. It was starting to feel stuffy in the church. He tried focusing on the people in the pews. There were less than a dozen, all apparently neighbors. No one from Punchline, at least not that he recognized.

What was up with that?

Fisher tightened his arms across his chest. There'd be more people at his funeral. He had a hell of a lot more enemies than this. They'd all come to dance on his grave. Hell, if everybody who hated him came, they could hold it at RFK Stadium. A long line of FBI supervisors would lead the procession.

The service concluded abruptly. The casket—closed—was wheeled down the aisle. Fisher ducked out before it reached him at the back.

Outside, he caught a glimpse of Kathy's assistant, James Edmunds, slinking around the side of the building. Edmunds took a sharp right toward the parking lot.

"Say, James, slow down a second," said Fisher, trotting after him.

"Oh." Edmunds's reaction told Fisher that he hadn't been avoiding him. "Hey, I need to get that hard drive back," said Edmunds. "Our systems people are a little torqued about it."

"No sweat," Fisher told him.

"Good. When?"

"Soon. There's paperwork to fill out and that sort of thing."

"Okay." Edmunds nodded, then turned to leave.

"Hey, wait up," said Fisher, falling in alongside him. Fisher had long legs, but Edmunds walked quickly.

"I gotta get back to work," he said. "I'm on my lunch break."

"Lunch? It's not even breakfast."

"I know. I gotta grab the light rail." He pointed. The station was only a block away; the line ran next to Icarus's building complex.

"Terhoussen wouldn't give you off?" asked Fisher, walking with him.

Edmunds shook his head. "Nobody's got off."

"Is he always such a jerk?"

"We have to get another satellite up," said Edmunds. "There's a deadline. Everybody's working around the clock. No breaks."

"Another satellite?"

"Yeah. By the end of the month."

"Who's launching it?"

"Don't know. Punchline, probably."

Fisher was surprised—Sandra, he was sure, would have mentioned it if that was the case. He filed the information away for future reference.

"Was there anyone else from Icarus here?" he asked.

"Not that I saw. Not even Debbie."

"Who's Debbie?"

"Debbie Ferris. Kathy's old assistant. I thought for sure she'd be here."

"She works for the company?"

"She did until eight or nine months ago. That's when they hired me. I replaced her."

"Full name?"

"Debra Ferris. She works for a clinic now. Stress Reduction of San Jose. They're psychiatrists, counselors. Like that. Damn—there's my train." Edmunds started to run. "They do hypnosis. Might help you with your smoking."

"Thanks," said Fisher. "I'm pretty good at it already though."

Telling Dolan about the other assistant came right out of the FBI Cooperate with Lesser Police Authorities handbook: Rule 8.2 a) Always share information that is of little consequential value.

Fisher also offered to have Dolan talk to her with him: Rule 17.3 c) Agents should suggest members of lesser police agencies to accompany them on interrogations when i) interrogations are unlikely to yield tangible results, and ii) members of lesser police agencies are likely to go on their own anyway.

Dolan agreed to come, allowing Fisher to implement something from his own rule book—always charge lunch to your partner's expense account. Even if it's only McDonald's.

Dolan took two calls while Fisher ate his Big Mac. One was from one of his compatriots back in the city, telling him that they had checked the video on the hotel without coming up with a possible suspect. The other was from the coroner, confirming that Kathy had died of a single shot to the forehead.

"They rule out suicide?" asked Fisher.

Dolan made a face.

"They found powder residue on her arm?" Fisher asked.

"No. But—"

"I hate buts."

"Yeah, so do I. Because of where the gun was found, locked door—"

"Hotel rooms always lock behind you."

"Hey, listen, I'm not the coroner. They left that possibility open. I gotta tell you—I think it's murder, you think it's murder, but we ain't got any evidence."

"You think she held the gun like this?" Fisher mimicked the angle, which he thought fairly unlikely. "And if she did, the weapon would have fallen differently."

"Yeah, I know, I know." Dolan seemed resigned—as in ready to give up.

"Suicide closes out the case though, right?"

Dolan shrugged. Fisher changed his tack.

"The thing that's interesting is the video," said Fisher.

"Maybe he's Spider-Man and got in from the window."

"They don't open. I checked. No, it's the coverage from the video camera," said Fisher. "He knew what he was doing—he came up from the stairs, stayed close to the wall. And he could duck around the camera downstairs somehow. My point is, he planned it."

"Yeah, all right. But none of that's helping us solve the case, right?"

"You look at video cameras in the neighborhood?" Fisher asked.

"What do you mean?"

"Cameras across the street, next door. Maybe there's an ATM."

"That's Grand Central. You know how many video cameras there are in the area?"

"Then it should be easy."

Dolan rolled his eyes, and went to work on his cheeseburger.

The clinic where Debra Ferris worked was a low-slung, one-story building with a pair of large, rect-angular metal slabs poised over its brown stucco body. The slabs looked as if they had been caught in midair.

Fisher wondered if the design was part of an employee incentive plan—work hard or the flying meteorites will crush you.

The receptionist told them that Ferris hadn't re-ported to work that morning, hadn't called in, and hadn't answered her phone.

"It's not like her," she said. "But the doctor-in-charge said to give her a little room. Sometimes, we all need a little room."

Fisher asked for her address.

Neither he nor Dolan said the obvious as they drove Dolan's rental to her house, a bungalow at the far side of a dead end about three miles away.

"If this were New York, I wouldn't try to force the door," said Dolan when she didn't answer the bell.

"Neither would I," said Fisher, reaching for his pick. "Good thing it's not locked."

Fisher pushed the door as soon as his pick clicked the tumbler clear. It stopped about halfway, bumping against Debra Ferris's prone foot.

"You want to call the locals, or should I?" asked Dolan.

6

GLENDALE FALLS, UPSTATE NEW YORK

The power substation sat at the end of a dirt road about a half mile from the New York State Thruway. The area was sparsely populated. Fewer than a thousand people lived in the town of Glendale Falls, and most were residents of the village, which lay at the bank of a large creek just to the south.

The creek was indirectly responsible for the substation's location. More than a hundred years before, it had been dammed up, first to supply power for gristmills, then, in the 1920s, for a small hydroelectric power station. The station had been abandoned in the late 1940s or early 1950s—no one in town now remembered precisely when—but the substation remained.

The station was small, both in physical size and in the amount of electricity that ran through it. That was one reason its technology was relatively old and simple; it simply wasn't considered important enough to upgrade. If some of the circuitry there failed and it deprived the area of power for a few hours, what was the harm? It could be easily fixed, and the inconvenience forgotten. It was a decision made more from neglect than necessity.

But under certain circumstances, the circuit was more strategic than it seemed at first glance. If another substation a hundred miles away—this one much larger and with considerably more power—was offline at the same time this one failed, the area affected by a failure at the Glendale Falls substation would be considerably larger.

More important, a switching station that brought nuclear energy into the regional grid could be affected as well—possibly overloaded, if the circumstances were right. At that point, the nuclear plant could be forced to take itself offline. Safety regulations—perfectly logical and adopted out of an abundance of caution—would deprive the regional grid of a considerable amount of power.

The result would not be a blackout. Rather, electricity would simply be purchased farther west, moving like a domino along the interconnected grid.

Of course, it would have to be purchased at spot rates, which at the moment were trending fairly high, due to the shortages in the New York metro area.

Of course, the odds of everything lining up precisely in that manner were fairly high. The nuclear power plant would have to have already shut down part of its yard for maintenance, the larger switching area would have to be out of service, one of the main transmission trunk lines would have to be temporarily disconnected . . .

And there would have to be some sort of catastrophic failure in Glendale Falls.

Or perhaps just a terrorist attack.

The transmission of high-voltage electricity over vast distances through wire was considered a ho-hum technology, absolutely commonplace in the twenty-first century. But it represented one of man's greatest engineering feats, no less impressive because of its seeming simplicity. The Romans had built an impressive empire on the foundation of their cities, which in turn depended on potable water, generally carried by aqueduct from sources beyond contamination. Power lines were the aqueducts of modern life.

In this case, the line was actually the smaller of four sets running through upstate New York. It was working as normal, well within design parameters, when at precisely 4:23 A.M. a radio-controlled aircraft approached the line. Radio-controlled aircraft can be difficult to fly, and even in the case where their control is being guided with the help of a computer, it can be nearly impossible to fly the plane precisely into a target such as a transmission.

For that reason, the explosives on the aircraft were detonated by a proximity fuse.

As the aircraft exploded, its radio-control unit sent a signal via satcom to a man who was hiking through the woods about a hundred yards from the Glendale Falls substation. He was behind schedule—he'd pulled his white van off the state thruway twenty minutes before, and should have been at the substation fence by now. But he'd run into a thick set of prickle bushes in the dark; attempting to backtrack he'd gotten lost, and by the time he decided to just push ahead he'd fallen nearly ten minutes behind his tight schedule. The buzz on his phone changed his trot to a run; the chain-link fence at the back of the station appeared within a few seconds, his target a few yards inside.

The fence was intended to deter animals rather than vandals, and he climbed it within seconds. Dropping to the ground, he rose and then backed himself against the fence, making sure he was properly oriented so he could find his way around the yard in the half-light. Getting lost once this morning was enough.

The man had been told that he had exactly five minutes after the signal to disable the circuit. In actual fact, he had considerably more time—in theory he could have taken all day—but he didn't know that, and the prospect of not being paid if he failed compelled him to hurry. He swung his pack off his shoulder, unzipped it, and grabbed the small packet of explosives from inside. The charge was overkill—there were actually easier ways to disable the bus—but necessary for the story that was an integral part of the operation.

The man set the charge, pushed the button on the simple watch timer that governed the detonator, then scrambled away. He was within sight of his van when the bomb exploded.

Within nanoseconds, half of upstate New York was without power. By the time most of the power was restored twenty minutes later, the price independent power suppliers were allowed to charge had tripled under contract. It would double again before the end of the day.

7

SAN JOSE

The lemon-fresh scent Fisher had noticed at Kathy's condo was missing at Debbie Ferris's. There was also no sign of a computer ever having been in the apartment. So he left Dolan with the crime scene people, and went back to the clinic, hoping to get a look at their computers.

"What makes you think I'm going to let you look at our computer system?" sputtered the assistant office manager when Fisher proposed it.

"Because Debra Ferris has just been found dead in her apartment, and maybe I can find something here to solve the crime."

The woman began screaming, then bolted from the reception area.

Fisher took that as a yes, and sat down at her computer. He was still looking at the list of files in the root directory when the head of the clinic, a psychiatrist in his late fifties, came out a few minutes later and demanded to know what he was doing.

Fisher held up his FBI credentials and continued to look through the computer.

"What do you think you're doing?" insisted the psychiatrist. "Those are patient records."

"I'm not interested in your patients," said Fisher, hedging—he wasn't interested in them *yet*. But then, he might never be. "I want to look at your e-mail and browsing history for something that might connect your employee to a woman who was murdered in New York. They used to work together."

"Aside from your charming personality, how am I supposed to know that you're really an FBI agent?" asked the psychiatrist.

"There's my credentials," said Fisher. "I also have pictures of the crime scene on my cell phone if you want to see them."

They reached a compromise—the office manager would go through the files with him, looking for anything out of place. But the manager proved to be too upset to do it, and eventually one of the counselors sat down with him. They found some soft porn and some coupon codes worth fifty dollars off on the next purchase at Sears.com, but nothing relating to Icarus. There were no e-mails from Kathy, and not even an indication that Debbie had followed the story of her death.

With no obvious leads, Fisher decided it wasn't worth confiscating the computer.

"The locals may want to look at it," he told the doctor as he left. "Erasing the porn is probably not a good idea. It'll only make them suspicious."

"Of what?" asked the psychologist.

Under other circumstances, Fisher might have made a bad joke. But it had been a long day, and so he simply shrugged.

Festoon woke him at five o'clock the next morning to tell him about a terrorist attack on the Glendale Falls substation.

"What does that have to do with two murders?" Fisher asked.

"Don't you understand, Fisher? The American power grid is under attack by demonic terrorists."

"Are all terrorists demonic?" asked Fisher, wincing as he caught a glimpse of the time, "or just the ones I deal with?"

Two hours later, Fisher was flying eastward, grumbling in his seat about the lack of reading material and wondering if it was too early to order a beer.

8

NEW MEXICO

Why would there be back pressure in the oxidizer line?

Sandra Chester got up from her computer. The incident team's preliminary examination of the disaster had flagged discrepancies in two different sets of instruments that monitored the fuel flow. One said everything was fine; the other reported a disruption in the flow which the valve controls attempted to compensate for.

Fatally, perhaps.

Or, alternatively, the disruption was the real problem, and no matter what the computerized controls tried, the rocket was doomed.

Huge difference.

Even the slightest burr in the assembly could be disastrous, but it had been examined meticulously, tested and reexamined.

It had to be the gauge, Sandra thought. But that, too, had been tested and retested.

Unfortunately, neither part had been recovered from the range. The search was continuing, but it was highly unlikely that they would find either part, at least in any condition to yield much information.

She was sure it couldn't be the tube. She'd looked at it herself, several times. Granted, visual inspections couldn't always find flaws, but their subcontractor had an excellent reputation, and would have fluoroscoped the entire piece and assembly before sending it on.

Which left the gauge, at heart a relatively simple circuit that had been used not only by her company but companies and governments around the world for more than a decade. Nothing in its history suggested a similar failure.

She needed fresh air.

Sandra put her workstation into hibernation and left her office. She nodded at the two engineers in the large room off the hall and walked to the stairway, trotting down to the landing.

It was overcast and threatening, though the odds were always against rain in the desert. She pushed open the door and stepped out, walking along the flagstone path past the picnic area and smokers' corral. She felt a pang—she'd only recently given up smoking, an occasional habit—but kept going, walking past the parking garage to the wide mesa behind the building.

Details of the launch day kept playing in her head. Andy Fisher showing up. As an obnoxious FBI agent.

Who would have thought, back in college. But you could say that about most people, couldn't you? Life led them on strange paths.

Andy—he'd always been intelligent. And a wise guy. Funny, though. Nice. Especially to her.

He seemed to have grown harder, much harder. The job must do that.

She'd had a slight crush. Many women did, she suspected. But he was with Kathy then.

Had his arrival at the range just been a coincidence? Or did he know something was going to happen?

If it was sabotage, wouldn't that explain why the rocket failed?

Sure, except for the fact that there should be telltale signs. And there weren't. Were there?

No. It looked like any other launch.

Failure. She had to accept it and move on. She had to find out what was wrong, and fix it.

Sandra stared in the direction of the range, barely visible from here.

Back to work, she told herself. She turned and headed toward the building, thinking of how much she wanted a cigarette.

9

GLENDALE FALLS

The tire tracks came from eighteen-inch wheels. Knowing that, investigators looked at E-ZPass records and narrowed down the possible vehicles to a list of just under five thousand. In most cases, checking out five thousand vehicles and their owners would stretch an investigative force beyond its limits, but this was no ordinary investigation. This was now a *national priority combined task force investigation*, a full-blown intraagency bonanza with regularly scheduled press briefings and high-level coordinating sessions.

Festoon was in his glory.

Fisher, on the other hand, was grouchy. He'd had to take a helicopter up from Westchester after his flight from California. It wasn't that he minded helicopters, per se. But this was a state police helicopter, and it came with zero coffee.

Clearly the troopers' tradition of high standards had hit a new low.

Fisher was dubious about the entire enterprise. He didn't think that the E-ZPass data was going to get them anywhere. For one thing, any terrorist with half a brain would realize that his comings and goings would be recorded on E-ZPass; he'd pay cash instead. Then they'd be relying on a tollbooth taker's memory.

And that was assuming that he actually went through the tollbooth when he got on the thruway. Fisher wouldn't. There were countless ways on and off the thruway, and even if you weren't familiar with the area, it didn't take more than a few moments on Google Earth to figure them out.

"So you don't think we should check the E-ZPass records?" asked Michael Macklin, who was bringing Fisher up to date. Macklin was the coordinator of the Homeland Security Special Counter-Terrorism Task Force, and had been sent up to New York to help the state police Bureau of Criminal Investigations, which was the lead agency in the investigation. Fisher had worked with Macklin before and liked him, though that wasn't exactly a character reference.

"I'm not saying you shouldn't check," said Fisher. "Just that I wouldn't count on it going anywhere."

"What would you count on?" asked the BCI lieutenant in charge of the case.

"Caffeine," said Fisher. "It's the one thing in life you can count on."

The lieutenant gave a little snort. He'd introduced himself as Joe Carloff. Fisher had to work hard not to call him Boris.

"So what do you think, Fish?" asked Macklin. "Muslim terror cell? You guys made that bust upstate a couple of months ago."

The bust: a pizza parlor worker who had tried to buy a concrete-filled grenade launcher. Even his father said he had the brain of an eight-year-old. This job required someone at least eleven.

"Incidents like this, they're usually local vandals," Fisher said. "Bored kids who are playing at being sociopath monsters. They start here, then they get MBAs, join the corporate world, go up the career ladder, and do real damage."

"I don't think this was a kid, Fish," said Macklin.

"Neither do I. And did I say you could call me Fish?"

Fisher got up and walked to the table where the coffeepot was set up. The BCI had commandeered two rooms in a trooper barracks not far from the substation to use as the headquarters for the investigation. The rooms weren't much—big spaces with a few desks pushed together, some phones and computers. But one thing you could say for the state police: they knew how to make coffee. And they kept it coming. A young trooper, hair in military buzz cut and gray uniform freshly dry-cleaned, stepped into the room with a fresh supply of Maxwell House and chilled milk.

"Geez, I'm s-sorry, Andy," stuttered Macklin. "You can call me Mack, if you want."

"You're not a Mack," Fisher told him. He pointed at the photo showing the remains of the incendiary device that had started the blaze. "Here's the thing that bugs me. This device is simple. You can get the directions on how to make it off the Internet. Right?"

"I guess."

"Look at the wiring, though. See how neat it is? The twists on the wires, the solder—perfect. The person that did this has serious skills."

"So he's an electrician in his spare time," said Carloff.

"Maybe. Or more likely a skilled bomb maker," said Fisher. "But here's the thing. If you're an experienced terrorist, not some numb nut who can be talked into shooting his own grandmother for the chance of screwing virgins in paradise, why would you pick a dumpy backwoods substation to blow up, instead of one an hour's drive away, where even if it didn't cause a massive blackout, you'd get at least twenty-four hours' worth of headlines?"

"This one caused a pretty good-sized blackout," said Macklin. "It knocked out the whole Northeast for a few hours. Pretty good for a little substation."

"Yeah," said Fisher. "Most wouldn't do that if they blew up, but this just happened to be the right one. So how do you think he knew?"

10

JERSEY CITY

"The Chinese, the Chinese, the Chinese—that's all I ever hear from you, Dennis. *The Chinese!*"

Loup watched as Dennis Van Gross seemed to shrink under his tirade, pushing back into the thickly padded seat. But it was one thing to intimidate Dennis, and another to get the Chinese off his back.

Or out of his neck, because they were more like vampires, trying to suck his blood.

"Icarus is our way out of this," Dennis said quietly. "They're salivating over it. Everybody wants the technology."

"It just blew up on a launch pad in New Mexico."

"That only makes them want it more."

"What's our cash position?"

Dennis laughed. It was so uncharacteristic that Loup didn't know how to react.

"We made plenty of money yesterday," he said.

"Jonathon, we're talking here about half a billion. Even I can't make that much in a day. Or two."

"What if we sell some of our plants to Tyenergy?" said Loup.

"So they can close them?"

Loup shrugged. Tyenergy was a nuclear power conglomerate; it owned a dozen nuclear power plants outright, and shares of another dozen. Though it was a publicly traded company, its board of directors was dominated by the CEO, Whitley Atkins. Atkins was the Genghis Khan of nuclear power, taking over everything in his path.

"I don't think you could get half a billion out of them. And besides, you do that, the money is all in the funds. We can't just move it over. That's jail, Jonathon."

Better than dealing with the Chinese, Loup thought.

"So what do I tell them?" Dennis asked finally.

"Tell the bastards I'll be at their goddamn meeting," Loup said finally. "But make sure there's no meal involved. I don't trust them not to poison me."

Chou Lai Wan wanted to meet in his lawyers' offices uptown, but Loup nixed that idea without discussion. They settled on a private club in Manhattan where Loup had a membership.

Wan's official title was executive secretary to the Chinese Trade Council in New York. It was a bland title for a man with enormous power. He was a diplomat connected somehow to the ruling Chinese government—not the official government, but the dozen or so party members and army generals who really ran things. He was smooth—and as far as Loup was concerned, little better than a Chinese mafia don.

The East Side Association was located in a five-story building on Fifth Avenue opposite Central

Park. Built primarily of gray-hued sandstone in the early 1900s, the building had survived long enough to be granted landmark status, though its actual design and appearance were so mundane that even the most carefully observant passerby might miss it.

This was not a liability for the club, which valued its obscurity to the point of neglecting to post a street number, let alone a sign, on the facade. Visitors—and there were never many—had to deduce the club's number by process of elimination. After climbing a flight of thick stone steps, they were met by a set of mahogany doors whose very thickness warned against entry. The doors were unlocked, but since there was no bell or knocker, the timid and unsure generally retreated. Inside the hall the atmosphere was cold, literally. The HVAC system was permanently set to keep the first floor at sixty-four degrees, purposely uncomfortable.

If a visitor simply stepped into the thickly carpeted hallway and did nothing more, he or she could stand for hours before being helped; in fact, help would never actually arrive. The doorman—or sergeant at arms as he was called on the club's official payroll sheet—was stationed at the far end of the hall, standing discreetly out of view (though monitoring the sidewalk in front of the building as well as the steps and hall with the aid of a video surveillance system). He only approached when the guest reached the threshold of the antechamber where he was stationed. Then he blocked the door—the man had been a tackle for the NFL Ravens and then a professional wrestler for a few years before finding his true calling—and asked the guest to whom they should be announced.

Chou Lai Wan arrived at the club with a phalanx of lawyers and aides. Having dealt with Loup before, he knew that the American would be late, and timed his arrival accordingly—it was more than thirty minutes past the appointed hour. Even so, he was pleasantly surprised when the doorman told him that Loup was waiting.

They tromped through the large common room. Filled with stiff leather chairs and lined by ceiling-high bookcases, the room was largely ceremonial; the seats were too uncomfortable and the temperature too chilly for anyone to actually use it. Unwanted guests and prospective members were sometimes seated here, just to heighten the luxuriousness of their eventual audience in the members' quarters, as the rest of the place was called.

A double flight of steps sat at the far end of the room. Whether by design or because measurements were not standardized at the time the building was erected, the risers were taller than customary elsewhere. Short-legged, Wan had to lift his legs awkwardly to avoid tripping.

The doorman led them to a large room on the third floor. A teak-inlay table sat in the middle of the room, taking up about half the floor space; most of the rest was given over to the oversized chairs that sat around it. A waiter stood at the far end, next to a bar setup and a table filled with crustless sandwich halves.

There were considerable refreshments here, but no Loup.

Wan took his seat with a frown. Before he finished looking around the room, one of the club attendants came in, lowered himself discreetly next to his chair, and asked if he was Mr. Wan.

"Yes," said Wan.

"Mr. Loup is waiting for you in the barroom. Just one guest is allowed there, sir," he added, straightening.

Wan considered sending one of his lieutenants, but decided that would needlessly prolong things. He told the others that he would rejoin them shortly, then followed the attendant up to the fifth floor and its penthouse barroom. Loup was standing on the patio overlooking the park, a glass of Scotch in his hand.

"Drink, Mr. Wan?" he asked.

"No, thank you."

Loup nodded, then turned back toward the park.

"There is the matter of the notes," said Wan. "We are calling them Friday at five, as the terms dictate."

"The terms allow that," said Loup. "They don't dictate it."

Wan didn't answer.

"There's no sense for us to be antagonistic," said Loup.

"I have tried working with you in the past, Mr. Loup. You resist it."

"I've already decided to help you get Icarus. That's what you want, isn't it?"

"Icarus is not worth half of what you owe, Mr. Loup."

"It's worth much more, isn't it? To China. For any number of reasons."

Loup drained the rest of the Scotch in his glass, enough so that it burned the back of his throat. He turned and held the glass up, signaling to the waiter who was watching back near the sliding glass doors to get a refill. Neither man spoke until Loup had a new glass.

"Orbiting solar arrays could solve your energy needs for decades if not centuries," Loup said. "Just as they would do for America. There are plenty of places for the receiving units, even more in your country than ours."

Loup took a sip of Scotch. He reminded himself it was meant to be drunk slowly, savored, not used as an antiseptic or painkiller.

"If China had the technology, and America didn't, there would be other advantages," he continued. "Competitive advantages because of raw material costs we'd still have to incur, revenue streams that you would get—"

"Mr. Loup, we're both well aware of the benefits of the technology. Let us concentrate on its transference."

"Good."

"I understand that Icarus is privately held. How do you plan to gain control?"

"They need operating capital. I'm the only one who can provide it. I give it to them on my terms."

Wan made a face.

"I know, it's more complicated than that," admitted Loup. "It's going to take time."

"You're testing my patience, Mr. Loup. You think that you hold all the cards. I am the one with the notes. You leveraged your assets far beyond what you actually had, and now your debt greatly exceeds your ability to pay. So you have nothing—no leverage, nothing."

"If you don't want to work with me on Icarus, there are other holdings that I can arrange to—"

"Your other holdings aren't worth that much."

The note of impatience in Wan's voice angered Loup.

"Look, let's talk like adults," said Loup. "Push me and I flush my company. I just go bankrupt. Don't think it's not set up to let me walk away without tears."

"We will hold you personally liable if that happens," said Wan. "There's no place on earth you can go to escape."

"To succeed here, you're going to have to do things my way. You're going to have to trust me."

"I doubt they'll ever trust you," said Wan. "That would be foolish."

"Trust isn't necessary," admitted Loup. "A certain amount of cooperation. And patience."

"Patience is a quality that has limits."

"Absolutely," said Loup. "Absolutely."

"You are a very strange man, Mr. Loup," said Wan. "Perhaps I will have that drink now."

11

SAN JOSE

It could not be said that T. Parker Terhoussen suffered fools gladly, even when he was lecturing them. The fact that he had known Congressman Gabriel Gonzalez for more than a decade, and, more important, that Gonzalez had been instrumental in obtaining several grants for the Icarus project, did not change the basic calculus: Gonzalez was a fool; talking to him was tedious.

Especially when the talk centered on other, greater fools.

Nonetheless, Terhoussen did his best to appear patient.

Until Gonzalez used the word "valid" to describe what the fools were saying.

"There are no negative environmental consequences at all," said Terhoussen, interrupting the congressman in mid-sentence. "None. This is a good solution for everyone."

"I don't mean that what they're saying is right." Gonzalez tried to quickly retreat. "What I mean is, they make arguments that sound reasonable. And because of that—"

"Reasonable?" Terhoussen slammed his fist on the coffee table that separated him from Gonzalez. The picture of Gonzalez and his two-year-old grandson, which had been sitting near the center of the table, collapsed on its face. "What is reasonable? Talk of death rays? They haven't a clue."

"They think of *Star Wars*—"

"It's *not Star Wars*. It's the same technology they hold next to their heads for hours every day. The same technology. Microwaves. Cell phones."

"Now, you've told me yourself it's more sophisticated than that."

"Sophisticated, yes. But the principles are the same. Transferring energy by microwaves is no more dangerous than moving it by wire."

Terhoussen felt himself starting to hyperventilate. He took a breath, and tried a different tack.

"We should talk about how many pounds of carbon dioxide are generated by natural gas plants in a typical year," he told the congressman. "Take just the plants that would generate as much electricity as Helios. It's nearly four billion metric tons! And that's just carbon dioxide. If we start talking about pollutants—"

"No one is going to dispute those arguments," said Gonzalez. "But the possibility of ozone being produced during your process—that's a problem."

"No ozone is going to be produced by the process. That's a red herring."

"You know, Doctor, don't take this the wrong way, but I don't believe you're the best advocate for your project."

"What do you mean?"

"You're too—you get emotional when you talk about it."

Terhoussen slipped back into the couch. He glanced around the office, eyes wandering as Gonzalez lectured him on the need for public relations. There were pictures on the wall showing Gonzalez with various public figures and celebrities, as if his job was to shake hands with people.

Maybe that was his job, Terhoussen thought. He certainly didn't have much brain power for anything else.

Whatever happened to Plato's philosopher kings?

"It's not enough to be good for the environment, Doc," continued the congressman. "You have to cultivate an image."

"This isn't a floor wax," said Terhoussen bitterly. "This is power for the next generation—for all time. This is as significant as Edison."

"Now, you take Tyenergy," said Gonzalez, ignoring him. "There's a company that is in control of its image. What do they do? They own nuclear power plants. Four or five years ago, they had the worst image you can imagine. Satan would have scored higher than a nuclear power company in a popularity poll. Even politicians would have. And you know how much the public loves us."

Gonzalez smiled, trying to lighten Terhoussen's dark mood.

"But now, by carefully presenting their case to the public—"

"Those bastards are out to ruin us!" shouted Terhoussen, no longer able to control his temper. "Tyenergy, the other nukes—they've been donating to the groups that are raising questions about us. They're behind the move in Congress to change the permitting process. They want to slow us down, then kill us. I wouldn't be surprised if they blew up my satellite."

"Calm down, Parker." Gonzalez glanced at the door.

"I've seen their lobbyists around. I've read the donor lists," added Terhoussen. "They've even given money to you."

"They've given a little, yes. So have you."

"Solar energy is better than nuclear power. Cleaner, safer, cheaper. A dozen Helios arrays in orbit and the U.S. can close all of its nuclear power plants and stop using coal."

Terhoussen winced internally at his own exaggeration—they couldn't close *both* nuclear and coal with only a dozen satellites. More would be needed, at least until the next generation of arrays.

Gonzalez wouldn't even remember the boast in twenty-four hours, he knew—but it bothered him greatly that he had resorted to exaggeration. Logic, empirical logic based on verifiable facts, should be enough to carry the day. He couldn't lose sight of that.

"Like I say, Doc, I think you get a little passionate about this. Maybe I can help you find a PR firm, or at least a girl somewhere who can help you make your case to the press. Or a guy," Gonzalez added, rising. "Should we go have lunch?"

"The Department of Energy grant?" said Terhoussen, reminding Gonzalez why he had come.

"Oh, don't worry about that." The congressman clapped him on the back. "As long as they see something in orbit—"

"But that's my point. We may be delayed."

"Well, they can't change the law." Gonzalez frowned. "Just get something up. That's all. You can do that, can't you?"

"We are going to," said Terhoussen.

He tried to calm himself down as they walked to the door. It was going to be hard eating through his clenched teeth.

12

NEW YORK CITY

Investigations had their own rhythm. Some were rap songs, smashing to a conclusion with an inevitable beat. Some were rock epics, whining and meandering across a vast terrain. Others were Mozartian operas, with finely wrought stanzas and fat ladies singing at the end.

And then there were the pieces composed by madmen and performed by elementary school bands.

The Icarus case, or the murder of Kathy Feder, or the blowing up of the substation in Glendale Falls, was the latter.

Definitely.

For nearly a week after the "incident" at Glendale Falls, the state police task force, with help from Homeland Security, plodded meticulously through literally hundreds of leads. As Fisher had suspected, using the E-ZPass records to try and locate the perpetrators turned out to be a dead end: Every one of the vehicles with eighteen-inch tires that had used the road around the time of the attack had an alibi.

A more old-fashioned approach worked better:

The state police checked lists of cars and other vehicles that had been stolen around the time of the incident. They had to go back several days and account for an unexpected tire swap, but eventually they did locate the vehicle, a white van—originally painted red—that had been abandoned at the train station in Tuxedo, New York, some three hundred miles from the substation.

"It took chutzpah to drive that far," said Macklin when the van was found.

"What do you expect?" answered Fisher. "It's hard to get a taxi up in Glendale."

The train that stopped at Tuxedo connected to New York City. There were two ticket machines on the platform. The task force obtained a list of the credit cards that were used to purchase tickets that day and dutifully checked each owner out. The two people who didn't have very good alibis were an eighty-year-old widower who lived across the street and a novelist who claimed he'd gone into the city to see his editor that day.

The novelist claimed to be working on a young adult book about Bat Boy, the fictional counterculture hero. The state troopers put him under surveillance for a few days before deciding both he and his book were dead ends.

Mostly, Fisher spun wheels. He talked to people, he drank coffee, he traveled, he drank coffee . . . His inevitable conclusion: There weren't enough connections to make everything cohere.

The attack on the substation was clearly an outlier. Except that it had to do with electricity, there was no connection that Fisher or that anyone could see. The only one in the world who saw any connection was

Festoon. In Fisher's view, he *was* the connection, trying to keep them together as part of his misguided attempt at empire building within the FBI.

An absolutely scary notion if taken to its logical end, something Fisher tried to avoid.

Another thing he tried to avoid was speaking with Bernie Stendanopolis, who had remained in California to coordinate the investigation. But Stendanopolis was about as avoidable as a tax collector, and at least once a day Fisher found himself having conversations like this:

Fisher: *Bernie, have you gotten a report from the rocket people at Punchline Orbiters yet?*
Bernie: *Punchline Orbiters?*
Fisher: *The rocket people, Bernie. Have they figured out why their rocket broke?*
Bernie: *Well, that's what they're investigating.*
Fisher: *No kidding. We want to look at whatever report they generate.*
Bernie: *Okay. And we want to do that why?*
Fisher: *Because we're the FBI, Bernie.*

Fisher could, of course, get the report from Sandra if he really needed it. But he had grown reluctant to talk to her. Somehow she made the case even more personal for him. Or rather, she reminded him of just how personal it was. And Andy Fisher didn't do personal.

What he did do was solve high-profile, high-technology cases. And this, for all its personal entanglements, looked like it might actually be one.

Fisher's working hypothesis was that the murders were connected, and that the accident was indirectly related to the murders: that whatever irregularities Kathy had detected were responsible, probably indirectly, for the rocket's failure.

That might implicate Sandra, another reason not to talk to her, but Fisher thought she was innocent. Partly, of course, that was because he knew her. But logic, too, was on his side.

Kathy was an accountant, not a rocket scientist, so Fisher figured that she had realized the contractor was skimping on a key ingredient or using some sort of inferior materials or workmanship in the rocket that screwed everything up. Or maybe it was in the satellite itself. Wherever it was, it had to be something Kathy had access to, and that would be recorded in a computer file somewhere.

The only problem with the theory was finding real evidence to support it. Stendanopolis—not completely incompetent, Fisher's rants to the contrary—had gotten copies of the bills and contracts Kathy had access to. These weren't terribly detailed, but they jibed with the engineering reports, which often included detailed photos and lab analysis provided as parts of the acceptance inspection. Stendanopolis had also found several NASA experts to check on the documents; not only did they appear to be in good shape, but the NASA people personally vouched for most of the subs, saying they were the best in the business.

Kathy had written no memos expressing concern, or sent e-mails indicating she had questions. She had visited several subcontractors, but the visits appeared to be routine meet-and-greet affairs.

The Bureau's forensic accountant said Icarus was thinly financed and probably teetering toward insolvency, but that wasn't exactly surprising. The firm seemed to be counting on a major Department of Energy demonstration grant, which was expected to be awarded as soon as the first satellite was launched. If that didn't happen, any cash problems would have to be solved by reorganization—a fancy word for bankruptcy. But with its concept so close to being proven, it seemed likely that Terhoussen could easily find an investor. Indeed, the money problems seemed to be as much a result of Terhoussen's stubbornness as anything else; he refused to sell stock or take on partners, even though there were plenty of people willing to pony up for a chance at the technology.

The respective murder investigations, meanwhile, plodded along. Except for the fact that both had been committed by professionals, the connections between Kathy's murder and Debbie Ferris's were tenuous. Even Bernie knew that.

Bernie: *Locals think Debbie Ferris owed some money to a loan shark and that's why she was killed.*

Fisher: *Since when do credit card companies kill people?*

Bernie: *Might not have just been credit cards. Those were at the limits. People who used to work with her say she liked to gamble. Rumor at Punchline was that she had big debts in Las Vegas. That's where the loan sharks come in.*

Fisher: *Police told you that?*

Bernie: *Nah. They're not saying anything. It's not like the good old days when the locals cooperated. Getting something out of these guys is like pulling teeth from a piranha.*

Fisher: *So where'd you hear that rumor?*

Bernie: *That little guy at the company, John Edmunds.*

Fisher: *James.*

Bernie: *Right. He's the only one over there who'll talk to anybody for more than a minute.*

Fisher: *That doesn't make him reliable, Bernie.*

Bernie: *No, but I have somebody working on it anyway.*

Fisher: *Are there loan sharks in San Jose?*

Bernie: *There's a pool hall.*

Fisher: *Case closed.*

Besides proving that Stendanopolis didn't get sarcasm, the conversation led Fisher to look at all of Debra Ferris's financial records, which had already been requested by the locals. While there were trips to Vegas—several over the past two years—there were no large withdrawals or deposits, and no records of debt. If Ferris gambled, she did it the old-fashioned way: in cash.

And so the investigation muddled onward, a mixture of false leads and nonleads, the investigators striving not just to unwrap the mystery but to dodge the bureaucratic power plays above them. It is very likely that it would have remained in this semi-limbo state for several months, had a group calling itself the Front for Environmental Power not blown up the New Bethlehem Nuclear Power Plant near New Bethlehem, Pennsylvania.

13

NEW BETHLEHEM, PENNSYLVANIA

The power plant was a so-called Safe BWR, or boiling water reactor. The word "safe" referred to design improvements that were supposed to fail-safe the reactor and the fluids in the event of a failure. Built by a coalition of European companies, it was one of the latest generation of nuclear power plants, with two reactors producing 1,100 megawatts of power. The cost was approximately $13 billion—and climbing due to delays in construction.

The plant was still several months from being loaded with fuel; the tests that were planned to follow, along with the inevitable curves in the permitting process, meant that it would be at least a year before New Bethlehem's energy was being fed into the grid. Nonetheless, it was seen by many as an important part of the solutions to the Northeast's chronic power shortages.

Which wasn't to say that the plant wasn't controversial. Many area residents remembered the Three Mile incident in eastern Pennsylvania with considerable dread. In March 1979, the nuclear power plant's cooling system had malfunctioned, causing a partial meltdown of the reactor core. A full meltdown could have been catastrophic—Chernobyl, a steam and chemical explosion that followed a power excursion or out-of-control chain reaction, directly killed fifty-six and probably added another four thousand cancer deaths to the region it affected.

At Three Mile Island, safety precautions and prompt action by personnel avoided any direct deaths or injuries. Even so, the release of coolant spread 43,000 curies of radioactivity throughout the region. The release may not have statistically increased local cancer rates—that was a matter of great controversy—but it had effectively killed the nuclear industry for years.

The New Bethlehem design was inherently much safer, and in fact the safety design could be viewed as an answer to Three Mile Island as well as Chernobyl. But that was little comfort to many people, who argued that no nuclear plant could be truly safe. Local residents packed the hearings on the plant for years. The crisis at Fukushima, Japan—another design and situation utterly unlike the one here—added even more angst and impetus to the opposition. Several groups were formed, first in an attempt to block its approval, and then in an effort to reverse that approval in court. The challenges had failed for various reasons; the last had been rejected by the state court just a few weeks before. In the meantime, protests and vigils were held in front of the construction site. At first, these were daily events. As the construction continued, however, the number of protestors steadily dwindled. The crowds shriveled to a dozen protestors, generally older women who showed up each

Friday at 7 A.M. with signs proclaiming NO NEW NUKES FOR NEW BETHLEHEM and HONK IF YOU'RE AGAINST NUCLEAR POWER before heading over to one of the local diners for breakfast. The only people who honked were construction workers on their way into the plant; a few were related to the protestors and in fact occasionally would bring them donuts and coffee.

The utility executives who had pushed for the construction of the plant knew that the dulling of the voices against the plant did not mean that it had won support. They viewed the present conditions as a lull in the storm, and busily prepared for the inevitable wave of protests when the fuel was brought on site in a few months.

Tuesday morning a week after the attack on Glendale Falls, a white van drove up to the main construction gate at New Bethlehem. It was early, about ten minutes before six o'clock. At six, the security shifts changed and the first wave of construction crews would arrive to take over from the night teams. The van looked like the canteen truck that came in every morning around that time, and the guards at the gate waved it through without inspecting it after the driver held up his ID card.

When the actual canteen truck arrived a few minutes after six, no one seemed to notice the contradiction, most likely because the shift had just changed and the new guards hadn't seen the other truck.

By then, the van had driven past two internal checkpoints—unmanned overnight—wended its way around the perimeter of one of the cooling towers, and approached the fence at the rear of the main reactor building. The gate was only about ten feet from the rear of the building; it had been constructed to allow concrete trucks to exit without having to make three-point turns during the pours.

The van's driver slowed as he came close to the chained gate. He was having trouble deciding whether to drive through and blow himself up with the truck as planned, or to simply set the backup fuse and escape into the nearby creek.

An hour before, Peter Greene had been resolute, dedicated to his cause and convinced that his death would mean much more than his life ever had.

Now he wasn't so sure. Now he realized that it would not be difficult to scramble down the embankment to his right, run to the water, and escape. Dying in the name of a cause was romantic from a distance, but up close it lost much of its allure. Peter Greene suddenly thought of all sorts of reasons to live. So rather than pressing his foot on the gas pedal as planned, he reached beneath the dashboard panel for the emergency detonator switch, which he had been told would give him sixty seconds to flee the vehicle.

Unfortunately for Peter, that was a lie. Pressing the switch ignited the explosives in the back of the van immediately.

Word of the attack hit Bloomberg News ten minutes later. The first report unfortunately was poorly worded, making it seem as if a live nuclear plant was destroyed. Even the bulletins three and six minutes later failed to mention that the nuclear fuel had not been loaded into the reactor.

Jonathon Loup expected the first mistake but was annoyed when it continued, primarily because he had no way to capitalize on it. Even with his precautions, additional trading now would be too easy to trace.

But there was no need to be greedy. By the end of the day, he calculated, he'd clear a little more than $2.5 million, enough to put off the Chinese for several weeks more.

What he would do beyond that, of course, remained an open question. Wan made it clear he would accept the interest payment only as goodwill toward Icarus's eventual takeover. Loup had promised Icarus would go to the Chinese, but he had no intention of delivering—even if Terhoussen came around.

Or maybe he would deliver. He couldn't be sure himself sometimes what he was thinking.

Indecision was the greatest sin for an investor. Indecision—far worse than greed.

Loup leaned back in his chair, staring at the ceiling, trying to think of a way out of the Chinese puzzle he had trapped himself in.

14

NEW BETHLEHEM

The road to New Bethlehem lay through cow country. The hillsides were pockmarked by dairy farms and the air was perfumed by the smell of manure wafting over the superhighways. Fisher rolled down the car window and breathed deeply as he drove. The smell reminded him of wet tobacco leaves in autumn.

Even at FBI speeds over the interstate, it took Fisher nearly six hours to get to the nuke plant, which pretty much guaranteed that he'd have no role in the initial investigation. This didn't bother Fisher at all, but it did irk Festoon, who felt that Fisher should have somehow anticipated the attack. He kept calling for updates every fifteen minutes, even though it should have been clear to him that Fisher was still on the road.

"By the time you get there, the state police will have muscled into the case," said Festoon when Fisher was about an hour away. "Just like in New York. And look at the mush they made of that."

"Think of it this way," Fisher told him. "The more agencies involved, the more chance there is to shift the blame when the shit hits the fan."

Festoon clearly hadn't thought of that.

"Maybe you should stop for lunch," he suggested.

The National Guard had cordoned off several square miles of land around the plant, giving the news media picturesque camera ops of cows and Hummers but no wrecked buildings, leading them to hire helicopters and equip photographers with outsize lenses. But keeping the media out of the plant site had only a minimal effect on crowd control there; besides the troops, there were more than two hundred police officers for security alone, three ambulance squads, two fire departments (one with a hook-and-ladder truck painted green), a rapid-response unit from the EPA, three different teams from the Department of Energy, and an assortment of congressional aides and other political hangers-on and kite-fliers, sent to determine which way the (hot) wind was blowing.

The answer was out, at hurricane speed.

The state attorney general had declared itself the lead agency for the investigation, with the attorney general helicoptering in to get a firsthand look at what was going on. His helicopter took a particularly meandering path over the nearby fields, taking it within close-up view of the TV vans—surely a coincidence, given that the damaged portion of the plant was on the other side of the hill.

As soon as Fisher arrived, he got to work on the most essential part of any investigation—finding a good cup of coffee. The National Guard had set up a mess tent near the main entrance, and the Red Cross was working urns there. Fisher was just filling up the largest cup he could find when a pair of uniformed state troopers marched in and announced that they were looking for Special Agent Fisher of the FBI.

Fisher turned around.

"What did that slimebag Fisher do now?" Fisher asked. "That jackass is always getting himself in trouble."

The troopers glanced at each other. Their battleship gray uniforms matched the sky, which had been steadily clouding up since morning.

"Uh, the AG is looking for him," said the trooper on the left. Even with his Smokey the Bear hat, he stood barely five-five. What he lacked in height, however, he made up for with the volume of his voice—the nearby tent poles shook violently as he spoke.

"AG would be the attorney general?" said Fisher.

"That's right, sir. Do you know Fisher?"

"Unfortunately."

"What agency are you with?" asked the other trooper. He was a little closer to medium height, though still lower than what Fisher generally thought of as the trooper standard.

"FBI," said Fisher. "How about yourself?"

The troopers exchanged another glance.

"Would you mind coming with us?" asked the runt.

Dressed in a gray pinstriped suit with a powder blue tie set off by a light salmon—never say pink—shirt, the state attorney general was holding court with several members of the state police Bureau of Criminal Investigation or BCI, the plainclothes detective division. Fisher recognized one of the men as Lou Agmar, the captain who headed the bureau's intelligence division.

Police intelligence was generally a contradiction

in terms, but Agmar was an exception. Even more inexplicable was the fact that he actually liked Fisher, an indication that even the most intelligent of men can have deep flaws.

He broke away from the group as soon as he saw Fisher.

"Andy Fisher, in the flesh," said Agmar. "How the hell are you?"

"Cranky," said Fisher. "How about yourself?"

"Baffled," said Agmar. "We don't have—"

"You're the FBI?" demanded the attorney general, swinging his face toward Fisher's.

"Special Agent Fisher."

"What the hell's going on here, Fisher?" The AG's face shaded red, which made a nice contrast with his white hair. "Have you guys been sleeping at the switch?"

"Probably," said Fisher.

"This could have been a major catastrophe. We could have had nuclear material all over the surrounding counties. We could have had a meltdown situation. Did you just say *probably*?"

There were plenty of ways to seriously screw with nuclear reactors, but blowing up their outlying buildings with car bombs wasn't actually one of them. And this one had not been loaded with fuel, a not insignificant point.

But Fisher didn't bother pointing this out. He'd learned it was a bad idea to interrupt a good rant, especially by a politician.

"I'll show you around," said Agmar, stepping in. "You have to be careful. We're still doing some of the forensics."

"Careful is my middle name," said Fisher.

The explosives had been mixed from fertilizer, not exactly a rare commodity in farm country. The state police were already checking for recent purchases and thefts; since the Oklahoma City bombing, ammonium nitrate vendors had kept records that made it easier to track purchases that were out of the ordinary. Whoever had made the bomb almost certainly knew that, though; Fisher expected that they'd be more likely to get meaningful leads from the van and the dead bomber.

The truck had been identified; the bomber had not.

"The explosion pulverized the body," said Agmar as he and Fisher stood at the edge of the crater the bomb had made. "Obliterated the front of the van."

"You're sure someone was in there?"

"Found a hand over there." Agmar pointed to the edge of the river. "Left hand."

"Nothing else?"

"Not so far. Most of the body would have gone that way, into the building as it exploded."

"So why is so much of the back of the van still there?" said Fisher.

"So much? That's barely an axle."

"It's the tires, some of the chassis." Fisher walked around toward it, treading around the flags that had been left denoting where evidence had been recovered. "The explosive would have been in the back, right?"

Agmar shrugged. "Had to be."

Not really. Fisher could tell from the blast pattern that it had been in the cab, rather than the back.

Interesting.

"Guy have an explosive belt?" he asked. "Vest?"

"Haven't found anything yet. Like I say—"

"You better get chemical samples."

"Already on it, Andy."

Explosions were idiosyncratic animals, each with its own set of decisions, some logical, some quirky and unpredictable. To Fisher, a car bomb that did more damage to the front of the vehicle than the rear—albeit a matter open to interpretation—meant that the bomb had been rigged purposely to produce that effect. Which meant that whoever had set it wanted to make it hard to identify the bomber.

Or rather, the driver.

"Truck wasn't filled to capacity," said Fisher.

"What do you mean?"

"From that axle, we're talking a panel type truck, right? Sort of thing sells coffee and sandwiches."

"Right. That's how we figure it got in."

"Okay. So if it was full of fertilizer, the whole back of that building would be gone. But it's not."

"Well . . ."

"Anybody taking responsibility?" said Fisher.

"Everybody and their mother," said Agmar. "I think even the Weathermen reunited and put out a videotape."

"Anything promising?"

"Nah. There's been a lot of opposition, things in the media. Protestors picket every day. But this is a bit beyond them."

"You sure?"

"They're mostly little old leftie ladies. Against the war, against nukes, against polyester in clothes."

"I feel their pain."

Fisher surveyed the damage. It was less severe than it looked—and yet in another way, far worse. The structure housing the reactor was too sturdy and too far away to have been damaged, but the explosion would put the entire project on hold. It would take months and maybe even years before it was back on schedule. There would be inspections and more inspections, probably public hearings—all sorts of fun.

In the meantime, they'd change security procedures. They'd beef up the guards, put more concrete barriers around. But in truth it was impossible to completely prevent a determined nutjob from wreaking havoc.

"How's this fit with what you got?" asked Agmar.

"It doesn't," said Fisher. "Which is why it's so interesting."

Fisher found the supervisory agent of the nearest local FBI office, exchanged important information with him about contact numbers and where to buy the cheapest cigarettes, then told him that he was going to do a little investigative work off-site.

"You have a lead already?" asked the agent.

"Absolutely," said Fisher. "I saw a good-looking diner on the way in."

The New Bethlehem Star Diner was old school, a gleaming silver bullet of a diner with a waitress named Flo and a menu heavy enough to anchor an aircraft carrier. The cast of regulars included a septic tank pumper with a crewcut flattop who smelled of lavender soap, a pair of American Legion vets in full regalia bemoaning the demise of Big Steel, and four women from the Tuesday afternoon bowling league who kept glancing at their watches and saying they had to get back for the kids after one more Coke.

There was also the unmistakable scent of cigarette smoke in the air, which Fisher's radar determined was coming from the kitchen.

Diner Nirvana.

"Whatcha havin', bub?" asked Flo as Fisher slid in at the counter. Her name was written above the pocket of her blouse.

"What's good?"

"Nothin'."

"Coffee and fries."

"Burn some potatoes!" yelled Flo as she took the coffeepot from beneath the urn.

"Is that fresh?" Fisher asked.

"You kiddin'? I made it myself two days ago." Flo set down the cup and poured it for him. She went right to the top. "You're the kind that likes it black. I can tell."

"Yup."

"Hurry up with them fries," Flo yelled. "He ain't got all day!"

There was a general grumble from the rear.

"Sometimes in the afternoon he falls asleep back there," confided Flo. "I gotta stay on him. Fries'll be ready in a minute. You want gravy?"

"Is there another way to eat fries?"

She narrowed her eyes. "Ketchup?"

"Lots."

"You'll do."

When the fries arrived a few minutes later, Fisher supplemented the gravy with a good helping of salt before emptying nearly half the bottle of ketchup on them. He pushed his coffee cup over for a refill.

"There's some lemon meringue pie," said Flo, pouring.

"No banana creme?"

"We got banana creme," she said approvingly.

Bona fides established, Fisher went to work, pumping Flo for information. She was a veritable fountain.

As Agmar had said, the anti's were mostly benign and had a good deal of sympathetic support in the community. It was widely believed that the owner of the property where the plant was to be built had helped channel campaign donations to the different officials whose approval had been necessary for the project. There had been a backlash against the local government, resulting in all new board members. But the newcomers had been warned that any action to rescind the approvals would be answered in court, with lawsuits that would cost millions to defend. The feds came down heavily on the side of the utility, claiming that the new power plant was critical to the country's national security.

Most people knew that was a mouthful of hogwash, Flo added, but with the feds and the lawyers lined up against them, there wasn't much they could do.

"So who'd want to blow up the plant?" Fisher asked.

"A lot of people, I suspect," said the waitress.

"But who'd do it?"

That was a much harder question to answer. The women with the signs weren't a threat, and none were directly related to farmers or fertilizer dealers, though one had served on the organizing board of the local farmers' market. A group of "college kid long-hairs" had passed out flyers against nuclear plants a few weeks back, said Flo; if anybody was going to blow up a place, she'd put her money on them.

"Except they didn't look like they could walk their way out of a broom closet," said Flo. "Bunch of sad sack losers. They were a dreary bunch. Not a smile among them."

Five had come into the diner for coffee. They'd asked if there was free Internet access and frowned even deeper when Flo told them there wasn't.

"What'd they think, they were in Starbucks?" said Fisher.

"God help us," said Flo, making the sign of the cross.

"You wouldn't happen to have any of those flyers?" asked Fisher.

"You're awful nosey for a stranger."

"FBI," said Fisher.

"Really?" Flo leaned close over the counter. "You know when I was in grammar school, I wrote a project paper about J. Edgar Hoover."

"Yeah?"

"Then I saw on TV that he wore dresses. Why wasn't that in any of the schoolbooks?"

"They always leave the best parts out," explained Fisher.

———

One of the group's flyers had been tacked to the bulletin board in the small vestibule beyond the diner's cash register. Hidden now by ads for babysitters, firewood, and all-you-can-eat church clam fries, it was a single-page diatribe against nuclear power and its assorted problems, printed in three different default Windows program fonts. Titled ANTI-NUKE MANIFESTO, it was signed "Plato, member of N-BAN."

"New Bethlehem Anti-Nuclear Plant," said Agmar when Fisher called to ask about the group. "We know about them. Inept bunch of college twerps."

"You have a membership list?"

"You don't think they're responsible, do you?"

"Hell no," said Fisher. "I just need to knock off a few interviews to convince my boss I'm working, rather than taking the cure down here."

The ringleader of N-BAN was a skinny twenty-three-year-old college dropout named Hank Canderfield, who worked at his parents' antique stall on the state highway. His hands began shaking as Fisher walked up to the front table.

"Nice pots," said Fisher, pointing at a shelf of Ming Dynasty vases.

"Ming," said Canderfield.

"What's with the dog?" Fisher pointed at a foo dog.

"It's a Chinese lion," said Canderfield.

Fisher let it go. "Baseball cards?" he asked, pointing at the display.

"Yeah, that's Reggie Jackson. First year with the Yankees. Good condition."

"Got any Mickey Mantles?"

"Baseball cards are just kind of a sideline," said Canderfield. "This is my parents' shop. Their real specialties are Chinese vases."

"Not really into it yourself, are you?"

Canderfield's pimple-pockmarked face turned a little whiter.

"Why are you asking?" he asked.

Fisher dug his wallet out of his pocket. "FBI. Why don't we go out back somewhere and have a smoke."

"H-h-how do you know I smoke?"

Fisher snapped the creds closed. "How does the FBI know anything, Hank?" The kid's fingertips were stained yellow, but Fisher wasn't one to give away his methods. "Besides, if you didn't already smoke, you'd want to now."

Canderfield smoked filtered Pall Malls, a choice Fisher would only make if stranded on a desert island in a hurricane. The kid practically inhaled the entire cigarette with his first toke. The nicotine didn't exactly calm him down.

"I didn't have anything to do with it. Nothing, nothing, nothing," he told Fisher, fumbling for another cigarette. "Nothing."

"With what?"

"Nothing."

"So what nothing did you have nothing to do with?"

"The nothing nothing. What you're here for."

"The explosion at the nuclear power plant?"

Canderfield dropped the cigarettes. They landed in a puddle. Canderfield scooped them up anyway, only to drop them again.

"Tell you what," said Fisher. "Why don't you close up shop and come with me?"

"Y-y-you can't arrest me."

"Who said anything about arresting you? Your cigarettes are all wet. I'm gonna buy you a new pack."

The cheapest smokes were sold at a small convenience market about two miles away. At a good fifty cents cheaper than the closest 7-Eleven, Fisher figured that they were black market cigarettes up from Virginia or maybe an Indian reservation.

He bought Canderfield a carton, after first making sure he was over twenty-one. Be just the thing to be busted for contributing to the delinquency of a juvenile delinquent.

They sat in Fisher's car, talking about N-BAN. Canderfield claimed that the organization had broken up several weeks before. It had never been much of an organization, he added, just a bunch of people who wanted to get the word out about the dangers of nuclear power.

"Your leaflet says it should be stopped at all costs," said Fisher.

"That's like, uh, a figure of speech."

"Anybody in the organization who would take it literally?"

Canderfield shook his head.

"You have a list of names?"

"I'm not rat-ratting out people. What is this, the Red Scare days? Like, like a b-blacklist?"

Fisher sighed.

"The thing is, Hank, somebody blew themselves up in the explosion. I don't think they intended to do that. But whoever put the bomb together wanted to make it real hard to ID the body. So what I'm saying is, I think one of your friends may have been murdered, and I'd like to figure out who it is."

That still sounded too much like "squealing" to Canderfield.

"Sooner or later, if it went down like that, we'll figure it out," added Fisher. "Because we'll get DNA, and there'll be other tests, and he's going to turn up missing. Helping me now might help you later."

The kid took out his cell phone. "Maybe I should call a lawyer."

"That's not a problem," said Fisher. "I can help you find a good one if you want."

Canderfield slid open the phone, exposing the keypad, then closed it. He played with it for a minute or so, flipping it open and closed nervously. As he did, the cigarette in his other hand burned down to the filter, singeing his fingers. He dropped it and the phone on the floor of the car, hopping out.

Canderfield went into the store in search of some ice. He returned with a beer instead. By then, Fisher had retrieved and copied all of the recent-call numbers on his phone.

"You still want to call a lawyer?" Fisher asked him as he nursed the beer.

"I just want to go home."

"All right. Tell me where you live. I'll drop you off."

"Drop me back at the antiques place."

"No good," said Fisher, backing from the space. He pointed to the beer. "You get in your car there, the state troopers who'll be watching you there will arrest you for DWI. They're just dying for an excuse like that. This is how these things work, Hank."

"I'm being watched?" Canderfield swiveled his head.

"Don't make it obvious that you know, all right?" Fisher put the car into drive.

After he dropped Canderfield off, Fisher gave the phone numbers to the local FBI agents, telling them that they were looking for a really depressed kid who wasn't going to be answering the phone in this lifetime. Then he called the U.S. attorney's office to get a warrant to search Canderfield's house and, more usefully, his phone records.

Agmar called him a few minutes later.

"So you're really hot on this Canderfield kid, huh?" The U.S. attorney had been instructed to cooperate with the state investigation, and the office had notified the AG of the warrant. "You think he did it?"

"I don't think he had anything to do with it, directly," said Fisher. "But I'm guessing he's got plenty of friends who fit the profile of the bomber."

Young. Depressed. Easily conned. And not necessarily trustworthy, at least when it came to killing themselves.

"What if I told you we already have some good suspects?" asked Agmar.

"I'm listening."

Fisher wasn't particularly surprised that the suspects were Islamic fundamentalists, nor that the information had come from the feds. He was surprised, however, that it had come from the DIA—the Defense Intelligence Agency, which wasn't known for domestic surveillance.

But if it had to come from the DIA, then it would naturally be Kowalski, Fisher's once and future nemesis. Kowalski was a self-proclaimed domestic terror diva.

"Yeah, he got up here an hour ago," said Agmar. "How'd you know who it was?"

"He follows me around all the time. He's my evil twin."

Kowalski—if he had a first name, it was known only to his mother—had apparently developed his intelligence by looking at NSA traffic reports. These detailed the number of communications a suspected terror group made and, to simplify somewhat, used statistical analysis to predict whether an "operation" was being planned. In most cases, these determinations were made without reference to the messages themselves; most were in seemingly innocuous language that, while thought to be a private code, gave no real indication of meaning. As far as Fisher was concerned, that by definition made the information unreliable.

Agmar thought otherwise.

"We're jumping off at eleven P.M.," said Agmar. "You want to come?"

"You're raiding these guys?"

"We can't afford to go soft. Media gets this, we're finished."

Unnamed Islam Conspiracy Group 23-PA-7 was, as the name hinted, an as-yet dimly known group of possibly affiliated individuals who were Muslims and had done something to arouse the suspicions of the federal government. Contrary to popular belief, this was not particularly easy to do, and Fisher had no doubt that at least one of the people involved in the group had some sort of nefarious past, if not felonious intentions. The problem was that almost nothing was known about the group.

There was, however, a good connection with New Bethlehem: A credit card that had been used to buy two cell phones connected with the group had also been used to rent a car and buy gas in the New Bethlehem area.

That was too much of a coincidence even for Fisher, and as he left the briefing prior to the raid, he contemplated the necessity of actually having to admit that Kowalski was right.

It was a horrible, sobering thought.

Conspiracy Group 23-PA-7 was known to gather occasionally at the home of one of its members, a Mr. Yahyah Benham, who owned five acres of semi-cleared land nearly a hundred miles southeast of the nuclear plant. The property had once been part of a farm and was surrounded on three sides by open fields, which would make it relatively easy to secure. A mixture of police, federal marshals, FBI agents, and several National Guardsmen would swoop down on the house by helicopter at precisely midnight and serve a search warrant, while state troopers secured the nearby road and bordering farm. The hope was to surprise the group with overwhelming force so that there would be no trouble.

Fisher donned his bulletproof vest and walked with Agmar to the state police helicopter that would take them to the raid. Five helicopters had been tasked for the raid. Three would make the initial assault; another would hover nearby with reserve troops; and the fifth, carrying Fisher, Agmar, and Kowalski, would come in with the warrant itself.

It was a real made-for-TV production, though Fisher couldn't spot any cameras.

The "target compound" was a small Cape Cod dating from the 1950s. By the time Agmar's helicopter approached to land, the backyard was blazing with spotlights and signal flares. Red and blue bubble-gum lights revolved in front of the house, and on the surrounding roads in all directions.

"Two suspects," announced Kowalski, who was monitoring transmissions from the assault team. "No resistance."

Fisher thought he sounded disappointed.

The Bell JetRanger put down in the neighbor's field. Fisher was the last one out, walking behind as the others ran toward the house. When he got there, Kowalski and Agmar were in the kitchen with the house's two Iranian-American occupants—Yahyah Benham, a very worried-looking man in his late sixties, who kept shaking his head, and his son Jalil, who sat at the table in a T-shirt and underwear. His T-shirt extolled the virtues of DX, a pro wrestling heel stable that flouted authority and communicated with hand gestures, none of which were polite.

Cute, if he'd been maybe twenty years younger.

The son was, in politically correct terms, mentally challenged. The father pleaded with Kowalski not to separate them when they took them to jail.

"Who said you're going to jail?" asked Fisher.

The question seemed to catch the older man off guard.

"I—"

"Have you done something wrong?"

"No, nothing. We are innocent. You'll keep us together? He needs someone to watch. He's like a child."

"Is this your cell phone?" Kowalski asked, coming in from the bedroom with a phone.

"I don't know," said Yahyah Benham.

"You don't know?" said Kowalski.

"I don't know."

"Maybe you better remember," said Agmar.

"My phone," said the younger man.

"It's mine," said his father.

"Well, that's one way to stay together," said Kowalski.

Fisher went into the living room to look around while the others continued to question them. He hadn't found anything interesting when Agmar came in to tell him that they were taking the two men over to the barracks.

"What's the deal on the cell phone?" Fisher asked.

"Maybe it's tied to the intercepts. I'll take it in and check."

"You taking them, too?"

"Absolutely."

"You don't have enough to hold them on," said Fisher.

"I got the cell phone. If it's tied to the calls, that's all I need."

Fisher was doubtful, but there was no sense arguing.

"Let me see the number," he said.

"Kowalski's checking for me."

"I'll check, too," said Fisher.

He wrote it down, then went out to call Stendanopolis and have one of his minions run it against the Bureau's terror lists. When he couldn't get a signal—they were pretty far out in the boonies—Fisher decided to use the sat phone in the command helicopter.

He was perhaps five yards from the chopper when a moving shadow far to his right caught his attention. He stopped and tried to make out what it was, but the glare of the helicopter searchlights made it impossible. Finally he decided to have a look, and began walking in its direction.

"Hey," he yelled, whistling to one of the National Guard soldiers. "Come with me."

The Guardsman—a private from near Philadelphia—ran to catch up. Just beyond the circle of light, Fisher came to a three-strand barbed-wire fence. He slipped through, then crossed over to a small building that looked like an old well house or root cellar. Built low against a slight slope, it was more roof than building, with a door at one end.

Fisher started to pull the door open, then saw something moving in the distance.

"Freeze!" he yelled, but of course the shadow didn't. He leapt after it.

I'm going to look awful stupid if this is a wayward cow, he thought to himself, pulling his pistol out.

"I said, 'freeze!' " he yelled.

It took several yards before the shadow finally stopped. Fisher went down to a knee, realizing the lights near the house would make him an easy target.

"Hands up!" he yelled.

Slowly, the shadow raised its hands. Fisher rose and began walking toward it. The Guardsman had stopped a few yards behind him and was trying to catch his breath.

"On the ground," said Fisher.

The shadow bent forward. Fisher put his hand on the shadow's head. He was a man in his mid-forties or fifties.

"What are you doing out here?" said Fisher.

"I'm not saying anything until I talk to my lawyer," said the shadow.

15

SOUTHWESTERN PENNSYLVANIA

The man Fisher cornered in the field called a lawyer in Philadelphia, who told him that he was required only to identify himself and arranged to meet him at the state trooper substation the task force was using as a temporary headquarters.

"I'll be there in an hour," said the attorney.

It took closer to two, but by then Fisher had checked back with Stendanopolis and made enough calls to figure out what was going on. At least with the man he'd tackled, Ahmed Kharjien.

Conspiracy Group 23-PA-7, it turned out, had been penetrated by an FBI mole—Ahmed Kharjien, who much to his credit and that of his handlers had carefully kept his cover. The Philadelphia "lawyer" turned out to be the special agent in charge of his operation; in layman's terms, his "control."

Of course. What Philadelphia attorney answers his phone at one in the morning, let alone gets out of bed to travel halfway across the state?

Fisher intercepted him in the parking lot.

"Andy Fisher. Shit. I might have known. What a screwjob."

"Dante Burns," answered Fisher. He'd met Burns two years before during a training session at the CIA. They'd been the only two Bureau agents there, which meant they were also the only two sane people there. This made for a real bonding experience.

"Shit, Fisher. What the hell did you bring our guy in for?"

"State attorney general thinks he and his friends blew up the New Bethlehem power plant this morning."

"No way," said Burns. "Who?"

"Ahmed and his friends here."

"No way. We've been following them for six months."

"That long and nothing to show for it?"

"They were getting ready to act."

"Looks like they beat you to it."

"No way. They wanted to take down a plane. Nothing like this."

"You sure?"

"I saw the news reports," said Burns. "This isn't them. They didn't buy no fertilizer."

"Positive?"

"This is bullshit, Andy. I can't believe you'd pull them in."

"Relax. It wasn't my idea," said Fisher. "How long has Ahmed been on the job?"

"A while."

"This his only case?"

"He's got a couple of things going."

"How did we get him? In exchange for us not pressing charges in a drug case?"

"Counterfeiting."

"He wasn't a terrorist to begin with?"

"No." Burns shook his head.

"You sure?"

"No way. We checked him out with the CIA."

"Oh, that's reassuring," said Fisher.

"No, I'm telling you. I spent time with him. He wasn't a terrorist. He's a thief. Con man. Good one, too."

"What about the rest of these guys?"

"You met them?"

Fisher nodded.

"This isn't exactly a hot cell," said Burns. He seemed a little embarrassed—as well he should be. But Fisher had to give him credit—many guys would claim the people they were following were Satan's own helpers. "The old man's old. The kid's—did you see him?"

"Reminds me of my boss."

"There's a guy who owns a pizza parlor. Two guys who just got out of jail. Those guys are more with it. But I don't see them capable of blowing up too much. And we'd know if they were planning to do it. I guarantee we'd know."

"The DIA has been tracking your group. The state attorney general thinks the cell phone they have inside was used to make some calls the DIA tracked. But it wasn't."

"No?"

"Hasn't been used. The funny thing is, the phone was bought in Pittsburgh with a clean credit card on the twenty-third. Same card bought another phone

the next day. Day after that, it rented a car in Pittsburgh. Used to buy gas that night near New Bethlehem. Hasn't been used since."

"What's the name on the card?"

"Belongs to a seventy-three-year-old man in Wyo-
ming. Account opened a month ago. Hasn't been
billed yet."

"Shit. You're saying our guy did it?"

"I don't think it was Benham. Do you?" Fisher
folded his arms. Burns said nothing. "You don't know
about the phones?" Fisher asked.

"No," Burns admitted.

"Trip to New Bethlehem?"

"I know he didn't go."

"You're sure about that? Check the date."

Burns shook his head. "I would have been told."

"You weren't told he was here. What's a trip to
New Bethlehem?"

"It's not in his area."

"Pittsburgh?"

"That I can't be sure of. He might have." Burns
frowned. "What else did they buy with that card?"

"Those are the only charges on the account."

"Shit."

"You guys bug the old man's house?" asked Fisher.

"No. We need a warrant for that. It hasn't been
worth the trouble."

"Is Ahmed wired?"

"Sometimes."

"Not tonight?"

Burns shook his head. "He can come on his own.
To keep contacts up."

"You don't have a trail team on him for his own
protection?"

"Not worth it here. We only have so many agents. Besides, sometimes being followed puts you in more danger."

"And it makes it harder for you to freelance."

"Yeah," admitted Burns. "I know."

Fisher let Burns talk to Ahmed first, leaning back against the wall and watching. Ahmed started out glad to see the agent, but he quickly realized he was in deep trouble.

He didn't have much of an excuse for not alerting Burns to the fact that he was coming up here. "Checking up on things," was his explanation.

"You go off alone a lot?" asked Fisher.

Ahmed blinked slowly. His eyes were large green ovals—sad-sack eyes, Fisher thought.

"What about the cell phones you bought for Benham?" added Fisher when he didn't answer. "Where's the other one?"

"What cell phones?" asked Ahmed.

Fisher pulled out the chair in front of him, spun it around slowly, then sat down. He let the time go slowly—it was always best to drag these little moments out, until each second was an ice pick on the side of the subject's skull.

"You bought a pair of cell phones with a credit card that didn't belong to you," Fisher said. "What happened to the credit card?"

"I didn't buy a cell phone."

"Two."

Ahmed shook his head.

Fisher leaned over the back of the chair. "Maybe seeing it will help your memory."

"Someone gave me a cell phone," said Ahmed nervously. "Is that what we're talking about?"

"When was this?"

Ahmed shook his head.

"Two weeks ago?" asked Burns.

"Around there."

"What if I said it was one week?" offered Fisher.

"Maybe one week."

"And why didn't you tell us?" asked Burns.

Ahmed shrugged.

"Why didn't you tell us you were coming up here?" Burns asked.

"I haven't had the chance yet. You said I don't have to tell you every move. To be natural. Well, I am trying to be natural. And now here—"

"Who gave you the cell phones?" Fisher asked.

"A man at the mosque."

"Who?" asked Fisher.

Ahmed shrugged.

"Is it on the surveillance tape?" Fisher asked Burns.

"We don't hook him up going into the mosque. Too risky. And it's a civil rights deal. Potentially."

"We're worried about the civil rights of terrorists?"

"Most people aren't terrorists."

"It was a rhetorical question," said Fisher. He turned back to Ahmed. "So tell me about this guy. What did he look like?"

Ahmed shrugged. "It was two weeks ago."

"Or one," corrected Fisher.

Ahmed glanced at Burns. "I think two."

"Was he tall, fat? Had you seen him before?" asked Burns.

"I hadn't seen him before."

Fisher glanced at his watch, then tapped Burns.

"I need to talk to you for a second," he said, rising.

Burns got up. Fisher started to leave the room, then stopped and looked at Ahmed.

"You want a Coke or something?" Fisher asked.

He shook his head. Fisher left the room with Burns, and walked down the hall.

"How badly do you figure he's playing you?" Fisher asked.

"What do you mean?"

"He tries to guess what the right answer to the question is before he answers," explained Fisher. "The time thing on when he got the cell phone—he got confused about what the right answer was, but tried to cover the bases."

"I think you're reading too much into that."

"Nah. You know I'm right. The cell phone was bought a week ago. The question is, does he know that? Or is he trying to throw us off and convince us he wasn't involved? How exactly is he playing the game?"

"He's just confused."

"You just don't want to think you've been played."

"Hey, Andy, come on."

"You're going to have to share the operation with the state people," Fisher told him. "And then you're going to have to keep Ahmed on ice for a while. He needs a much better explanation of the cell phones, for starters."

"All right, I agree with that. The cell phones. He goes on ice. But if I tell the state people about the operation, there's no way I'm going to be able to continue it."

"You got anything to charge these guys with?"

"Nothing solid," said Burns. "Talk. You know how these things go. You work on them for months until you get them to the right stage."

"Did he promise them money if they helped him?" Fisher asked.

"Maybe. Sometimes we do that."

"Does he do that?"

"Andy, listen. I can't micromanage every little—"

"You're going to have to review every case he's involved in," said Fisher, who didn't much care for excuses. "But it's more than likely something you don't know about that we're interested in."

Burns nodded, reluctantly.

"Work something out with Agmar," Fisher told him. "And keep your guy real close."

"You don't think he was involved in the plant attack, do you?"

"Ordinarily I would. But this lead came from DIA, and you know they never get anything right."

16

SAN JOSE

Every scientist had a moment of inner discovery, when he or she realized that they were a scientist, that investigating nature or changing it was his or her life work.

For T. Parker Terhoussen, that moment was his earliest memory. He was on the beach, at his family's summer house in Massachusetts. It was a very sunny day. He was making a sand castle with a cousin. It was a grand edifice, with a center keep and several turrets at the side, a pair of moats and walls. The cousin placed a piece of tinfoil at the top of the center tower. The sun glittered off the foil. Terhoussen placed his hand near it, feeling a wave of heat.

He didn't realize, of course, that this was energy, much less think that it could be tapped. But he did feel a surge of curiosity about the sensation, and the fascination quickly kindled an interest in the physical world.

His wealthy family had all the connections to get him into practically any college he wanted: Harvard, Yale, Princeton. He chose MIT, the one school where those connections didn't much matter. He was so precociously smart that the school paid for him to attend—an irony that was not lost on him.

When he was twenty-five, Terhoussen had worked on a problem involving the conversion of chemical energy into electric energy. The work had put him into whisper contention for a Nobel Prize in Chemistry. He didn't win the award, but given his age he wasn't surprised, nor disappointed. He *was* crushed, however, by what happened to his discovery:

Nothing.

Terhoussen had been working at the time for a large multinational corporation. In exchange for his salary and a modest bonus, he had signed over the rights for any patentable discoveries he made. The contract allowed the company to use those patents as it saw fit—or to *not* use them.

Terhoussen's discoveries would have made most batteries in use at the time more efficient, slightly cheaper, and most important, considerably longer lasting. This would have greatly affected the company's bottom line. The discoveries and the work related to them were boxed and filed in a large secure warehouse, essentially forgotten for a few decades until a team of Japanese scientists made a parallel discovery. Their work was considered to have revolutionized the industry; Terhoussen's was reduced to a small-type footnote on Wikipedia.

By then, Terhoussen had moved on. He'd also reached several conclusions regarding himself and his work, the most important of which was that he would never work for a large multinational company again. And in fact for the past twenty years he had owned his own company, though as he had discovered to his chagrin, that gave him less than the total control he had anticipated.

Energy had remained his primary concern, though over the years he had worked in fields as diverse as genetics and neurophysics. After working to reduce the size and increase the potency of solar cells in 2008, Terhoussen created Icarus to fulfill his lifelong fascination with the sun. His aim was as easy to state as it was audacious: He would construct a system that would eliminate the need for *all* other sources of energy on the planet.

From photoelectric toy cars to roof-mounted hot water heaters to a massive thermal solar project in Alvarado, Spain, people around the world were trying to put the sun's rays to work. Those terrestrial projects, however, had several built-in limitations, starting with the fact that the sun's energy was greatly diluted by the time it reached the Earth's surface. Earth-bound systems required large footprints for effect or efficiency.

Terhoussen had decided, quite logically, that the obvious solution was to capture the energy in space, where neither filter nor size were issues. Once captured and converted, the energy could be beamed to Earth in the form of microwaves. They would be "caught"—Terhoussen's term—by special antenna systems and then introduced to the national electric grid.

This was not a new idea, not even to the general public. Novelists, visionaries, and madmen had talked of such plans in general terms for years. More seriously, *Scientific American* had devoted an entire issue to the concept in 2007. Various articles in trade journals and on popular Web sites had discussed the premise—and a few of the difficulties—for years.

Terhoussen believed most of the difficulties could be solved by constructing a modular, infinitely scalable system. Where previous visions—they were too primitive to even call designs—had seen huge arrays necessarily linked together in orbiting infrastructures larger than several football stadiums—his were contained in assemblies that were only slightly bigger than beach balls. Once lofted into orbit, the balls unfolded panels, claiming territory measured in meters rather than miles. They worked together, but did not need to be physically interconnected, eliminating the need for costly spacewalks. If one malfunctioned, there was no need to turn off the entire system to replace it. And the unfolded petals, as he called them, were modular as well; losing one did not shut down the entire unit. Finally, the satellites had a limited ability to maneuver, making any repair or replacement relatively easy. These innovations in particular made Terhoussen's system more economical than even the most idealistic seer had predicted.

Economical was a relative term. Terhoussen came from a family of considerable wealth, a good portion of which he had inherited on his thirty-fifth birthday. He had invested that money, together with his own savings, into Icarus, and still had to borrow to keep the company going. Government money, the proverbial golden calf, had been limited and hard to come by.

An enormous amount of money was needed at every stage. A simple launch cost $50 million—and that was a relative bargain, possible only because Punchline was trying to prove itself.

The destruction of the first satellite, as devastating as it seemed, was actually an opportunity for the company. The satellite was covered by insurance—a mandatory portion of the launch costs. Terhoussen could borrow against that insurance for the short term. He could use the second satellite to get the federal grant. Between the grant and the insurance money, he could build half a dozen more satellites, enough to get the system started. Once it began generating electricity, he would have a revenue stream sufficient enough to get financing on his own terms. He'd be done with Loup, whom he knew was hovering around with cash because he saw an opportunity to get his hooks into the company. He'd be done with all the other hovering vultures and carrion eaters pecking at him.

Terhoussen would rather take the company's secrets to the grave than let anyone else get part of Icarus. He had cut them off again and again. No one else was going to get in his way.

He squeezed his eyes together, trying to push off his fatigue. His body was tired, but he had to move. He needed to convince Punchline to go ahead with the launch, despite their hesitation. He had to convince them that the first loss was just an accident, as their own internal report hinted.

Too much work to be done. Nothing was going to crush his dream now.

17

NEW MEXICO

Sandra Chester rubbed her thumb across her chin, watching as the engineers finished the bench test on the rocket's pressure monitoring system.

"At spec," said the lead test engineer, Gene Ng. "It's good to go."

"Good," said Sandra.

They looked at each other for a long moment.

"I'm going to clear the launch," said Ng finally.

Sandra didn't answer.

"All the systems are green," continued Ng. "There is absolutely no problem here. The data is all in."

"Then why did we crash ten days ago?" asked Sandra.

"If we wait for the final report, we won't launch for a year," said Ng. "That's the end of us. You don't want that. Phillip doesn't want that."

"No one wants that." Sandra shook her head. "But we don't know why the rocket blew up."

"I think it was an impurity with the fuel," said Ng.

"That doesn't work out in the simulations."

"It could. Or the tubing was imperfect."

"Unlikely."

"Possible."

"Do what you have to do," said Sandra. "I know Icarus has been pushing for the launch. Terhoussen even tried calling me."

Ng nodded.

It wasn't that they didn't know what had happened. They did: Pressure had built up in one of the tubes feeding oxidizer into the pump assembly. The buildup had raised the pressure in the tube, and caused the initial explosion.

The question was why had it happened in the first place.

All of the data on the pump, the logical cause for the pressure backup, looked fine. In fact, they had recovered it and put it on a test bench . . . where it worked fine. Sandra had made some minor changes, replacing the tubing with slightly thicker pipes and altering the feed. But the changes didn't really account for the problem, at least not in her mind.

"Whatever happens, I want the booster's inducer impellers under a microscope," she told Ng.

"Already done."

The inducer was responsible for maintaining head pressure into the thrust chamber, and was another logical culprit for the problem—except it, too, had been recovered and appeared in perfect working order.

"I'm going to get some lunch," Sandra said finally. "Want to come?"

"No, I have to write all this up."

"All right. See you later."

Sandra brooded about the rocket's failure as she walked from the test area to the elevators. Her mind played the explosion over and over again. She'd had failures before, but nothing like this—nothing so spectacular, or mysterious.

The inducers looked like metal propellers, and worked the same way. The system was mechanical, with a long history of success—you could track it back *at least* to the early Atlas rockets.

Bad machining?

Impossible. It would never have made it out of the fabricator's. And she'd inspected it herself.

Punchline shared a cafeteria with several other businesses at the park. Sandra walked out the back door and into the sun, striding up the cement path past the row of cactus and other native plants. There was an awning reserved for smokers, empty at the moment.

She hadn't smoked in years and years, and had never been a heavy smoker at all, yet she felt a twinge as she passed.

Andy still smoked. More than he had in college, she thought. Must be a job hazard.

She thought of calling him. Just to talk.

But of course, she couldn't do that. She didn't want to come off like a jittery little girl.

Truth be told, she felt attracted to him. Why, though? He was sardonic and off-hand and cynical. Good-looking. But he smelled of coffee and tobacco.

Maybe it was nicotine lust.

She smiled at herself.

Underneath it all, he cared about what he was doing. And Kathy. He still cared about her. It was obvious in his eyes, in his manner.

Andy Fisher, an FBI agent! Well at least he'd be a good one.

She continued into the cafeteria. The hot food line

had a special on beef stroganoff. Sandra decided to stick with a hamburger.

What if the data in the sensor was wrong? She assumed that it was right—everyone assumed that it was right—because the explosion had started in that line.

But what if the information was false? If the sensor was wrong, which systems were affected? If the temperature of the fuel or the oxidizer was out of spec . . .

Sandra mulled the permutations as her burger was cooked. She was so distracted that the cook had to wave his hand in front of her face to get her attention.

"Sorry," she said, reaching for the plate.

He smiled. He was used to dealing with airy scientists.

Back in her office, Sandra began going through the flight data one more time, comparing it to the recent test results as well as the previous launch and simulations. A software tool showed and compared different values, highlighting outliers. With the exception of the pressure numbers in the one tube, there were no meaningful differences. In fact, the numbers from the sensors on the side of the rocket where the explosion began tracked precisely with the last launch.

Sandra did notice one thing, however: The prelaunch satellite data dump had lasted about thirty seconds longer at the launch than the simulated prelaunches. Which seemed odd, since the prelaunches used Icarus's dataflow.

Why? she wondered.

Had something there screwed them up?

It was highly unlikely. Impossible even.

And yet it was the only thing that seemed different between the two launches. She went into the files and retrieved the data records.

The raw telemetry was meaningless, essentially a foreign language that needed to be translated. Sandra called up the e-mail program on her computer and started to write an inquiry to Icarus's satellite supervisor, asking for a deciphered transcript. She got about one sentence into it before deciding that a phone call would be faster.

She got his voice mail and hung up.

Struggling with the e-mail again, she decided it would be easier to leave a message to have him call her. Then she thought of talking to Terhoussen—he knew everything anyway. He had told her to call if she wanted to discuss the launch.

He answered on the second ring.

"Dr. Terhoussen, good afternoon." She was always a little formal with Terhoussen, both because of his manner and the fact that he reminded her of her grad school thesis mentors. "This is Sandra Chester. I've been going over some of the launch data and I found an anomaly. I was wondering if we could get a transcript of—"

"What exactly are you asking for?" snapped Terhoussen.

"Your transmission with the satellite. We—"

"Why?"

Well, if you let me finish a sentence, I'll explain, thought Sandra.

"The transmission time when you uploaded instructions to the satellite was different on launch day," she told him.

"So?"

"I'm wondering if you can explain that."

"What would that have to do with the launch?"

"I don't know. I just—"

"The launch must go through," he said abruptly.

"The launch—"

"I spoke to Phillip an hour ago. He assured me the launch would be scheduled. It is contracted."

"Without knowing why the booster exploded—"

"Phillip assured me there would be a launch. Your company is obligated to launch my satellite. A great deal is riding on the timetable."

"I understand."

"No, I don't believe you do understand, Ms. Chester. This is a project with national security implications. The future of our country. The world."

"Dr. Terhoussen, I fully understand the situation." Sandra emphasized the "Dr." His general lack of respect was one thing, but the way he had used Ms. put her over the edge. "I called because there seems to be an anomaly in the data flow to the satellite prior to launch and I want to rule that out as a factor."

"If you can advance a theory on how our satellite contributed to your failure, I would be very pleased to listen," said Terhoussen. "If not, I'm afraid I have other things to attend to."

"I know it's far-fetched. Still, I'd like to understand everything that's going . . ."

Sandra stopped talking. Terhoussen had hung up.

She slammed the phone down, then sat, elbow on the desk, chin in her hand, trying to calm down. There was no way that telemetry from the satellite, or to it, had caused the explosion.

Was there?

Sandra sent an e-mail to the propellant team, ordering a simulation of what would happen if the maneuvering rockets on the satellite had sparked during takeoff. Then she called her telemetry chief, asking if he had a copy of the instructions sent to the satellite.

He did. But it was raw code, encrypted to boot. It might as well be written in Sanskrit.

She had just hung up when she heard a knock on the door. She turned and saw Phillip Sihar, the company president, shifting nervously from foot to foot.

"Phil, come in," she said.

"Yes. Yes, I will."

Sihar closed the door behind him. Even though he was the head of the company, he was shy by nature and avoided direct confrontation when he could. He might send out a nasty e-mail, and then turn around in the hall a few minutes later to avoid seeing its recipient.

"Dr. Terhoussen just told me you agreed to launch next week."

"Yes, he's been pushing. You know the contract."

"I really, really have to advise against it."

"Everyone else has signed off, Sandra."

"That's not relevant." She thought of different terms, but held her tongue.

"We're obligated to launch. The contract specifies it. Even NASA has signed off."

"You're worried about a contract? We don't know why the rocket exploded, Phil."

"You can correct the only possible problems—the tubing and the fuel."

"There's no hard evidence that either caused the problem."

"One or the other," said Sihar. "The only possibilities. You said so. Your team said so."

"But I have no data."

"Icarus insists on launching."

"They're willing to risk another satellite?"

Sihar raised his shoulders in a half-shrug. Sandra knew that Icarus must be under enormous economic pressure to demonstrate a success. Now she realized that Punchline Orbiters was under the same pressure. Unlike Icarus, Punchline was owned by several investors; Sihar had founded the company, but retained very little of the stock.

"I think there may be something beyond a simple error here," Sandra said.

She noticed for the first time that Sihar's hands were shaking. Catching her glance, he clasped them together, trying to stop them.

"What are you saying?" he asked.

"There were some anomalies in the data. For some reason, Icarus talked to its satellite for about twice the regular length."

"How would that be related to the accident?"

"I don't know that it is."

"Dr. Chester." Sihar sat down in one of her chairs. "Sandra. Sometimes we have to admit that our work is not . . . perfect."

"I don't think it's perfect," she said quickly. The words jumped from her mouth, louder, harsher than she wished. Sandra immediately regretted them.

"Your design is solid. We already have had success," said Sihar. "An accident like this is not a major setback. You've corrected the problem."

"I'm going to run some simulations involving the telemetry data," Sandra said calmly. "Just to see if it's possible that the length of the message introduced an error. If the system wasn't expecting a long message, or if something in the message tripped us up somehow—"

"Of course," said Sihar. "It should be checked."

Sandra spent the rest of the day organizing herself, going through e-mail, checking the schedules on small projects, listing the dozens of tasks she had to complete before the launch. She drew up long lists, trying to focus.

It was difficult.

Finally, there were no other possible delays. She threw herself back against the problem, hoping to find the solution—the answer to the crash—through sheer force of will.

She would recheck everything, not just the telemetry. Every possible thing.

18

PENNSYLVANIA

Andy Fisher was in the car on his way back to New Bethlehem when Sandra Chester called. He saw Punchline in the address box and turned on the phone.

"Fisher," he said, flipping the phone open and hitting the intercom. "Talk to me."

"Andy?"

"Hey Rocket Scientist Lady, go ahead."

"I hate it when people say that," snapped Sandra.

Fisher heard another voice in his head:

Sometimes, you're too much of a wise guy for your own good.

Kathy's. Again.

"Hey, listen, I'm sorry," he told Sandra. "I wasn't making fun. I was just being a jerk. Sorry."

"I didn't mean to snap at you."

"Take exit eight in exactly one mile," said the voice module of the GPS.

"Excuse me?" said Sandra.

"Just my GPS. What's up?"

"I was hoping you might be able to help me with something," she said. "The FBI, I mean."

"I'd be happy to help. What do you need?"

"I have some satellite telemetry that's encrypted so that it can't be read. I'm wondering if the FBI can help decrypt it."

"You don't know your own code?"

"It's not our encryption."

"Sandra—you want me to break the law?"

"Oh. Uh—"

"No, no, I love that. Tell me more."

Sandra explained that the satellite code belonged to Icarus, and while she admitted it was a long shot, there was a possibility that the code had somehow screwed up her rocket. Without seeing the instructions themselves, her team couldn't decide one way or the other.

"Icarus won't tell you?"

"It's not a priority for them. Our contract gives us access to it, but I'm sure I'm not going to get it for quite a while."

"Hmmm."

"I don't want to get you in trouble," she said. "Forget I asked."

"No, no, I like getting in trouble," said Fisher. "And asking me to break the law. I love that in a woman."

Actually, it wasn't breaking the law at all, or at least not the letter of the law. The contracts covering the launch agreement allowed Sandra's company to review all telemetry, and handing it over voluntarily as part of an FBI investigation was hardly a legal issue. The real problem for Fisher was finding someone competent enough to decrypt it. And to do it sometime this century.

The Bureau did have people like that. Unfortunately, most of them were mad at him, and finding the right person would take time, something he was short of at the moment. So he handed the job off to Stendanopolis in San Francisco.

By the time he got off the phone—Stendanopolis wanted to talk about expense vouchers, which made hanging up easy—Fisher was about a half mile from the trooper barracks. He stopped off at a deli for a snack, only to find that they didn't have any fresh coffee.

Or stale coffee, for that matter.

"Nobody buys coffee around here after four o'clock," said the teenager behind the counter apologetically.

"Four o'clock?" said Fisher. "I've heard of rolling up the sidewalks, but not the caffeine."

The girl shrugged. As a consolation, she offered him a two-for-one deal on the fruit pockets—an almost healthy-sounding name for sugar pastry stuffed with sugar and a few slices of apple. He bought the pockets, along with some potato chips and a Red Bull. Nothing like a well-rounded dinner on the road.

He was just finishing eating when his BlackBerry buzzed. The supervisory agent handling the FBI side of the New Bethlehem investigation was updating him via e-mail.

We've been looking at the phone numbers that kid called, the one you ran down. One kid showed up in the police records because he went to the hospital about a year ago. Tried to kill himself. Reply if you want the address.

"Duh," muttered Fisher, hitting Reply.

Peter Greene lived with his parents in a dark gray Cape Cod in a town about thirty miles from New Bethlehem. The housing development looked like a suburb to nowhere. Most of the houses were built in the early 1960s to accommodate families working at an electronics plant on the nearby state highway. The plant had been one of the early manufacturers of integrated circuits and glass-etched chips used to make processor wafers. But it had bet on the wrong technology and went bust in the 1970s. The buildings were now abandoned, the area suspected of being a grayfield pollution site which no one dared examine.

Most of the residents from that era were long gone as well. Now the people who lived here were a collection of civil servants—the county center was two towns away—and workers in lower-level white-collar jobs, clerks in banks and supermarket cashiers.

The grass at the Greenes' was a little shaggy. The driveway sloped down from the road—a steep plunge if it snowed, Fisher thought, pausing at the curb before pulling in.

The driveway was empty. Fisher walked down to the backyard, looking around. There was an aboveground swimming pool, covered for the winter. It wasn't a big pool, but it filled about a third of the yard.

Fisher went around to the front and leaned on the

bell at the door. There was no answer. He rang the bell again, then tried the screen door. It was locked.

A light came on inside. A short, middle-aged woman unlocked and then pulled open the door.

"Yes?"

"My name's Andy Fisher. I'm with the FBI," said Fisher, flashing his ID. "I'm wondering if your son is around."

The look in the woman's eyes—a mixture of apprehension, fear, and confusion—nailed it for Fisher.

"Can I come in for a minute?" he added, knowing she was going to have a hard time answering.

Mrs. Greene hadn't seen him in three days. He hadn't taken a suitcase or a backpack, or brought along extra clothes. There was no girlfriend, at least not that she knew—one of the reasons, she thought, that he was "always so down."

"I liked the fact that he was interested in the nuclear plant," she told Fisher. "It was a group. They had a cause."

"Did he know a lot about nuclear power?"

"No." She put her hand around her waist, holding it. The thing that impressed Fisher about Peter's room was how dark it was; two of the three lights in the overhead fixture were out, and it was paneled in a dark-colored wood veneer. "Well, he did a project about nuclear power in high school his junior year. He got an A."

Fisher didn't really need to look, but she insisted. He waited on the couch while she ran and got it.

Neither one of them said anything about Peter being involved in the bombing. Fisher knew he didn't need to. He looked at the report when she returned, nodding as she leafed through it. There was a picture of Three Mile Island on the front. In the conclusion, Peter said that nuclear waste was too big a problem to deal with.

Fisher got a good description of what Peter was probably wearing, and managed to talk his mother out of a picture of him in his winter coat—a nondescript green field jacket.

"I wonder if he did his own laundry," said Fisher.

"Peter?" His mother smiled. "You don't know children, Agent Fisher."

"No, I don't. Think there's some dirty clothes around?"

"Everything gets washed every night."

"No socks under the bed?"

Fisher got down and looked. There was a pair of white athletic socks tossed near the wall.

"Maybe you do know children," said Mrs. Greene as he retrieved them.

They were still sweaty, which meant there'd be plenty of DNA material, more than enough for an ID. Fisher put the socks into a plastic bag. Mrs. Greene didn't ask why, and Fisher didn't volunteer. They had a pact going; if neither one of them made things explicit, they could both go on with their business.

Back in the kitchen, Fisher wrote his cell number on the small dry-erase pad they used for messages.

"If you hear from him," said Fisher, "please call me. All right?"

"Oh yes. You sure you don't want any coffee?"

"Thanks," said Fisher. "But I have a whole bunch of things I have to do right now. I'm sorry."

Back at the barracks, the forensics coordinator

told him whoever was driving the van had been wearing a green jacket and a lower-end pair of New Balance athletic shoes.

Fisher glanced at Peter's feet in the photo. There was an N on the side of his shoes.

"You can use the DNA in this sock to see if it links to the bomber," he said, handing over the plastic Baggie. "Assuming you can find enough genetic material in the shoes or the truck."

"We have."

"Yeah, I was afraid so," said Fisher, feeling bad about the kid's mom.

19

SAN DIEGO

They called him Em.

It was a nickname, one he'd gotten in the military, even before Afghanistan. The origins were so obscure now that not even he could remember how it had come about, though it had something to do with his middle initial and a joke someone had made in school. The people who really knew him called him Em, and the people who knew him vaguely called him Em, and even he generally thought of himself as Em. The name had grown to fit him.

Few people really knew him. One person now, the man he answered to. Everyone else knew someone they thought was him, but wasn't.

Em glanced over his shoulder as he walked into the Internet café. These places were notorious as havens for thieves and spies and drug dealers. It was best to assume that everyone inside fit into one of those categories, even if most were tourists. Or looked like tourists.

He paid cash for a card with a coded access number, then went to find an open machine. There was only one available, at the very end of the room, but he hesitated when he saw the man at the station next to it was drinking a beer in a brown paper bag.

God, he wanted a drink.

Em had not had a drink in two months. They had been the roughest months of his life, far worse than the time when things fell apart for him in Europe.

His abstinence was self-imposed. He had tried to cut down on his drinking several times in the past, but this time it was for real; this time was complete abstinence. He knew if he had a drink, just one drink, he would have many, and if he had many, he would not be able to work, and if he could not work, he would be cast off. Em had been warned. He was lucky to have his job. He had gotten this chance only because his former commander and friend was in charge here.

But he needed a drink.

He focused, signed into the Gmail account. There were ten e-mails.

Nine were spam. The tenth contained a number: 5,401.

It was a time: 10:45 A.M.

It meant that he should be online exactly at that moment. If he was, and if he was signed into the right account, he would get an instant message.

By chance, he had five minutes to spare. He checked the weather in random parts of the country, lingering over the radar displays.

The message came to him exactly on the dot. It was a telephone number.

He had a half hour to call, but pay phones were scarce and hard to find. He was starting to think he would have to use his emergency prepaid phone when he spotted a phone in front of a small market.

He was just about to hit the brakes and swerve into the parking lot when he noticed the roof lights of a police cruiser two cars behind him.

It meant nothing. It was a coincidence.

Em slowed but did not turn in, continuing instead to the next intersection. He turned right.

So did the police car.

Em signaled, turning into the mall. The police car's lights came on.

He glanced downward without moving his head, looking at the shadow wedged between the passenger seat and the center console. With his left hand on the wheel, he slid his right to the pistol, ready if he needed it.

The policeman walked up to his window.

"License and registration," said the cop.

Em took his wallet out and started to hand it over.

"Take the license from the wallet, please."

An honest cop, Em thought, handing it over.

It's routine, he told himself as the policeman walked back to the patrol car to check the ID. The license was from out of state. Em expected it to pass, but there was always a chance there would be a problem.

No need to panic, he told himself. No need to shoot the cop.

If he *had* to shoot him, he could deal with it. If he had to.

It was always the unexpected that tripped a man up. He remembered The Wolf telling him this many years ago, when he took him under his wing. You planned and you planned, but it was always what you didn't plan for that surprised you.

Which was why you planned. This way, you had an out.

The Wolf was a notorious drinker himself. It had killed him in the end.

The policeman got out of his car and walked up the side.

"Your left brake light is out," said the cop, handing him back his license and registration. "There's a shop in the mall, the far end over there. Buy a light and fix it. I'll forget about the ticket."

"Yes, sir. Thank you," said Em, pretending to be relieved.

"Have a good day."

He drove down the side aisle of the lot, turned right, and found the auto parts store. The clerk had seen the whole incident, and thought it was funny. He sold him a Phillips head screwdriver to take the bulb out.

"A quarter of the price of a ticket," said the clerk when Em objected to the twenty-dollar tab for the tool. "Your lucky day."

"I need to call someone and tell them I'll be late," he said. "Is there a pay phone around here?"

"There may be one across the street," said the clerk. "Is it a quick call?"

"It's quick."

"Here." The clerk took out his cell phone. "You can use my phone."

He hesitated, not wanting to share the number. But the number would be useless as soon as the call was over. And he didn't have time anyway; there was only a minute or so left.

He went to the front of the store and dialed.

The man on the other end answered on the first ring.

"Sandra Chester at Punchline Orbiters is a problem. She must be dealt with."

The line went dead.

"I ran into a bit of a car problem," Em said, though he knew he was only speaking to himself. "I'm going to be a little late. But I'll get there. Eventually. And after that—I would like the vacation you promised."

THREE

Twists and Turns

1

PENNSYLVANIA

Even before the DNA from his sock was analyzed, Fisher was so sure that Peter Greene was the dead bomber that he had the local FBI agents pull as much information on him as they could.

In the meantime, he went to talk to Ahmed Kharjien, the double agent who'd been snared by the DIA's false leads.

Or maybe not false. He clearly was doing something behind Burns's back, though what exactly it was wasn't clear.

Burns had stashed Ahmed up in a motel about fifty miles south of Philadelphia. A team of agents was watching him around the clock. Burns had thought about putting him in jail for a few days, to make it clear how angry he was, but he was scheduled to testify in a government case soon, and the U.S. attorney who was handling the trial didn't want him rattled any more than absolutely necessary.

"No way he had anything to do with the bombing," Burns told Fisher when he met him outside the motel. "None of those guys did. They're the gang that couldn't shoot straight."

Fisher avoided asking the obvious question: If that was the case, why was Burns wasting his time with them?

"The guy he got the cell phones from. That's who I want," said Fisher. "I need a name. Beyond the dead guy whose Social Security number they filched."

"I've been sweating him on it," said Burns. "He doesn't know who he is—just some guy in a mosque who wanted to do him a favor and gave it to him in case he wanted to be contacted. He left it with the old man as a safe phone. The guy he got it from didn't even tell him the number."

That was a slightly different story than what they'd started with. Not necessarily better, or more accurate. Just different.

"Did you check the credit card account?" added Burns.

"Oh yeah. The old guy's Social Security was used on a whole slew of accounts. It's probably written on bathroom walls all over Russia."

"That sucks."

"I was thinking of having him hook up with the guy who gave him the phones."

"We gotta keep him on ice until the trial. He's lucky he's not in chains."

"He got a phone number or something from this guy, right?"

"No."

"I have a number we can try," said Fisher. "Let's give it a shot."

"Where'd you get it?"

"It's to a cell phone. The phone was used at the

place where the others were bought. It's on a different network, and it happens to be the only cell call in that area within, I think it's ten or fifteen minutes."

"I don't get it," said Burns. "Why would that be significant?"

"Because it went to a phone booth out of state."

"That's confusing."

"But interesting."

"How'd you find that out?"

"Remember Bernie Stendanopolis?"

"Bernie What's-the-Right-Form?"

"Yeah. He's working with me on this. He's got some people and one of them got it for me."

"You're working with Bernie? There's a match made in hell."

"It works out pretty well, actually. As long as he stays in San Francisco."

There were only six calls made from the phone in question, and all had been to phone booths. The last call had been made a few hours before; according to the cell phone company, the caller was in western Pennsylvania not far from New Bethlehem.

Ahmed was sitting on the bed, watching television, when Fisher and Burns knocked on his door. His Bureau "minder" was sitting at the room's small desk, reading *The Washington Post* on his laptop.

"Watching porn on the government dime?" asked Fisher.

"It's CNN," said Ahmed, defensively.

"Same thing," said Fisher. "Why don't we grab some coffee? Just the two of us."

It was an order, not a suggestion, and Ahmed knew it. He pulled on his shoes and followed Fisher out of the room. They drove alone to a diner Fisher had spotted a half mile away. Burns and the minder followed at a distance.

"Pretty nice racket you got," said Fisher. "I hear Burnsy set you up with a Mercedes, expense account, Platinum American Express. Nice."

"I am helping the government. I love this country."

"Come on, Ahmed. You have to at least *try* to make me believe you."

Fisher slid over his coffee cup for the passing waitress to refill.

"I'm a patriot."

"Me, too," said Fisher. "But only on the weekends. The rest of the time I'm a money-grubbing slime who's trying to fatten my bank account while staying out of jail. Oh, wait. That's you I'm talking about. My mistake."

Ahmed squirreled his face into a frown, then rose and started for the door. As soon as he spotted Burns sitting in a booth near the cash register, he turned back around.

"What I want you to do is call this number," said Fisher, sliding over his cell phone as Ahmed sat down. "Tell whoever answers you want to have a meeting."

"Where?"

"Here would be great. If that doesn't work, try for another restaurant somewhere. Someplace you'd meet."

"How did I get this number?"

"Tell him he gave it to you."

Fisher waited as he dialed. The problem with watching a con artist pull a con was that you didn't know how far it went.

The phone rang four times, then sent him to voice mail. Ahmed held the phone away from his ear so

Fisher could hear the canned voice telling him to leave a message.

Fisher twirled his finger, telling him to do so.

"This is Ahmed Kharjien," he said. "Please call."

He hung up, then started to slide the phone back to Fisher.

"Hold on to it," said Fisher. "Let's sit for a while, see what happens."

"If you wish."

"What are you, the genie of the lamp?" said Fisher sharply, deciding to turn up the heat a bit. "Granting me wishes?"

Ahmed blinked at him.

"Tell me about the guy who gave you the cell phones," said Fisher. "What's his name?"

Ahmed shrugged.

"Stranger hands you a cell phone and you don't ask his name?"

"I think it was Manu."

"Manu? That's not very Arab."

"He's not Arab. He comes from Malaysia. There are many Muslims there."

"How do you know he's from Malaysia?"

"Someone said."

Ahmed began explaining how he worked, visiting different mosques at different intervals, basically talking up different members. Most times, people were suspicious of him, and building relationships took time. Manu also seemed to be an outsider, looking to curry favor with anyone—hence the cell phones. He claimed to be a wholesaler and had many things "brothers could use."

"Brothers with malicious intent?" suggested Fisher.

"Things are never that explicit. Not at first."

"This guy sounds like he could be you," said Fisher. "You sure he wasn't working for the Bureau?"

Ahmed shrugged. He had a certain obeisance in his manner, the sort of look a dog had when broken. But he became more fluid as he talked, more confident. It wouldn't take much for him to seem charming if you were an outcast yourself, someone like Yahyah Benham or Peter Greene.

"So what was counterfeiting like?" Fisher asked.

Ahmed shrugged. "A job."

"You were good at it?"

"Enough to get by."

"How'd you do it?"

"Copy machine."

"Copy machine?"

Ahmed smiled, a bit of pride showing through his mask.

Finally, thought Fisher. *I'm getting through.*

"Most people don't pay attention," he said. "You would be surprised. People start talking, they forget what they are doing. Even when they know something is wrong, they can't put their finger on it."

"Then you pass the bills."

Another shrug.

Most of the people who did what Ahmed did were small-time crooks. With some polish, they might be used car salesmen. Working as a pseudo-terrorist for the FBI was typically the best gig they ever had.

So was Ahmed dumb enough to screw up the gig of a lifetime? Only if he was a truly committed terrorist. Fisher had a hard time buying that, but he knew appearances could be deceiving.

The waitress brought Fisher some french fries. The cell phone rang as he poured on the ketchup.

"What do I tell him?" Ahmed asked, instantly nervous.

Fisher realized he must not have expected a call back. So maybe he wasn't entirely lying about how distant the connection was.

Hmmm.

"Tell him you want to meet," said Fisher. "You're taking him up on his offer to help. And you need money."

"If he says no?"

"Get a meeting. Here, if possible."

"Where did I get the number?"

"He gave you the number. When he catches you in a lie, confess that you looked at his cell phone."

"If he doesn't catch me?"

"He will."

He did. Ahmed confessed masterfully. The conversation was over in a minute.

"Tomorrow in Harrisburg," he told Fisher. "At a McDonald's. Three o'clock."

"Good," said Fisher. "I'm dying for a Big Mac."

"Not literally, I hope," said Burns.

2

NEW MEXICO

There was no trick to killing a person. Anyone could do it.

Getting away with it was more difficult. There was always a certain amount of luck involved, even with careful planning.

Em planned carefully. But he had a tendency, a natural inclination, to want to act instinctually. Instinctual action was important during battle—it had helped him to great successes as a soldier—but for his job now it was a liability. It had led to trouble in Europe several times before the fiasco that had nearly led to his disgrace, not to mention his death. He knew he had to plan, and he did plan, though at times he felt as if he was fighting his own true self.

The way Em saw it, planning made him think about what he was doing too much. It was one thing to focus on mechanics—how do I make this fire look like just a fire—and quite another to start thinking about the person in the fire. It was difficult to separate the facts you needed about the person from other facts that made the person real. Once they were real, they were less the enemy, more a victim. And if you had any sympathy at all for victims, if you had even once been slightly religious, as Em had, their being real caused you problems.

That was the funny thing about drinking. A few drinks made the work easier, since it calmed the mind. At some point though, too many . . . too many were fatal.

Em looked at his hands. They were steady. They hadn't been in New York. So he was making progress.

The first step was to gather information. The garage door to Sandra Chester's condo opened at exactly 7:23 A.M. She backed her car—a two-year-old Porsche Cayenne SUV wagon—out to the street as the door descended. By the time she reached the road, his scanner had recorded the code to the opener.

Her drive to work was leisurely. There weren't many cars on the local roads even at rush hour, and he had to stay far back so he wouldn't be seen. But since he knew where she was going, this wasn't particularly difficult. About ten minutes from the office she stopped at an Exxon station. Em drove past, noting that she had stopped to go into the convenience market rather than fill up with gas. At the next intersection he found a place to turn around and went back, resisting the temptation to pull in and get a closer look. By the time he turned around again she was already back on the road and heading to work. He followed her into the industrial park, passing the entrance to the parking garage where she was just going through the gate. The garage required a magnetic key card. It was a security precaution easily fooled, though it implied other difficulties—like video cameras in the garage.

Em circled through the park. There were several different parking areas, some gated, some not. A few looked like they had video cameras. It was early, not yet eight, and so it was difficult to tell which buildings might be sparsely occupied.

He'd come back in a few hours for that.

A FedEx substation sat at the far end of the complex. It didn't open until 8:30 A.M., but there were boxes outside that accepted overnight envelopes. He parked and walked slowly to the box. Unsure of whether he was being watched by a surveillance camera, he reached into the supply bin and took out an envelope, then went back to his car to fill it out. Miming confusion, he got out, went over to the door, fiddled with the envelope, then checked his watch as if wondering whether to stay until someone came to answer his question. Finally he pretended that he had decided to stay, locked his car, and went for a walk, as if killing time.

It took a little more than ten minutes for him to reach the garage where Sandra had parked. There were cameras near the stairwells, and one at the entrance, but most of the rows weren't covered. He determined that he could escape the video eyes entirely by staying close to the wall on the first level, then going up the side ramp.

Sandra's car was on the second level, parked on the side toward the building. He squatted at the edge of the ramp, making sure that there was no camera watching it. Finally assured he was safe, he pulled himself up by the rail, swinging into the narrow lane in front of the curbs that marked the parking slots. He walked quickly to her car, dropped to his knees, and then crouch-walked to the back fender. He reached into his pocket and took out a device about half the size of a cell phone. It was a GPS locator, which would allow him to track the car practically anywhere across North America. He punched a code on the small keypad to activate it, made sure it was set to its longest interval—transmitting its location every three minutes to preserve the battery—and reached up under the car to put it in place.

Once, he had been setting a similar device on a car in Rome, only to discover the vehicle had already been bugged. He was annoyed at the time—he had to move to the other side of the vehicle to place his locator, and this exposed him to the traffic. Now it seemed funny.

Locator placed, he slipped out of the garage and walked to his car. The FedEx office still wasn't open. He made a show of going to the door, looking frustrated, then turning back to the car.

He'd almost reached it when a woman's voice called out behind him.

"Sir—wait! Wait!"

Instinctively, he put his hand to the front of his waistband, covering the small Glock nestled there.

Calm, he told himself.

"Sir?"

He turned slowly. A young woman dressed in a FedEx uniform was standing at the door, one hand holding it open.

"Did you want to send that?" she asked.

It took him a second to formulate an answer.

"I had a question, actually."

In the four steps it took for him to reach her, he had regained his equilibrium.

"I wondered if it's possible to put in the recipient's

account number—if I do that, do I need a note or something from them?" Em asked.

"A note?"

"That's why I had a question." He smiled. "Some sort of permission from them?"

"No. You'll need their account number, of course. And their phone number would be a good idea. The address, obviously. If you use the account number, generally we assume you have the right to do that. They said you could?"

"I have to check with them. Save some money. Okay. That was my question."

"That's it?"

"That's it." He smiled. "I'll be by later. Tomorrow at the latest."

The incident at the FedEx office filled Em with dread. It wasn't fear so much as agitation. His heart pumped as if he'd had too much coffee. He drove for an hour, hoping it would dissipate.

What he wanted, of course, was a drink. He knew better than that.

Driving on the long expanses of New Mexico highway, Em tried to push his mind away from the present. But that offered little solace. His thoughts slipped around, floating like droplets of oil on water, spread by the waves. Then one by one they began to pool in Afghanistan.

He had many memories of Afghanistan. A good number were horrible—the helicopter that had crashed, in flames, a few meters from him. The little girls, butchered by the Taliban. But there were other memories. Many were pleasant—walking with Giant on patrol, laughing at his jokes. Most were neutral—the colonel and his habit of scanning the horizon silently for twenty minutes or more, as if he were absorbing it into his bloodstream.

Em pulled into a gas station, filled the tank, and went inside to get something to drink. He kept his eyes focused on the floor as he walked past the beer cooler.

Outside, he pulled the car into a parking spot and sipped his iced tea.

The war didn't haunt him, not the way it haunted some others. Thinking about it was actually calming. Very calming.

He had begun thinking about the war during his worst days after the fiasco in Europe. He had given some thought to organizing his memories of it—if not into a book exactly, at least into something that could be given to others.

At this stage in his life, Em knew it was unlikely he would ever have children himself. But he had two young nephews, nine and ten, whom he liked to think admired him. He wanted them to know who he was—partly to impress them, it was true, but also to pass some hard-earned knowledge on.

Em wasn't much of a writer. And making recordings was not a particularly good idea in his line of work. It was not that he would be stupid enough to give some direct link to his assignments, let alone confess to what he was doing. But ambient noise behind the recordings might somehow give him away—a train that only passed at a certain time, whistling in the background, might be a piece of evidence somehow for a conviction. Or so he imagined.

But sitting in his car, sipping iced tea, he saw it

more as a choice: drink, or remember Afghanistan. Record his memories for his nephews.

There was nothing else to do for a while now anyway. Killing the scientist would be easy, if he took his time, if he kept calm. In the meantime, this would give him something constructive to do.

Getting a tape recorder proved difficult. Em stopped in a large grocery store, hoping there might be an electronics section; they sold tapes but no recorder. None of the small stores nearby had anything like electronics.

Plenty of alcohol, though. There were two liquor stores.

There was a Radio Shack in the next mall. The clerk, a young man of about twenty, fiddled with his tie as Em looked around.

"Maybe I can help you," the clerk finally said.

"I need a tape recorder," Em told him. "Something portable."

"Tape recorder—nobody carries those anymore," said the young man.

"This sticker says you do."

Em pointed at a metal peg, where mini-cassette recorders usually hung. The store had sold out its last one recently; new ones were on the way. The clerk told Em that he should buy a voice recorder instead.

"These are much better," he told him, steering him to the display. "You just download the file. You can e-mail them—they're MP3s. Everything's digital now, man. And the price is just about the same, when you figure tape in."

"They hard to work?"

"Easier than a tape recorder."

Em doubted that was true. But looking at the recorder, he saw it had simple controls—play and record, which were basically all he needed.

"Zip code?" said the clerk when he took it to the register.

"Zip code?"

"It's for marketing purposes."

"I'm not from around here."

"I can tell from your accent."

Em gave him 10020.

"Where's that?" asked the clerk.

"New York," said Em, guessing.

"Name?"

"Why?"

"We keep track of our customers."

Em almost backed out, but thought it would make him look too suspicious. He made up something, paid with cash, then left the store.

His agitation at stasis not banished but under control, Em returned to the task at hand.

He wanted to look at her condo. But he needed another car, and he didn't want to use his backup vehicle either. What he needed was a van.

"Forty-nine ninety-five," said the woman at the counter of the Rent-A-Wreck franchise out near the airport. "Andja taxes. Six forty-three, two dollah suh-charge. Damage waiv-uh fourteen ninety-five. Personal accident . . ."

The woman reeled off a menu of insurance and other charges that quadrupled the base price. Since he wasn't paying for it himself he didn't care; he just handed over his credit card.

"Take it all," he told her.

"Ain't from around here, are you?"

Em shook his head. "Does it show?"

She smiled. She was flirting with him. In her mid-thirties, still very pretty—but the temptation was easily put off.

Em found an electrician's truck with magnetic signs in the parking lot of a nearby mall. He took the signs; when he got closer to Sandra's condo unit, he stopped and put them on the van's door. He parked at the edge of her property, positioning the truck so that it was possible he was going into any of several units, including two across the street. Then, with a bag of tools in his hand, he walked up her driveway, whistling.

The garage door, prodded by the preprogrammed radio control in his hand, opened as he approached. Inside, he paused to put on his gloves, then went to the door at the side. After looking for wires or other signs of a burglar alarm, he pulled a small circuit detector from his pocket and did a more thorough check. When that didn't turn up anything, he tried the doorknob.

It was locked, but this was only a temporary problem. He opened the tool bag and took what looked like a small key gun from the top tray. The gun was a lock-pick tool, with slotted key pieces that could be selected and adjusted; the lock opened easily.

Propping the door open a crack with his foot, Em took a telescoping spy cam from his pocket and extended it through the crack, looking to see if there was an alarm control on the nearby wall. When he didn't spot one, he turned his attention gradually to the rest of the hallway, pulling the wand out to its fullest extension. Unlike many similar devices, this one did not plug into an external viewer, and he had to squint to see the image in the bud-sized viewer at the end. Scanning the nearby rooms took several minutes; he moved methodically, pushing back mentally against the urge to move ahead, against the instincts that told him that there were no alarms here. Finally assured, he pulled the wand back and pushed the door open, stepping into Sandra Chester's home.

The place smelled vaguely of coffee and toasted muffin. Em was in a hall that led from the front door to the great room at the back; the kitchen was opposite him.

He took a quick look around the kitchen. The morning dishes—a cup, a plate with crumbs—were in the sink. The refrigerator was nearly empty, except for the bottom shelf, which was filled with beer, at least a half-dozen different varieties in bottles haphazardly packed at the bottom—the remains of a party, he suspected.

He closed the door, looked around.

He could poison her food.

A car passed outside. Em waited, then walked quietly down the hall to the great room at the back of the condo. It was intended as a combination living and dining room, but there was no dining room furniture, which made it seem even larger. He paused at the threshold from the hall, looking first for motion detectors or cameras. Then he walked through it, circling the pair of couches set in the middle of the space. There were two consoles set against the wall at the side, pushed together. He imagined they would hold a buffet.

She liked to host parties.

He imagined himself here, with her and her friends. A moment's fantasy—but work, too, learning who his prey was. Then he moved on to the bedroom.

Some women's rooms smelled of perfume. This had a vaguely soapish smell, lavender mingling with something more utilitarian. The room was sparsely furnished—a queen-sized bed, a dresser, a chair with a shirt neatly folded over it. Shoes in the corner—two pair.

On the walls, three large posters. The one nearest the door featured an astronaut jumping off the lunar lander to step on the moon.

One small step for mankind . . . read the script.

The other two, opposite the bed, were of artworks by Rothko and Kandinsky, advertising shows long gone. Both were abstracts.

There was a big walk-in closet. If he decided to kill her here, he could wait inside, then do it.

The house would be easy to blow up as well. A small bomb in the gas-fired furnace, or perhaps behind the stove.

The possibilities circulated in his mind as he completed his walk-through, checking the utility closet, going upstairs to her study. The study was the most personal room in the condo, and by far the messiest, with papers and reports and books and magazines in several piles scattered around. There were three computers, including a laptop. Spying on her would have been child's play, but that wasn't his job.

Killing her was. And the hardest thing about that would be deciding how to do it.

In her bed as she slept?

The garage on her way to her car?

A bomb in the car—easier.

He thought about it as he relocked the door and left the house.

3

NEW BETHLEHEM

"I think your friend blew himself up as one last fuck you to the world," said Fisher, pushing himself back from the table in the interview room.

Canderfield scratched his forearm, gazing absently at the wall behind Fisher. He had rubbed his skin raw. "He wasn't my friend."

"He wasn't your enemy."

"No one was supposed to do something like this! God!"

Tears leaked from Canderfield's eyes. Fisher was skeptical. Remorse was a difficult emotion to read, and he didn't have enough context to fit the tears into. Canderfield had waived his right to an attorney and given the state detectives the names of the others who were in his small group. None of them had criminal records; most were just bored, B-plus students at the local community college. Preliminary interviews showed most would have good alibis. Except for the fact that a member of their group had driven the truck to the plant, everyone would have dismissed them as postadolescent wannabes.

Impossible to do now. Peter Greene had damned all of them. Once his identity was confirmed through DNA, it was bound to be released to the media. After that, it would be only a few hours before some of their names made their way to the reporters.

"Why do you think your friend would blow himself up?" asked Fisher. "Did he believe in the cause that much?"

"He—I think he was depressed."

"It takes more than that," said Fisher. "Was he on medication?"

"I don't think so. No."

"Unlike you."

Canderfield shrugged.

"Prozac?" asked Fisher.

"Zoloft."

"It helps?"

"Most days. Not today."

"I don't think he actually meant to kill himself," said Fisher. He pushed forward, sliding his forearms down along the table, folding them in front of him. "I think someone told him to bring the van to the plant. He probably knew there was a bomb there, but didn't think it would go off until he was out. If I were looking at a map of the plant, I would think I'd have an easy time getting out."

Canderfield stared at him, a blank, almost dumbstruck expression on his face.

Was he *that* good—could he look so ignorant, so out of it, and actually be the mastermind?

"Maybe he thought the bomb was too small to do real damage," said Fisher. "Maybe he was just sending a message. Like the protestors. And then got double-crossed."

Canderfield didn't answer. Fisher had genuinely pushed him too far.

So was it Ahmed? But Ahmed wasn't a mastermind. Maybe he was someone playing both ends against the middle, skimming a little off the top of both sides as he went. That might fit, it could fit—but it left him with the question of who was really behind the attack.

"Who came up with the map of the plant?" Fisher asked. "Was that something you did?"

"Map?" Canderfield shook his head.

"Yeah, the place was mapped out."

"You found a map?"

"Did you draw it?" asked Fisher. "Who knew the layout of the plant?"

"You can get plenty of maps—the newspaper had a map. Google Earth—"

"Google Earth is a couple of years old. The plant's not even there," said Fisher. "I looked this morning. Virtual Earth, Flash Earth—they're all pretty far behind. You can't see the checkpoints. Somebody prepared the van. What was it you did?" Fisher leaned back in his chair, stretching. "Did you do the bomb?"

"No." Canderfield was emphatic. "I didn't do any bomb."

"Go up there and map it out for them?" said Fisher.

"I wanted to talk the workers into striking," the kid blurted. "I thought I could."

"Uh-huh."

"I went in one day and that's all I did."

"Because you were in charge of the group."

"I wasn't in charge."

"Who was?"

"There was no leader. We weren't even a group. Not really."

They went around on that for a while, around and around, Fisher pushing gently now, Canderfield still resisting. Gradually, Fisher assured himself that Canderfield wasn't lying, not in the main—the group was too amorphous to have a leader.

But he had gone there, gone around and talked to the people he knew. He naively thought that they would agree with him and decide not to work. And when he got back, he diagramed the place for the others, who were anxious to know what it was like.

"You made copies of the map?" asked Fisher.

"It wasn't really a map."

"You made copies?"

Canderfield shook his head.

"You still have it?"

"No."

"Where did it go?"

"I don't know."

He could have blamed the dead kid, Fisher thought, but didn't. It seemed legitimate, not a clever move to push off suspicion.

"So where does Peter fit into all of this?" said Fisher.

"He was just one of the other people."

"Why would he blow the place up?"

"He wouldn't."

"Who would?"

"Simon." The name gushed out of him. "This guy Simon contacted us like, a week or two weeks ago. We met him. He was a nut. He wanted to help us."

"What kind of nut?"

Canderfield shrugged. It took Fisher another half hour, two cups of coffee, and a bathroom break to get the full details from Canderfield:

Ten days before, a man who called himself Simon had contacted them, and made it clear that he would help them in any way—money especially—in their protests against the plant. And if protests weren't enough, he was prepared to do anything.

"You could tell the guy was slimy," said Canderfield. "A real slime."

"How?" asked Fisher.

"Always looking around. His clothes—a little off. Like he bought them to try to blend in, except he didn't."

"What did he look like?"

"More Spanish than Arab. I don't know where he was from."

"Malaysia?"

"I don't know. Maybe."

4

PENNSYLVANIA

Like most McDonald's, the restaurant Manu had named was located on a highway not far from a busy intersection. It had a small parking lot, sharing the overflow with a neighboring strip mall and an older building that until recently had been an upscale restaurant but was now empty and advertised for sale. Burns called the real estate agent and managed to convince her to let the FBI use it for surveillance. This wasn't particularly hard to do: She sounded as if she was going to have an orgasm on the phone as soon as he said he was with the FBI.

They put a dozen cars with two agents apiece into the area, moving around or parking in what they hoped were inconspicuous spots. Four other teams stood by, ready to rotate in as the time for the appointment drew close. Ahmed was taken to a motel about a half mile away to wait. The plan was to send Ahmed in, get an ID on Manu, then pick him up in the parking lot quietly. Burns had some hope that in the process they would manage to avoid implicating Ahmed, though that seemed forlorn at best.

Fisher would have preferred just putting Manu under surveillance, but that wasn't practical. Peter Greene's name had not yet leaked out to the press, but that was bound to happen any moment. The state attorney's office and the troopers were running their mouths like PR flacks paid by the syllable. In fact, the loose lips had convinced Fisher that no locals could be used as backups on the operation, a decision Burns readily agreed to.

Fisher pulled into the mall lot behind the McDonald's around ten to three, ahead of the meeting. He parked, then sauntered over to the restaurant.

"Big Mac, large fries, strawberry shake," he told the young man at the counter.

"Should I supersize that?" asked the clerk.

"What, make it a bigger Big Mac?" asked Fisher.

"Well, no, it would just be a Big Mac."

"So my Big Mac would be a small Mac if I supersized it?"

"Uh—"

"The sign says I can get a free refill on the drink," said Fisher. "So what you're really asking is, do I want to be way overcharged for a few extra fries and a less than super hamburger?"

"Uh—"

"Tell you what," said Fisher. "Give me a Big Mac and two orders of fries and we'll call it even."

The clerk was so befuddled he forgot to charge Fisher for the burger.

A mother with two preschool boys was just finishing a late lunch at the next to last table in the seating area on the side. Fisher grabbed a newspaper and sat behind them, making faces at the kids while he pulled out his phone and a Bluetooth receiver to find out what was going on. Though wearing a wire, to have an actual conversation he had to use the phone.

"Good thing you straightened them out on the burger pricing," said Burns sarcastically.

"Had to," said Fisher. "The accounting department watches me like a hawk. Where's our boy?"

"Ahmed's getting out of the car now. Manu hasn't shown yet. Not that we've seen."

Fisher dumped about half a shaker's worth of salt on his tray's paper insert and began eating. In his experience, McDonald's french fries had a very short half-life: They had to be eaten before they reached room temperature. Once cooled, the fat on their skin hardened, and they went from tasting like very hot cardboard to lukewarm plasterboard soaked in recycled motor oil. This was not necessarily fatal, but called for much more salt.

Fisher could see Ahmed in the reflection at the front window. He walked to the counter, ordered a cup of coffee, and took a seat near the front window, exactly as he'd been briefed.

So far, everything was going according to plan. Which worried Fisher a great deal. Operations like this worked according to a law of inverse proportions— the longer it took for something to screw up, the worse the screwup was going to be.

"No sign of Manu," reported Burns.

"Bang-bang," shouted one of the nearby children. "You're dead."

Fisher looked over. The kid was pointing a toy gun at him. "Don't shoot the nice man, honey," said the boy's mother, turning around. Eyelids drooping, shoulders hanging toward the floor, she looked like an exhausted marathon runner—or a typical mother of a preschooler.

"Fish? What's going on?" asked Burns.

"Just a kid," said Fisher. "You can't see that on video?"

"Not getting a good image," said Burns.

They'd planted a small video camera in the corner, but apparently someone had shifted a nearby garbage can, partly obscuring the image. It was too late to fix it.

Which made Fisher feel better. It was the necessary flaw in the operation.

Of course, a superstitious agent would always say that bad things came in threes . . . Maybe the french fries counted. They were slightly soggy.

Not that he was superstitious.

"We got a car with a dark-colored Asian or Hispanic coming through the parking lot," said one of the FBI agents. "He went through the place before— Okay, this may be him."

The car swung around through the parking lot, then went over to the drive-through lane. Fisher looked at the kids and the woman next to him. When he'd sat down, they'd looked like they were ready to leave. But the woman had just returned from the soda counter with a pair of refills and fresh straws.

The kid who'd "shot" him earlier took a straw, opened the end, then blew the paper in Fisher's direction. Then he began blowing bubbles into his soft drink.

Cute, thought Fisher. Until the kid turned around and spit some of the soda on Fisher's newspaper.

"Jeremy, what are you doing!" scolded the mother, returning. "Look what you did to that man's newspaper!"

Jeremy was so impressed with his mother's admonition that he spit a fresh load of soda toward her. Then he began giggling uncontrollably.

"I'm sorry, sir. I'm sorry," said the woman, grabbing for a napkin.

"It's all right," said Fisher, thinking the kid had a future as an FBI supervisor.

The woman's fussing over the mess and her kids blocked Fisher's view momentarily, making it impossible for him to see Ahmed as Manu came into the restaurant. By the time she finally corralled her kids and sat back down, the two men were talking in the booth.

Burns was listening to the conversation with the aid of a device that worked by collecting the vibrations off the front window. The device was impossible to detect, but it was also not very good at screening out ambient sounds, and the noise level of the McDonald's made it hard to hear what was going on.

"Fisher, can you get a little closer?" asked Burns. "I'm having trouble hearing them."

But Fisher could tell that wasn't going to work. The young mother and her boys were gathering their things to leave, and moving now would look suspicious.

Manu said something to Ahmed, slapped his hand on the table, then rose and moved quickly toward the door.

"He's moving," said Fisher.

"Shit," said Burns in Fisher's ear.

A state police car had chosen that moment to pull into the parking lot. It had no connection with the operation—the two troopers had been running a speed trap down the highway—but their arrival came at a bad time. About half of the FBI detail was still on the nearby roads and parking lots, delayed as they made sure Manu didn't have a trail team watching him before moving in.

"Go!" Burns said over the radio. "Grab him."

The two agents assigned for the collar began walking from the mall parking lot toward Manu's car; another pair pulled their car over right in front of the restaurant. But neither team had a chance to get close to him. Seeing him dart out the door, the state troopers concluded that he was trying to skip out without paying. The driver reached down, hit his lights and siren, while the officer in the passenger seat jumped out and tried to corral Manu.

Manu ran back into the restaurant.

Fisher, still sitting at the back table, eyed the side door, calculating when to jump up and grab Manu as he pushed it open. But Manu wasn't looking for an easy escape—instead, he scooped up the little boy who'd been bothering Fisher earlier, then, holding him to his chest, ran to Ahmed.

"You fucker," he said.

From Fisher's vantage, it looked as if he was going to throw the kid into Ahmed. But Fisher was wrong—he'd taken a pistol out from under his shirt and fired twice point-blank into Ahmed's belly.

It was a large target, impossible to miss at that range. Ahmed slumped to the left, falling down between the chairs, groaning.

One of the state troopers had followed Manu in.

He was too shocked to react, his pistol still in his holster.

"Out of the restaurant!" Manu yelled at him. He held the gun up to the boy's head. "Out!"

Fisher leaned closer to the table. With the newspaper up, he slid his own pistol from beneath his jacket and leaned it against the table.

The boy's mother was standing by the counter, frozen in fear.

"You, what are you doing?" Manu yelled, turning toward Fisher.

"I was just reading the sports section," said Fisher calmly.

"Get out!"

"I'm not finished with my fries," said Fisher.

"Out!" yelled Manu, taking the gun away from the boy's head and pointing it at him.

It was exactly what Fisher had hoped for. His bullet struck Manu square in the forehead.

5

SAN JOSE

"It's that Russian," said Terhoussen's secretary. "Line one. And remember, you're supposed to talk to DOE today."

"I remember."

"You asked me to remind you."

Terhoussen frowned at the phone before picking it up.

"Dr. Terhoussen," he said stiffly.

"Doctor, thank you for taking my call," said Gavril Konovalav. His English was excellent, barely accented. "I wanted to pursue the matter I raised in New York, prior to the unfortunate incident."

"Hmmmm," said Terhoussen noncommittally.

"A launch contract would be very beneficial to you, on good terms. The space agency is anxious to attract new customers, and you would bring a certain prestige factor. Because of that, a very good price could be negotiated."

"How good?" said Terhoussen.

"In a long-term contract, very good," said Konovalav. "With a dozen launches, the price would be brought down to the neighborhood of forty million. You won't get anywhere near that price from the Europeans. Even better from your perspective, there is flexibility. We can schedule launches every week for the next two years if you wish. I know you have heard of our capacity."

"I have a launch·contract in place."

"Yes, but that is with a company that lacks a track record," said Konovalav. "Or should I say, lacks a positive track record?"

"Who exactly are you representing today, Mr. Konovalav? The Space Agency, or Gazprom?"

"Gazprom?" Gazprom was the state energy company; most of its money currently came from natural gas sales to Europe.

"I know they'd be interested in my technology," said Terhoussen.

"I have many masters," said Konovalav. Rather than being defensive, he suddenly sounded excited. "If you're looking for financing for your company, that too can be arranged. The failure of your launch must have presented difficulties. We could make them a thing of the past."

"I'm not interested in financing."

"I just wanted to mention it. A launch contract— you should be interested in that. Your goals are admirable, Doctor, but you have to be conscious of the costs as you proceed. If you can get five launches for the price of three—doesn't that make sense?"

"At the present time I have a contract that my attorneys say is airtight. If that changes, I'll talk to you."

Terhoussen hung up. Konovalav was after more than just a contract—Gazprom and the Russian government would love an opportunity to get a close-up look at the system, which a launch would allow them to do.

Still, the amount of savings he might be able to negotiate might be significant. And Konovalav wasn't exaggerating about the Russian Space Agency's unused capacity.

It would be a deal with the devil. Not as bad as the French, perhaps, but still bad.

The vultures seemed to be circling.

Terhoussen pulled up the contact program so he could call the Department of Energy to make sure the grant was on track.

6

PENNSYLVANIA

Under other circumstances, Fisher might have been congratulated. He might even have congratulated himself.

But he had just killed their best lead on the bombing case, and he didn't feel too much like breaking out the champagne. He *did* feel like having a cup of coffee, but the troopers who took control of the scene wouldn't let him go back into the kitchen to grab one.

"Come on," he told the trooper barring his way. "Do you think the CSI people are going to want to measure the amount of coffee in the pots?"

"I'm glad you can make jokes about this, Fish," said Burns, who was standing next to the counter.

"Who's joking?"

"You realize we're going to have a media statement on this," said Burns. "You're going to have to be in it."

"Why?"

"For one thing there were witnesses. What are we going to say?"

"He caught them skimping on the special sauce?"

"Yeah, you can laugh. Real funny. Ha, ha. I just lost a witness in two cases. Big cases."

Technically, he hadn't lost Ahmed yet—he'd been taken to the hospital code one, in cardiac arrest. The bullets had hit his bulletproof vest, but they hadn't counted on a heart attack.

"Medics gave him a fifty-fifty chance," said Fisher. "Besides. Do you really think you can trust him to tell the truth?"

"Shit. What the hell do we tell the media?"

"These guys were meeting, there was an argument, troopers broke it up," said Fisher. "Make them the heroes. End of story."

"We'll take the credit," said the BCI lieutenant standing nearby.

"The only credit you're going to get is for having screwed this puppy into the ground," snapped Burns. He was mad at the troopers, extremely, and not in the mood to make them look good.

The lieutenant bristled. "You should have given us a heads-up. That's standard operating procedure. You screwed up, not us."

Fisher decided to let them argue the point a little and walked outside. The woman and her two kids, though unhurt, had been taken to the hospital for observation. No one else had been injured.

A pair of Burns's men were standing next to Manu's car, waiting for a forensics team. Fisher thought that was a waste; he wanted to open the car and see what they could find out about the deceased.

"You're going to have to take it up with the boss," said the skinnier of the two agents. He had smooth, tan skin, stretched over handsome features that made him look like a male model.

"Burns isn't in charge of the case. I am," said Fisher.

"This guy killed our source," said the model. "We own this car right now."

"You shot the guy in the head?" said the other agent. He was a medium-sized black guy, almost the exact opposite of the model: a bit of a paunch, shirt coming out of his pants, a trace of lunch on his tie.

The sort of FBI agent you'd trust your life with, unlike his partner.

Fisher shrugged. "Only shot I had."

"Tight nerves."

"I can understand him getting pissed off at the kid though," added Fisher. "Kind of annoying."

"Hey, Fish, I'm supposed to take your gun," said Burns, coming outside.

"Why?"

"Standard procedure," said Burns. "If I don't, the staties will. You know, you're supposed to go on administrative leave, too. And counseling."

"You want me to see a shrink? That won't go well."

"Hey, I'm not your boss," said Burns. "You work it out on your own. But the gun has to be turned in. The state guys aren't going to let it go. They need it for the investigation. You know the drill."

"I'll give it to you if you open up Manu's car. We have to get over to his place before word of this gets around. Assuming he didn't have a trail team."

"He didn't have a freaking trail team. We would have seen it," said the model.

Fisher shrugged. Everybody was in a bad mood, and for once he couldn't blame them. He handed over his pistol.

"I should probably ask you for the little toy you have strapped to your ankle," added Burns.

"I'll give you that if you insist, but if you want the one strapped to my groin, you're going to have to get it yourself."

Burns didn't confiscate Fisher's other weapons, and Fisher wasn't placed on administrative leave, though he offered to go when Festoon called him a short time later.

"The hell with that. You're staying on this case," said Festoon. "Why the hell do I have to call you to find out about these things? Burns checked right in. That's the way an agent is supposed to operate. No surprises for his supervisor."

"He's a good agent."

"That's not the point, Fisher. This is a critical case here. I need to be informed. You have to keep me up to date. This is national media. The DirBur is involved! Why the hell did you shoot this asshole, anyway? Do you always have to be a hero?"

"Looked like he was going to plug the kid if he got too excited," said Fisher. "And he was already pretty excited."

Festoon told him he was damn lucky he hadn't hit the kid. Luck had nothing to do with it, but Fisher let the comment ride as Festoon continued to rage. Finally he got another call, and eased his boss off the line.

The call was from one of Burns's men, telling him that they had a search warrant for Manu's apartment. Fisher told him he'd meet him there.

Manu lived alone in a two-bedroom unit in a

condo development a stone's throw from the highway. Fisher located it, checked around to make sure
it was empty and wasn't being watched, then called
the owner to see about getting in.

"My name is Fisher. I'm with the FBI."

"If this is about my taxes, you have to talk to my
accountant. I don't know anything about them."

"It's about one of your tenants. I have a warrant to
search his apartment."

"What?"

"Turns out you rented a place to a terrorist who
tried to shoot a four-year-old in the head." Fisher
glanced at his watch. "Look, I don't want to put you
out. If you're tied up I'll just break the door down.
I may wait until word of this spreads through so there
are some television news crews around."

"I'll be over in five minutes."

"Manu" was a fake name—no surprise there. The
license plate on the car he drove came back to a
woman named Glinda Bautista, a Filipino who the
records said resided at the condo address. But there
was no trace of her in the apartment. Fisher found
two different passports, one from the Philippines
and one from Great Britain, both under the name of
Thomas Powers. There were licenses and credit cards
that went along with them. His computer was pass-
word protected.

Otherwise, the apartment could have belonged to a
monk. The furnishings were mostly things that could
be bought at Target, if not Wal-Mart. The kitchen
was well stocked with dried rice and beans, and there
were enough canned vegetables to last a millennium,

but the only meat was a small piece of chicken buried under ice and frost in the freezer. His clothes—jeans, T-shirts, two long-sleeve button-down flannel shirts—filled a single drawer in the modest dresser.

The toilet bowl looked as if it hadn't been cleaned in a few years, but Fisher had seen worse displays in his own apartment.

The landlord knew nothing about Manu cum Powers, except that he paid his rent on time. He hadn't even bothered to do a credit check when he rented the apartment some eight months before.

"Always paid cash," said the condo owner. He'd been a Chrysler dealer some years before. Luckily for him, he'd invested his money in a few condos as rental units nearly a decade ago; when the auto company went bankrupt, it put him out of business.

"How'd you get the money?" Fisher asked.

"Mailed it in an envelope."

"Not afraid of somebody stealing it out of the mail?"

"Federal offense to fool with the mail."

Paying in cash also had advantages for the landlord—which explained the anxiety about the IRS.

"His phone has caller ID," said Robinson, the FBI agent who'd brought the search warrant. "We can get a head start checking out some of these numbers."

Fisher went over and watched as Robinson paged through. Most read "unknown" and "private" on the ID—telemarketers, probably flouting the No Call law.

One stood out: It had a 917 area code.

"Cell phone in New York," said Fisher.

"Could be anywhere," said Robinson.

Fisher wrote down the number, then picked up the

phone and tried the number. It rang several times, then transferred over to voice mail.

Except that the message said voice mail had never been set up.

It took about a half hour, but Christian Carr, the Bureau's resident phone guru, called Fisher back with information about the number.

"The network is Verizon," he told Fisher, "but you knew that because of the message, right?"

"Yeah."

"Well, here's something you don't know. The guy who bought the phone works at the Chinese embassy."

7

JERSEY CITY

Jonathon Loup reached across his desk to his phone and pressed the intercom button.

"You better come downstairs," said Dennis.

The tone in Dennis's voice as well as his words tipped Loup off. He slipped his left hand to his mouse and brought up the surveillance screen, zooming in on the main feed from the trading room.

Armed men surrounded Dennis.

Asians.

"Tell Mr. Wan I'll be down when I'm ready," said Loup.

But even as the words left his mouth, he heard sounds outside his office. He hesitated a moment, then reached his left hand to the underside of the desk to release the lock. Two men in suits sprang through the door a half second after the lock buzzed free. They had small submachine guns—type 61 Scorpions, easily concealed Czech weapons that looked more like toys than real guns.

Wan came in behind them.

"You're very resourceful, Mr. Wan," said Loup

calmly. "I was told that it would be impossible to get past my security."

"Like many things in America, those claims were overrated," said Wan. "Your interest payment was short."

"Twenty thousand dollars, Wan. Come on."

"For some of us, Mr. Loup, that is a considerable sum."

"Listen, I'll write you a personal check." Loup started to reach for his drawer.

"Keep your hands where we can see them, Mr. Loup. I am afraid money no longer interests my employer. You will provide access to Icarus's blueprints and data."

"In time, sure."

"Now."

"I've explained our relationship. I'm a creditor, not a stockholder. You know the difference."

"Introduce me to Dr. Terhoussen."

"I don't think that'd be wise. He's paranoid as it is."

"I will meet him within the week."

Wan said something to the others in Chinese. They started to leave the office.

"Listen, Wan, this was unnecessary," said Loup. "You can call me, for crap sake."

Wan turned and walked toward him. He didn't touch him, didn't come within three feet of him, yet Loup could feel his violence. For one of the few times in his life, he felt completely vulnerable—an ant, watching the heel of a shoe descend toward him.

"I will tell you what is necessary, and what isn't," said Wan. "There are no more velvet gloves."

This time, Loup let him have the last word. He sat

in his chair and leaned back, staring at the ceiling until Dennis came in.

"Boss?"

"Fire the guards," said Loup.

"They're all unconscious. They hit the two guys outside with some sort of high-powered tranquilizers. They tapped into the power somehow and got around the security system."

Loup put up his hand. He didn't care how Wan had gotten in. The question was what to do next.

"Jonathon?"

"Where are we on the oil futures for this month?"

"We're short."

"Go long. Everything in them."

"Boss—"

"Long."

"They've climbed thirteen percent over the past few days. They're due for a fall."

"Hopefully everyone's thinking that. Go. Do it. I have other work." He rose. "Forget what I said about firing those guys downstairs. Get them to the hospital."

"You don't think that'll raise too many questions?"

Dennis. Always thinking. And he had the good judgment not to mention that he had warned Loup about the possible consequences of a short payment.

"Right," said Loup. "Do you know a doctor who can keep his mouth shut?"

"I know a doctor who lost a lot of money in the stock market last year. Maybe if I explain some of the situation to him—"

"Just some of the situation."

"Yes. Just some. And the fee would be paid in cash."

"Do it."

8

PENNSYLVANIA

The connection to the Chinese—as tenuous and tortured as it might seem—greatly complicated the case, and, more importantly Festoon's life. Now an investigation that he had shepherded—nay, that he had ridden to the heights of the national security/criminal justice bureaucracy—presented complications beyond even his ambitious imagination. While at first blush this was a very positive development—a chance to get involved not simply with the upper echelons of the FBI and CIA, but the State Department as well—Festoon discovered that it was a potential snake pit. What looked like an opportunity for advancement from one perspective turned to a dangerous career-ending disaster from another.

What if Fisher was wrong? What if there was no Chinese connection? What if the Chinese connection was just the tip of the iceberg—hadn't there been hints earlier on that the Russians were involved? Maybe another foreign government was using the Chinese. The British were very smart. They could play just about anyone. Perhaps there was an international conspiracy bigger than the conspiracy itself.

Worse, given that he had been working on this case for an incredible amount of time now—it seemed like months, if not years—shouldn't Fisher have shut down this vast conspiracy by now?

What about his boss? What about the FBI itself?

The terrible damage to the nuclear power plant might have been averted if only the FBI had acted more quickly. How long could America hold its breath while these miscreants, these terrorists, these demons, roamed freely?

Why were they free? Because Fisher had to have a coffee break?

"It's more like dinner," said Fisher. He was sitting in a diner a few miles from Harrisburg, where he'd just finished a hot meatloaf sandwich, extra gravy, hold the relish cup. Now he had an important decision to make: cheesecake for dessert, or apple pie?

"You're eating, and I'm having an ulcer," said Festoon. "You don't understand the pressure I'm under. This is a big case. Huge. Attacks all over the country. Now the Chinese are involved. And THE RUSSIANS."

Festoon said it like that, in capital letters: THE RUSSIANS.

"Where do the Russians come in?" asked Fisher.

"They're all over the Icarus thing. They were out there during the launch."

"So were the French, the Swedes, and the Japanese."

"I don't trust the Japanese," agreed Festoon.

"Never trust anyone that eats raw fish and brags

about it," agreed Fisher. "But how are they connected to this?"

"It's all one case, Fisher. Icarus. The substation. McDonald's. It's all related."

"Kathy's murder?"

Fisher twinged as the name escaped his mouth.

Rule Number One: Never ever refer to a murder victim by their first name. Ever. It shows an emotional attachment. And if there *is* an emotional attachment—see Rule Number One.

But Festoon was too consumed by his paranoia to pick up on it.

"They are all related, Fisher. You're working on them. You know they're related."

"I don't see how. The nuke plant, Icarus, and the substation—different things."

"You're the common denominator."

"All right, I'll skip dessert," said Fisher. "How long before we can get all the records on those phones connected to the Chinese?"

"The phones. Oh, yes . . . I'm working on it personally."

Damn, thought Fisher. That meant he'd never get them.

The Chinese intelligence service, like all spies, were meticulous about certain things, and sloppy about others. They bought cell phones over the counter regularly, rotating them into service for a few weeks and even months before tossing them. Apparently they felt that the way they used them—passing code words disguised as everyday conversation—precluded the FBI or CIA from getting anything of value even if they were listening in. But the mere fact that the phones were being used could be helpful, especially in a case like this.

Fisher wanted to work backward from the phone he had found, seeing if a call from the man he'd shot had initiated other calls, and if so, where those calls had been. It wasn't much, but at the moment he didn't have anything else.

"Are you going to pick up this Lee character?" asked Festoon.

"My guess is that Lee is a low-level schmuck who won't say anything if we pick him up, because he won't know anything," said Fisher. "And that's assuming that he's even the one who bought the phones in the first place. That's why I want all those records."

"You already know he bought those phones."

"Sure, but he used his own ID. He never would have done that if he was high on the food chain."

"Maybe that's just to throw us off," said Festoon. "They know that we know, so they pretend that they don't, knowing we realize they do but don't, so they can then do what we don't think they won't do. It's spy versus spy, Fisher. Spy versus spy."

"Uh-huh."

"I think we need more men on this," said Festoon. "I'll request more."

"You'll have the whole Bureau working for you if you keep this up," said Fisher.

"Yes," said Festoon triumphantly. "With luck."

Fisher was halfway to his car when his cell phone rang again. He noticed that the number was an FBI exchange. Hoping it might be information on Lee—

with any luck, his phones were already under surveillance—he unfolded his phone and answered.

"This is Fisher," he said. "Talk to me."

"Special Agent Fisher? This is Adrian Minx, from the Office of Public Affairs."

"What affairs are you investigating?"

"That's a good one, Special Agent. I've never heard that before."

"Sorry. You can call me Fisher."

"I'm sure. I understand you played a special role in a hostage situation this afternoon."

"As a matter of fact—"

"Special Agent, that's just the sort of story we like to advertise here at the Office of Public Affairs. A real feel-good picture of what the Bureau can do."

"Splattering people all over the front window of a McDonald's?"

"Just an FYI here: We wouldn't want to use the word 'splatter' for the media."

"I could see that."

"The thing is, Special Agent Fisher, we don't get too many opportunities to express our mission in a positive way like this. You saved a child's life."

"Not to mention avoided the cost of a trial, and appeal," said Fisher. "Two more pluses."

"Well, yes."

Minx drew a long breath.

"What exactly is it you want from me, Adrian?"

"*Good Morning America* wants to talk to you. *The Today Show, Sixty Minutes*—I can get you on them all. The country is starving for a hero, Special Agent. Starving. What do you say?"

"I just had dinner."

"Excuse me?"

"I'm not going on television," said Fisher. "I'm in the middle of a case. What the hell time is it over there, anyway?"

"It's ten after seven."

"You're a public servant. What the hell are you still doing in the office after five?"

Fisher wasn't averse to making a direct connection between the Chinese and the kid who'd blown himself up. He just didn't see a real benefit for the Chinese.

Sabotage the U.S. power supply?

It was something they might want to encourage on general principles—but only if relations between the two countries were, say, at the stage they were at in the 1950s. The way Fisher saw it, the United States owed China too much money to start messing around with its power plants, or anything that hampered the country's ability to pay China back.

Still, he had to go where the evidence was, and at the moment, that's where it was. As for the theory that all of the attacks were connected—that was too far-fetched. The attack on the substation in Glendale Falls had no obvious connection to the strike on the nuclear plant. Granted, it too seemed to be an attack by an obscure group—so obscure the investigators had no clue who was behind it. But it seemed to Fisher random noise in the system, unrelated to either the bombing or Kathy's murder.

Fisher lit a cigarette, then checked the GPS for the route back to New York.

9

NEW MILFORD, NEW JERSEY

Nearly three years before, Jonathon Loup had invested in a company that owned oil tankers. The idea wasn't so much to transport oil, but rather to buy at a low point in the market and hold on to it for a few months until the price went up. After a vast run-up in the price of crude, the market had temporarily crashed, and Loup felt he could do better with the actual product rather than just trading futures or stocks.

But the deal had gone sour due to the avariciousness of one of his partners, a shady pseudo-mafia type whose name was Leonard Mandolfi but who insisted that Loup (and everyone else) call him Big Leo. As soon as the deal crashed, Big Leo made himself difficult to find. Since he owed Loup quite a bit of money, Loup had hired someone to find him and get it back.

The man he hired ran a security firm that was itself slightly shady. Its name was Ironworks International, and while it had a long résumé of impressive jobs—among other things, it had provided security for food convoys in Iraq and the Sudan—it also had a reputation for handling jobs that other firms wouldn't take. Its principal and founder was an ex-Army Ranger captain named Chris Freeman. Six foot eight and built like a weightlifter, Freeman had a physical presence that could only be described as intimidating. He cultivated that impression, though he could just as easily have impressed people with his intelligence—he'd gotten an engineering degree before joining the Army.

Freeman had gotten Loup his money back, taking a good percentage of it as pay. He'd also helped set up the security at his offices—again, at a very high rate. He was expensive, too expensive to hire on full time, but he was also effective and efficient.

They met in a small bar one of Freeman's friends owned next to a bowling alley. Loup got there a few minutes early, but Freeman was already waiting, sitting alone at a booth in the back.

"What happened in Pennsylvania?" said Loup, sliding into his seat. "Somebody got killed at that power plant."

Instead of answering, Freeman pushed his empty glass to the edge of the table. A waiter quickly appeared. Loup ordered a bourbon, straight up.

"You should be specific when you place an order," said Freeman when the waiter left. "If you weren't sitting with me, you'd get the cheapest rotgut they have."

Loup shrugged. He only ordered bourbon when he didn't care what he was drinking. Scotch was a different story.

"This isn't just vodka," said Freeman, continuing to make his point. "This is Blue Ice. Very big difference."

"What about New Bethlehem?"

"I don't know anything about it."

"Listen—"

Freeman leaned across the table. "The person involved exceeded his portfolio. It worked itself out. It's not a problem for you. You shouldn't read the newspapers," added Freeman, leaning back.

"I have to," said Loup. "The Chinese came to visit me this morning."

He watched Freeman's face turn into a scowl. Freeman did not like the Chinese, or the Russians for that matter. It was more than just his Army prejudices. They had failed to pay him properly for a job he'd done for them years before. It was the sort of thing a man like Freeman never forgot.

"And?" said Freeman.

"They're really becoming a problem. They don't even want the money now. They want Icarus. They want the technology. They came into my place with guns. I was twenty thousand short, and they wanted to kill me."

"You gotta pay your debts."

Freeman straightened as the waiter returned with the drinks. Loup took a sip. The fact that he didn't particularly like bourbon kept him from drinking too much. Which was a good thing, because he was in the mood to drink.

"I can't see letting them get their hands on this technology," said Loup. "You know what they'll do—take it, build it themselves with their slave labor, then sell it back to us at exorbitant prices. If they do that. They might not—they might just jack the price of oil up, keep it going up, keep putting the screws to us."

"We did it to ourselves," said Freeman. He took his glass of vodka and downed it in one gulp. "We sold ourselves for pennies on the dollar."

"Not all of us."

"Look at how you make money, Loup. You don't build things. You don't even trade real things. It's all paper. What do you make?"

"I'm making electricity," said Loup, feeling defensive. "This is something that will help this country."

Freeman pushed his glass out to the edge of the table.

"I need to improve my security," said Loup. "That's number one."

"You'll have to move if they've already hit you." He shook his head. "It's not just that they know where you are. You need a better spot. A more easily defended position."

"I understand that. There are plenty of places."

"You need the right place."

Loup nodded. The implication was that Freeman would have to find the right place—and that it was going to be expensive.

But it was necessary. Just as it was necessary not to ask questions when things got more . . . messy.

The waiter came for Freeman's glass. He glanced at Loup's, still half full, then retreated.

"How long is this going to take? Icarus is launching another satellite next week, and I need to be in a good position."

"This isn't like dealing with some asshole who's pretending to be a made man," said Freeman.

"I know that. But—"

He stopped, hearing some people come up behind him. They sat in the booth across from them, two white couples, mid-twenties. They'd just come from a movie, and were earnestly discussing it.

Loup signaled with his head to the waiter.

"I'm sorry, this section is reserved," he told the people.

"Reserved?" said one of the men. "For what?"

"We expect a pretty large party."

"At this hour. Give me a break."

"I'm sorry, sir," insisted the waiter. "You'll have to move."

"This is bullshit."

Freeman leaned over. "You really ought to do as he says," he told the man.

Loup could see the indecision on the man's face. He was big, but not as big as Freeman. He glanced across the table at the other male, who was more perplexed than anything.

"We'll just go somewhere else," said the other man's date.

"There are plenty of booths in the other section," said the waiter. "It was my fault for not meeting you at the door."

The man started to get up. Loup could tell that he hadn't decided what to do.

"Their first round's on me," Freeman told the waiter.

"We ain't taking your money," said the man. He turned to the others. "Let's get the hell out of here."

They left.

Loup shook his head. "If they had any class, they would have taken your drinks. Then paid you back by buying us a round. They might have made a friend."

"I don't need friends," said Freeman. He looked up at the waiter. "Bring Mr. Loup another drink."

10

NEW MEXICO

Sandra Chester knelt down on the floor in front of the computer workstation as if she were praying.

"Run it again," she told the operator.

Michael Abelard hit the Control key, cueing the simulation. Numbers flashed and rolled in the two boxes on the screen. A line graph in the lower left-hand corner of the display shot upward, began leveling off, then suddenly plummeted.

"That matches the profile of the explosion precisely," said Abelard. He was the head of the propellant team, which at her request had been modeling possible malfunctions to see what had happened to the rocket.

"Merge the charts and let me see," said Sandra.

"I can't without a lot more work. But I can show you them next to each other. And you can see the numbers. The variance—"

"Put the windows as close together as you can."

Sandra watched. The line on the left was from the actual launch and accident; the one on the right was a simulation that increased the temperature in the oxidizer line 320 percent. In the simulation, the high temperature created a spot in the nearby tank. The heat radiated across to another pipe holding the fuel.

"When it reaches that temperature, it explodes?" asked Sandra.

"Well, the line ruptures," said Abelard. "That I know exactly. We haven't modeled the explosion. That's not really what we're set up for."

"But the profile is exactly the same as what we recorded?"

"Exactly."

"So that's what happened."

"It couldn't have. We'd have seen the temperature rise. And the pressure. The data would be completely different. You know that."

"You're assuming the instruments were correct."

Abelard blinked. He had no reason not to. "Well, even if they weren't, you'd have to figure out how the temperature rose."

An increase in the pressure in the line would increase the temperature; it was a simple formula taught in basic physics classes. The problem was, the instruments didn't show the temperature or pressure rising.

"Let's skip the instruments for now," she said. "How could the temperature increase that high? If the valve turns off—"

"It didn't."

"If it did. The pressure would increase. Then what happens?"

"Temperature would go up. Emergency protocol kicks in."

"Auto 34," said Sandra, referring to the computer protocol that governed the feeding of fuel into the rocket motors and the overall guidance system. Auto 34 would have ultimately shut down the rocket and signaled for a destruct.

"We can follow the temperature all the way through the event," said Abelard, turning to one of his assistants. "The only thing that's off spec is that little blip in the pressure right before the explosion."

"You can see that's not nearly enough to cause the problem," said the assistant, coming over. "The heat increase there is minimal."

"What if that's not it?"

"You mean that instrument was faulty?"

"No, I mean what if the problem is in one of the other lines. What if that pressure sensor is right— what if the problem is in one of the others? What will the reading be here?"

Abelard looked at his assistant, who shook his head. They hadn't modeled it.

"It won't take too long to find out," said Abelard, straightening in front of the keyboard.

Outside, Em drove the Impala past the front of the building, slowing as he counted the lit office spaces on the floor where Sandra Chester had her office.

There were three. Too many to take a chance.

The parking garage blocked part of the other side of the building, but he'd seen two lights there as well. He wasn't sure how many people that translated into. Five, he guessed, at a minimum, but without going into the building he couldn't tell. And he couldn't go into the building, at least not tonight. There were surveillance cameras at the outside doors, and he didn't care to be recorded.

If he wanted to kill her tonight—Em was undecided—the best bet might be to catch her in the garage alone. To do that he needed to find a place where he could wait out of the sight of the cameras, and still easily reach his car after it was done. His car had to be put someplace where it wouldn't be captured on the surveillance tapes. And of course her car had to be out of view as well.

The road narrowed at the far end of the complex, extending along a culvert that at one time had brought water to a farm. Em thought of leaving the car there, but it would be obvious and out of place to anyone patrolling down the road. What he really wanted was a building parking lot, where it would be unobtrusive.

And not recorded.

The perfect lot didn't exist in this complex. But there was one across the street, a half mile away across an open field. And after taking a last look around and making sure he hadn't missed a video camera, he turned out of the complex and headed there.

It took longer than Abelard had thought to construct the new model. It wasn't just a matter of changing a few variables—his original model simply didn't bother to account for what happened in the other parts of the system; there seemed no need to add them at the time. The formula proved elusive—changes in the main tank and the engine lowered the pressure at first, or *could* lower the pressure, or raise it, depending on the variables used.

"Or" was a killer; it showed the deficiency in the model.

"I'm kinda hungry," said Abelard as it neared nine o'clock. "You want to knock off?"

"I'll keep working on it," said Sandra. "You can go home."

Abelard looked at his assistant. "How 'bout we order a pizza?"

Sandra readily agreed.

Em parked the rental in the exact middle of the lot. Taking no chances, he slipped the door open and got out with his head tilted toward the ground. He took a step toward the closest building, then veered to the right, walking down the exact center of the parking lane until he came to a curb. The lot was unlit, but there was enough ambient light to see the concrete curbstone easily. He stepped up into the weeds and walked about ten yards in, squatting finally to get his bearings. Unkempt grass, twisted shrubs, and trees dotted the dark landscape ahead. He'd chosen not to take his night goggles; the moon was out and if he was spotted or caught on camera they would immediately draw attention to him. But scrub and the shadows made the terrain harder to negotiate; he bumped against some logs and a discarded cement block, then wandered into a clump of brambles. He was cursing by the time he reached the road.

Headlights veered from the office park. Em dropped to a knee, hesitated, then went down to all fours, hiding behind the grass as the car came into view. He rose slowly after it passed, waiting for the taillights to disappear. As soon as they were faint glimmers of red he rose into a sprinter's stance and bolted across the highway.

The strain in his legs as his muscles stretched felt good. He kept running after he reached the other side of the road, leaping across the sidewalk and continuing into the grass, which was better cut on this side. The tendons in his thighs pulled taut.

He'd run like this in Afghanistan all the time.

One time, in particular—under fire at the base of the hill they called E-342.

A mortar shell burst a few meters away. Someone in the company went down.

Em closed his eyes and ran. Adrenaline took him to the back of the parking garage. He hesitated for a moment, blanking momentarily on the layout of the cameras.

I'm letting my energy carry me away, he thought to himself.

Breathe slowly.

Em lowered himself to his haunches, filling his lungs, emptying his lungs, trying to pace his body.

He spread out, moving at first on his hands and knees as he hunkered next to the wall. There was plenty of light to see in the garage.

Heels.

She was coming.

"They don't deliver pizza after eight," said Abelard, looking up from the phone.

"I'll go get it," said his assistant.

"No, you guys stay here and work on the model," said Sandra. "It'll only take me a few minutes."

"Can you get some soda, too?"

She pulled over a pad to write down their requests.

There was something about the footsteps that struck Em wrong. But it was too late to stop.

He rose, extending his arm. The woman walked from his left to his right.

It wasn't Sandra Chester.

It was too late. The woman saw him, saw the gun. He was already squeezing the trigger.

The .22 caliber bullet flew into her forehead, smashing through her skull and tunneling into the gray matter of her brain.

He lowered his arm. Killing the woman was better than having a potential witness.

But it ruined everything. He had to leave now. His haste, his excitement to get the job done, his distractions, his fatigue.

This had all happened before, in Europe.

"Sorry for the mistake," said Em, rolling back into the shadows.

The night had a slight chill to it as Sandra stepped out of the rear door to the building and walked across to the parking lot. Her mind was a jumble of mathematical formulas, pipe diagrams, and pepperoni.

Almost to the door of the parking garage, she heard a popping noise above her, the sound a can of soda might make if shaken on a hot summer day. Except there was no fizz, no reason for that sound or any other sound.

Fear paralyzed her. It was nameless, irrational—but she couldn't move.

She forced herself to open the door.

There's nothing here, she told herself.

Em worked his way about seventy feet down toward the corner where he could jump to the ground when he heard the fresh set of footsteps climbing the shallow staircase. He stopped and balanced on the ledge, listening as the steps shuffled slowly up the open staircase.

Were they women's feet? Was it Sandra Chester?

He began sliding back along the wall.

Sandra reached the threshold of the level where her car was and stopped short, clutching her purse. The fear she'd felt downstairs clung to her, like a foul odor enmeshed in her clothes. And then morphed into something else, something more pleasant and nostalgic, a parallel in time bridged by the emotion:

Back at college one night, Andy Fisher walking her to her car after class. For some reason she had been all paranoid. She didn't ask him to come; he seemed to sense it.

She almost jumped as her cell phone began to buzz in her pocketbook. Sandra pulled it out and answered without looking at the number.

"Andy?" she said.

"No, it's me," said Abelard. "Andy who?"

"Oh, just—I thought it was a friend. What's up?"

"You think it would be all right if you brought back a few beers?"

"Sure," she said. "Yes, I will."

"And some Red Bull? A lot of Red Bull."

"Right."

Sandra snapped the phone closed and stepped out into the garage. She heard something on her left, back near the wall. As she turned, her eye caught a glimpse of something ahead on the ground. A small rug.

It was a person.

Someone had fallen.

"Are you all right?" she yelled.

It was a person—there was blood.

Blood!

"Oh, my God!" Sandra yelled, running forward.

Em listened, sure it was her.

He was on the opposite end of the garage. In order to get a shot, he'd have to cross back along the wall that ran near the stairwell. Otherwise two cameras would catch him.

Go! The hell with the cameras. Just get it done.

But here was the problem—if it was Sandra Chester, being on the video camera would be bad. If it wasn't Sandra Chester, then being on the video camera would be catastrophic, a repeat of Europe.

He turned back, then started climbing down.

Sandra pushed the woman over, thinking she might give her CPR. But then she saw the blood ooze from her head, a gentle ripple in the middle of a low puddle.

She let the woman slip back to the ground.

Call 9-1-1, she thought to herself. *9-1-1.*

She grabbed at her phone. Her finger shook. She pushed down, willed herself to make the call.

"There's been a shooting," she told the dispatcher. "A shooting. In the parking garage."

"Is the shooter still there?"

"Oh, my God, I didn't think of that."

Sandra dropped down next to her car.

"It's all right now, relax," said the 9-1-1 dispatcher. "I'm here with you. The police are on their way. You'll hear their siren shortly."

"All right," said Sandra, forcing the words from her mouth.

"They're almost there."

But they weren't almost there. The seconds slipped into a minute, two, three.

Finally, a siren in the distance.

"I can hear them," said Sandra.

"Stay down," said the dispatcher. "Describe what you're wearing."

A pair of police cars careened up the ramp, lights flashing.

"I can see their lights," said Sandra.

"Stay where you are until they call for you," said the dispatcher.

The first police car skidded to a stop near the body. The car doors opened and the officers leapt out.

"Sandra Chester!" yelled an officer. "Sandra?"

"I'm here," she said.

"Stay where you are. Stay there until we tell you," he yelled back.

"I am," she said, leaning against her car.

It took only a minute for the police to check the area, but it seemed like an eternity. The policeman's arm around her felt incredibly warm, reassuring as her father's would have been.

When they were sure that the garage was clear, the

police told Sandra she could call Abelard and tell him she was okay. He and his assistant were already downstairs, standing with some other police officers.

"God, we were worried," said Abelard.

"I'm fine," Sandra told him.

"Who was it?"

"I don't know. Someone from Nortel."

"Jeez, they almost never work late."

"I know. Oh, the pizza."

"The hell with the pizza."

"I don't feel much like eating right now anyway," said Sandra.

"We got the model to work," he told her.

"Good."

"You were right. The gauge comes up exactly like that if the pressure rises in one of the other tubes. So we just have to figure out why that happened, and we can solve our problem."

"And why it didn't show up on the instruments."

"That, too."

"A hot spot in the other tube. Which is what causes the explosion."

"Except there's no way there was a hot spot there."

"We don't know that. We haven't recovered the tube. Which would fit—"

"Yeah, but you'd see the data. And it's not there."

"We just have to figure out if it's possible, and then what would have caused it," said Sandra.

"Well, sure," said Abelard.

Sandra glanced at the body of the woman lying on the ground. The problem with the rocket seemed almost petty now.

"Let's take the rest of the night off and work on it tomorrow," she said.

11

NEW YORK CITY

To succeed, he needed two lies and a little luck—not the best foundation for a plan.

But Loup had no other choice. He was too far along. And besides, if he didn't stop them, Wan would find some way to get Icarus. It was clear from the way he was speaking the other day—that was the mission now. That may have been the mission from the very beginning. They wanted that technology and they were going to get it, legitimately if they could, but with force if necessary. He had bared his teeth the other day, coming into the place with guns.

Guns, the bastard. Which proved everything he'd heard about Wan. He was just a thug wrapped in diplomatic immunity. He deserved what he was going to get.

With a little luck.

Loup turned down the side street, walking in the general direction of Battery Park. The small electronics shop was exactly where Freeman said it would be.

Loup went to the counter and waited. The shop

was one of several run by a Hasidic family who lived at the edge of Bensonhurst. Loup realized he'd been here before—he'd stopped in occasionally when he worked on Wall Street. In fact he'd come here on 9/11 for a flashlight. The day was still fresh in his mind.

"Sir?"

"I need a SIM card," Loup told the clerk. "For a cell phone."

"I know what a SIM card is," said the man, reaching to the keychain at his belt. "Do you need an unlocked cell phone?"

"It's all right. I have one." He wanted to buy them at different places to make sure there was no chance of being traced.

"We have T-Mobile, AT&T—"

"T-Mobile."

"Five free minutes, or twenty? Twenty's a better deal. It's only eleven ninety-five before tax. Five will cost you five dollars. Tax extra."

"The twenty. The minutes aren't free if you pay for them, are they?" added Loup, reaching in his pocket for a twenty-dollar bill.

"Mmmm," said the young man.

"A few years ago, there was an older man. I think his name was Menachum," said Loup as he took his change. "Does he still work here?"

The young man shook his head.

"Work somewhere else?" asked Loup.

The young man shrugged.

"Same family own the place?"

"For thirty years."

The clerk raised his eyes, signaling to the next customer. Loup wanted to ask if Menachum had died—he suddenly felt as if he was his friend. But it was out of place, and he had much to do besides. He stuffed the SIM card in his pocket, and hailed a cab to take him up to Forty-seventh Street, where he knew he could get a cheap cell phone. That done, he walked another block uptown and hailed a cab to Grand Central Terminal. He could have walked the few blocks, but it was easier in the cab to see if he was being followed. He thought Wan might have someone watching for him.

It didn't look like it.

It was just past noon. The train station was relatively quiet. A light murmur rose toward the high ceiling as the crowd from a recently arrived train came through the doors downstairs. There were more sounds of plates and trays being shuffled in the food court below. Loup walked past the bar at the left to Michael Jordan's. He gave his name and was shown to a table.

Thirty seconds after he sat down, a skinny man dressed in a black business suit came and sat across from him. The man's face looked Asian, but he could have been from any of a dozen countries, from Malaysia to Japan to the Philippines. He was in fact Chinese, one of Wan's several henchmen. Loup knew him as Thomas Zhou; he had come to America as a college student and, after briefly returning to mainland China upon graduation, had worked in the United States as a deal scout and all-around handyman before being added to Wan's staff. To Loup, he seemed a less refined version of his boss, perhaps an apprentice assigned to him for finishing. He was very good with numbers—Loup had watched him rattle through some figures, in Chinese of course, on an early deal with Wan.

Loup would have preferred Wan at the meeting, but Zhou would do. In some ways, he was perfect.

"Where's Mr. Wan?" Loup asked.

"He's busy. You're not in any position to demand his time."

"I didn't demand anything," said Loup. "I simply wanted his advice. Terhoussen is being stubborn."

"That's your problem."

"Yes, and I'm working on it."

"You're not getting any money or more time."

"I'm not asking for money." Loup looked up as the waiter approached. "Drink?"

"Water."

Loup ordered a bourbon.

"Terhoussen is due to get money from the Department of Energy after next week's launch," said Loup. "That's my problem. If that doesn't go off, he'll be under a lot of pressure. That's my chance. So I just need a few weeks."

Wan's man frowned, but said nothing. They sat there in silence for a moment, neither one speaking. Finally, Zhou leaned forward, starting to rise.

Loup felt a twinge of panic. Everything depended on Zhou staying and having lunch.

But panic was a good thing. It was fear, but it was also energy, and energy could be strength. It had gotten Loup through many trades in the early days, and many deals as he'd climbed up his ladder. Panic, controlled, was an asset.

An idea sparked, a strategy. Instinct took over. Panic was replaced by a different sensation, one of excitement, the feeling of being on a motorcycle in perfect balance, accelerating.

"Thomas, the fact that you're here—is Wan giving you more responsibility finally?"

Loup's tone was confidential, almost fatherly. Zhou frowned.

"I have a great deal of responsibility."

"In a way." Loup looked up as the waiter approached with his drink. "I'll have the meatloaf," he said peremptorily. "My friend—"

"I'm going to go," said Zhou.

"Have lunch," said Loup, reaching out his hand. "Spend a few minutes talking. This is a more . . . private matter between us. Something your boss doesn't have to get involved in."

Zhou gave him a look that Loup recognized well.

Ambition. It was mixed with deep contempt, but was definitely there. Strong. Impossible to resist.

Zhou settled into the seat.

"He'll have the bass," Loup told the waiter. Then he looked at Zhou. "It's very good."

The waiter nodded, then retreated.

"You should work for me," said Loup. "There's a great deal of money to be made for the right person."

"If you were capable of making a great deal of money, you would not be in the position you're in now," said Zhou.

"No, Thomas, you don't understand. A momentary reversal—Mr. Wan happened to be in the right place at the right time to capitalize on it. For that I salute him. A momentary miscalculation—hubris, really. Arrogance. It's an American disease. You don't have it," Loup added quickly, playing to his audience now, completely in control. "But believe me, it's a fatal flaw. One difficult to overcome."

He talked about the possibilities of their working together until their food arrived. He could tell that Zhou was not interested in joining him, though the prospect of making millions of dollars was a heady temptation. He was still young, and though treated well, would spend many years toiling in the trenches before reaching Wan's status.

"I think you'll like the bass," said Loup as the food was placed on the table. "This meatloaf—supposedly the recipe comes from Michael Jordan's mother. Do you have recipes like that?"

"I eat what is in front of me," said Zhou.

"Of course."

Loup took a few bites, watching surreptitiously as Zhou picked over his food. Timing was everything. Finally, with Zhou three-fourths through the bass and seemingly ready to leave, Loup excused himself.

"I'm going to run to the men's," he said. "Be right back."

He spotted the waiter as he walked toward the back.

"Check," he mouthed, miming a signature.

Loup reached the vestibule to the restrooms, then turned to watch. Zhou's back was to him. Loup could barely see the waiter through the crowd.

There was always a chance that Zhou would pay with cash—if, say, he was under strict orders to deliver his message and return. It was the weak link in the chain that held Loup's plan together. He thought it unlikely, however—less likely than Zhou insisting Loup pay.

To Wan, paying a bill was a sign of power, the right of the more important man. Zhou was acting in his boss's place. And he felt he was more important than Loup—he took a credit card from his wallet and laid it on the leatherette folder that contained the bill.

Now Loup had to wait. He had chosen the restaurant purposely for its layout and his access to the management if necessary—the night manager was a relative of one of his traders.

The waiter picked up the bill and headed toward the credit card machine nearby.

"My friend paid?" said Loup, intercepting him. "No, no, it's mine."

He took the folder, removed the card, and gave the waiter his, making sure to use his American Express Platinum as Zhou had. The waiter smiled, then went to the machine.

Loup stepped into the restroom quickly. He pulled a small card reader from his pocket and inserted Zhou's card. The red LED at the top blinked green.

Done.

He was fast, but not quite fast enough—the waiter was already returning to the table with the card and check. He put them down in front of Loup's empty seat.

Loup strode quickly to the table as Zhou reached for the folder.

"Let me take that," Loup said, knocking it from Zhou's hand. It fell to the floor, scattering its contents.

"I've already paid," said Zhou.

"You sure?"

"We always pay our bills."

Loup palmed his card, substituting Zhou's. He handed up the card, then the slip.

Had Zhou taken the time to look at the name, he

would have seen that it was not his. In that case, Loup would explain that he was treating Zhou and intended it as a surprise. It was thin, but wouldn't matter—he already had what he needed. Zhou could stomp away now, and everything would be fine.

Better in fact. Or at least easier.

But Zhou didn't bother looking. He was in a hurry, late for another appointment, and slightly angry with himself for accepting the delay.

"Remember what we spoke of—you have until next week," he told Loup, pushing the receipt away.

"I may need some more time," said Loup.

"You'll get none."

The tone was harsh, and vaguely triumphant. It made Loup feel so pleasant that he thought of ordering a glass of wine to finish his meal. But it was too late; he had a train to catch. And in fact, he'd have to rush not to miss it.

Poughkeepsie was the farthest stop from New York City on the Hudson Line. It took roughly two hours for the train to get there. Loup bought a book—a CSI thriller by Jerome Preisler—and read much of it on the way up. The ride would have been pleasant if the train had been cleaner.

He'd never been to Poughkeepsie before. The train station was a real station, but it was roughly on par with Hoboken: hinting at a faded glory that never really was. He walked out the front, down the street where snow was still gathered in small piles, and turned toward the river. He'd never been here before, and the area seemed a bit sketchy—a large high-rise with graffiti on the curb and on some of the facade, older buildings in different stages of renovation. But it was perfect for his purposes.

There was a park at the base of the street, just before the river. He took out the cell phone he'd bought a few hours before, and his small voice recorder, then dialed the number Freeman had given him.

"Homeland Security," said a voice. "This is Michael Macklin."

It sounded live, and Loup almost started to talk. Then he realized it was a recording.

". . . I'm not here right now. Please leave a message and I'll get back to you."

Loup pressed the Play button on the voice recorder.

"There's going to be an attack on a ship . . ."

A car drove down the road behind him. Loup nearly pressed the Stop button prematurely. He turned, saw it was just some kids. They eyed him suspiciously, but moved on.

The voice recorder stopped, the file finished. Loup killed the phone, then threw it into the river.

He glanced at his watch. He had fifteen minutes before the next train, and he definitely wanted to be on it. He started for the station, walking at first, then starting to run.

12

UPSTATE NEW YORK

Fisher spent the morning reacquainting himself with
the cuisine of Glendale Falls, New York. Said cuisine
consisted of a) fast-food hamburgers, b) slightly soggy
hot dogs sold by a vendor who parked near the only
traffic light in town, and c) a diner whose menu
boasted "all food mad to odor."

Fisher chose the diner. He was a little mad himself
after ordering the home fries, which were more like
french fries than self-respecting breakfast fare,
though the French would surely be insulted by the
comparison.

So would a potato.

Fortunately, the coffee made up for the food. Fisher
drowned his sorrows in caffeine as he took out his
phone and caught up on the various tenets of his
cases. The first person he called was Roberta Di Sarcina, the financial analyst who'd been assigned to
look at the Icarus information. Roberta's voice had
the exact tone and timbre of a D-10 bulldozer pushing through a load of exploded shale. She was one of
those people whose physical attributes, personality,

and voice were in perfect harmony—except for her thick-framed reading glasses, she looked like a hunchback troll.

"Andy Fisher," she said as she picked up the phone. "To what do I owe the pleasure? Wait, don't tell me. You're calling for advice about your 401k. I advise Maxwell House. Those cans last forever."

"Good morning, Roberta."

"Heh, heh." When she laughed, Roberta's bulldozer voice went down an octave; she became a clamshell, pulling up muck from an overfed delta.

"So what can you tell me about Icarus?" Fisher asked.

"They're broke."

"Broke, as in, their technology doesn't work?"

"Technology? Who cares about technology, Andy?"

Fisher heard the telltale toke of a cigarette being inhaled.

"Smoking in your office again, huh?" said Fisher. "You're not afraid of Festoon catching you?"

"I don't work for Festoon, that ninny," said Roberta. "Didn't you hear? My transfer came through last week. I'm with Peterson now."

"Why are you on my case, then? Figuratively speaking."

"I'm on loan. Everybody else heard you were involved and ran away." She took another puff. "And you're one to talk about cigarettes in the office."

"I speak only in admiration," said Fisher.

"I'll bet. Icarus may have fantastic technology. They may save the world. But what they don't have is dough-ray-me. No moola, Fisher. Green. Money-money-money."

Fisher held the phone away from his ear. Roberta tended to get a lot louder when she laughed.

"Yeah, I heard they were short," said Fisher. "How broke are they?"

"Well."

This was obviously a difficult question. Roberta took a very long drag on the cigarette before answering.

"There are different shades of broke," she said finally. "I mean, their balance sheet is nothing, except for the patents. And their worth is whatever I say it is. You know about patents?"

"Should I?"

"Normally, you'd want to set up the company and license the patents, blah-blah-blah, but in this case the company owns them. I'm guessing it was the only way they got the money they needed. But bad strategy. This guy Terhoussen? Should've held on to them personally."

"What's the advantage?"

"Tons, honeysuckle. Tons. We're talking control—you control the company, you control the patents. You control the patents, you make the cookies."

"Terhoussen owns the whole company," said Fisher. "So he figures he's got the company, he's got the patents."

"But the company is in hock, right? Borrows money—the patents are collateral. Debtors call in their notes, the debtors own the company. The debtors own the patents. The debtors own everything."

"I love it when you talk with something in your mouth," said Fisher.

"This is the typical undercapitalized BS you see all the time in Silicon Valley. I'll bet they fly around in Gulfstreams doing dog and pony shows, take investors out for steak. Porterhouse. Aged Angus porterhouse. Maybe you should pretend to be an investor, Andy. You could get a couple of steaks out of it, at least."

"What I'm trying to figure out is whether there was something underhanded going on, maybe skimming off the top or something," said Fisher. "Someone pocketing a million here, a million there."

"Mmmmmm."

"Mmmmm yes, or mmmm no?" asked Fisher.

"Mmmmmm I don't know. Could be, but doesn't look likely. It would have to be with the subcontractor payments."

Fisher could hear Di Sarcina's fingers tapping furiously on the keyboard.

"I think it would be pretty hard to skim money off the top of this corporation," she said. "There's just not that much to skim."

"How about a few months back?"

"Months? No. They seem to have been running pretty close to the bone for a while. The data you got for us goes back two years. I don't know, maybe before that. The subs might have been paid a lot of upfront. Still, from what I can see, this wouldn't be the sort of company ripe for plucking."

She cursed softly. Fisher pictured her looking down at her pants and realizing she had dropped ashes on them.

"I just had these washed," she mumbled.

"You oughta wear gray pants," said Fisher. "Hide the ashes."

"Oh yeah, I'm really going to start taking tips from you, Mr. Fashionplate."

"So you think the company is worthless?"

"Hell no. It's in debt, sure. But the patents, the technology? Those are worth a fortune. Assuming they work. Has GE tried to buy it?"

"Got me."

"One of these days I'm going to put together a Fisher Index and I'll make a killing. Every time you open a new investigation, the markets go wacko-crazy. You've got the energy markets roiled."

"Is that a good thing?"

"It is if you buy and sell nuclear power. And look at fast food. I'd say your visit to McDonald's made the stockholders a couple of millions overnight."

"How? Didn't the stock go down?"

"Sure. At first. Everybody sold on the terror hit, then realized there was no real threat and bought, bought, bought."

"Let me ask you something—when the substation here blew up, could somebody make money on that?"

"Do you listen when I talk?" asked Roberta.

"Sometimes. Not usually."

"Of course someone could make money. As soon as the news hit the wire, energy prices began to spike. So anyone who controlled the contracts, directly or indirectly, for power did well. Unless they were short."

"What's that mean?"

"Short means that they gambled the prices were going to go down. It's like stock. Think bananas."

"Uh, okay."

"Say I'm of the opinion that bananas are going to drop in price over the next week," said Roberta. "But you don't think that. They're going for ten bucks a bunch right now. You think they'll go up."

"Expensive bananas."

"They're made out of gold. So I buy a bunch and I tell you, I'll sell you my bunch for nine bucks, but you can't have them until next week."

"Sounds like a good deal," said Fisher. "They're selling for ten bucks right now."

"Right. It *sounds* like a good deal. To you. All right. Now here's the thing. I don't have a bunch. I'm betting I can buy them before next week, at a cheaper price than nine bucks. And guess what—the price drops and I buy them for seven bucks. I deliver them to you and make two dollars on the deal."

"You can do that with energy?"

"Sure," said Roberta. "And it works the other way, too." Roberta ran through an opposite scenario, explaining how futures contracts worked when prices were rising. "The point is, you can make money whether it goes up or down—if you guess right."

"Or if you know what's going to happen," said Fisher. "So if I knew that someone was going to blow up the substation—"

"I don't know why people say you're dumb as a crustacean," said Roberta, pausing to exhale. "I'd rate you a marmot, at least."

Roberta's theory about stock manipulation and energy purchasing didn't apply to Icarus, which as a privately held entity had no stock to trade. But the incidents at both the nuclear power plant and the substation affected literally thousands of companies, directly and indirectly.

Which naturally made Fisher curious.

Compiling a list of anyone who had benefited from

both was impossible. Even if such a list was confined to just the stock market, there were so many "plays" that could be made that any list would be hopelessly long and incomplete. Sales of energy as a commodity weren't a good indicator, either. For one thing, while regulation had increased since Enron, there were still wide gaps in reporting requirements and the ability to track complicated transactions.

None of these arguments swayed Fisher in the least. He told Roberta to look at the incidents and see where the spikes had come. Then he wanted her to correlate those with other spikes over the past six months, and look for incidents related to those spikes. Once they had that list, they might be able to see what the connections were.

"I'm gonna need more help," said Roberta. "You don't know how much data you're asking for."

"I'll fix it with Festoon."

"That'll be the day."

"I'll call him right now."

"You do that, and I'll spring for the cigarettes next time you're here."

"Just let me breathe the air in your office for a half hour," said Fisher. "I won't have to smoke for a week."

Fisher flipped through his e-mails, dismissing them with a flick of his thumb, until he came to one from Kathy's friend Erin.

He hesitated, then opened it.

Andy, I'm sorry for what I said in the diner about you becoming a cynic after Kathy broke things off. I

know you're not really as cynical as you pretend
to be.

"Yes I am," he muttered to himself before continuing to read.

I never really understood why she did that to you. It's
not nice to speak ill of the dead, and especially
Kathy, whom I love like a sister—better than my sister. She was my sister, and is.
    You must be hurting, too, and I hope you'll forgive me.
    Call me sometime.

    e

Fisher clicked out of the e-mail program and
brought up his phone book, thinking to call Erin. But
he stopped, finger poised over the button.
    What was he going to say?
    You don't owe me an apology.
    Losing Kathy didn't make me cynical.
    What he'd like to say was that she wasn't the one
who walked away. But that wouldn't be honest. And
if there was one thing Fisher was more than cynical,
it was honest. Excruciatingly honest.
    He did want to talk to her. But he also didn't. And
in the end, he decided his energy was better spent
concentrating on the case.

Fisher hoped he'd get Festoon's voice mail. But his
boss picked up on the first ring.
    Some days luck just wasn't your friend.

"Less than twenty-four hours ago, you told me none of these cases were connected," said Festoon after Fisher explained why he'd called. "Now you're looking for *more* cases?"

"It may have to do with money," said Fisher.

"Bullshit, Fisher. This is a war we're in. With the Chinese. And the Russians. Maybe the Russians."

"Maybe they all need the money," said Fisher.

Sovereign funds—basically, fronts for foreign governments—were active in all facets of the energy market. So it was possible.

Theoretically.

"She doesn't even work directly for me," said Festoon. "She should ask her own boss if she needs help."

"This is head count," Fisher said. "Yesterday, you were bragging about your plans to get the entire agency under you."

"I don't need any more head count," said Festoon, annoyed. "I just got a memo this morning about a new performance matrix that's going to discount head count. Head count is out."

"All right. If you want to give up control of the investigation, that's fine," said Fisher. "Tell me who I'm supposed to report to."

"What?"

"If this turns into something to do with the stock market, and Barbara's boss is the one with the head count," said Fisher, "then I guess he's the one with the power."

"We'll see about that," said Festoon. "Stay on top of this."

Fisher had barely hung up when Stendanopolis called to update him on the rocket transmissions.

"Samie Markoff started on it last night," Stendanopolis told him. "She says it's going to take a while. Telemetry's a bitch. Weird thing about it—she says there are two different encryptions."

"Like a double code?"

"No, like the middle has a different encryption in it. She called it a piggyback carrier—like it was hitching a ride."

"Like a virus?"

"Damned if I know. You want me to tell the scientist that?"

"I'll tell her," said Fisher.

"By the way, Samie wanted to know where I got her number."

"I hope you lied."

"An FBI agent never lies. I told her you gave it to me. By the way, there was a murder last night in the parking garage behind the Punchline Orbiters building."

"What?" All Fisher could think of was Sandra.

"Yeah, they're still working on it, but—"

"Bernie, who was it?"

"I don't have the ID. Victim didn't work at Punchline, though. She was shot once in the head. Twenty-two caliber. Autopsy won't be ready for a while."

"Lucky shot?"

"Right in the forehead, probably as she walked to her car. That's a lot of luck."

"True."

"Guess who found the body. Your rocket scientist, Sandra Chester."

"Why the hell didn't you tell me that to begin with?" said Fisher.

"Geez, I was getting to it. Calm down, Fish. It's not like she's a suspect, or anything."

"Is she all right?"

"Yeah, I guess. I didn't talk to her myself."

A car flew onto the highway from a side road, cutting Fisher off. He slammed on the brakes and jerked his wheel hard right, barely managing to avoid the other vehicle. In the process, the cell phone flew from his hand to the floor. He straightened the car, then reached down to scoop it up.

"You're talking while you're driving?" asked Stendanopolis, incredulous.

"You don't think I'd pull off the road for you, do you?"

"That's against the law, Fisher. You could get a ticket."

"That's why I carry your ID with me. Cop pulls me over, you get the ticket, not me."

"Ha ha."

"You think I'm kidding? Check your wallet."

Fisher hung up, knowing Stendanopolis would do just that. Then he thumbed the recent calls directory to find Sandra's number, and pressed it.

"Hey, are you okay?" he asked as soon as he heard her voice. Then he realized he'd gone directly to voice mail.

"Leave a message at the tone," she said.

He opened his mouth, but suddenly felt tongue-tied. He hung up without saying a word.

The expression Macklin gave Fisher when he walked in late that afternoon bordered on religious ecstasy.

"I was just about to call you," he told Fisher.

"And here I am."

"And here you are. Someone is going to blow up a tanker in New York Harbor."

"New York Harbor?"

"New Jersey, actually. Come here and listen to this. Somebody called my voice mail about a half hour ago."

Fisher listened to the recording.

"You trace it?" asked Fisher.

"We're working on it. The caller ID looks like a cell phone. It was somewhere in the Northeast."

"That'll narrow it down."

Upwards of 90,000 barrels of crude oil were imported to the East Coast each month, with a good portion of it going to refineries in New Jersey. The vulnerability of the area's petroleum facilities to terrorists was well known in the counterterrorism community. Despite a variety of improvements in security and any number of safety features, it was generally conceded that there was no way to completely thwart a determined attack. And a successful attack would have an immediate effect on the commodities market—the sudden icing of New York and New Jersey harbor areas in 2000 had nearly doubled distillate prices in a matter of hours.

It fit with the money pattern.

There was, however, one thing that bothered Fisher about the warning. There hadn't been any warning in the other two attacks.

Of course, he was assuming they were related, which maybe they weren't. He listened to the message again. There was no mention of a connection; he was the one jumping to conclusions.

A logical jump, but still a jump.

"If the attack is going to be tomorrow," said Macklin, "we have to do something right away."

"Yeah," Fisher conceded.

"Thank God for patriotic Americans."

"Patriotic Americans don't use voice scramblers," said Fisher, taking out his phone to call Festoon. He answered on the first ring—always a bad sign.

"You want to blow up a ship in New York Harbor?" Festoon screamed into the phone after Fisher told him his plan. "Are you out of your fucking mind?"

"Better be careful of the profanity," Fisher told him. "We have you on speakerphone and Macklin is very sensitive."

"We are *not* blowing up an oil tanker," said Festoon. "No way."

"We'll get an empty one," said Fisher. "Once we blow it up, we can see who benefits. It's the only way to figure out the conspiracy."

Fisher explained Roberta's theory that the attacks were being used to manipulate energy prices and the stock market.

"How does it tie into your murder?" asked Festoon. "Or the rocket explosion?"

"I'm not sure it does. I think we have a couple of different cases here. This will help me figure it out."

"We could have the crime of the century for all I care, Fisher. You're still not going to blow up an oil tanker."

"We can let the terrorists blow it up if you want," said Fisher.

"We're not doing that, either."

"It's only sailing to New Jersey," said Macklin. "It's not like we'd lose anything important."

The alternative to letting the tanker blow up was to stop it from blowing up. The problem was how exactly to do that.

The tanker was a medium-sized ship about thirty years old named the *Green Star*. It was sailing from Western Africa to a refinery in northern New Jersey opposite Staten Island. Registered in Antigua, it was owned by a Greek shipping company, had a small Filipino crew and a spotless record—just the sort of ship that would be low on a surveillance list.

The *Green Star* was capable of carrying about 120,000 deadweight tons of liquid cargo, which if fully loaded would translate into approximately 864,000 barrels—about three times what the refinery where it was docking processed in a day. That alone would make a serious dent in the local energy supply. Worse, if the tanker shut down the channel or blocked the docking area, the impact would be severe.

Fisher suggested boarding the ship at sea, making sure it wasn't booby-trapped—a definite possibility, he thought—and then sailing it into the harbor to see if anyone attacked. They could plot a course where other traffic wouldn't be disturbed if it was sunk. And rather than going to the docking area near the refinery, they could stop at a deserted wharf about a half mile away.

The plan made sense. The problem was implementing it.

The Coast Guard had jurisdiction over the harbor and surrounding waters, and between that and Macklin's involvement, the Guard thought they should be the lead agency in any operation dealing with the ship. The oil tanker, however, was still in international waters, making the Navy the logical lead agency—in the admirals' eyes, of course.

"What about the FBI?" suggested Festoon.

"When you get something larger than a rowboat," answered the admirals, "then we'll talk."

The result was a tense planning session at the Coast Guard Station New York on Staten Island a few hours after Macklin first received the tip. Macklin and Fisher were picked up by a Coast Guard helicopter—Fisher checked for bombs after boarding—and whisked southward. They got there well after the meeting had started; by then, the Coast Guard and Naval commanders were negotiating over the honor of firing the first warning shot—a Navy Seahawk helicopter, or a small Coast Guard harbor boat.

"You're not going to get a chance to fire a warning shot," said Fisher. "As soon as you show up, somebody aboard the ship presses the destruct button."

"Who are you?" asked Vice Admiral Stephen Kusund. Kusund was the commander of the Coast Guard's Atlantic Area Command, based in Portsmouth, Virginia.

"Fisher. FBI."

"I've heard about you," said Admiral Kelsey Tanner, the Navy's representative at the planning session. "You plugged that guy in the McDonald's."

"They were out of Happy Meals that day and I got a little ornery."

Tanner frowned.

"Let's say we get aboard the ship," said Kusund. "What if there are suicide bombers aboard as well?"

"That's why we get aboard out to sea," said Fisher. "We don't come into the harbor until we're sure the ship is clear."

"Into the harbor where it can be easily targeted," said the Coast Guard officer.

"Look at it this way," said Fisher. "If they're prepared to make an attack, and they don't see this ship, do you think they'll go home? Or try and sink a different one?"

Fisher left Macklin to fend off the objections as he ambled over to the side of the room. The Navy and Coast Guard were at war, and everyone knows you can't fight a war on an empty stomach. So the hosts had put out a good spread—sandwiches, potato salad, corned beef hash. The only thing missing was a carving station.

"All right, so let's say we do this. We have to surprise them," said Admiral Tanner. "That means we send the SEALs."

"Not so fast," said Kusund. "The Guard has its own response team."

"This isn't a job for a response team," said Tanner. "This is what SEALs live for."

"I have to agree," said Fisher, his mouth full of roast beef and rye. "We go in with the SEALs. They secure the ship. Coast Guard comes over the horizon. Just in time for the photo op."

"We're not in it for the photo op," said Kusund.

"Of course not," said Fisher. "But you'll be in it anyway."

"I think Mr. Fisher makes a good argument," said Admiral Tanner. "I can have a team of SEALs ready to go before dusk."

"Where do I meet them?" asked Fisher.

"You're going to give the briefing?" Admiral Tanner asked.

"I'm going in with them."

"With all due respect, Agent Fisher. I'm sure you're very capable as an investigator. And your, uh, heroics yesterday notwithstanding, but these are very highly trained young men."

"Yeah, I figure they probably know what they're doing when it comes to taking over a ship," said Fisher. "Otherwise I'd insist on using the FBI CRT team."

"I suggest you set up your operational headquarters at a Navy facility. We'd be happy to supply you with everything you need. Secretaries. Plenty of coffee. Even a smoking area."

"Thanks, but somebody else is covering the paperwork. When can I get a chopper?"

"The Coast Guard could work with your CRT team," offered Kusund. "We can have our response team work with your people. That ship will be secured by daybreak."

One of Tanner's aides leaned over and whispered in his ear.

"A helo will take you to the SEALs within the hour," Tanner told Fisher. "They're already en route."

Fisher glanced at Kusund, thinking maybe he would throw in a flat-panel TV. But the best he could do was a ride in a cutter.

"I'll stick with the SEALs," said Fisher. "I just have one question."

The others looked at him expectantly. Fisher turned to the banquet table.

"Do you have any real mustard here?" he asked. "All I see is this fancy French stuff."

13

UNDISCLOSED LOCATION, NEW JERSEY

Two hours later, Fisher stepped off a Navy helicopter in the parking lot of an undisclosed location in southeastern New Jersey. He had never been to an officially undisclosed location before, and was disappointed to find that this one looked quite a bit like an abandoned warehouse facility. It looked so much like one that if it weren't for the men with submachine guns, he would have thought he was in the wrong place.

"Fishman is here," said one of the men as the helicopter left. Dressed in a black ninja outfit, he was talking into his sleeve.

Fisher stopped and pulled a package of cigarettes from his pocket.

"Excuse me, sir," said the SEAL. "This is a U.S. facility. There's no smoking."

"The world is a screwed-up place," said Fisher, putting the cigarette in his mouth. "You want one?"

"I don't smoke, sir. And yes, it is screwed up."

"I'll take a cigarette," said another of the ninja-clad

sailors, coming over from the other side of the temporary helipad.

Fisher held out the pack.

"You're FBI?" asked the SEAL.

"That's what they claim."

"What's that stand for? Fornicators, Bums, and Intelligence officers?"

"Ignoramuses, actually." Fisher would have asked if SEAL stood for Scumbags, Eunuchs, and Ass Lickers, but had learned long ago never to test a man with a submachine gun in his hand.

"You're the guy who nailed the terrorist yesterday," said the sailor.

"They were out of ketchup," said Fisher. "Desperate times."

"Come, J. Edgar," said the first SEAL. "Captain's inside."

Fisher followed him toward a low-slung cement block building, wondering if Jimmy Hoffa was buried around here somewhere.

If the SEAL captain had said his name was Stalin, Fisher would have believed him. He had the moustache and the black hair, though not quite the belly of the famous dictator.

And his personality matched to a T.

"Who the hell are you?" he snapped as Fisher came in. His name was Captain James Tallahassee, like the city. He had the distinction of being a mustang—an officer who'd first joined the Navy as an enlisted man, risen through the ranks, then gone to officer training and joined what chief petty officers called "the other side."

They used other terms as well.

Tallahassee stood over a table that consisted of a large piece of plywood supported by a pair of sawhorses. Plans for a ship had been unfurled on the table; two other officers, Lieutenant Reid and Lieutenant Cortez, were examining the plans.

"I'm Fisher."

The commander frowned. Fisher went to the end of the table and leaned down over the plans.

"If they're going to blow this sucker up, they'll have explosives on both ends of the hull," he said, pointing. "They don't just want a big boom, they want oil all over the ocean so it'll sweat the tree huggers."

Reid grinned. He'd been making the same argument.

"Maybe they want it to burn," said the other lieutenant. "What then?"

"They don't need it to burn," said Fisher. "But if they do want that, say for the news video, they'll try to get it really hot. Which means special explosives in the hold. More or less the same place, right?"

"They're doing this for show?" Tallahassee's voice approximated the snarl of an angered sea lion.

"It's definitely for show," said Fisher. "Theater of the absurd."

"There's nothing on the deck out of the ordinary," said Cortez. He pushed over a pair of high-altitude photographs taken approximately an hour before. Though they had been shot from over sixty thousand feet, they were in sharp focus.

"You could have anything in these pipes," said Fisher. "Something on the hull. It could be anywhere. It's just not big."

"Or this could be all lousy intelligence," said Tallahassee pointedly. "After all, the tip came from the FBI."

"Actually, Homeland Security," said Fisher.

"Oh, that makes me feel one hell of a lot better about it."

The SEALs were pretty good at taking over ships—in fact, they could take over just about anything smaller than a country, and could take over most of those as well, given a little air support and several cases of Red Bull. The trick here was getting enough SEALs on the ship quickly enough to make sure that no one aboard had time to blow it up.

Actually, that was only the first trick. The second was taking care of whatever the terrorists were planning to do if they didn't have explosives or their people aboard.

"The thing is, we're going to want them alive after they attack the ship," said Fisher. "That's the whole point."

"Tell you what," offered Tallahassee. "We'll make sure to get DNA samples after we fry them."

"The whole reason I got you guys is so we get them alive," said Fisher. "If you can't do it, I'll get somebody else."

"What? You planning on calling Ronald McDonald?" Tallahassee spit the words out.

"Hey, one clown's as good as another."

"Har, har," said Tallahassee. "If keeping these guys alive was so important, why'd you nail that guy in the forehead?"

"I was having a bad day."

"I think we just get aboard the ship and then worry

about it," said Reid. "The goal is to keep as many alive as possible. But we can't get too picky."

"Probably right," said Fisher. "When do we leave?"

"What do you mean 'we,' kemo sabe?" said Tallahassee.

"We as in us," said Fisher. "I'm assuming you're coming."

"I am. You're not."

"This is my mission."

"This is *my* mission. You're not even the a-hole who got the intelligence."

"Yeah, but I'm coming anyway," said Fisher. He pulled his cigarette down to the nub.

"You mean chopper in once we have it secure, right?" asked Reid.

"No. I'm there the whole way. In the boats with the assault teams. Call the admiral. He'll tell you it's already cleared."

"Screw the admiral," said Tallahassee, exhibiting his unit's well-known respect for the upper echelons. "I'm not arm wrestling you here, Fisher. I don't care if you are a hotshot in the FBI. That doesn't hold water with me. I don't want you fuckin' anything up."

Fisher shrugged. "If you don't want to talk to the admiral, call J. R. Harkins. Ask him if he'd take me along."

"Chief Harkins?" Tallahassee narrowed his stare. "You know Daddy Longlegs?"

Everybody else in the room looked at Fisher, then back at Tallahassee. Chief Petty Officer James Richard "Daddy Longlegs" Harkins was the subject of many of Tallahassee's stories—he had served under the officer several times, beginning with Tallahassee's first assignment with the SEALs. He was part "sea daddy," part guardian angel, and pretty much the archetypal SEAL.

He was also one hard-bitten SOB. He wouldn't vouch for the head of the Navy without seeing him in combat first.

"What are you setting me up for, Fisher?" asked Tallahassee.

"I don't know the number off the top of my head, or I'd call him myself."

Tallahassee made a face. "Wait outside. Everybody. Outside. You, too, Fisher."

Five minutes later, Tallahassee opened the door. He still had his cell phone in his hand.

"All right, everybody back to work," he barked. "Fisher, get yourself kitted out."

"Yes, sir," said Fisher.

"Twice?" said Tallahassee. "You saved his butt *twice*? Under fire in Central America?"

"Yeah, it's hard to believe," admitted Fisher. "Once, that you could say was a mistake. But there's really no excuse for twice."

FOUR

SE(a) A(ir) L(and) and Cigarettes

1

UNDISCLOSED LOCATION, NEW JERSEY

Fisher spent the next hour driving around to various sporting goods and specialty stores, grabbing a wet suit and related gear. A SEAL named Tiny came with him. Ordinarily, Fisher might have been annoyed at the fact that he had a shadow, but in this case it proved useful—the store clerks took one look at Tiny and immediately fetched whatever Fisher asked.

Tiny took a liking to Fisher as they shopped, and even offered to lend him a waterproof rucksack, which Fisher needed to carry his gear—his Colt, spare ammunition, cell phone, sunglasses, six packs of cigarettes, and three Bic lighters.

"You gonna wear your sunglasses at night?" said Tiny as he watched Fisher pack.

"Ninety percent of being cool is looking cool," said Fisher.

"What's the other ten percent?"

"Shooting first."

———

Fisher used the break to call Dolan, the New York detective who was working on Kathy Feder's murder.

Nothing new.

"Did you look at the hotel employees?" Fisher asked.

"Been all over that. All over everything."

Dolan was hoping for some sort of connection with the San Jose murder, but hadn't found one yet. He didn't say it, but Fisher knew he was fighting time. If no evidence turned up soon, the case would be pushed to the side.

Maybe it already was.

Fisher heard Tiny coming back. "Hey, thanks, I'll keep in touch," he told Dolan, hanging up.

Fisher was assigned to Reid's group, which included Tiny as well. A pair of Coast Guard Dolphin helicopters came for them; stuffing just Tiny, let alone the other seven SEALs and Fisher, into the little chopper was a feat on par with what the Japanese accomplished on bullet trains at rush hour in Tokyo. Fisher held his breath as the helicopter wheezed its way into the sky.

"This takes us out to the boat," yelled Reid over the rotors' noise. "We go from the boat to the rafts, from the rafts to the ship. You got questions?"

"The questions I have, you don't have answers to," said Fisher.

He hooked his arm around one of the web belts and gazed through the small window at the gray air above the water. The sun was just setting. If things went according to plan—something the SEALs assured him never happened—they would board the ship at 0100 military time—one o'clock in the morning.

The way Tallahassee described it, they would have control at 0105, unless they ran into trouble, in which case they would be in command by 0103.

Tallahassee's eyes had sparkled when he said that. He was hoping for trouble.

Fisher, on the other hand, was hoping for a little air. The packed helicopter smelled of sweat, metal, and seaweed.

"All right. Stiletto's about five yards starboard," said Reid as the chopper dropped into a hover. "Jump in and swim."

"Jump?" said Fisher.

"Yeah. Too much hassle to land on the thing when we can just jump and swim over."

"What about fast-roping?"

"That's for sissies."

"Fish jump," said Tiny. He wrapped an arm around Fisher. "He jumps with Tiny."

"That's all right. I can go on my own," said Fisher, but it was too late—the SEAL pulled him across the helo deck, and suddenly they were free falling through five or six feet to the water.

Or eight or twelve or twenty. Freed of the rest of the SEAL team, the helicopter had steadily risen from the waves.

It had also moved to the northeast, a fact Fisher realized when he broke the surface and saw a series of small shadows in the water ahead, moving steadily toward a bigger shadow in the distance.

Fisher stretched his arms and started to follow. He'd never been a particularly adept swimmer, nor could he say that he liked the activity very much, but there was nothing like being dropped in the middle of the ocean to focus one's effort.

Fisher managed to reach the Stiletto SEAL boat just ahead of two of the SEALs. That raised his standing another half notch with the group. The fact that he was willing to share his cigarettes did even more.

"Cigs are out once we hit the inflatables," said Tallahassee, who'd somehow materialized on the boat before anyone else. "Ten minutes. And stay topside."

"Up this way," said one of the smokers, thumbing Fisher up a ladder at the rear of the craft. Ruck on his back, sneakers squeaking, he climbed up to the top of the boat, standing on the stern deck.

"Stern" and "deck" were relative terms—the boat was radically different than any seagoing vessel Fisher had been on. It looked more like a child's extra-large eraser than a seagoing craft. Twenty-seven meters long and twelve meters wide, the craft had faceted, knifelike lines designed to make it hard for radar to pick up. It was also low to the water and flat, hard to pick out on the horizon. Its hull looked like a double-M, allowing it to skim over the waves at high speeds. It was so fast that to get his cigarette lit Fisher had to turn toward the stern and duck his head from the wind.

"You're with the FBI?" asked the SEAL who was crouched next to him.

"Yeah."

"I'm Navy."

"I figured. Boat and all."

"You like the FBI?"

"Uh-huh. You?"

"It's a living. My specialty is demolitions."

"You get to blow things up?"

"Sometimes. Not enough."

"How would you blow up a rocket?" Fisher asked.

"A rocket. That would be fun."

The SEAL began ticking off the many ways, starting with plastic explosives strapped to the booster. He was up to 178—a pinpoint laser on the fuel tank—when a bellow from Tallahassee announced that the assault team should get ready to board the inflatables for insertion pronto, or face insertion themselves. Fisher followed the others down the ladder to the diving platform, where Tallahassee was standing with Reid and two other sailors.

The Stiletto was essentially a floating garage, able to launch a thirty-foot rigid-hulled inflatable from its interior, spitting it out like a seagoing Pez dispenser. But this operation was going to involve several craft—none of which were aboard the Stiletto.

Which to Fisher looked like a problem.

"They're on their way," growled Tallahassee, apparently reading his mind. "Patience."

Reid pointed upward. "Listen."

Fisher heard the drone of a C-130 Hercules a few seconds before he spotted the aircraft jutting in over the water. Something seemed to break off the rear of the plane; in the next instant, the Hercules veered off. Two more appeared behind it, then a third and fourth. Each dropped something and turned off.

The objects began to move toward the Stiletto, skating across the water like water bugs over a pond. They were NSW RIBs, or Naval Special Warfare Rigid Inflatable Boats, thirty-six-foot-long excuses for twin Caterpillar diesels, which didn't feel as if they were working hard until they topped forty-five knots. But what was special about these engines was the fact that they were nearly as quiet as the motor on a Prius; the boats moved up to the Stiletto fantail like a silent film parade.

Black, the boats were almost impossible to see, even a few yards away. They had no superstructure to speak of, just low-slung metal brackets for a radar drum. When it was his turn to board, Fisher reached out for the guide rope on the starboard hull and tried to feel his way. Tiny, sensing that the FBI agent was going to fall into the drink, gave him a hand, lifting him by the rear and hoisting him forward. Unfortunately, Tiny misjudged Fisher's weight and the force of his assistance nearly drove Fisher through the hull.

"We're all here?" said Reid as Tiny clambered in. "Good. Let's move it."

Fisher grappled for a handhold as the boat sped off. Seawater sprayed everywhere.

"How you doing, Fisher?" asked Reid.

"I could use a good cup of coffee," he said.

A metal canister flew at him from the stern.

"Made it myself," said the sailor. "Don't burn yourself."

Fisher wondered what would have happened if he'd asked for a beer.

It took about twenty minutes for the RIBs to get close enough to spot the tanker in the distance. Clouds had moved in. The night was pitch black. Between the radar and their night glasses, the crew had no trouble finding the ship. The SEALs hunkered down, staring ahead as the boat spun into a pattern that would bring it parallel to the port side of the tanker.

"No lines. Sorry," said the crewman at the bow.

There were a number of ways of sneaking aboard a ship. Lines trailing from the deck or rail, though a sign of poor seamanship, were common, and made climbing aboard an easy task. Alternatively, grappling hooks with lines attached could be shot onto the deck. SEALs even practiced using large suction cups to walk up the hull, Spider-Man–like.

These SEALs, however, had their own way of doing things.

"Get the ladder ready," said Reid.

Tiny and one of the other sailors grabbed a long aluminum beam from the side of the boat. The beam extended about fifteen feet high; Tiny pulled a lever at the bottom and a set of rungs sprang down on one side.

Meanwhile, Reid was talking to the rest of the teams.

"Get us up close, now!" he yelled to the RIB crew. The tanker's engines were so loud he had to shout to make himself heard.

The boat veered toward the tanker. As the small craft pulled close, the man at the wheel cut back on the throttle, falling into place alongside the ship.

Tiny rose, the ladder in his hand. Another SEAL and Reid pulled a second, slightly longer one from the bottom of the boat. They put them together, and Tiny set the contraption into a boot at the side of the RIB.

"Up! Up! Up!" yelled Reid.

By the time Fisher got to the ladder, the rest of the team had disappeared over the rail above. He grabbed a peg and pulled himself upward, then reached for a second. As his fingers grabbed the metal, the ladder began to sway. He pulled his right leg up onto the peg, hoping this would make it more stable. All this did was move the ladder the other way. Fisher pushed up another rung, hoping for balance, but as he did a particularly large wave hit the RIB head on. The ladder shot upward, giving Fisher a brief sensation of weightlessness. Then he felt as if he weighed a million pounds, the ladder slamming downward.

In the next moment the ladder slapped hard against the side of the tanker, smashing Fisher's fingers. His skull, already vibrating with the tanker's engines, shook back and forth. A rogue wave pulled Fisher and the ladder away from the ship's side. He glanced down and saw only blackness.

He started climbing in earnest, reaching the deck in a matter of moments. The night exploded, bursting white: flash-bang grenades, used to startle the crew as the SEALs rushed the bridge.

The engines abruptly stopped. The night turned quiet.

Fisher shrugged the rucksack off and grabbed his pistol. More explosions. Fisher started moving toward the superstructure, legs wobbly, balance unsure. The middle of the deck area was covered by a raised platform, which topped pipes and other machinery above the oil tanks. As Fisher started to gain momentum, he saw someone climbing up on the platform, headed toward the bow.

Fisher grabbed hold of a large U-shaped pipe to his right and jumped, hoping to use his handhold to lever himself onto the platform. Instead, he slipped on the wet surface and crashed his elbow against it, bounding into one of the massive angle irons that held the deck cover in place. His gun fell from his hand, but now he was mad; he got to his feet, pulled himself up onto the platform, and began running toward the bow of the ship.

The man jumped off the platform and headed for the bow. Fisher threw himself into a slide, grabbing the man's leg as the man grappled with a life ring, hoping to use it to escape. They fell together, the man squirming like a squid.

A gun fired behind them.

Fisher crawled over the man, trying to subdue him—and keep him from being shot. Suddenly he felt himself being pulled upright and lifted to his feet.

"Tiny has him," shouted one of the SEALs. "Relax, FBI."

Fisher fell back. Floodlights flicked on—the SEALs now had full control of the ship.

Tiny slipped a pair of zip-lock handcuffs around the wrists of the man Fisher had wrestled to the deck, then picked him up. The man was jabbering in Spanish, speaking too fast for Fisher to decipher. But the gist of what he was saying was clear enough—he didn't have his proper work papers, and begged the men not to arrest him.

"Is there a bomb on the boat?" Fisher asked.

"Bomb?"

"Explosivo," said Fisher. "Explosives?"

"¡Explosivo! ¡No!" shouted the man. "No! There are no explosives—this is an oil tanker. Who would blow it up?"

On the bridge, the ship's captain was asking Tallahassee a similar question. Two of his men had locked themselves in a storage room belowdecks. Either they, too, were afraid that their papers weren't in order, or they didn't trust the mate's assurances that the SEALs weren't pirates. They refused to undo the lock.

The crew was Filipino. The captain was French, his English heavily accented. He'd been sleeping when the SEALs woke him with their flash-bangs and was still dressed in his pajamas.

Stripes.

"You could have requested *le permission* to come aboard," stuttered the captain, mixing languages and grammar in his anger. "Why are you acting as if we are criminals?"

"Relax," said Tallahassee. He pointed to Fisher. "This man is from the FBI. He's going to explain the whole thing."

"Smoke?" Fisher asked, holding out a slightly crumpled, not quite soggy pack of cigarettes.

The Frenchman shook his head.

"We got a report that this ship was going to be blown up, and we wanted to make sure that someone aboard wasn't going to do it," said Fisher.

"No one would blow up this ship. No one," said the captain. "Not in this crew."

Tallahassee rolled his eyes.

"I'm sure you're right," Fisher told the captain. "We're worried about an attack closer to the port. That's why we're going to ride with you to the dock. After we make sure there are no bombs aboard."

"I have to tell my company of this," said the captain.

"No," said Fisher. "I'm afraid that can't happen. We need *un silence de mort.*"

"A silence of the dead?" said the captain.

"Right. Or we'll end up with just the dead."

By the time dawn broke, the *Green Star* had taken on a harbor pilot and was aiming for the wide channel between New Jersey and Staten Island, heading in the direction of the Verrazano-Narrows Bridge, saluting garbage scows and coal barges every fifty yards. The two holdouts had released themselves from the storage locker, and the crew was working at their stations, albeit nervously, as the SEALs watched from the shadows. The Coast Guard cutter *Vigorous* was trailing the tanker by a respectful distance, just out of sight. The SEAL boats had gone north as well, trying to stay as inconspicuous as possible. News of the takeover had not leaked out.

"What are the odds this is a waste of time?" asked Tallahassee, as he and Fisher stood on the bridge.

"Even money," said Fisher.

"If they're going to do it, it'll be a speedboat," said Tallahassee. "Take it right into the side."

"I don't think so," said Fisher. "Not this time of the year."

"What would you do?"

"I'd get something no one would suspect. A police boat would be perfect. Maybe a tug. Of course, if I really wanted to screw with our minds, I'd hijack the Stiletto and plow it right through the side like a dagger."

Tallahassee's frown deepened.

"You know, Fisher," he said. "You got a little SEAL in you."

"Thanks."

"I'm not sure that's a compliment."

2

JERSEY CITY

Jonathon Loup paced anxiously around his office. On his desk, a high-powered scanner breezed through the maritime radio bands. It stopped occasionally with transmissions from tugs and water taxis. Each time it did, Loup paused, listening, worried that he had missed something.

There were many contingencies to the plan, branching paths of possibility. But they all depended on the government people being relatively intelligent.

Why hadn't they gone to the tanker?

Freeman said they might not believe the tip. That was okay. They were prepared for that. If that happened, the plan would move to Branch B. If they did, Branch A.

What if the Homeland Security man didn't get the message, and *nothing* happened?

It would, eventually. Branch Z.

Something would happen.

Loup leaned over his computer and hit Refresh, updating Google News.

Nothing he was interested in.

The scanner paused. Loup listened expectantly. But it was just a broadcast from a boat captain, greeting another, asking how the channel was.

"Clear sailing," came the reply.

Freeman has it all figured out, Loup told himself. *Just follow the plan.*

Follow the plan. Path B.

Loup shut down his computer. Then he opened his right-hand drawer and took out a pistol. The gun was a precaution Freeman hadn't counseled, but Loup felt it was necessary.

Downstairs, the trading room was empty, all of the computers and other gear gone. His people had been moved to a temporary location in Yonkers that Freeman had found; their permanent base would be ready in a few weeks. By then, all of this would be behind him. And most likely he'd have a clear shot at Icarus. Without the Chinese interference.

Two of Freeman's men were waiting at the front. One of the men touched his radio set as Loup came out, calling the car.

Loup took out his BlackBerry while they waited for it to arrive. He sent two text messages. The first was to Dennis: *Be ready*.

The second was to Freeman.

Path B.

The car came up. The two men moved in a well-practiced scramble, hustling Loup to the vehicle. It was all a bit much, Loup thought—except that it wasn't. The Chinese had proven they could be vicious. And if they ever figured out what he was doing, they'd come at him with everything they had. Diplomatic cover or not.

Two men and an armored car wouldn't be nearly enough.

"What's the traffic like to New York today?" Loup asked his driver.

"Same as always. Bad."

"Get onto 95 South."

"South?"

Loup didn't answer. The driver spun west, heading toward 78 so he could get on the highway. The bulk of the traffic was heading for the tunnel to the north, but there were still a good number of cars on the road in front of them. Loup drew a breath, trying to stretch it out, trying to relax. It was all easy now, everything was easy.

They'd gone all of a mile when suddenly the limo ground to a halt. The traffic ahead was jammed.

"What's going on?" Loup asked the driver.

"I don't know. Got to be an accident. This just happened—there's nothing on the traffic sites."

"See if you can get off at Avenue E," suggested Loup, mentioning the exit for Port Jersey Boulevard. But that was backed up just as badly.

Loup glanced at his watch. It was nearly 8:30. He needed to be in Manhattan no later than 9:30 for the second call—and the start of a string of appointments, none of which he wanted to blow off. The world didn't stop because of this one piece of business, as nasty as it was.

But there was no way they were going to make it at this rate. He'd have to make the call from here, rather than driving farther south as planned.

"I'm going to get out and make a phone call while we're stuck," he told the bodyguards and driver. "You're to wait here."

"Our job is to protect you."

"Do as I say. It's not that I don't trust you," added Loup. It was an obvious lie, but he felt compelled to say it anyway. "It just has to be done this way. When I'm done, we're going to Manhattan. Quickest way to Battery Park."

"Quickest way?" asked the driver.

"Yes. Forget what I said about 95."

"If we get off at the junkyard, I can drive along the railroad tracks and swing back on in the other direction," said the driver. "Bumpy, we'll get around almost all the traffic."

"Bumpy's fine," said Loup, opening the car door.

3

ABOARD THE TANKER *GREEN STAR*

The main entrance to New York Harbor runs almost due north-south, the mouth of the Hudson River spitting into the Atlantic Ocean at the southern tip of Brooklyn. The river is actually an estuary of the ocean there, saltwater running several miles northward, well past the George Washington Bridge and the close-in suburbs.

The most famous landmark in the harbor is the Statue of Liberty, which stands with beacon blazing about a mile and three-quarters from Manhattan's tip. In the popular imagination, every ship passes the statue before docking, crew and passengers alike crowding the rail to stare in awe at the greenish lady.

The reality is somewhat different, and not just because of inbred cynicism. Much of what is now called the Port of New York lies south of the statue—and in fact is in New Jersey.

Case in point: the dockyards the *Green Star* was heading toward, which lay west of Staten Island, closer to Newark than Manhattan. To get there, the tanker had to pass through Raritan Bay, a large pool of water between Staten Island and Monmouth County, New Jersey, and then go up the Arthur Kill, as the channel between New Jersey and Staten Island was known.

By now the traffic had picked up considerably. There were commercial boats, tugs, and all manner of barges lugging things around. A cruise ship lumbered past as they headed up into Raritan Bay. Passengers who weren't hung over and a few who were clung to the rails, waving at anything that passed.

Fisher tried focusing on what was going on around them, but the more he stared, the more he thought of Kathy.

She'd tried to talk him into going sailing once. He told her he'd rather have bricks tied to his feet and be dropped upside down from the nearest dock.

It wasn't *quite* true. He could have done without the bricks.

"Ferry at ten o'clock," said Tallahassee as they passed under the Outerbridge Crossing.

"That belong there?" Fisher asked the pilot.

"Ain't usual," said Tallahassee. The area around them was all industrial.

"Not unusual, either," said the pilot. "Could be going for repairs. There are a lot of ferries on the water."

The pilot had been handpicked by the Coast Guard because he was the most experienced man available, but the white whiskers on his chin didn't translate into calmness. His eyes blinked every time he talked, and the blood vessels at his temples looked like blue balloons ready to burst.

"I don't like it," said Tallahassee as the ferry continued in their general direction. "Cutter's too far back, and I'm not sure the chopper can take out something that big."

Fisher raised his binoculars. The ferry was about a mile away, sailing southward directly toward them.

"I don't see anybody on the deck," added the SEAL captain. "You?"

Fisher turned to the ship's captain. "Let's slow down."

The order was passed.

"Still coming," said Tallahassee. He turned to his communications specialist, whose satcom radio had the Coast Guard's mission commander preselected. "Get one of the Coast Guard boats to hail it," he told him.

The nearest Coast Guard boat was a twenty-five-foot small response boat, a craft roughly the size of the SEAL vessel they'd used the night before. It had a machine gun at the bow and a pair of Hondas at the stern, and immediately cut across channel traffic and began approaching the ferry.

The ferry suddenly picked up speed.

"Not answering their hails," said the como man.

Tallahassee began barking orders, calling the helicopters in, alerting his men. Almost instantly, the heavy thud of Marine Whiskey Cobras—attack helicopters that had flown all night from New River, North Carolina—pounded the air.

The ferry was five hundred yards away.

"Are there people on board?" Fisher asked.

"Two I can see," said Tallahassee.

Fisher darted out of the door at the side of the bridge and clambered up the ladder to the top of the superstructure to the lookout point. As he climbed onto the deck, he saw two small speedboats, nineteen and twenty-one feet long respectively, heading toward them from the opposite direction, out of Staten Island. They were going fast, bows high against the waves.

And there was no one in them.

"Boat! Boats on the starboard side! Take out the boats!" shouted Fisher. "Speedboats at five o'clock! *Take out the boats!*"

One of the SEALs near the stern began firing his LW-50 machine gun. The next second, what looked like a D battery shot from the tanker and hit the speedboat square in the prow. The fiberglass splattered, but the boat continued to move, lowering steadily until a few seconds later, when a second grenade hit it amidships. This time there was a tremendous explosion, the grenade setting off the five hundred pounds of plastic explosives stuffed into the boat's passenger section.

One of the Cobras swung down, its tail wagging like a dog's as the pilot lined up his shot. White smoke puffed from the winglets on both sides. The air frothed, and the second speedboat ignited in a fireball.

The thunderclap that followed was so loud that Fisher and everyone else aboard the tanker lost their hearing for a few moments.

The ferry, meanwhile, passed them, continuing on as if nothing had happened.

Fisher clicked his fingers, then darted down the ladder, hopped over the rail, and scrambled toward the davit aft of the superstructure.

Then he stopped, not quite sure how to lower the open boat it held.

"Like this," growled Tallahassee behind him.

The SEAL captain raised his arms and whistled; two of his men jumped down from the railing above and helped swing the boat out. Fisher, Tallahassee, and two of the sailors got in; instantly the boat was dropped toward the water. It hit stern first, rocking sharply.

"We have to get to the ferry," said Fisher.

"No shit," said Tallahassee.

One of his men set up the outboard at the rear. The engine revved, and they spun in a wide arc away from the *Green Star*.

The ferry had picked up speed. White furls of water shot from the underside, frothing out like the contrail of a rocket.

Even so, the lifeboat began gaining steadily. As the four hundred yards between them shrank to three hundred, one of the Cobra attack helicopters swung in front of the ferry, buzzing the forward deck in an effort to get it to stop.

It didn't. Instead, a rocket-propelled grenade flew from the lower deck of the ferry. The grenade hit the housing above the chopper's engine, exploding in a black and red burst. Aircraft parts rained across the water as the helicopter sputtered into the river.

"Damn," said Tallahassee.

"We need the people on the ferry alive," said Fisher.

"Yeah, well that ain't going to be easy now," said Tallahassee as someone appeared at the stern of the ferry. "Duck!"

The man on the ferry began firing an automatic rifle in their direction. The others ducked; Fisher, unconvinced that the fiberglass hull offered much protection, took out his Colt and began firing.

His first shot was wide left, his second wide right. His third hit the top of the ferry.

He didn't fire a fourth. A fusillade from the SEALs sent him racing for cover.

"Get ready to board!" yelled Tallahassee as they closed. The ferry had altered course, running on a diagonal toward the shoreline. The other boats on the water ahead flailed desperately to get out of the way.

A hundred yards. Seventy-five. The SEALs gripped the gunwales of the boat, ready to spring aboard. The Cobra began firing at the ferry's wheelhouse.

Fifty yards.

"Watch out!" yelled one of the SEALs.

In the next moment, a rock flew toward the lifeboat.

Except it wasn't a rock. It was a grenade, fired from the interior of the ferry.

The odds on hitting a lifeboat doing close to twenty-five knots from another vessel doing perhaps eighteen cannot be very good. The variables—wind, loft, fuel component, etc.—are many; the target relatively small and moving. In this case, the variables conspired to send the grenade about two yards too far to the right. And while it's often said that close counts in horseshoes and grenades, in this case the projectile sailed harmlessly into the water, and if it exploded it did so far under the waves where it presented no danger.

It was the second rocket-propelled grenade that did all the damage.

Fisher jumped at the last possible moment, plunging into the water as the warhead ignited. He swirled around for a moment, dazed, then pushed back for the surface. A swell grabbed him and threw him into a floating splinter of the boat as he broke water. He took hold, kicking his legs as if the flotsam were a surf-board as he pulled it under his chest. Five feet long and shaped like the state of Delaware, the board provided just enough buoyancy for him to clear his eyes.

The ferry was tantalizingly close, no more than five yards away. The Cobra had shot up the wheel-house, damaging the controls and quieting the engine. But the vessel still had plenty of momentum, and Fisher couldn't catch up.

He was just about to head toward shore when he realized the heavy whoop of the Cobra was getting closer. He turned around and saw the helicopter gun-ship skimming toward him.

He put his hand up for a ride.

"Way to go, Marines," he yelled, thinking the chopper would swoop in for him. But the pilot had other things in mind—namely, raking the side of the ferry with his gun.

The wash from the helo pushed Fisher forward—then downward. He lost the board he'd been using. He kicked and flailed, realizing that without it he was going to have trouble reaching shore.

His hand hit something hard—the side of the ferry.

Fisher tried to grab the hull, but his fingers could find nothing to grab on to. He clawed at the side, kicking and trying to will his way onto the small ship. The current pushed his body sideways, parallel to the hull, but the bigger craft started slipping away.

He tried another grab, only to have something smack him in the side of the head.

A tire, attached to the ferry to keep it from being damaged when pulling up alongside a dock or another boat.

Fisher grabbed for the tire that had hit him, but missed. He saw another on his right and leapt at it, poking his fingers into the open rim behind the whitewall.

Firestone. *Where the rubber meets the road.* Or in this case, the FBI agent.

Fisher pulled himself up, clambering onto the narrow deck behind the railing. Trying to jump over the top, he slipped and rolled unceremoniously to the deck, landing flat on his back near one of the doors to the ferry's cabin. He got to his knees just as someone came running out of the cabin door. They collided, sending the man's AR-15 to the deck. Fisher lurched for the gun, grabbed it, and pointed it at the man's face.

Dazed, the man remained slumped on the deck, semiconscious.

"Drop the weapon!" yelled someone near the stern.

Fisher glanced upward—it was one of the SEALs.

"Don't shoot him now," barked Tallahassee, appearing behind the sailor who'd mistaken Fisher for one of the ferry crew members. "We may need him for a human shield later on."

"Thanks," said Fisher.

"Don't mention it."

Fisher looked at the sailor. "Cuff this guy. We got to get to the bridge. There may be a bomb there."

He ran toward a set of steel steps and started

climbing. They ended on an observation deck open to the air and outfitted with benches. Another ladder led upward from the fore of the deck to the rear of the wheelhouse. As Fisher ran toward it, automatic rifle fire splintered the benches to his right. He dove down, his ribs crunching against the rifle butt.

Tallahassee, back by the stern, started firing at the gunman, who took cover behind the metal benches. Fisher crawled to the ladder, pulled the rifle's strap over his shoulder, and jumped upward, going up the steps as if his life was at stake—which it was, since the man behind him was once more firing in his direction.

Reaching the top, Fisher dove headfirst toward the doorway onto the bridge, out of the gunman's range. The structure had been chewed to pieces by the Cobra's cannon. Shards of glass, metal, and plastic littered the floor like confetti left over from a parade.

There was no one, dead or alive, on the bridge. Fisher took a look at what had been the control panel. He'd seen car wrecks in better shape. Parts of the wheel were in three different corners; its mount now resembled an umbrella stand.

Fisher went back to the bulkhead and looked out toward the observation deck. The man who'd been firing at him was wedged between a pair of tables near the middle of the deck. Tallahassee was still back by the stern. They exchanged shots every few seconds, but the metal furniture sitting between them made it impossible for them to hit each other.

Fisher wanted to get the guy alive if at all possible, but there was no telling how long it would be before he ran out of ammunition.

He obviously had plenty. A short but furious flurry of bullets chased Fisher back from the doorway and eliminated the idea that he might be able to sneak down the steps and grab the guy from the rear.

"FBI!" shouted Fisher. "Give yourself up and we'll go easy on you!"

A hail of bullets spit through the metal above Fisher's head as he hunkered on the ground.

"I'm losing my patience!" yelled Fisher.

More bullets, then a loud click—the magazine had run dry.

Fisher got up and started to go out, only to hit the deck as a fresh volley clanged into the metal around him. The gunman had reloaded quicker than he'd expected.

Fisher retreated. Thinking he might be able to flank the gunman from the side, he leaned over the remains of the forward bulkhead. The Cobra had demolished the narrow deck and railing that had circled the superstructure, and what remained clearly wouldn't hold him.

Fisher slipped over to the port side of the bridge. The bullets from the Cobra had torn away much of the thin bulkhead separating the bridge from a storeroom. A godawful, yet piquant stench rose from it.

The storeroom had housed a season's worth supply of condiments. Boxes of mustard, vinegar, and ketchup containers were stacked deck to ceiling. Several had been smashed by flying shrapnel, creating an odor so hideous that tears began running from Fisher's eyes.

This gave him an idea.

Splat!

Splat-splat-splat-crash-splat!

Fisher rained bottle after plastic bottle of mustard on the gunman's position, lobbing them through the damaged roof of the bridge. His first few shots were wide, but the return fire soon let him know that he was finding his mark. The gunman fired furiously, first because he was unsure of what was being thrown, and then out of frustration.

Fisher switched to vinegar, then ketchup, alternating all three in quick succession. The return gunfire became increasingly erratic, then sporadic.

Finally there was a shout from below.

"Cease fire! Cease fire!" yelled Tallahassee. "He's out of bullets. He's surrendering."

Good thing, thought Fisher. All he had left were a few jars of sweet relish.

4

BATTERY PARK, NEW YORK CITY

It was a chilly but sunny day, the sort that hints of spring without overpromising.

Loup, trailed at a respectful distance by his two bodyguards, found a bench at Battery Park and sat down, gazing southeastward. He could see a pair of helicopter gunships well off in the distance. There were other helicopters as well—Coast Guard rescue aircraft, two Blackhawks, a police chopper, three or four television traffic 'copters.

It *was* working.

It was going to be a good day. A very, very good day. He didn't even have to check what the markets were doing to know it was going to be a good day—a very good day.

Loup glanced around casually, making sure he wasn't being watched—the few people here were all staring at the helicopters—then pulled a cell phone from his pocket. It was a prepaid phone, one that he wanted to be traced. He dialed Wan's contact number. While he waited for the message to end, he took out his voice recorder.

He pressed the Play button for Wan's voice mail.

"Things have not gone well," said a voice constructed from television audio.

He pressed the Stop button, but left the phone on as he walked to the edge of the water. Changing his mind, he turned and walked toward an open garbage can. He dropped it in, then walked away.

A glorious day, he thought, looking at the sky. A very glorious day.

5

NEW JERSEY HARBOR

By the time the second gunman surrendered, the ferry was surrounded by SEAL boats and a half-dozen Coast Guard and police patrol craft. The cutter hove into view just in time for the photo op, as every network cut to live feeds from helicopters in the harbor. The Coast Guard called over a tugboat to secure the ferry. Two NYPD boats came down with a team of U.S. marshals and FBI agents from the New York office to help Fisher take custody of the prisoners. A forensics team was called in to go over the ferry for evidence. Before they arrived, one of the SEALs discovered the remains of what looked like a remote control unit on the observation deck near the ladder to the bridge. It had been severely damaged during the assault.

"Just a guess," said Tallahassee, pointing it out to Fisher, "but that's probably what they steered the speedboats with."

"Can you do two boats with one?" asked Fisher, looking at the box. A 30 mm bullet had hit it in the corner; it looked like a giant rat had taken a bite out of it.

"Sure. You just switch frequencies," said Tallahassee. "Easy enough."

"Hmmm," said Fisher.

The police were already searching the shoreline where the explosive-laden boats had been launched. Tallahassee told Fisher that the boats could have been set up there the night before, then started by remote control as the tanker approached.

"Sophisticated," added Tallahassee.

"Clever, maybe," allowed Fisher. "If it was sophisticated, we wouldn't have found it."

The SEALs found several more rifles and weapons scattered around the ferry. While the damage to the bridge and surrounding structure was severe, the hull itself had only a few small leaks. They could be controlled by pumps until the ferry was taken to a dock.

The crew of the downed Cobra had been rescued; they would be remembered in history as the only gunship crew ever downed by a ferry.

The prisoners were locked up aboard the cutter, waiting for the reporters to leave so they could be choppered back to land. Fisher had the Coast Guard take them out one at a time, so he'd be able to keep them separate. It also gave him a chance to talk to both of them outside their cell.

The man he'd pelted with condiments looked to be aspiring to become a jailhouse lawyer.

"I ain't talkin'," he said as the helicopter descended. "I have constitutional rights. I have the Fifth Amendment."

Fisher shrugged. "You don't know anything I want to know anyway."

"Fifth Amendment. That's what I know."

"Do you know you're going to prison for the rest of your life?" one of the marshals holding him asked. "Attempted murder, government agent."

"That's not a life sentence," said the man, correctly, as it happened.

"Who hired you?" asked Fisher.

The gunman replied with an anatomically impossible suggestion.

The second thug was more cooperative. He said his name was Richard Tarken, gave his age as thirty-two, and claimed to be a homeless Vietnam vet.

Twenty years older and Fisher might have believed him.

He said he and his companion had been hired the night before and told to show up at a pier in Hoboken before dawn. The ferry was waiting when they arrived.

"They told us just to drive the ferry south, that's all. Nothing would happen."

"Who's they?" asked Fisher.

The man glanced up at the helicopter arriving for him, but didn't answer.

"How'd you get the guns?" Fisher asked.

Another glance, but no answer.

"What about that grenade launcher?" asked Fisher.

"They were all on board. Gabe wanted to use them. I never shot anyone."

"What's Gabe's last name?" asked Fisher.

Tarken shook his head. "Just Gabe."

"Who hired you?" asked Fisher.

Another shake of the head. "I don't know names."

"We'll keep you safe," said Fisher. "We'll take you to a military base where no one can touch you."

Tarken frowned but said nothing.

Fisher flew with the two men and a security detail to a secure area at the Staten Island Coast Guard station, which was a problem for Fisher—his clothes were sopped and smelled of ketchup. A liaison officer had found a pair of dungarees in Fisher's size, along with a pullover sweatshirt. But she couldn't find shoes, socks, or underwear.

It wasn't the first time Fisher had interrogated someone commando-style, but it was the first time he'd done so in his bare feet. The cold floor numbed his toes as he waited in the interview room with a deputy U.S. attorney, who introduced himself as Paul Gonzalez.

As Fisher filled him in on the relevant parts of the case, Gonzalez glanced down at his feet.

"I thought the Bureau was paying agents fairly well these days," said the attorney. "I can loan you a few dollars if you need it."

Tarken was escorted in before Fisher could ask for the attorney's shoes instead. Gonzalez introduced himself, then read the man his rights. He emphasized that Tarken had the right to an attorney with a little more gusto than Fisher would have liked.

"Let's start with your name," suggested Fisher.

"Do I have to answer that?" asked Tarken.

"Of course not," said Gonzalez. "You have a constitutional right not to incriminate yourself."

"You already told me your name was Tarken," said Fisher, annoyed. "Richard Tarken. Is that true?"

The prisoner nodded.

"Look, we can figure out a deal here," said Fisher. "You're a little guy in all this. You didn't want to kill those people on the tanker, or blow up the nuclear power plant."

"What nuclear power plant?"

"Or the substation."

"I don't know what you're talking about."

He didn't, clearly; Fisher could tell from the confused expression on his face.

"Was it hard to steer the boats?"

"To steer the ferry?"

"The boats with the explosives."

Tarken gave him a blank stare.

"So who hired you?" Fisher asked.

"People. I don't know. Maybe I do need a lawyer."

"We can get you one," Gonzalez assured him cheerfully.

"What town would we call?" asked Fisher. "For an attorney?"

Hoboken.

Where, it turned out, Tarken was well known to the police. According to his rap sheet, he'd been charged with more than a dozen crimes, though none were more serious than petty burglary.

"Disorderly conduct, vagrancy things," said an officer who'd dealt with him. "Plenty of charges we didn't even file. Your typical homeless stuff. Sad case, when you think about it. He's got an IQ around eighty."

The cop tentatively identified Tarken's "partner" as Gabriel Penske. Gabe had a much longer rap sheet, and visions of grandeur to match. He tested on the opposite end of the intellectual scale—well into genius range—but he was also clearly a nutjob, as the officer put it. He'd been a Marine—for about six months before being discharged as a wackjob.

"You know the guy is not wrapped too tight if the Marines got rid of him," said the cop. "They took my brother-in-law and made him a goddamn colonel."

As soon as it was clear that Fisher knew his name, Gabe called his lawyer. The attorney arrived at the Coast Guard base a little past three. Apparently smelling a civil rights bonanza after the phone call, he stormed into the interview room proclaiming that Gabe's civil rights had been violated.

Gonzalez began to pale as the attorney ranted, citing various statutes and amendments to the Constitution, all of which had allegedly been violated by Gabe's arrest. Fisher watched the smug look on Gabe's face grow as the lawyer continued. He waited until his cheeks were puffed just to bursting.

"I'm sure you have a pretty good case," Fisher said finally, interrupting the lawyer. "The thing is, Gabe isn't going to spend a dime of the millions you win for him because he's going to be in jail for attempted murder of a federal agent, grand theft—the ferry—piracy, assault, a couple of dozen terrorism counts—"

"Terrorism?" The lawyer turned to Gabe.

"He tried to sink the oil tanker," said Fisher, eyes locked on Gabe.

"What are you talking about, oil tanker?" answered Gabe. "All we did was sail the ferry. I didn't know it was stolen."

"You were controlling the speedboats, right?"

"What speedboats? I haven't a clue what you're talking about."

"The two guys who hired you didn't tell you?"

"What?"

"The two guys didn't want you to ram the tanker?"

"It was only one guy."

"The black guy with the moustache?"

"He didn't have no moustache. And he was as white as you. Whiter."

"I advise you to say nothing further," said the lawyer, putting his hand on Gabe's arm.

Fisher rose.

"Where are you going?" Gonzalez asked.

"To see about getting a pair of dry shoes. My toes are frozen."

NYPD had already started searching Staten Island for the speedboats' launch point. It wasn't a complete waste of time, but then neither was waiting in line to buy lottery tickets. Fisher figured the odds of either paying off were about the same.

He got a helicopter back to the undisclosed location, changed, then drove to the closest diner and got himself some lunch. While he was waiting for his BLT to arrive, he called Roberta, the Bureau's forensic accountant.

"Good day to be in oil futures," she told him.

"I'll bet."

"I have a list of all the trades."

"Yeah?"

"It's longer than the Manhattan phone book. It'll take us years to sort through this all."

"Great."

"We're putting it into a database where we can filter it against the other incidents and see what we get. Here's something interesting, though. The news of the attack broke on Bloomberg News at exactly 8:28 A.M."

"Why is that interesting?"

"The attack didn't begin until after the Cobras arrived, right?"

"Yeah, I guess," said Fisher. "Right around then."

"According to the Marines, their helicopters weren't there until 0835. If I remember my little hand and my big hand, that's about seven minutes *after* the news broke on Bloomberg."

Bloomberg News had picked up the story from a radio station in Newark, which aired the news around 8:25 A.M., then fed it to Bloomberg via a stringer arrangement with the service. The reporter who had put the story together was a tall, thin woman named Geraldine Higgins. She had a nose that would have made a parrot jealous, but a wondrous radio voice; it was worth keeping your eyes closed for.

Fisher kept his open when she met him in the foyer of the station offices. The place smelled of burnt coffee and moldy newspapers; a little too much Sumatra for Fisher's taste, but he was never one to judge joe by its aroma.

Higgins took Fisher to a conference room down the hall, where the news director and the station manager were waiting. Both men—middle-aged, one fatter than the other—went to great lengths to avoid staring at Higgins's nose. They offered Fisher coffee.

He accepted out of scientific curiosity—as he had expected, the brewmaster had leaned a little too heavily on the Indonesian beans, though all in all this was a forgivable offense.

Fisher started off with generic questions about where the information had come from—an eyewitness who was watching the attack, supposedly—then gradually asked for more specific details. The station hadn't recorded the call, since it came in on a sales line rather than one of the news lines.

"Who would know that number?" Fisher asked.

"Anyone, I guess," said the woman. She turned to the news director, giving Fisher a full broadside view of her schnozzle.

"It's printed on business cards, brochures, that sort of thing," said the news director. "It's in the phone book."

"What did the caller ID say?" Fisher asked.

"Private."

"Exactly where did he say he was calling from?" asked Fisher.

"Didn't say exactly. Just that he could see what was happening. So it must have been in New Jersey somewhere."

"You think you could get that number for me?" said Fisher, turning to the station manager. "We can get a subpoena for it, but if you call it'll save time."

"You think they'll give it to us if it's private?"

"They might if they thought the caller was harassing you. Or if you said it was an employee you were trying to track down."

The others exchanged a glance.

"Don't you have a lot of witnesses already?" said the station manager.

"Not like this one," said Fisher. "He saw it before it happened."

The phone call had come from a cell phone using a tower near Bayonne, New Jersey. Whoever had called not only had an incredible ability to see the future, but could see through buildings to the river miles away.

Fisher handed off the number to the New York office to check into, then went back over to New Jersey to have a look at the place where the ferry had been stolen from.

The boatyard straddled the Jersey City-Hoboken line. It handled a wide range of craft, from yachts to tugs, along with the occasional ferry. The craft had been tied up at one of the piers for several days, waiting for an overhaul of the bridge instrument panel, but was otherwise in good shape, as the day's events had proven. Security at the yard was beyond lax, which was typical of the small yards on both coasts. There was neither a gate nor a fence on the land side, and many nights the owner forgot to lock the office. He'd been there for more than forty years and never had a problem.

"Now my re-port-tation is ruined," said the owner, Luigi Giacomo. He met Fisher on the pier just outside his office. He was about a quarter of the way down a thick Cuban cigar.

"All afternoon, newspapers, TV calling me," added Giacomo. Born in Italy, he immigrated to the United States as a baby immediately after World War II, a fact he had volunteered twice to Fisher after being introduced. "They keep asking, why did you let them steal the ferry. I didn't let them steal the ferry. They took it. They took it before I opened."

"From where?"

"Right there."

He pointed his stogie toward an empty space on the wharf directly ahead. The ferry would have been the first ship anyone saw coming into the yard. From the way the owner described it, it would also be among the easiest to steal—the ignition wasn't keyed, and once under way even a dunce could handle it.

And one had, Fisher thought.

"You not go very fast. But she's very forgiving the way she sails. She's a good pony for someone who doesn't know how to ride horses, if you know what I mean."

"You see anyone hanging around here who looked suspicious yesterday or the day before?" asked Fisher.

Giacomo took a long, pensive pull on his cigar, twisting it slightly.

"Suspicious? Everyone is suspicious. I am suspicious. Even you. You are very suspicious, eh?" He laughed.

"Nobody who stood out?" said Fisher.

Giacomo shook his head. There was no sense asking about video camera surveillance. Fisher took a walk out of the parking lot, gazing around the street. The area was industrial, or more correctly had been industrial, until sending industry overseas became a national obsession. Now it was mostly abandoned. A few large brick buildings dating from the 1920s or '30s dominated the nearby landscape. The parking lots were mostly cratered concrete or pulverized asphalt, all overgrown with weeds. The marina's was the lone exception.

Fisher walked out to the street, surveying the area in hopes of finding a coffee shop—Sumatra always left him needing a re-hit a few hours later. He didn't see a shop. But he did spot a fairly new Toyota Corolla, parked on the street across from the marina.

"Your car?" he asked Giacomo.

"This is my Jeep," said Giacomo. "I drive only American cars."

"Jeeps are Italian," said Fisher. "Fiat took the company over a few years ago."

"Ah, no wonder it is driving funny lately."

6

NEW MEXICO

Sandra Chester rolled over in the bed, pulling the sheet up over her body. Her legs and chest felt clammy, even though the air conditioner was on, even though the New Mexico night was typically dry.

She couldn't sleep. She hadn't been able to sleep since she got home. She'd taken a bath and read a book and tried to sleep, but she couldn't.

It wasn't just the murder in the parking garage. Certainly that had upset her—unsettled was a better word, she told herself; upset sounded too much like she was an oversensitive female.

There was nothing wrong with being sensitive or being female. The problem was with men. As soon as they saw the combination, they expected that, despite all your accomplishments and all your achievements, you were at heart a six-year-old deathly afraid of spiders, ready to wilt and call for Daddy at the first sign of upset.

The problem was, she did feel like that. Worse. She felt as if she was falling into a pit, a bottomless hole.

The police had speculated that the murder was a domestic dispute. Most murders were, said the one who had walked her to her car when they were done. Husband or boyfriend got mad at something, and bam, there it was. Boyfriend or estranged husband, that was the number one suspect. Case would be wrapped up in twenty-four hours.

The policeman who had said this had a baby face and the tone of a man ninety years old. Sandra guessed he was twenty-five, if that. She wondered how many dead bodies he'd ever seen in his life, let alone how many murders.

She couldn't help but compare him to Andy.

Andy. She wanted to call him, just to hear his reassuring voice. But she didn't want to come off like a weak female.

It wasn't the murder that had sent her retreating. It was her own failure, the failure of the rocket to launch properly, the utter failure of her career, her worthlessness, her black hole. Her failure was a recording, playing over and over in her head, repeating itself as she tried desperately to shake it loose. It tied her up in the sheets, even as she repeated to herself that it wasn't true. The rocket's failure had been a mistake or an accident, but only that—not the negation of everything she had done in life.

The failure of one rocket was nothing. Goddard had failed—how many times had he failed. They used to talk about it all the time in grad school. Robert H. Goddard, father of modern rocketry, the man who had launched the first liquid-fueled rocket in history.

March 16, 1926.

There wasn't television yet. Aircraft were still new. Most were made of fabric.

Goddard's work at Roswell amounted to failure after failure, disaster after disaster.

Sandra sat up in bed. She'd felt the irrational despair before. The worst was during her work on her Ph.D. She was supposed to meet with her doctorate supervisor first thing in the morning, and she hadn't been able to sleep at all, not a wink, not a lick. But she'd stayed in bed, certain she was going to do horribly at their meeting, certain that he was going to tell her that she simply didn't have what it took, that she was a phony, a pretender, a *girl* and not a rocket scientist.

She'd given herself a pep talk. She'd given herself several pep talks. None worked.

If you don't face him, he'll think he's right.

He's a sexist asshole. He thinks that because you're a girl, you can't cut it.

You're a woman, not a girl.

But it was thinking about her father that got her out of bed. She visualized him scolding her for giving up. The thought of his stern face—and the disappointment that went with it—pushed her from the bed.

The irony wasn't lost on her. To be a woman, she had to call on the memory of the one person who had valued her as a girl.

Her fear had been utterly unfounded. Her Ph.D. director had asked for the meeting because he had to give up mentoring her. He had pancreatic cancer, a few months to live.

"That's what they claim," he'd told her, forcing a smile. "But I know better."

He was dead inside of two months.

And she'd felt like a fool for being so scared, for almost giving in to the despair.

Sandra threw off the covers. Telling herself she'd feel better once she hit the shower, she walked to the kitchen and turned on the coffeemaker.

The water helped, a little. So did the coffee.

Her jeans felt a little loose as she dressed. That was one benefit of feeling down, she thought. It made her lose weight.

Not that she really needed to be concerned.

Her neighbor was sitting out under her overhang across the way as Sandra came out of the house to leave. She'd left her car out the night before, so tired she worried that she would bump the side of the garage door coming in.

The neighbor waved. Sandra decided to go over and say hello.

"How are you, Connie?" she asked.

"Very well, very well. Who is that young man coming around?"

"Which young man?" said Sandra.

Her voice was so sharp that the neighbor almost stepped back.

"Oh, I thought I saw someone drive up to your house before. I just thought it might be a boyfriend."

"Which day?"

"Oh, I'm sure I was mistaken. No, it must have been one of the other units. Jerald's. He's always having those musician friends over."

"Sure."

"You should come over for tea one evening," said Connie as Sandra started to leave. "I have another video of my grandson performing."

Her grandson played the trumpet. Not very well. Not even for a fourth grader.

"I'm so busy at work right now," said Sandra. "But maybe soon."

"Maybe soon," echoed Connie.

7

NEWARK, NEW JERSEY

The Corolla had been rented at Newark International Airport the night before by a man who signed his name as Thiweruriro#$#Xwerrwerwerr, an indecipherable squiggle that in no way matched the simple name on the credit card—Thomas Hhou. In turn, the simple name on the credit card in no way matched any of the records in the New York Division of Motor Vehicles—a substantial achievement, according to the overnight clerk who looked it up for Fisher.

The clerk's job was basically to deal with inquiries from police agencies, and she seemed chosen especially for it. She was surly, uncooperative, and cranky.

Those were her good qualities.

"No match means no match," she told Fisher. "It means, no match."

"Did you run the address?"

"Did you tell me to run the address? I'm not a mind reader, you know."

"I thought maybe you might use a little initiative."

"I've heard of that."

The address was also nonexistent. Fisher had her go through a search of similar names and close addresses, largely because she was such a doll to deal with. When he was done amusing himself, he called the Bureau credit card liaison, who of course had gone home hours before. Then he called his own card contact: Ms. Margaret.

Ms. Margaret was a supervisor of customer service for a firm in India that handled all of the major credit card companies. Fisher had first encountered her while questioning a charge for an extended warranty that he didn't order. As it happened, his encounter with Ms. Margaret was so worthwhile that he ended up paying for the warranty, writing it off on a voucher as a business expense. When questioned about it, he said it was the best investment he had ever made.

Fisher had since learned that Ms. Margaret's real name was Mehadevi Nida Matroka Yamuna, but she preferred Ms. Margaret. While not an official channel for FBI account inquiries, she had access to considerably more information than the liaisons typically did, and was several times more helpful. Then again, Fisher didn't think it was relevant to mention that he was calling on official Bureau business.

"I need to speak to Ms. Margaret," he said after entering the credit card account number and wading through the phone menu to reach a live person. The system, of course, was set up to deny direct access to the supervisor, or indeed any human at all. Fisher knew from experience, however, that once put on hold by an operator—or anyone—he could get to Ms. Margaret's extension by pressing a succession of keys in rapid order, fooling the computers into thinking it was an internal transfer.

"This is Mr. Raymond," said the man who answered the call. "Perhaps I can help you."

"Ms. Margaret is who I want to talk to," said Fisher. "If you'd just put me on hold—"

"I am an accredited account representative, Mr. Hhou," said the man, looking at the account information on his computer. "I am specially trained to assist you. By the way, would you mind taking a brief survey at the end of this phone call?"

"I'd love to take a survey," said Fisher. "As soon as I'm done talking to Ms. Margaret."

"I notice that you're calling from a private number today, Mr. Hhou," said Mr. Raymond. "Is your home phone not available?"

"What do you have for my home phone?" asked Fisher.

"914-456-0541. Is that not correct?"

"As a matter of fact, it is," said Fisher. The number matched the number that had been used on the car registration; unfortunately it had come back as non-assigned—a ghost number, undoubtedly chosen because it was a dead end.

"And you are calling from your business?" asked Mr. Raymond.

"I'm calling from my cell phone."

"Ah, I see. The one you rented from T-Mobile yesterday?"

Pay dirt, thought Fisher.

"Wait a second," he said. "I don't remember making that purchase. What store was that?"

Mr. Raymond sucked air for a few seconds.

"I am going to transfer you to the fraud department," he answered. "Please hold the line, Mr. Hhou."

The members of the "fraud department" were actually other phone reps with exactly the same powers; the transfer was designed solely to impress on the caller how seriously the company took fraud. Fisher knew this and didn't care—as soon as he was on hold, he punched in Ms. Margaret's extension.

She picked up on the first ring.

"Ms. Margaret," she said in her singsong voice. "Please tell me your card number."

"My friend Andy Fisher told me to talk to you," said Fisher. "My name is Hhou. Someone used my card to buy a phone yesterday, and I'm pissed."

"Mr. Hhou, Mr. Hhou, please calm down. We should not use profanity over the phone. We should be polite at all times."

"I'll try."

"Am I pronouncing your name correctly? Is it Hou?"

"It's Hhou," said Fisher. "Almost as if you were stuttering."

"I see. My bad. I apologize."

Her command of American slang had improved considerably over the past few months. Fisher stood to gain much of the credit. His explanation of "pissed" had been a true bonding moment.

"Andy Fisher told me you could help straighten it out," said Fisher, playing Hhou.

"Mr. Fisher? Ah yes, Mr. Andrew Fisher. He is a very good account."

Not an exaggeration: His late charges probably paid her salary.

"Can you help me?" asked Fisher. "There is a case of fraud—"

"Are you sure that you did not buy this phone, Mr. Hhou?"

"I'm positive. What store was it?"

"Big Buy."

"Where? In Jersey City?"

"No, the one in Paramus."

"Can you fax me a copy of the bill?"

"That will take twenty-four hours."

Fisher gave her Bernie's fax number out in San Diego.

"Are there other recent charges?" Fisher asked.

"There is a car rental. And a restaurant. Would you like those faxed when they come through the system as well?"

"Please. Those are all the charges?"

"Well, they are all that are in our system. Sometimes it may take a day, two days to come through. And with some customers, small customers, it could take a week or more. It depends very much on their processor."

"Right. I understand."

"Very well, Mr. Hhou, I am sorry this happened to you. I'm going to place a hold on your account—"

"No, no, that's okay," said Fisher.

"But Mr. Hhou, if someone is using your card—"

"You know what—I just remembered. I bought that phone."

"Mr. Hhou?"

"It was me. It might have been me. Fax me the receipt so I can tell."

"You know, Mr. Hhou, you remind me of your friend Mr. Fisher very much," said Ms. Margaret. "He too is always forgetting the charges he makes and asking to see copies."

"I think it's something in the water over here," said Fisher.

The manager at Big Buy was one of those rare Americans actually impressed by FBI credentials, and gave Fisher the list of phone numbers that had been activated that week. Fisher hoped Hhou—or whoever was using the name—had purchased several phones under different aliases around the same time; each number would be checked out.

The store closed while Fisher was getting the information, and it was dark and very cold by the time he came out. He hadn't had either a cigarette or coffee in the past half hour—an incredibly long time without artificial stimulation. He tucked a Camel into the corner of his mouth and lit it, luxuriating in the sheer thrill of raw nicotine, tar, and other addictive substances as they careened into his system.

As he walked toward his car, a glint of neon caught his eye. A diner sat across the highway, shoehorned between two overpasses and the entrance to a mall. It was about a hundred yards away as the bird flew, but in the car it might well be unreachable—it was on the other side of the highway, a place in New Jersey that could only be reached through a series of misdirection plays that made English roundabouts seem straightforward.

Aware of this, Fisher ignored the signs, found a spot where the highway median was reduced to a raised curb, and shot across through traffic. Landing safely on the other side, he veered across the highway ramp and found a spot to park in front of the restaurant.

From the outside, the Best Joisey Diner looked to be about the size of a photo booth. Once inside, however, the diner appeared impressively massive, with mirrored walls and ceilings projecting the customer into a veritable Versailles of eating pleasure. The Best Joisey Diner had recently undergone renovations intended to lift it to the cutting edge of dinerdom. An electronic eye opened the door as a customer walked up the outside stairs. The pies in the front case didn't revolve, they shuffled, sliding on shelves in a flickering pattern that would have made a blackjack dealer dizzy. The booths were made of recycled plastic composite whose luster was enhanced by LCDs embedded in the framework. If you stood near the cash register and squinted just right, you saw that the blinking lights spelled out BEST JOISEY DINER.

Actually the lights in the "I" were out, but Fisher got the idea.

"Ready, hon?" asked the hostess. The diner itself might be cutting edge, but she was purely retro, with frosted yellow hair and makeup caked thicker than the meringue on the lemon pie.

Fisher followed her to a booth about halfway down the main aisle. The mirrors on the walls and ceiling made it impossible to judge distance or location; if he went to the restroom, he'd have to leave a trail of dill pickle slices. Fortunately, there were plenty in the complimentary relish dish, which also came stocked with white onions and capers.

"Coffee?" said Fisher.

"It's on its way, hon," said the waitress. Immediately behind her appeared a woman of indeterminate age, weight, and height in a gray checkered waitress uniform, cup in one hand, steaming metal carafe in the other.

"Ya wanna menu?" she asked.

"Sure."

"Press da button on the side of the booth," she told Fisher.

Fisher looked to his right. All he saw was a bottle of ketchup, a stack of sugars, and salt and pepper shakers.

"Ya gotta press da button, hon," said the waitress, reaching across to show him.

The button was virtual, created by a beam of light visible only from certain angles or when it came in contact with a hand. As soon as the waitress's fingers crossed it, a menu appeared in front of Fisher. This too was virtual—a full-color, 3-D hologram menu arranged to look like an authentic diner menu. On the cover was a virtual banana split (785 calories, declared the parenthesis below it). The different sections were tabbed on the side; there was also an alphabetical cross-section at the bottom and a search page.

"Too early to get scrambled eggs and hash browns?" asked Fisher without flipping through the menu.

"Hon, this is a diner. You can *always* get breakfast. Uderwise, what's the point?"

"Exactly," said Fisher.

Fisher took a sip of the coffee. It was hot enough to burn his upper lip, and tasted as if it had reheated at least twice over the past hour.

Heaven.

The eggs and potatoes proved no less fulfilling:

Rubbery and burnt, respectively, they restored his faith in the future of American cuisine.

Refreshed, he called Bernie Stendanopolis in San Jose and gave him a brief rundown of the day's events, pausing for Bernie's occasional "wow" and "holy shit." It occurred to Fisher that Bernie was in many ways a perfect supervisor: He did paperwork and could brown-nose with the best of them.

Getting results in an investigation was another story.

"There is nothing that links any of these murders, except for the obvious," said Stendanopolis when Fisher asked what was going on in California.

"The obvious being what?"

"They're dead."

Terhoussen was pushing ahead for the launch of the next rocket, scheduled for next week. The push had to do with a federal grant, Stendanopolis said. Without the grant, Icarus was in big trouble.

"Interesting," said Fisher.

"Say, Samie called about that decryption thing. She was wondering if maybe you could get someone at the rocket company to give them some background on the instruction set."

"Not a problem," said Fisher, who wanted an excuse to call Sandra anyway. "Anything new on that murder in the parking garage?"

"Negatory. Gotta be a random coincidence."

Hearing Stendanopolis say it, Fisher realized it couldn't possibly be.

"Gotta go," he told Stendanopolis. "Gotta make a phone call."

8

NEW MEXICO

Sandra Chester had just drawn a bath when she heard her cell phone ring in the other room. She debated blowing it off, but in the end was too conscientious. She tugged her bathrobe closed and went out into the bedroom, grabbing it just before it rolled over to voice mail.

"Yes?"

"This is Andy. I hear you saw a murder."

"Andy!" Sandra felt her voice catch in her throat. "I didn't see it. I came into the parking garage. It must have happened a while before."

Fisher was quiet for a moment. Sandra worried that she sounded too excited, too scared.

"It was nothing," she told him. "Really."

"I was going to call you about it. I was worried about you."

"I'm fine. Of course I'm fine."

"You know, I can get some people to watch you."

"Andy, please." Suddenly she felt defensive, and needed to change the subject. "Is anything else up? Did you get that telemetry decrypted?"

"Apparently they want some more help from your people figuring out the data. Can you do that?"

"I have a couple of people who could."

"Good. There's something interesting about it. There are two different encryption sets. The technical people think that means there's two different streams of information, as if one was encased in the other."

"What do you mean?"

"We were wondering if one of them is an envelope, like you deliver a message to a subsystem."

"You're describing a virus."

"Maybe."

"Have you talked to Icarus about it?"

"I'd rather they didn't know we're looking at this yet," said Fisher. "Assuming you didn't tell them."

"I didn't." Sandra pulled her robe closed at the top. "So you think this wasn't an accident."

"I don't know enough to think yet," said Fisher. "All I'm doing right now is drinking coffee and trying not to piss into the wind."

"Do you always have to make a bad joke?"

"Come on. Some of them aren't bad."

She sighed. "Andy, they're terrible."

"They're making you smile."

"I'm frowning," she said. But then she laughed.

"I hear you're going to launch another rocket."

"That's right."

"You sound like you don't want to."

"I do want to. Once I'm sure what happened to the last one."

"The company must have a theory."

"Not a good one."

"But I'll bet you do."

"It doesn't matter what I think. It's not my company. We're obligated."

"Yeah, but what's your theory?" Fisher asked.

"We ran a simulation. If the heat spiked in one of the feeder tubes on the other side of the assembly, it would increase pressure quickly. The pressure increase would stop valve DX-3, which in turn would cause a backup in the system and the explosion exactly where it occurred."

"But the problem with that is you don't know what caused the heat, right?"

"Very good."

"It's also not shown in the instruments."

"Excellent."

"So how do you know it happened?" he asked.

"Because it's the only real explanation. A problem with the fuel or the tubing—those are the official reasons at this point—would have been caught."

"All right. So where could the heat have come from?"

"I don't know. In theory, nowhere. I can't explain it."

Fisher was silent for a moment. Sandra guessed what he was thinking—no possible heat source, instrument readings all completely at spec.

Bad theory.

"Tell me about that murder in the parking garage last night," said Fisher. "What was the deal on that?"

He was like a boxer, always circling back. Sandra took a deep breath, then started to recount what had happened.

————

Em saw the light on in the back as he drove past. That was the master bath. Maybe she was turning in early.

So be it. After last night's fiasco, he wasn't about to take any chances. The units were too close together to risk killing her here. And besides, he'd killed the other woman in her house. He didn't want to establish a pattern, even if it was several states away.

Some assignments were star-crossed.

Years before, in Italy, he had had to take care of a priest. That was extremely difficult. Italy wasn't like America. It was harder to fit in. And the subject—the priest—had an erratic schedule, obligations in several different cities outside of the Vatican, where he worked as a secretary to an important commission. He was always moving around, making his habits hard to predict.

And then there was the fact that he was a priest. Psychologically, that made things more difficult.

A car backed out of the driveway ahead, just barely missing him. The driver, looking belatedly in his mirror, cranked his wheel and then hit the gas, as if speeding away would somehow make things right.

Em closed his eyes, opened them, then put the car in gear. His hands were shaking so bad that he thought he might have to stop. He could feel his chest heaving.

Relax, he told himself. Relax.

His stomach was still upside down when he reached his hotel room. He resisted the mini-fridge, and lay down on the bed, practically vibrating with nervous energy.

He remembered a time in Afghanistan, toward the end, when everyone in the unit wanted to be done with it, wanted to be home. He'd gone days with this same feeling in his stomach, this same pit, turning over and over.

Em tried to replace the memory with a better one, one from earlier in the war. He remembered the voice recorder, and got up to record.

Except that he'd forgotten to get a battery.

He lay back down, but sleep wouldn't come. Finally, Em put on his clothes and went downstairs.

The elevator opened across from the bar. A large-screen television was playing a news program. Em stopped short.

They were U.S. Marines. In Afghanistan.

He walked over slowly, pulled out a stool, and began to watch.

"Drink?" asked the bartender.

Surprised, Em jerked around.

"Beer?" asked the bartender. She was a woman, in her twenties, not beautiful but not ugly, either.

"No. Nothing."

"Nothing?"

"Um—some seltzer?"

"Sure."

The bartender filled a glass.

"You wouldn't happen to know where I can get a battery for this, would you?" asked Em, holding the voice recorder out.

"Takes triple-A? Check that vending machine out in the corner of the lobby," said the bartender. "Has razors, toothbrushes. I think there's batteries."

"Thanks."

"You in Afghanistan?" asked the bartender.

"Why?"

"The way you were looking at the screen."

"Long time ago," said Em, getting up.

9

PARAMUS, NEW JERSEY

Fisher spent the night in a Holiday Inn, trying to ignore the groans of the ice machine across the hall, and the squeals of the couple next door. He woke up around six, went down and harangued the kitchen for some coffee. Back upstairs, he checked out the news.

The terror attack on the tanker was headline number one. The Coast Guard got the lion's share of credit—not surprising, since the SEALs had followed standard operating procedure and officially vanished from the story. The FBI wasn't mentioned.

As far as Fisher was concerned, that was perfect. He guessed, however, that Festoon wasn't going to be happy about that—a fact that probably accounted for at least half of the two dozen voice and text messages his boss had sent him overnight. All were variations on a theme:

Call me.
Call me!
CALL ME!!!!!
Call me now!
And so on.

The Wall Street Journal report noted that this was the second attack involving energy in the past week, but that was as far as the reporter went with the connection. *The New York Times* had a story talking about the potentially devastating effects the explosion *could* have had, mentioning the effect on gasoline prices. The story estimated that it could have doubled them inside a week. It didn't explain the math, but it did get the gist of the situation:

> *Supply of crude oil isn't just the problem. The availability of refineries has become the limiting factor. Refineries are expensive to run, and many are using older technology . . .*

The problems were well known, declared the writer, exacerbated by management philosophies that emphasized short-term corporate profit over long-term societal benefits.

"But that's the purpose of capitalism," he added, verbally throwing up his hands.

Fisher couldn't figure out if the story was supposed to be a closet endorsement of socialism, or a subtle satire of the way economics theory was taught, at least to journalists.

What annoyed him was the fact that the media attention inadvertently highlighted the refinery—and by extension, the others in the area—as a ripe target for terrorists. Crazoid nuts hearing about the attack wouldn't focus on the fact that it had been thwarted; they'd think they could do it better.

They could easily be right.

None of the stories mentioned the early phone call to the radio station. So far, at least, the radio station had kept quiet about it; Fisher hoped they'd maintain radio silence a bit longer.

Fisher was just about to go downstairs for some more coffee when his BlackBerry rang. He recognized from the preface that the number belonged to the FBI's New York City office, and picked it up.

"Fisher."

"You're Fisher, right?" said the agent, who didn't bother to identify himself.

"That's what I just said."

"The cell phone that was used to call the radio station. We've run down the other numbers it was used to call."

"And?"

"Bob Rolison wants to meet with you right away. He's en route from his house right now. Can you find a place called Jerome's Diner on West Forty-second Street, New York?"

"I know it very well. Tell him first one there gets to pinch the waitress."

Jerome's Diner was more a coffee shop than a real diner, though it did feature Formica counters, grease-stained booths, and fruit flies the size of humming-birds. Fisher got there first and secured a booth along the side that let him look out on Forty-second Street.

Rolison supervised surveillance operations in the city. His unit kept tabs on various and sundry foreign agents, suspected agents, wannabe agents, and non-agents operating in the New York area. The UN made this a big job; there were probably as many spies per square inch in the city as there had been in Berlin during the Cold War.

Rolison also happened to be an extremely efficient agent, one of the few supervisors Fisher got along with. This was largely because a) he had never actually worked for him, and b) Rolison knew a good Rueben when he saw one.

"Causing trouble again, huh?" said Rolison, sliding into the booth. He flashed a grin, wrinkling his freckled and unshaved face.

"You owe me a coffee," said Fisher.

"How's that?"

"I bought one a few days back for one of your people at the Hyatt."

"What was he doing?"

"Holding up a wall."

"You made him?"

"I just about tripped over him."

"Oatmeal?" the waitress asked, coming over with coffee.

"That's right," said Rolison. He ate here often.

"Oatmeal?" asked Fisher.

"Good for my stomach. Never know what the rest of the day will bring."

Not a good sign, Fisher thought, though he wasn't sure if it was a comment on the restaurant or Rolison's job.

"I have a transcript for you." Rolison reached into his back pocket and took out a piece of paper. The entire conversation consisted of a single, short sentence:

Things did not go well.

Even more interesting was the information at the bottom stating where and when the call had been made—from Battery Park, just about the time Fisher and Tallahassee were chasing down the men on the ferry.

"Mean anything special?" Rolison asked.

"Only the obvious," said Fisher. "Who got the call?"

"Guy by the name of Chou Lai Wan. He has an office around the corner."

"At the Chinese consulate?"

"You catch on, Fisher. You may have a future in this business. You know who he is?"

Fisher simply shook his head, taking the high road and avoiding the obvious "Who Lai?" joke. Kathy had said he joked too much.

Sandra. Sandra said that.

"You should see his car. Very nice Mercedes. Twelve cylinder," said Rolison. "Supposedly he's a trade official, working deals for the government."

He pressed his lips together in a goofy grin and fluttered his eyes. Then he grew serious again.

"He's a principal for a number of Chinese companies. Hard to separate his government post from his private role. That's always the way with the Chinese. We've been watching him off and on over the past eighteen months. He does industrial espionage and has some deals running on the side. But we have bupkus on him. Nothing to kick him out with."

"Let me guess: He has diplomatic status, so of course you can't touch him."

"You get smarter every time I see you, Fish. You know who your caller is? The person who made that call about things not going well?"

Fisher shook his head. "Used some sort of fake name."

"Ah." Rolison dug into his pocket for another piece of paper. This one was a laser-printed surveillance photo. "Thomas Zhou. He works for Wan."

"The name on the credit card account is Hhou," said Fisher.

"Nah. It's Zhou. The address on that credit card is the same."

"He's using his own address, but not his right name?"

"If you look, it's just the building number, not the apartment. The wrong name would let him skip out of the bill if he had to."

"I thought the Chinese always paid their bills," said Fisher.

"Everybody needs an escape hatch," said Rolison.

"I don't like that he used his own credit card," said Fisher. "Even if it is a different name. He's gotta have dozens."

"You'd be surprised. So far, we can't find another card, under this name or his own. So tell me about the call." Rolison pointed at the message.

"It came from someone who knew about the attack on the tanker yesterday," said Fisher, folding up the paper. "He tipped off the radio station, but he called a little early. And from too far away."

"Why?"

"It was a setup to make money."

"The Chinese aren't exactly broke."

"That's a point." But that didn't mean it wasn't him, thought Fisher. On the contrary—Wan might have something going on the side. Or maybe Zhou did.

"So this call to Wan is telling his boss that things fell apart," said Fisher. "Except that your sheet says it was made from Battery Park. Staten Island's between him and the tanker."

"Maybe they had someone on board, or on the shore, and he's getting radio signals, relaying them."

"Yeah, maybe."

Rolison laughed. "You look disappointed."

"I'm wondering if I should trust the banana pancakes."

The fact that Wan was a high-ranking diplomat greatly complicated matters. Diplomats were protected by international law. While questioning one was not impossible, it would provoke extraordinary cover-your-butt action from all quarters of the Bureau.

Zhou was much farther down the food chain, but his boss was sure to raise a holy tornado if he was questioned about the attack.

"You want to see where this guy works?" asked Rolison.

"Thought you'd never ask."

Rolison threw a twenty on the table to cover the tab.

"You know, you owe me fifty bucks from that poker game two years ago," said Fisher as they walked out.

"I paid that off the next day."

"No, you tried to give me those Knicks tickets."

"I *did* give them to you."

"Even if I liked the Knicks, I couldn't have used them," said Fisher. "I was going to Italy."

"That's not my problem."

The Chinese mission was a large complex of office buildings fronting on Twelfth Avenue not far from the waterfront on the Hudson River. Like all foreign missions, it was under twenty-four-hour surveillance by the FBI, which used a variety of methods to keep tabs on the place. The Chinese, of course, knew they were being watched, and on occasion played a cat-and-mouse game with the agents, using different methods to lose trail teams or disguise people coming in and out of the building. For the most part, however, they came and went openly, accepting the Bureau's nosiness as part of the cost of doing business. It was probably a tenth of what American diplomats were subjected to in Beijing.

"Where's Wan now, do you know?" Fisher asked Rolison, as they eyed the corner of the building from two blocks away.

"Probably still sleeping. He doesn't usually get in until ten. Rents a house on Long Island's gold coast."

"What about Zhou?"

"Not sure."

Zhou wasn't important enough to keep under constant surveillance, but Rolison took Fisher over to see his apartment on the Upper East Side near Yorkville. Though the area was one of the finest in Manhattan, the apartment building itself was nothing special; there wasn't even a doorman.

"How many hoops would I have to jump through to get Zhou followed?" Fisher asked.

"That's not a problem," said Rolison. "I can get somebody on him right now."

"Twenty-four/seven?"

"Sure."

Fisher stared at the building. It looked as if it had been shoehorned in between its two larger and more ornate neighbors, though the truth was just the opposite—it had preceded both.

"You're thinking of talking to Zhou?" said Rolison.

"What I really want to do is sweat him," said Fisher. "And his boss."

"You'll never make any of these guys nervous," said Rolison. "And you're not going to get anywhere near Wan without a personal okay from the secretary of state."

"He's that high up?"

"With what we owe the Chinese, their doorman's that important. He's a diplomat. You have to kiss ten million rings. It's easier getting in to interview the pope."

Among the things bothering Fisher about Zhou/ Hhou was that it meant Festoon was right: A foreign government, or at least its agents, was involved in a massive conspiracy to disrupt the American economy through energy price manipulation.

Fisher had always operated under the premise that anything Festoon said or thought should be regarded as the inverse of truth, or truth to the $^{-1}$ power. If Festoon was right—or even *kind* of right—the universe might require an entire rethink. It would be like discovering that zero wasn't really zero, or that Camels were really Marlboros with their filters hacked off. Life would never be the same.

Faced with this radical paradigm shift, Fisher did what men of Fisher's ilk always did—he went to have a smoke.

In this case, the smoke was at the secure detention center at Fort Dix, New Jersey, where Tarken and Gabe, the two ferryboat hijackers, had been taken.

"You can't talk to me without my lawyer," said Gabe when he was brought into the interview room.

"And I ain't gonna say anything with him here besides."

"If you ain't going to say anything, it doesn't make much difference, does it?" Fisher took his cigarette box out of his pocket and shook one out. He stuck it in his mouth, then pretended to realize that Gabe might want one, too. He held up the box.

"Is that supposed to be a good-cop thing?" asked Gabe derisively.

"How's that?"

"You try to get on my good side?"

"You don't have a good side."

"Damn straight."

"But you do smoke."

"In the joint."

"The joint?" Fisher tapped out a cigarette. Gabe was chained, his hands held close to his waist. Fisher held it up to Gabe's mouth, then lit it for him. "That's an old expression."

"Yeah, I'm older than I look," said Gabe, talking through the side of his mouth.

"How old's that?"

"Twenty-one. Take these handcuffs off."

"Let's not get crazy," said Fisher.

Gabe scrunched down and managed to take the cigarette in his fingers. "What is it you want?" he asked.

"Description of the guy who hired you."

He smirked. "Wait for my lawyer."

"That's all right," said Fisher. "I already know who it was."

Gabe smirked again. It was a *you are one dumb-shit cop, you know it?* look.

"Was it the black guy, or the Asian guy?" Fisher asked.

Gabe squinted, reached down, and took the cigarette in his fingers. "Wait for my lawyer."

The squint was all Fisher wanted.

"You can take him," he told the guards.

"I haven't finished my smoke," said Gabe. "I have a right."

"Last time I checked, that one wasn't in the Constitution," replied Fisher, grabbing it and stubbing it out.

Tarken was visibly nervous as he was led into the room. He didn't smoke, so Fisher cut straight to the point.

"The guy who hired you. Was he Asian?"

"Asian?"

"Japanese? Chinese? Korean?"

Tarken shrugged.

"Did he look like me?" Fisher asked.

Tarken shrugged again.

"I could show you some pictures," offered Fisher.

"Wasn't like a Jap or a Chink," said Tarken.

Fisher showed him a half-dozen photos, including Zhou's.

"None of them," said Tarken. "He was just, you know, American."

"White?"

Tarken nodded.

"Talk about who he worked for?"

"We didn't get into that," said Tarken.

"Thanks," said Fisher, getting up.

Diminished capacity or not, Tarken seemed sufficiently prejudiced to know that it wasn't Wan who had hired him.

Or Hhou, for that matter. Or Zhou. If Zhou was Hhou.

While Fisher was talking to Tarken, the credit card company located and made a copy of the Hhou account charges. He found them as a PDF file in his e-mail. Fisher was hoping to find another telephone—or two, or three—charged to the card, but there wasn't anything like that. The card hadn't been used in the past few days, and there was only one charge he didn't know about—the purchase of 10.2 gallons of regular gas at a station on Staten Island at 9:53 the night before the ferry incident.

Fisher found the station off Victory Boulevard, wedged into a triangle between a bank and a strip mall. He persuaded the clerk to call the owner and get permission to check back on the surveillance tape, only to find that the tape was recorded over every twenty-four hours.

He had better luck, but more red tape, at the bank, where the ATM kept digital images for forty-five days. Once the necessary bank vice presidents had signed off, security got Fisher images ten minutes before and ten minutes after the charge card had been used. A dozen people had driven into the gas station during that time; the camera caught some but not all of their faces. Most were in the shadows, and those who weren't looked nothing like Zhou. As for their cars, there was too little available for a positive identification.

Fisher had no evidence linking Zhou to the terrorist incident; the name might even make it hard to definitively link him to the credit card used at the gas station. But there might be more evidence linked to another card—he told Rolison to ask the liaison to use pattern linking to see if there might be another account tied to him.

The technique looked at one set of charges, found patterns in them, and then looked for parallel patterns in another card. For example, say one card showed that Zhou always ate at a certain restaurant most Tuesday and Thursday nights, and that the bill always came within a certain range. Records could be scanned to find cards that had similar patterns, fitting into the other charges like two hands clasping.

Fisher asked Rolison to work on that, figuring that the liaison would be more likely to take a complicated request from him. In the meantime, he concentrated on tying Zhou personally to the card.

No one at the restaurants admitted to remembering him; Fisher suspected that they were so nervous about illegal immigrant investigations that they would deny knowing their own grandmothers if it kept them out of trouble. The only restaurant not in Chinatown was Michael Jordan's in Grand Central Terminal. Not exactly a place where a person was likely to be remembered, especially since there was only one charge made there since the card account was opened.

Rolison suggested checking on the other people who had bought gas at the station and had dinner in the restaurants—perhaps they had seen Zhou and could describe him or his car. Fisher got another idea, and called his friend Pinkie O'Rourke.

"You know that dinner of fried clams I owe you?" he told O'Rourke.

"God help me," said O'Rourke, who was a lieutenant in the New York City MTA police department. "Andy Fisher is going to pay off a bet?"

"No, I was hoping to make it two dinners."

An hour later, Fisher squeezed in behind O'Rourke and a pair of video technicians, watching as the techies dialed and tapped their way through the high-tech surveillance system that watched Grand Central Terminal. Six photos of the gas station customers, printed on eight-by-eleven paper and so grainy they looked as if they'd been taken through a screen door, were spread out on the control console for reference, along with a picture of Zhou from Rolison's surveillance teams.

The entrance to the restaurant, one of the balconies, was in full view of one of the cameras. They started at 12:35, when the bill had been processed.

Ten minutes later, Zhou walked out of the restaurant.

Which wasn't *exactly* what Fisher wanted. For by the time he had arrived at the video surveillance booth, he had decided that Zhou had given some thug his credit card to use.

But there he was. So at least there was definitive, or semidefinitive, proof that he and Hhou were the same person.

"I'm going to need a copy of that," Fisher told O'Rourke. "Any chance I can find out who he was with?"

"Maybe they came in together," said one of the techies.

They switched cameras and, working backward,

found him coming in. He was alone. Another camera showed a few people waiting at the bar; he walked right past.

"Let me see him leaving again," said Fisher.

He watched Zhou walk out—confident, purposeful. He knew where he was going.

Fisher stared at the screen, then looked over at the door, the only surface of the room besides the ceiling and floor not covered with a display or control panel.

Why would Zhou meet someone here?

There was scant evidence to draw any conclusions, but Fisher drew them anyway.

It was a meeting, business obviously, since it was in the middle of the day. Someone else had picked the location, someone who either worked nearby or was planning to use the train. Or maybe Zhou was planning to use the train.

"Fisher, you with us?" asked O'Rourke.

Fisher turned back to the screen. The video was still running. He stared at the screen, eyes unfocused. Then a set of neurons in an obscure, uncharted part of his brain fired in rapid succession.

"Stop that a second," he said. "Back up a couple of frames."

The techie moved the image back. The camera had a perfect head-on shot of a man he'd seen before, though he couldn't place him precisely.

"Search that image, can you?" Fisher said.

The computer found him sitting at a table with another man, just out of view. They ran the clip forward from that point.

"You think that's Zhou he's sitting with?" asked O'Rourke.

Fisher didn't think anything; he was trying to coax

his memory into connecting the man's face with a name. Normally this required either copious amounts of tar, nicotine, and cancer-causing chemicals, or obscene levels of caffeine in the bloodstream. Without access to these higher forms of inspiration, Fisher struggled.

"The time is in the right ballpark," said one of the techies.

"Could be him," said O'Rourke.

"How far does this thing go back?" asked Fisher.

"We keep seven days, more or—"

"I know who he is," said Fisher, snapping his fingers. "He told me to put my cigarette out."

"Well that narrows it down to half the world," said O'Rourke.

10

YONKERS

The man Fisher had seen in the video was at that moment directing a series of trades from his new facility on the waterfront in Yonkers, anxiously rubbing his chin as the traders worked the computers. Oil had dropped faster than they had anticipated, and they were trying desperately to adjust their strategies. The attack yesterday morning had apparently wreaked havoc with some other traders' strategies, provoking a precipitous fall today. There was nothing to do except ride it out; the numbers showed that they were still two hundred thousand or so ahead, though it had taken a superhuman effort to do so.

Money was nice—very nice—but not the goal of the operation. The real upshot was that it distracted Loup from other things, such as checking on Terhoussen and canvassing his sources to find out whether Wan had been fingered for the attacks yet.

Everything depended on the feds being smart enough to pick up the bread crumbs. Freeman had claimed they were. A successful operation, he said, depended on being at least somewhat subtle. But

Loup wasn't sure. In his opinion, it was difficult to underestimate the intelligence of government bureaucrats.

He rubbed his chin, trying to settle down. He couldn't think about it. He had to focus on the trades.

"Oil keeps pushing up," said Dennis.

"Mmmmm."

"Market's going to close soon and we're going to have to roll up some of these positions. You sure we want to be short?"

"Yes, damn it."

"Short everything?"

Once the arrests were made, the market would plunge dramatically.

Of course, if there were no arrests . . .

But then he'd have much bigger problems.

"Just hold to the course," Loup told his assistant. "Things will work out. Tomorrow if not today."

"We're gambling here, boss," said Dennis.

"Just hold to the course."

11

NEW YORK

Fisher remembered Jonathon Loup's name even before he looked at the online program for the alternative energy conference. It was an interesting coincidence—or not.

Even more interesting, Loup's face was found in the video banks again. Not much longer after leaving the restaurant, he'd headed down a long platform and boarded a train.

Was it just a coincidence that he'd kept his head down when he neared the first video camera on the platform? That camera was actually a decoy; the area was covered by two other cameras, hidden in the girders above.

Loup, enough of a player in the energy business that he had a private plane, taking a commuter train?

"Can we find out where that train goes?" Fisher asked O'Rourke.

"Poughkeepsie," said the techie running the video. "I take it every night."

But before Fisher could consider the actual permutations and possibilities—before he could even go outside the terminal for a cigarette break—Rolison called.

"How fast you think your man Zhou drives?" he asked.

"Got me," said Fisher.

"I'd say he flies," answered Rolison. "Either that or he was in two places at the same time the other night."

Not quite the same time—five minutes apart. But that was nowhere long enough for him to be both on Staten Island, where his card indicated he was buying gas, and in Chinatown, where another card claimed he had just paid for dinner. The other card was held in the name of Chue and addressed to a Manhattan post office box; it had been found by analyzing the Hhue charges and looking for similar patterns.

"This other card looks like a personal card," Rolison told Fisher. "A lot more stuff on it. No phones though, no cameras, electronics—nothing even close to incriminating. But those Chinese restaurants are the same. He eats four or five nights a week, roughly at the same time. Pretty predictable fellow."

"He wouldn't have an escort service on there by any chance, would he?" Fisher asked.

"Escort?"

"They usually go by names like Pink Pleasures or Escort Inc., that sort of thing."

"I know what to look for," said Rolison. "Believe me, if he used something like that, I'd know about it."

"Where is he?" Fisher asked.

"At the embassy with Wan. Should be heading home soon. Why?"

"Because I'm investigating a case of credit card

fraud," said Fisher. "And it looks like he's the victim."

Zhou took his time getting home, which didn't bother Fisher—exploring the neighborhood for a good place to get coffee, he found serviceable cannolis as well. He was just polishing one off when the surveillance team called over and said Zhou had gone up to his apartment.

Rolison was waiting near the entrance to Zhou's building.

"No way I'm letting you up there alone," Rolison told him.

"If you're not there, you don't know about it."

"If I'm not there, you're liable to throw him out the window."

"I haven't done that in over six months," said Fisher.

"Some would say you're due."

They were met in the lobby by the doorman. Standing about six four, he looked as if he had been imposing once but was now rapidly going to seed. His impressively wide shoulders sagged toward a basketball-shaped belly. His suit, though relatively new, was folded in all the wrong places.

He did, however, have an excellent get-outta-here voice.

"Can I help you?" he croaked as Fisher walked in.

Fisher unfolded his ID.

"Where ya goin'?" asked the doorman.

"We know the way," said Rolison.

"I gotta announce ya."

"So announce us," said Fisher, heading for the elevator.

"Listen, it's my job."

Fisher pressed the elevator button.

"Give me a break," said the doorman. "Come on."

The elevator took its time coming down.

"I can shut that elevator down, you know," warned the doorman.

"That would be pretty foolish," said Rolison.

The door opened. Fisher got in.

"Listen—" said the doorman.

"Zhou in 3C," said Fisher. "Wait until we're on the floor to announce us, all right? I don't want him to go to too much trouble before we get there."

Upstairs, the building smelled of pumpkin pie and cinnamon—clearly not Zhou's doing.

Fisher knocked on the door. There was no answer at first.

"I don't see why you told him we were coming," said Rolison.

"Relax," said Fisher. "He's the victim here, remember? Naturally, we'd want to be announced. No reason not to."

He knocked again. This time there was a shuffle inside, and a scraping sound as the metal door was lifted off the eye guard.

"Yes?" asked Zhou.

"Mr. Zhou, my name is Andy Fisher. I'm with the Federal Bureau of Investigation. I'm terribly sorry to bother you, but I wonder if I could talk to you."

"You're with the FBI?"

"That's right."

"I have nothing to say."

Fisher leaned toward the door. "I'm sorry?"

"I have nothing to say."

"I realize you're probably wondering why I'm here," said Fisher. He put his eye up against the little spyglass, trading eyeballs with Zhou. "It has to do with a credit card case. I think you may have been a victim of identity theft. As a matter of fact, I'm pretty sure you have been."

The locks on the door began clicking and clacking. Zhou, barefoot and dressed in just his work slacks and undershirt, opened the door about halfway.

"Credit card?" he said.

"It's kind of a sensitive issue," said Fisher. "Which is why we came to talk to you in person. It might be better if we talked inside your apartment."

Zhou pulled the door back and stepped out of the way.

The apartment was small, with a kitchen and a living room whose couch folded open as a bed. It was probably the smallest apartment in the building, thought Fisher as he walked into the living room. He sat on the small upholstered chair, leaving Rolison to share the couch with Zhou.

There was an open laptop running on the coffee table. Zhou closed the lid without turning it off. Fisher resisted—just barely—the urge to pick it up and see what he'd been up to.

"There is a problem?" asked Zhou.

"We found an account with your address on it, but we don't believe the card is yours," said Fisher. He reached into his jacket pocket and unfolded the Hhou bill. "Any of these charges mean anything to you?"

Zhou took the paper. Fisher watched his eyes. He was trying to figure out what was going on.

Would Zhou deny the account was his? The name was wrong; it would be easy to say that was a mistake. But that might come back to bite him—what if the FBI agents went to the building and discovered there was no Hhou there, or worse, found someone who recognized him?

Worse for Zhou was the fact that they were here at all—were they playing a trick? If so, he wanted as much information about it as possible. If not, he didn't want to arouse suspicion.

"I don't know about this," said Zhou, his Chinese accent suddenly very heavy. "My English reading is not best."

"I can read them for you," said Fisher, snatching the bill back. "Did you go to lunch at Michael Jordan's a few days ago?"

"Michael?"

"It's a restaurant at Grand Central Terminal," said Rolison.

"I go to lunch at many places. Perhaps I should call the embassy," said Zhou, getting up. "I work for the Chinese embassy."

"Good idea," said Fisher. He waited until Zhou picked up the phone. "I didn't want to get you in trouble with them if this was really your bill. You never know how people are going to react. I mean, we're in this business to protect people, not get them in trouble with their employers."

Zhou, now unsure what else might be on the bill, put the phone down. "It is probably too late to call."

"There's a ring of card counterfeiters," said Fisher. "What they do is glom onto existing accounts, legitimate accounts. I've been working on it for a while."

He spun a harrowing tale of an investigation that

would have made J. Edgar proud. A ring of bandits in Russia opened accounts using names similar to but not actually the same as people who had legitimate accounts. Charges were made, money withdrawn. Vodka and caviar were consumed.

Zhou's card might be an important break in the case, said Fisher. With Zhou's cooperation, they might be able to trace their way all the way back to thieves who had set the whole operation up. Of course, it would take a little bit of work, but Zhou and Fisher would do it together. They'd set a little trap over the course of a few weeks. Fisher would basically move in—

"Can I see the bill?" asked Zhou.

Fisher gave it back.

"There are not many charges here. Restaurants."

"Are you sure?" asked Rolison.

It was an ad lib, but it was well timed.

"You see, sometimes businesses list themselves as restaurants for billing purposes," explained Fisher. "That's what's going on here."

"These places are restaurants," said Zhou. "I know them all. I eat there."

"Just eat?" asked Fisher. He cocked his head slightly, in what he hoped was a knowing way.

Zhou nodded solemnly.

Fisher let his chest fall. "These are your charges? But the name there—it's Hhou. Not Zhou."

"Many people get that wrong," said Zhou.

"You wouldn't correct that?" asked Rolison.

Zhou shrugged. "I see it many months I open the account," he said. It was remarkable how his English could worsen as time went on.

"Are they your charges?" Fisher asked.

"I'll have to—I have to check. But what if they were?"

"If they are your charges, then they're your charges," said Fisher. He sounded as if he had just lost a sure bet. "I mean—you know, it's a dead end here. I'd be sorry for bothering you. But if they're not, which I hope they aren't your charges, then maybe you can help me break this. We could work together—"

"The problem tonight is that I'm very busy. I have a date." Zhou smiled weakly.

"Sure," said Rolison, rising.

"We'd really like to get this solved right away," said Fisher. "Can you tell me if the account belongs to you or not?"

Rolison, sensing Fisher's next move, gave him an apocalyptic death stare, trying to warn him off. But it was too late.

"Yes, as I think about it, I think these are my charges," said Zhou.

"You bought a telephone at Big Buy?" asked Fisher. "You're sure?"

Zhou looked at the statement. "It's not on this bill."

"My mistake," said Fisher. "It happened after that statement closed. It's on this one."

Fisher took the updated statement from his pocket. Zhou glanced at it.

"Yes, yes," said Zhou. "My own phone was acting up. I hope there's no law against it."

He smiled, thinking he was making a joke. Fisher pointed to the next charge on the account.

"And you were on Staten Island two nights ago?"

"Staten Island?"

"That gas charge."

Zhou was confused, but at this point all he wanted to do was be rid of the annoying agents.

"I'm sure these are all my charges," he said. "No need for alarms or investigation."

Fisher jumped up. Rolison buried his face in his hands.

"Thomas Zhou, you're under arrest for suspicion of a terrorist act against the United States of America," said Fisher. "You want to talk to the highest-priced lawyer you can find before you say anything else."

12

NEW YORK

"That was dirty pool, Fisher," said Rolison when they were alone in the elevator. Zhou had already been escorted downstairs—gently—by the surveillance team. Fisher had confiscated his laptop.

"I didn't know he was going to confess."

"He didn't confess. He just said the credit card was his."

"What was I supposed to do? Let him go? He just put himself at the scene of the crime."

"Oh bullshit. He put himself on Staten Island. You know how many people live on Staten Island? You know how many people drive through Staten Island? You have nothing. Not a thing."

Rolison continued, berating Fisher for making an arrest without the proper preparation in the case, let alone following Bureau protocol for dealing with a foreign diplomat. Fisher should have, could have, left the apartment, and if he thought there was enough evidence, should have presented to the U.S. attorney on the case, as well as called the New York supervisory agent, the State Department liaison . . .

"What about the guy on the corner who makes the cannolis?" asked Fisher. "Don't leave him out."

"Zhou is going to be out of custody and out of the country inside two hours," said Rolison.

"Only if you let him go."

"We have no evidence to hold him. You don't even have the phone. You don't have the card that was used to buy it. You can't link the phone to the crime. Even if you could, what did he do? He made a crank call. He predicted the future. He—"

"Fortune-telling without a license is a crime in New Jersey," said Fisher. "Worst case, I got him on that."

"Crap. His lawyers will meet us at the building for cryin' out loud. They're going to see the names are different and demand he be released."

"So release him," said Fisher.

"Release him?"

"He didn't do it," said Fisher. "And you got no reason to hold him."

Rolison was wrong about how long it would take the lawyers to get to the federal building: They didn't arrive until nearly a half hour after Zhou had been taken inside. But there was a bonus: Zhou's boss Wan was with them.

Fisher regretted missing him, but he had something more important to do—copy the contents of the laptop's hard drive before it had to be returned.

"You're lucky it only went into sleep mode," said the geek who examined it. He worked in the basement of a building across the street from the federal offices. Fisher thought the basement location might explain the fact that he wore extra-large eyeglasses and blinked a lot. His name was Morrison, but Fisher thought Mole more descriptive.

"It has a scrubber program that erases data files every time it turns off. It replaces their characters with zeroes, then turns them to ones, then back to zeroes. Impossible to decrypt."

Mole made a copy, even though he warned Fisher that there was nothing of use on the laptop. There were only basic programs: MS Word, Excel, Outlook. None had data files anywhere, and each history was clean. Zhou had been running a game—Age of Empires, Asian Edition—when Fisher arrived. He seemed to favor the Japanese.

"No e-mails, no instant messages, no nothing," said the geek. "It doesn't even look like he uses Outlook. Everything's set to default."

"Then why does he scrub the files when he turns it off?" Fisher asked.

"Maybe he loses Age of Empires a lot and doesn't want anyone to know."

A rainbow coalition of federal officials had turned up at the federal office building, alerted to the arrest not by Fisher or Rolison, but by the Chinese embassy. This was wrong on many levels, as Festoon put it in one of the several voice mail messages he left for Fisher—several of the calmer messages, that is.

Fisher, who knew pretty much what the reaction would be, didn't bother listening to his voice mail, or answering his text messages.

He did, however, make a call to a night editor he

knew at CNN, just in case the word of the arrest hadn't spread that far.

It hadn't, but by the time Fisher emerged with the laptop, television trucks and camera crews had surrounded the federal office building.

Under other circumstances, Fisher might have gone back upstairs to see who had come for Zhou. But he had other things to do. So he slipped the laptop to one of the guards, telling him to give it to Rolison, then took a leisurely stroll to the PATH train station. He got out in Jersey City and caught a cab to Jonathon Loup's building.

There was no one there. Which didn't surprise Fisher as much as the fact that the door was open, and the place completely empty.

13

SAN JOSE

They didn't understand what it took to succeed. It wasn't just a matter of the vision. The vision was critical, but it was nothing without the drive, without the desire.

People blocked you at every turn. Even the people who you brought on to help—in the end they became impediments. They didn't understand.

"The second satellite is on the launch vehicle and ready," the systems engineer was saying, "but given the problems we had, and some of our own testing requirements, another two or three weeks would be useful . . ."

T. Parker Terhoussen lowered his head to his hand, propping it on the table and rubbing his forehead as the engineer continued. He might understand the system, but he had no understanding of the need for progress—or the more immediate need for money. They were burning through it even faster than Terhoussen expected without Kathy Feder to control it.

There were so many impediments. So many barriers.

Terhoussen wasn't going to let any of them stand. He was going to succeed. The satellite was going to be launched. The system was going to be demonstrated. The electricity would flow.

He pounded the table and stood up abruptly. The others in the room, all engineers, were shocked by the outburst.

"We must do this, and we must do it on schedule," he said. "No more roadblocks. If there are problems, fix them. Or find a way around them. We are at an historic moment."

Then he turned abruptly and left the room.

14

NEW MEXICO

Sandra Chester's engineers spent three hours with the encryption expert without any real sign of progress.

That just made her even more positive that Icarus's transmission had something to do with the malfunction.

Or rather, sabotage. That was the right term for it.

The simulation her team had prepared proved that the best explanation for the rocket's failure was an unexplained increase in pressure. The instruments—conveniently destroyed—didn't show that increase because they had somehow been compromised. Whatever had come in that transmission had told the rocket to feed false data, probably by interfering with the code to clear old data and record.

She was sure she was right. It fit completely together.

But there was no hard evidence. And in truth, she couldn't even think of a motive—why would Icarus destroy its own satellite?

"Going for lunch, boss?"

Sandra looked up and saw Gene Ng in the doorway.

"I'm on my way," she said. "What about you?"

"Me, too. I'll walk over with you."

"Thanks," she said, getting up. "Anything new on that transmission?"

"Nah. Ms. Markoff said she had some other ideas and she'd call if she needed us."

"Maybe if we gave her the instruction set for the dummy launch?"

"Already did."

"Maybe my friend at NASA, Yogi—"

"She's already talked to a bunch of people there," said Ng. "I think it's the encryption that's the real problem."

"Gene, is there a way for the data from the last launch to accidentally be transmitted again?" she asked.

"What do you mean?"

"The readings are stored, right? They're always read into flash memory modules as they're transmitted."

"Sure. But we have a new set for each launch."

"What about the test?"

"Temporary storage clears before launch."

"What if it didn't?"

"Can't happen."

"Are you sure?"

Ng shrugged. "The ground instruments would pick up the problem. Test parameters are nothing like the flight numbers."

"What if nothing's transmitted?"

"We'd see error messages." Ng shook his head. "I don't think that's possible."

"Probably not." Sandra picked up her pocketbook. "Well, keep working on it."

"We do have the launch coming up. We're up against it, timewise."

"I know, I know. But this is really important," she told him, pulling the door closed behind her.

15

YONKERS

When news of Zhou's arrest made the radio, Loup was halfway to the temporary apartment Freeman had found for him in White Plains. He was driving himself; his driver had off, and the bodyguards were in the car behind him. He immediately pulled over, jacking the volume on the news to hear the report.

"Details are sketchy at this time," said the newscaster breathlessly. "But informed sources say that the FBI, with help from the NYPD, made an arrest in the case early this evening—"

Loup jumped against his seat belt as he heard a sharp rap on the car window. It was one of the bodyguards, wondering why he'd pulled over.

"I have to go back to the office," he told him. "Things are moving."

16

JERSEY CITY

Surprised by Loup's decision to vacate the Jersey City quarters, Fisher did what he always did when he was perplexed—he found the nearest diner and ordered a coffee.

"Keep them coming," he told the waitress, settling into the booth at the back of the Silver Arrow Rest Stop. The interior was decorated in a country and western theme, which struck Fisher as an interesting change from the normal diner formats. It was still definitely a diner: The tables smelled of freshly squirted ammonia, and the house specialties included five different varieties of hot open-face sandwiches. But everything had a western name—Last Roundup Roast Beef and Rye, for example. Fisher ordered a plate of Texas Tatters—home fries—to go with his coffee, and took out his phone.

Roberta Di Sarcina, the financial analyst helping him with the case, picked up on the first ring.

"You're calling me on my cell phone?" she said as soon as she answered.

"It's after five. You're not in the office."

"Damn straight. Why haven't you answered your phone all day?"

"Too busy saving the world," said Fisher.

"I know who's benefiting from these attacks," she said triumphantly. "I'm pretty sure he's the one behind it all."

"I already know who it is," said Fisher. "What I have to figure out is where he is."

"Jonathon Loup? You know it's Jonathon Loup?"

"Yeah."

"Damn."

"But you confirmed it," said Fisher, trying to cheer her up.

"He's pretty clever, I have to say. He didn't trade until just after the incident started. If it weren't for that—"

"What I need is his location."

"He's probably still pacing his trading floor," said Roberta. "They were trading like mad when I left the office a little while ago. Making a killing, too. He was short when everyone else was long, and now he's getting the rebound as well."

"Nah, he's not there. I just came back," said Fisher. "He cleaned out. It's empty."

"Empty?"

"Looks like they cleared out a couple of days ago. You sure he's still trading?"

"I'm telling you, he was trading like a fiend just a few hours ago. Or at least his people were."

"From where?"

"I don't know. You told me he had a regular trading operation, so I assume—"

"Is there a way to trace those orders?" asked Fisher. "Can we tap the phone line?"

"It'll take hours, if not days. First, we have to get a subpoena."

"Here's something better—how about we hold one of the orders up."

"What?"

"Send a message back that the trades are being stopped. Have him call the order in. Trace that call."

"I don't know if we can do that."

"Roberta, who was the guy in the SEC who wanted to date you a few months ago?"

"He was only after my 401k. Wait a second, you're not suggesting I use a personal connection to skirt the law."

"Suggesting? No . . ."

17

NEW MEXICO

Em woke to light streaming through the windows, the sun on a low angle. It was after three P.M.

The voice recorder was blinking at the side of the bed. He'd fallen asleep, talking about Kabul.

He showered and squared away his room, vaguely angry with himself. He left it clean as he always did, in perfect shape in case anything happened, then went to get something to eat. When he was done, he swung over to the parking lot where he had stashed his backup rental car, to make sure it was still clean. On the way, he passed one of the ravines he planned to use to dispose of the gun. It was deep, but far from perfect—a raging river or a furnace would have been much preferable. But life was rarely perfect.

The voice recorder was a problem. He didn't want to get rid of it, obviously, but carrying it with him could be a problem. If it was ever discovered by his employers he would be in serious trouble, no matter what was on it. If, God forbid, he happened to be arrested and the recorder was itemized among his things, that would be the end of any help. So he needed to stash it somewhere that he could get it later on.

The logical place to hide it was in the backup car. The only problem was that there was always a chance he wouldn't be able to return to the car; if that happened, another operative would be sent to do so, cleaning up loose ends a few days after the job was done. That meant he had to be clever about where he left it. They wouldn't look too hard, but if it was out on the seat . . .

The car was parked in the lot of a bowling alley. Rather than walking straight up to it—it was possible, he thought, that someone was watching—Em went inside the building. There was a small lounge, empty, to the left of the entry—the smell of booze was strong.

He took a breath, then walked into the lanes.

"Help ya?" asked a man, surprising Em as he walked in.

"The bar?" It was all he could think of.

"Closed," said the man.

"Oh." Em felt a surge of relief. He tried not to show it.

"Special on bowling right now," said the man. "Two bucks a game. You're wide open. How many games?"

"Just one," said Em.

"We sell them in twos."

"Two. Okay." Em dug into his pocket.

"Rent some shoes?" said the man, pointing. "We got lockers. You don't have to worry."

The man pointed to the wall.

"Put a quarter in, turn the key and take it out," said the man. "You don't have a quarter, I'll give you one.

Don't lose the key, though. Master's been gone ten years at least."

Em took his shoes off and stashed them inside—then left his recorder there as well.

Bowling helped him relax. His body had stopped aching for alcohol, and his mind was no longer thinking about Afghanistan. He bowled a 128 and a 167, with several strikes. Not bad for someone who knew almost nothing about the sport.

Leaving his recorder in the locker was a simple matter. The man was waiting on several other customers—a noon boomlet in business.

Outside, Em stashed the key in one of the magnetic boxes beneath the frame he used for his spares, pushing it farther back so it was harder than the others to find. Feeling much calmer than he had for the past few days, he walked over to his other car, confident he was going to get the job done today.

18

YONKERS

By the time Loup arrived at his temporary office, the night crew was rushing to keep up with the mad swing in the Asian markets. Dennis, who'd left to go to dinner and then his hotel room a short while before, had been called and was on his way. Loup decided to have the rest of the day people come in as well. Oil futures were plunging—they were going to make an even bigger killing than he had hoped.

Of course, the best part of it was that Wan and his operation were now under considerable scrutiny. He had no doubt that Wan as well as Zhou would be picked up and sent back to China.

Eventually, he'd have to pay the Chinese back, of course. And the way things were going tonight, he might have the money by the end of the week.

Loup rubbed his hands together, childlike, as he looked at the screens tabulating his option plays. He'd been down nearly three-quarters of a million dollars when he'd gone home. Now he was up almost a hundred million.

Forget about paying off the Chinese. At this rate, he'd be able to corner the market on Exxon.

"Shit," said one of the traders.

"What?" he asked, going over quickly.

"Trade was held up. Shit. What the hell?"

Red letters started appearing on all the screens. Loup suddenly felt every muscle in his body tense.

"The exchanges—are they shut?" he asked.

"No," said the trader next to him. "They need verification. There's some sort of problem with the lot number here. Probably a glitch."

Was it? Or was Wan somehow on to him?

"I'm supposed to call."

"Use my cell phone," Loup told him.

"Your cell phone?"

He started to reach into his pocket for the phone Freeman had given him that he said couldn't be traced. But Freeman had warned him to use it only to call him. And Freeman's warnings were not to be taken lightly.

"Use yours, and I'll pay you for the call," said Loup. "I don't want our number traced tonight."

"All right, boss."

Loup stepped back. Other trades were going through. This was just a glitch.

His pocket began to buzz. Freeman's phone.

Loup walked to the far end of the open warehouse room before taking it out and hitting the Call button.

"I heard the news already," Loup told him. "Good work."

"How much do you trust Dennis?" Freeman's sharp tone as well as the question took him by surprise.

"I—"

"Get out of there. *Now!*"

The rattle of a submachine gun outside told him the warning had come about sixty seconds too late.

19

NEAR THE HUDSON RIVER

By the time Roberta got back to him with the information about where Loup's operation was located, Fisher was standing on the dock in Luigi Giacomo's boatyard, waiting for a Coast Guard helicopter.

"They used a cell phone to clear the order," said Roberta. "I don't have the address but I do have GPS coordinates."

"Text them to me," said Fisher, spotting the helicopter zooming toward him. He slipped the phone back in his pocket, then waved as the chopper took a short circle overhead. The helo plopped down a few seconds later.

"You Fisher?" yelled the crew chief as he jumped in.

"Yeah."

"Where we going?"

"Hang on." Fisher took out his cell phone and retrieved the message Roberta had just sent. "Does this make sense?" he asked, handing it over. The crew chief handed it up to the copilot.

"Yeah, we can find that. Right on the water," said the copilot. "Hey, did you read the rest of this? It says you're supposed to call somebody named Looney Pants."

"That's my boss," said Fisher, taking the phone back. "How long before we get there?"

"Five minutes, unless you're in a hurry."

"Three would be better," said Fisher.

As soon as he heard the bullets, Jonathon Loup dropped to the floor, paralyzed by panic.

He knew he should get up. He knew he had to move. But he couldn't, not for several long seconds.

The bullets were coming from *his* people. There was plenty of time to get out. If he moved now.

Loup pushed himself to his feet. Someone grabbed the back of his shirt.

"This way," barked the man. He was one of the bodyguards. "Come on," he said, dragging Loup backward.

"All right, all right."

Loup tried to turn and walk with him, tried to appear calm for the others, but he stumbled and nearly fell. The other man held him tightly, pulling him along.

A door at the side of the main room led to the basement; another member of the security team was standing there, gun level.

There were more bursts of gunfire outside.

"Everybody stay on the floor!" yelled the bodyguard who was holding Loup. "Down!"

"It'll be okay," said Loup.

Feeling they weren't reacting fast enough, the bodyguard fired a burst from his submachine gun. Loup tried to reach back and grab the man, but he slipped instead, and fell down the steps. The other man caught him.

"Why are you shooting them!" yelled Loup.

"I didn't shoot them," said the other guard, rushing down. "I told them to get down and they didn't. We're here to protect you, not them."

There was more gunfire outside, louder.

It was dank in the basement. The only light came from a red glow in the distance, at the far end of the wall, the side closest to the river.

"Come on," yelled someone near the light. "They'll be inside any second."

"But the others," said Loup.

"It's you they want," said the man who had grabbed him earlier. "Come on. Move!"

Fisher steadied himself between the two pilots, looking out the front windscreen as the helicopter hurried northward. The bearings Roberta had given him corresponded to an old wharf along the river in Yonkers, just north of New York City. It was an area of old warehouses, nestled so close to a massive sewer plant that even the hardiest riverfront developer wouldn't take a chance on rehabbing.

"What kind of situation are you expecting?" asked the copilot.

"Lots of guys making money," said Fisher.

"You think you need backup?"

"Maybe some wheelbarrows," said Fisher. Then

he thought better of it. "You got a patrol boat around somewhere?"

"We have a patrol craft down by the bridge. Ten minutes away."

"See if they can come up. What are the Yonkers police like?"

"No idea."

"Call them and have them meet me," said Fisher, as the helicopter began angling toward land.

Loup ran through the open door and out onto the narrow landing flanking the building. Pebbles and bits of glass crunched beneath the soles of his shoes as he ran. The air smelled like water, heavy with the odor of the river. The shooting continued behind him. A boat revved its engine at the end of the wharf, fifty feet away.

Loup started for it. By the time he was halfway, his lungs were screaming in agony.

Everything had happened so quickly—the phone call, the shooting. Maybe it was a setup.

It had to be a setup, Loup thought.

He stopped short.

"What are you doing?" yelled the bodyguard behind him, catching up.

"How do I know Freeman didn't set this all up?" asked Loup.

"Come on, asshole." The man grabbed him, pushing him toward the water. "If Chris was going to kill you you'd already be dead."

It was good logic. But just as Loup started to run, something whizzed overhead. The boat exploded in flame.

"Holy shit!" yelled the helicopter copilot as a fireball exploded at the edge of the river. "What the hell is going on over there?"

"Looks like a billing dispute," said Fisher, moving to the back. "Get me as close to the fire as you can without getting burned."

Loup rolled on the dirt and battered cement, unsure how he had fallen to the wharf. There was another loud bang behind him as something exploded in the building.

"They have RPGs!" yelled Loup's bodyguard. "Get into the water!"

The metallic rap of a silenced MP5N submachine gun followed. Loup started crawling toward the edge of the dock. The boat that had been his escape route continued to burn, its glow turning everything red.

He was in hell.

Bullets splattered to his right, ricocheting into cement splinters. Then the gunfire stopped, and for a moment he heard nothing, then a few groans, and in the distance a helicopter.

Loup started to pull himself up. Suddenly his right leg hurt, then his left. It was as if a bee had stung him, once, twice, three times. Then the pain became more intense. There was another sound, metallic, and a wave of nausea rode over him. He felt himself pulled upward. He thought he had fainted, thought he was dreaming—but then he fell back hard, spinning onto his back.

A man with a Beretta 9 mm stood over him.

"This is what happens to people who double-cross Mr. Wan!" yelled the man, extending the pistol toward Loup's forehead.

"Put the gun down!" said Fisher through the chopper's PA system. "You're under arrest!"

The man on the wharf didn't react.

"Can he hear me?" Fisher asked the crew chief.

"He hears ya," said the crew chief as the man on the ground aimed his gun toward the helicopter.

The pilots turned the chopper hard toward the gunman, dazing him temporarily with a burst of wind and grit. The man slipped and fell; scrambling to his feet as the helicopter banked, he ran toward the river.

"Down, I need to get down!" yelled Fisher.

"Don't be a fool!" said the crew chief. "The patrol boat's on its way. Let them take care of this."

"Get the pilot to land me on the wharf."

"No room to land."

"Then get the chopper low enough so I can jump. Let's go!"

The helicopter fluttered lower. Fisher saw the gravel of the wharf in front of him, then pitched out through the door.

The ground was farther than he thought. And harder.

He groaned and cursed as he rolled. Flattened, he grabbed his pistol from his holster. But there was no one to fire at—half of Wan's men had fled into a boat on the water; the other half were in two vans speeding down Riverhead Avenue, away from the approaching police cars whose sirens had helped warn them away.

Loup's bodyguards were dead.

As was Loup, who lay faceup, a bullet hole in his forehead.

"Damn," said Fisher, gazing downward. "Why the hell did you have to get yourself shot for? Damn." He kicked the ground. "You ruined my day, you know that?"

FIVE

Damsel in Distress

1

YONKERS

Fisher stood on the landing next to the warehouse, gritting his teeth. Then he heard a yell from inside the building, and realized there were still people in there. He spotted the door and ran to it, wrapping his hand in his jacket sleeve as he pulled at the handle, worried it might be hot. But there was little to burn in the basement. A few wisps of smoke and steam escaped from the gap above the door.

"Hey!" yelled Fisher, taking a step inside, but unable to see.

"Help! Help!" yelled someone.

"Where are you?" said Fisher, plunging into the darkness.

"Here!"

"Where the hell is that?" he shot back. "Keep talking! Talk!"

The person who'd called to him coughed. Fisher angled in the direction of the sound, his eyes adjusting to the dim light. He heard a rumble above him, as if a bowling ball were being rolled across the floor above. He looked up and realized the sound had come from flames racing across the rafters, the old wooden floor easy fuel.

"Talk to me!" shouted Fisher, pushing on.

The person moaned instead. Fisher saw something move. He jerked forward, then reached down and grabbed at the black lump in front of him. He got hold of the back of the man's shirt.

As he pulled him to his feet, there was another rumble behind them. Fisher turned in time to see part of the ceiling collapse, sparks raining down as the beams gave way.

"Not good," he muttered.

The air was thick with smoke. The man Fisher had grabbed coughed viciously, his body shaking. Fisher turned to his left, thinking he might be able to drag him back up the stairs. But the space above the stairs glowed red.

"We're going out the way I came," Fisher said, pushing his shoulder under the man's arm.

Fingernails dug into Fisher's arm and side. Fisher decided that meant *Fantastic, let's hop right along.*

Fisher put his head down and willed himself forward. A fallen beam burned on the cement floor, a long string of red and black, flames and embers.

"Hold your breath," Fisher said. "More damn smoke down here than in the restroom at the Super Bowl."

The entire building began to rumble. Embers fell in huge chunks. Fisher ran toward the door as a large part of the ceiling collapsed. A shock of air pushed against him—

And then they were out.

Fisher fell onto his back. His rescuee rolled on top of him.

"Ever think of going on a diet?" grumbled Fisher, crawling out from under him.

The first fireman reached Fisher a minute later. By then the warehouse, its timbers old, was a massive wall of flames.

"You gotta get off this wharf," the fireman shouted. "Are there more people inside?"

"I don't know," said Fisher.

"There's an ambulance up by the road."

"You can take him there, but he's under arrest."

"What?"

"Until I can figure out what's going on. FBI," added Fisher, belatedly pulling out his ID.

The fireman helped the man up, and all three started walking back toward the road.

"Why am I under arrest?" asked the man. "I didn't do anything. Thugs came in and started shooting at us."

"Who?" asked Fisher.

"I have no idea. I'm a trader."

"You work for Loup?" Fisher asked.

"I'm not saying anything until I know what the hell's going on."

The ambulance was just pulling up in front, a pair of Yonkers policemen directing it in. Fisher called them over, told them he was an FBI agent, and after making sure they were suitably impressed, told them the man he'd rescued was his prisoner.

"I shouldn't be arrested," insisted the man. "What have I done? I haven't done anything."

"You're a material witness at the moment," said Fisher. He turned to the cops. "I'll collect him later. But I don't want him walking out of the hospital. His life is probably in danger."

A paramedic took the trader and helped him into the back of the ambulance and the policemen watched. Another, this one a woman, took Fisher's elbow.

"You have first-degree burns," she said. "Were you in the fire?"

"I'm all right," said Fisher.

"Did you swallow smoke?"

The paramedic was short, with a thin, pretty face and a body that seemed perfectly curved even beneath the stodgy blue uniform she wore.

"Sir?"

"I'm okay," he insisted. "I've gotten worse burns from my toaster."

"It's about *time* you called me!" said Festoon a few minutes later when Fisher dialed his cell phone. "Where the hell have you been?"

"Running down your conspiracy theory."

"My conspiracy theory? My conspiracy theory?"

"Don't worry, boss, I'm giving you full credit on this. I'm no glory hog."

"Fisher, the secretary of state—*the* Secretary of state—just called me at home. Why the *hell* did you arrest a Chinese diplomat for terrorism?"

"I didn't know about the arson and murder at the time."

"Murder? Arson? What the hell is going on? Where are you anyway? What are those sirens in the background?"

Fisher sketched out what he knew, and some of what he was guessing—that Jonathon Loup was working with the Chinese, in the person of Wan's assistant Thomas Zhou, to manipulate energy prices and otherwise benefit. Somewhere along the way, very recently, there had been a falling-out. Fisher was only guessing that the tip-off to Homeland Security about the oil tanker had come from Loup, though at the moment he didn't have evidence to that effect, aside from the fact that he had boarded a train heading to the place where the call had been made.

"But we'll have a lot more evidence inside his office here," Fisher told Festoon. "Which is why I need the best crime scene people here by daybreak."

Part of the building collapsed behind him. At the rate this was going, another dozen fire companies might be more useful.

"Where is this Loup?" asked Festoon.

"I'm looking at him."

"Is he going to cooperate?" asked Festoon.

"I wouldn't bet on it."

After hanging up with Festoon, Fisher called Rolison, partly to tell him what was going on, and partly to tell him to hang tough with Zhou.

"I intend on it," said Rolison. "Guess what. The boats in the ferry attack? They were rented, not stolen. They used phony credit cards at both places. We haven't been able to track the names yet."

"Okay."

"One of the clerks wanted more ID. So they gave them a driver's license. The name's wrong, but guess whose number is on it. Zhou's. Looks like you got this guy nailed twelve ways to Saturday."

"Does Wan know that?"

"Oh, yeah. He was in here raising a stink when I got the information. He left real fast when I told him. The lawyers are still here, though."

"Where was it you said Wan lived?"

"I didn't. And I won't. No way, Fisher. No way. You go through channels on this from now on."

Fisher would have gotten Wan's address eventually, but before he had a chance to decide what he would say to make Rolison relent, he got a call from Stendanopolis on the West Coast. Bernie had just been called by Festoon, who was wondering what the hell he was doing in California when all the action was back east in New York.

"I hope you told him you were holding down the fort," Fisher said.

"I told him things were jelling out here. Did Samie get a hold of you?"

"Not yet," said Fisher. He looked at his Black-Berry. He'd missed several calls, including hers.

"One of her people cracked that code. It goes into the telemetry unit and sets something in the rocket so that it sends false signals, or old signals—I don't know the technical details. She's still working on it if you want to talk to her."

"Did you tell Sandra that?"

"The rocket lady? No, I figured I'd talk to you first."

"Good," said Fisher. "I'll handle it."

"So the Chinese blew up the rocket, huh? Wow."

"Don't jump to conclusions, Bernie."

"But you had that guy arrested."

"He had nothing to do with the rocket."

"Damn, Fish. Talking to you makes my head hurt."

2

NEW MEXICO

Gene Ng was right about the way the instrument data worked—each launch vehicle had its own set.

But the ground unit was always the same. And maybe, Sandra thought, that was the key.

The investigation had focused on the launch vehicle—not the ground sensors receiving the information. They'd naturally assumed that they were right, and for good reason. They simply recorded what they got from the rocket. And as long as the data was within expected parameters, they'd never be questioned.

The more Sandra thought about it, the more she became convinced that the instrument data from the area where the explosion occurred had to be wrong—there was no way it could have tracked so perfectly with the last launch. But if the numbers didn't come from the rocket, maybe they came from the ground unit.

Or rather, they were wrong in the unit the whole time.

She pulled the manual describing the software

programming for the units—several pages of very dense prose and many flowcharts—and determined that it might not be very hard to leave the data intact. All you really had to do was delete the instruction that reset the "flags" relating to the flash memory.

Was the unknown transmission responsible? There was no way to be sure until it was decrypted. Perhaps. Or maybe it just turned off the instrument transmission from the launch vehicle, and something in the ground unit prevented them from realizing there was a problem.

Possible, in theory. But who would do all that? And more important, why?

If the transmission from Icarus was involved, then Icarus had destroyed its own satellite.

Unlikely.

Yet the more she thought about it, the more it seemed the only possible explanation.

She went over to the launch center and looked at the gear. It didn't seem to have been tampered with. But what would she look for?

Sandra stared at the console. She was alone in the bunker. It was after six, and there was no one else at the site, save a lone security man at the fence.

Thoughts cascaded through her mind, technical problems mixing with emotions. She thought of her father, and Andy Fisher, and Kathy; she thought of her dream to build rockets and send them to space.

Terhoussen a saboteur and murderer?

It didn't seem possible. He was dismissive, aloof, cold—a whole thesaurus of adjectives that grouped with those sorts of terms.

But he was also a genius and a visionary.

And what was the definition of that? Someone who would do anything to see his dream succeed?

What would she do to succeed?

Anything. Or nearly anything. And maybe that was the problem—maybe she didn't want to accept the fact that she had overlooked something and made a mistake.

Her cell phone rang. It was her boss, Phillip Sihar. He wanted to talk to her before she went home for the night.

"As a matter of fact, I wanted to talk to you," she told him. "I'm over at the test range. It'll take me a few minutes."

"Take your time."

Em watched through the binoculars as Sandra Chester's car cleared the gates of the launch area. He waited a few moments before following her, waiting to make sure she had a good lead.

It was still daylight. It would be better, easier, if he took her at night. For now, all he would do was hang back and see where she went.

Sandra's cell phone rang soon after she turned out of the gate, the jangle startling her as she drove. She had to stretch to get it, flicking it open just before the caller would have gone to voice mail.

"This is Dr. Chester."

"Sandra, this is Andy. What's up?"

"Oh, how are you, Andy?"

"Long story," said Fisher. "What are you doing?"

"I—I don't know. I wanted to talk to you. I have a theory," she said.

She stopped speaking, her mouth suddenly dry. Her theory seemed too far-fetched to share with him.

"Listen, we're working on that encryption," said Fisher. It was hard to hear him with all the background noise on his phone.

"Where are you? There's so much noise in the background. Police sirens. Is that a helicopter?"

"Just a typical night in New York," said Fisher. She heard him fiddle with the phone. "That any better?"

"Not really."

She glanced up and saw a car approaching in her rearview mirror. It was a small speck in the right-hand corner.

"You still there?" asked Fisher.

Sandra watched the car growing in the mirror. It was moving incredibly fast.

"Can I call you back when I get to my office?" she asked Fisher. "I'm on the road and I don't like talking while I'm driving."

"Tell me about your theory first."

There was something about the car behind her— it was moving way too fast. Crazily.

Sandra felt the pit open in her chest. She dropped the phone on the seat next to her. The car behind her was closing in. A tandem truck came over the rise ahead.

The idiot was going to try to pass her and slam head-on into the truck.

She pulled off the road. The car whizzed by.

Em saw Sandra pulled off to the side of the road ahead. The crazy driver in the Impala had nearly hit her.

He'd also nearly hit Em. Jerk must have been on meth.

Should he pull over? He could pretend there had been an accident, get her to look at his car . . .

No. Too risky in daylight. He edged into the other lane as he drew close to her car, and turned his head, making sure she wouldn't get a look at his face.

Sandra sat shaking in the car for nearly a full minute after the speeder passed. Finally she took a breath, then a deeper one. She reached over and picked up the phone.

"Andy, are you still there?" she asked.

"Where are you?"

"I'm between the test range and my office. Some jackass just tried to kill me."

"What?"

"No, nothing. I didn't mean it like that. Just some jackass driver. Probably a drunk." She took another breath. "My theory is a little—maybe it's paranoid. The instrument readings may be from the last launch. I'm going to have some tests run on the receiving unit in the morning."

"Listen, I don't want you to do anything until I get out there, okay?"

Something in his tone touched something inside her. It seemed patronizing, as if he didn't trust her.

Or was she just being overly sensitive? God, she hated acting like a little girl.

"I don't need you to tell me what to do, Andy."

"Hey, that's not what I meant."

"I have to go," she said. "I'll call you tomorrow."

"Listen, Sandra. Hey—"

She clicked off the phone, ending the call.

3

YONKERS

"Hey! You Fisher?"

"Who wants to know?" said Fisher, debating whether to call Sandra back or not. With all the red lights flashing, he couldn't make out who was walking down the street toward him.

He was wearing a suit. So he had to be either a detective or—

"Johnson, New York office," said the agent, flashing his FBI credentials. "Man, everybody in the world is looking for you."

"It's that lottery ticket I bought a year ago, right?"

"You gotta call Rolison. You gotta call your boss. I think there's somebody from the State Department that wants to talk to you yesterday."

Fisher glanced toward the river. The Coast Guard patrol craft and helicopter were out in the middle of the river, playing their searchlights on the water.

"You hear what I said?" asked Johnson.

"Hold on a second."

Fisher hit the redial on his phone. Sandra didn't answer.

"Hey," he told her voice mail when it connected. "This is Andy. Listen, you took what I said completely the wrong way. You have an interesting theory but we have to flesh it out. Call me back. Just don't talk to anybody else about it until you see me, all right? I'll be there tomorrow—tonight if I can swing it. All right? Call me back."

He snapped the phone shut and looked at Johnson.

"Women," said Fisher.

"Uh, listen, Agent Fisher—"

"Andy," said Fisher. "How long you been with the Bureau?"

"Me?" Johnson curled his arms in front of his chest. "Two years."

"You think you could take charge of this scene?"

"Take charge?"

"The people who blew this up probably worked for the Chinese—for Wan and the guy on ice downtown, Zhou. I think some of them are in the river. The Coast Guard may have grabbed them. If that happened, you want them separate from Zhou. Have the Yonkers cops put them in some sort of isolation. Call me and I'll tell you what to do."

"Call you?" Johnson held out his hands. "You never answer your phone. That's the whole reason I'm here."

"In the meantime, make sure this warehouse, the whole area is secure. It's off-limits from this point on. Get the fire department and the police to stay out of it."

"What are you going to be doing?"

"Going to New Mexico to see a damsel in distress."

4

NEW MEXICO

Sandra stopped in her office before going up to see Phillip Sihar. She splashed water on her face, gathering herself together, then redid her makeup and lipstick.

The woman staring back at her in the restroom mirror had bags under her eyes.

Of course she did. She hadn't slept.

Sandra closed up her bag and started for Sihar's office. Fisher's tone had annoyed her, but he'd only been echoing her own doubts. Still, the right thing to do was to delay the launch.

"Ah, Sandra, good," said Sihar, rising as she came in. "How are things at the range?"

"They're good."

"We are ready for the launch?"

"Well . . ."

"I told Dr. Terhoussen that you remain reticent to give approval," said Sihar. "That was the word I used. Reticent."

"That's a good word," said Sandra, surprised. "I am reticent."

Sihar shifted in the chair. It was a fancy mesh and steel model, advertised as being adjustable in a hundred different ways to fit the human body. Whatever ways he had tried, they hadn't worked; he looked nearly as uncomfortable as a human could be, short of torture.

"I don't think we should launch until the investigation is complete," Sandra added.

"Yes, I know that is your position. And I have never gone against your opinion. I told Dr. Terhoussen this, too."

"Thank you," she said.

"Yes, I said that my top scientist, my right hand, has questions of the launch, reticence," said Sihar. "So I do not know how to proceed."

Sihar's awkward English told Sandra that another shoe was about to drop. Still, the fact that he had at least brought up her reluctance to Terhoussen was a sign of respect.

"He wants to talk to us—to you especially," said Sihar. "We'll have dinner."

"When?"

"Tonight. I offered to pick him up at the airport, but he already had arrangements. So he will meet us at Corscico's in Alamogordo. We should leave soon," Sihar added, glancing at his watch. "It will take us an hour to get there."

"Tonight? I'd really rather not."

"Did you have plans?"

Sandra thought about lying, but it was too foreign to her nature. She shook her head.

"We're going together, you and I?" she said.

"Yes. I will drive."

"Let me just lock up my office, and I'll be ready."

5

NEW YORK

To get from New York to White Sands airport—the
closest airport to Punchline's offices—would have
meant waiting until the morning, and then spending
the better part of a day catching planes and making
connections.

That was far too much airport coffee for Fisher.

A year before, he had done some work on a case
involving the U.S. Air Force. The work had pissed a
lot of people off. Most of them were no longer with
the service.

It had also helped two or three people get pro-
moted, including one who made general.

The general answered on the second ring.

"Sorry to call you at home, General," Fisher told
him, without any other introduction. "The thing is, I
have this critical case and I need to get to New Mexico ASAP. Faster than that, if possible."

"Andy Fisher?"

"I really need a hand here. I hate to call in favors,
but it's important."

"What time is it? What are you telling me, Fisher?"

"I'm telling you that I was checking my files and saw a sheet of paper relating to a Ms. Danafellow and I was wondering how in the world it got there."

The general sucked a very large and hurtful gulp of air.

"Where exactly are you?"

Thirty minutes later, Fisher stepped out of a New York State Police helicopter—another favor bank cash-in—and ran across the concrete apron to a waiting Gulfstream G100, known to the U.S. Air Force as a C-38. It was a small executive-class aircraft capable of cruising just under the speed of sound. Usually used by high-ranking Air Force and government officials—on occasion, the speaker of the house was ferried home in this particular aircraft—it was equipped with a full suite of communications gear—a fact the crewman in charge of making Fisher's flight "*com*-for-able" emphasized.

The crewman was a tech sergeant whom Fisher suspected had been shanghaied into the assignment, or at least had not expected to be flying tonight; he and the pilots as well as the plane were designated as backups in case another aircraft needed servicing. Fisher didn't particularly care about the job assignments, however, or the sergeant's drawn-out pronunciation of fricative consonants; all he wanted to do was get to New Mexico as quickly as possible.

"Four hours, tops," the sergeant told him. "You do have to turn off your cell phone, because we're about to take off."

"I have to turn it off?"

"Haven't you ever flown in an airplane before? It can screw up the radar stuff."

"That's just bullshit, isn't it?" asked Fisher.

"Maybe. But if it messes up the microwave in the galley, you won't be able to have popcorn with the movie."

Fisher held up the phone and killed the power.

"I'm guessing you want coffee," said the sergeant.

"The stronger the better," said Fisher.

"Milk?"

"Milk's for sissies."

The sergeant nodded approvingly. "Buckle up while I make the joe."

Two cups of coffee and approximately three hundred miles later, Fisher had the sergeant acquaint him with the communications gear. The sergeant hadn't been exaggerating—the plane's systems allowed Fisher to talk, e-mail, text, and IM with anyone anywhere in the world. He could do it in any number of encryptions, and a machine would translate into nearly every known language, including those of several extinct American Indian tribes. The aircraft also had access to an immense directory of contact information; essentially, he could reach out and touch anyone in the world.

Fisher used the system to access his voice mail and began listening to the accumulated messages. None were from Sandra; the bulk were from his boss, easily ignored.

And then there was Tommy Dolan, the New York

City detective investigating Kathy's murder. His message was a simple "Call me."

Fisher tapped the number Dolan had left; he got the detective's voice mail. He left a message, then he had the sergeant help him locate Dolan's home phone.

Dolan answered with a grunt meant to warn off bosses seeking overtime work.

"This is Fisher. FBI. You wanted to talk to me about Feder."

"Oh, Fisher." Dolan's tone changed, becoming almost abjectly apologetic, and Fisher realized immediately why he'd called. "Listen, I thought I owed you a heads-up."

"Nothing, huh?"

Dolan started talking about his other assignments. Even though the murder had received a huge amount of attention in the local media, that attention was now gone. Without any real leads, his boss had shifted manpower away, and though officially the investigation continued . . .

"So you didn't find any connection to Santa Clara?" said Fisher.

"Nothing physical."

The financial condition of the company was the link, but getting from that to the actual murders would be difficult.

"What do you think of Terhoussen as a suspect?" said Fisher.

"Terhoussen? The company president?"

"Yeah."

"I can't see him killing somebody."

"Company is in financial trouble," said Fisher. "The only person who seems to know everything that's going on is worried, maybe going to turn him in—"

"Way different kind of crime scene, Fish. You know that. It's going to be messy, or there's going to be signs that he cleaned up."

"Unless he hired somebody."

"Sure. But you have evidence? That he's involved, I mean."

"Nothing direct."

"The only way I could think it works," said Dolan, "is that he comes into New York, has some sort of argument with her, goes to some bar out in Brooklyn, finds a Russian illegal, pulls a wad of cash out and tells him to go to town." Dolan whistled. "Not gonna happen."

"What if Terhoussen was in town earlier," said Fisher. "Or maybe he hired somebody in California, and they flew to New York."

"Lot easier to kill somebody on their home turf. And besides, Terhoussen told us he came in that morning, and came straight from the airport," said Dolan.

"You checked on that?"

"I got somebody at JetBlue says his name was on the manifest. Hey, listen, Fish," Dolan added, "my wife is making faces at me, if you know what I mean."

"Did you check that room for bugging devices?" asked Fisher.

"Where?"

"The hotel room. Terhoussen's room, too."

"Bugs?"

"Yeah. There were a lot of spies at the conference. I wonder if they were being bugged."

"No. Never even thought of it."

It was probably too late to check now—definitely too late—but Fisher offered to arrange to do so anyway. Dolan reluctantly agreed.

"You think a spy killed her?" he asked.

"No," said Fisher. "But maybe they know who did."

The spy connection was improbable, but Fisher called Rolison anyway. He didn't want NYPD to drop the case, and as long as they had to let someone in to sweep the room, it was still active.

"Where the hell are you?" asked Rolison. "Your boss is calling me every ten minutes."

"You hook Wan into the attack on Loup's place yet?"

"Ain't gonna happen, Andy. You know that."

"Are you trying?"

"Shit yeah, I'm trying. And by the way, I heard you shanghaied one of Peter Roscoe's guys into watching the place for you."

"He looked like a bright kid," said Fisher. "Listen, I need a pair of rooms swept for bugs in Manhattan. Who do I talk to about that?"

"You're looking for Fritzy Sherman. You know him?"

"No. What's his number?"

"You ain't gonna get him at this hour." Rolison gave him the number anyway.

"You pulling credit card accounts and travel information on Loup?" Fisher asked.

"Loup? Of course. I got somebody sitting with the Visa people right now. American Express is—"

"Can you do me a favor and add a couple of names? Actually, a whole company of names."

"This is related?"

"Tangentially. I think."

The people Rolison was working with were efficient, and had the information for him within an
hour. Fisher needed help—and another cup of
coffee—from the sergeant, but he was able to open
spreadsheet files showing charges Icarus's various
employees had made over the past year. Nearly two
dozen employees were authorized to use company
credit cards, and the FBI bank liaison had pulled all of
the accounts. She had also cross-referenced, using the
account information to pull personal accounts as well.

The result, unfortunately, was too much information. Fisher had over a hundred accounts to look at,
with charges stretching back over the previous year.

Terhoussen was the one he was most interested in.
But his information showed only one purchase of a
New York–bound plane ticket over the past twelve
months. And there were no New York charges until
the day of the murder, either. The first charge was
dinner, not far from the hotel, about an hour after the
plane landed. There was a restaurant charge on
AmEx in Chicago at 10:45 that morning, right before
his flight.

It did not appear that anyone else who worked for
the company had flown to anywhere other than New
Mexico over the past few months.

With one exception—James Edmunds, Kathy's
assistant, who'd been to New York for a few days.

And who, Fisher recalled, had made a point of
saying that he had never been there in his life.

Which left about a one-week hole in his memory, if
the charges on this personal card were to be believed.
They'd been posted six weeks before the conference.

"Say, you think we could change our flight plan?"
Fisher asked the sergeant.

6

NEW MEXICO

Phillip Sihar was in a particularly expansive mood as they drove to the restaurant, telling Sandra first about his visions for the company—a launch every two weeks by 2012—and then talking about the importance of space in general. The existence of the human race, he said, depended entirely on exploration of outer space. Humans had already blown their chance on Earth; if the race was going to survive beyond the next millennium, it would have to do so outside of the solar system. Adam and Eve—or rather, two hundred Adams, two hundred Eves—would settle down on a new planet and take another shot at it.

"You may think I'm crazy," Sihar said, "but I believe we've been down this road before. It's very possible we originated somewhere else. Neanderthal man died out. They're gone. We killed them. We were smarter. An alien culture."

Sandra didn't say anything. When Sihar got like this, he was looking for an audience, not a discussion.

And besides, she wasn't in the mood to talk about the future of the human race, or space exploration. She was thinking about what she was going to say to Terhoussen.

She wanted to confront him. No, what she wanted to do was scratch his eyes out for ruining her rocket. The urge burned deep within her, the impulse so strong it tensed all her muscles, and she found her fingers folded into fists when she looked down at them, halfway to the restaurant.

She reminded herself that she was a scientist, and a scientist waited for facts. A scientist channeled passion. You couldn't be a scientist without passion— there were so many reversals, so many obstacles, that if you didn't have passion, you would never survive. But you channeled it and used it to get you up on the mornings when you felt you couldn't climb out of the dark hole.

She would gather information, as a scientist. And then she would give it to Andy.

Now she felt bad for hanging up on him. She'd listened to his message twice.

She'd call him after dinner.

No, it'd be too late. He'd either be sleeping or on the plane coming out.

It will be good to see him.

The idea surprised her. It was true, certainly, but it still did seem a little surprising.

They reached the restaurant ahead of Terhoussen. Sihar was still on his talking jag, barely taking a breath as they were shown to the table. The country's power problems were just the tip of the iceberg, he said. They were going to be solved, though perhaps not by Terhoussen. Though he believed in Terhoussen's ideas, he didn't have 100 percent confidence in the scientist's ability to run a company, a necessary skill for success in the field, for practical success. Even a man like Thomas Alva Edison had trouble translating his inventions, and those of his shop, into marketplace successes.

Edison was Sihar's favorite role model. He always used Edison's full name, pronouncing AL-va with a heavy emphasis on the first syllable.

"Energy is the easy problem," said Sihar, waving his hand as the waitress approached with their drinks. "Energy can be solved. And then the climate. In ten years, the work on that will materialize, as the crisis continues. The weather changes will force solutions. But what we cannot cure is the anger. Everyone at their heart, very angry. This causes the war. This is what will kill us in the end."

Having reached his philosophical end point, Sihar took his drink, a Scotch and water neat. Sandra had Pellegrino, carbonated Italian mineral water. The small bubbles burst in her mouth, the fizz tickling.

She looked up and saw Terhoussen walking across the room, brushing off the waitress's approach.

He looked straight at her, arrogant, confident.

"Doc-tor Terhoussen, you have made it to join us," said Sihar, his awkward choice of words broadcasting his nervousness.

"Yes," said Terhoussen, sitting.

The waitress followed Terhoussen to the table. Sihar held up his drink for a refill. Terhoussen ordered a light beer, then looked at Sandra.

"We have several beers," said the waitress.

"Whatever," he said dismissively, not even bothering to turn toward her. "Why do you think the launch should not proceed?"

"I think we should wait until we know precisely what the cause of the accident was," said Sandra. His sharp tone somehow made things easy for her. "You don't want to lose another satellite."

"Am I going to lose another satellite?" Terhoussen turned and glared at Sihar. "This was a one-time anomaly. Your people said so. The NASA people seemed to agree."

"Well," started Sihar.

"Even a one-time anomaly has to be explained," said Sandra.

"The report said the pressure built up," said Terhoussen. "Clearly this is because of a manufacturing defect. Poor machining."

"It's possible," said Sandra.

"You improved the piping and your inspections." Terhoussen ignored the returning waitress, much as a man walking down a sidewalk would ignore an ant. "So then there should be no more anomalies."

Sihar began to talk, trying to steer the subject into more neutral ground by complaining about the paperwork involved with the insurance companies. This was a highly specialized field, and it was not possible to fully insure the rocket against failure, not at a reasonable price. The satellite was fully covered, but the technicalities involving the rocket made for many headaches.

"Your satellite was fully insured," said Sandra, interrupting as Sihar took a sip of his Scotch.

"Of course," snapped Terhoussen.

"Have you even been paid yet?" she asked.

He waved his hand. "These things take time. Don't worry about my affairs—concentrate on your own."

"I'm just wondering why you're so willing to risk such an expensive piece of equipment."

"The underwriters give us problems, too," said Sihar. "This is not something to worry about. The expensive part of the system is the idea, not the satellite itself."

"I would think the expensive part is the implementation," said Sandra.

"Money cannot be a substitute for vision," said Sihar. He leaned toward Terhoussen. "If you will permit me to say, you are a visionary."

Terhoussen ignored him. "When would you launch?" he asked Sandra.

"When I have a definitive cause."

"And when would that be?" His tone implied he expected the answer would be never.

"It might take some months. Certainly weeks."

"I lose my funding without a successful demonstration by the end of the month," said Terhoussen. "The money goes back into the pool, and I have to demonstrate my worthiness again. The political process makes it highly likely that we won't get it—even though our system is nearly ready to go online. Our money will go to build some bridge in the Alaskan tundra."

The words practically spit from his mouth.

"You don't understand," Terhoussen continued. "This is the way it works in America. Some crackpot congressman or senator wants to run for another term, and the only plan capable of supplying electricity for the next hundred years is crushed."

He wasn't just arrogant, Sandra thought; he despised anyone that stood in his way. Maybe even people in general.

So he was capable of murder. Definitely.

The waitress took their order. Sihar began talking about NASA, of the difficulties in dealing with them. Terhoussen sat silently. Deciding she needed to re-group, Sandra excused herself to go to the restroom.

There were times when risk had to be avoided. The difficulty was knowing when they were.

Terhoussen leaned back in his seat. Sihar contin-ued talking about NASA. He had started by talking about how dysfunctional the agency was, but now he had moved on, expressing his admiration for the people there. Despite their bureaucratic problems, the agency employed some of the brightest people he had ever met. They were capable of great things, said Sihar, if the administration would get out of their way, if the politics were flushed from the system, if . . .

If, if, if. That was how great ideas died, thought Terhoussen.

If.

"I had a consultant check over your preliminary report," Terhoussen told Sihar abruptly, cutting him off. "He believes that you are covering up for sloppy practices. To him, the cause was clearly a malfunc-tion in the piping. There's plenty of precedent."

"Sloppy?" Sihar's eyes narrowed. "I assure you, we do not cut corners."

"The past is immaterial." Terhoussen waved his hand. "It's the future I'm worried about. That satel-lite must reach orbit. And your contract guarantees me a launch."

"Well, the way it is worded—"

"It's airtight. I had my lawyers double-check it. I double-checked it. We need to launch on schedule," Terhoussen added, leaning forward. "Do you believe in this project?"

"Of course. I've said so from the beginning. No one else has backed you the way I have."

"That's true," said Terhoussen. "So now I need you to back up that belief with actions. I need the launch."

Sandra could see Sihar's pout from across the room as she returned to the table. Clearly Terhoussen had said something that deflated him, though that might have been something as simple as telling him that his vision of man's future in space was daffy.

The waitress arrived right behind her with their food. Sandra unfolded her napkin meticulously, observing the two men clandestinely, waiting for one of them to speak.

It was Sihar who broke the silence.

"This eggplant is very good," he said. "Delicious."

"Hmmmm," said Terhoussen.

"And your fish, Doctor?" Sihar asked.

"Fish."

Sihar managed an ironic smile. Sandra could tell that he was coaxing himself back into a good mood. He turned to her. "Your pasta?"

"It's very good," she said, though in truth she barely tasted it. "So, Doctor, what would you have done if the launch vehicle hadn't blown up?"

"I'd be in Arizona right now, overseeing the process of generation," he said. "We would be preparing to connect to the power grid."

"That quickly?"

"You're a woman with some ambition, are you not?"

"Well, yes. Of course."

"Then you must learn not to accept delays. You must always move forward. People delay for no reason. For trivia. This one wishes to spend the afternoon talking to their girlfriend. This one thinks that a ball game is of interest. What are these things? What use are they?"

"Not everything is of immediate use," said Sihar, trying to interject himself into the conversation.

"I've heard rumors that your company was close to bankruptcy," said Sandra.

"Rumors." Terhoussen picked up his napkin and wiped his mouth.

"Without the launch, you'll go bankrupt," said Sandra.

"Without the launch, the penalties you will owe my company will more than take care of any financial difficulty," said Terhoussen. "Concentrate on your job, on proper inspections."

"I'm trying."

"Good. Then we are all agreed. The launch will proceed." Terhoussen pushed his chair back from the table. "If you'll excuse me, I have other business."

7

SANTA CLARA

The local detective handling the Debra Ferris murder case had gone to Sacramento on another case, and given the hour—a little before ten—the desk sergeant could only offer a beat cop to help Fisher.

Which was just fine with him. Preferable, even. The cop had only been on the force for a few months, and Fisher was the first FBI agent he'd ever met in the flesh. *Ruin 'em while they're young* was a motto to live by.

The first thing he noted when they drove up to Edmunds's condo was the Porsche Boxster parked in the driveway.

"Who's visiting?" Fisher asked the cop.

"Dunno."

"I thought maybe you'd ask your computer there," said Fisher.

"Oh, yeah. Right."

The officer pointed the little camera on the dashboard at the car, and within moments the registration information came back.

The car belonged to James Edmunds.

"What's a car like that go for, you figure?" Fisher asked.

"Fifty, sixty thou. Depends on the options. Porsche can have a lot of options."

"Used, maybe less, right?"

"Looks like he got it new," said the policeman, looking at the registration data. "It's less than a year old."

"Leased?"

"No, this would say." The cop pointed at the screen. "Besides, the plate would be different if it was leased. You see how it's bent up at the corners? That's an old plate. Was probably on whatever car he used to have."

"Which would be what?"

The officer hit the touch screen. Another registration came up. "Used to be on a Honda Civic. Six-year-old Honda Civic."

"Maybe he got a good deal on the loan," said Fisher.

"Nah." The cop flicked back to the previous screen. "No lien holder, see? He bought that car with cash."

In the kingdom of Silicon Valley, where stock options and ridiculous windfalls had once been the rule, it was not exceptional for an administrative assistant to buy a Porsche. Still, it was a talking point, and Fisher opened with it as soon as Edmunds came to the door.

"Nice car," Fisher said. "Yours—or a girlfriend's?"

"Um, just me," said Edmunds, who'd thrown on a pair of jeans before answering the door. "Who are you?"

"Andy Fisher, remember? Investigating Kathy Feder's death."

"Oh, yeah." Edmunds nodded. "Yeah."

"This is Officer Winston," said Fisher, gesturing to the cop. "He's riding shotgun. Can we come in?"

"Did you find out who killed her?"

"I can't really discuss the case out here," said Fisher. "I don't want to wake the neighbors up."

"Oh, yeah. All right. Okay."

Edmunds pulled the door back and let them in. The condo was furnished in a mix heavily favoring hand-me-downs, with the exception of an IKEA television stand. That investment had been necessitated by a sixty-inch, top-of-the-line LCD TV, which was flanked by a pricy set of speakers.

"Coffee?" Fisher asked.

"Coffee?" echoed Edmunds.

"I'm just asking because Officer Winston looks like he could use some."

"Sure, I can make some coffee," said Edmunds.

Fisher followed him into the kitchen. "You were right," he told Edmunds.

"What?"

"Kathy didn't have any boyfriends. Why do you think that was?"

"Um—I don't know." Edmunds measured out two scoops of Chock Full o'Nuts, then started to push the basket back into Mr. Coffee.

"Better make the whole pot. Here, let me." Fisher took the can and began dumping coffee into the filter. "I think she probably worked too much. That's my theory."

"About Ms. Feder? Yeah, I think you're probably right."

"So she knew everything going on there. Everything."

Edmunds's eyes seemed to wake up suddenly, the lids moving wider apart.

"When you went to New York City," Fisher asked, filling the pot with water, "what did you do?"

"New York?"

"You have coffee cups in here someplace?" asked Fisher, opening the cabinets.

"Uh, up here, yeah." Edmunds took out two cups.

"None for yourself?" Fisher asked.

"I don't drink coffee after six o'clock."

"You probably want to tonight," said Fisher. "Does this Pause and Serve thing work?"

"Uh, not too well."

"I can wait." Fisher folded his arms in front of his chest. "So. New York?"

"I was in New York," said Edmunds. "Like two months ago. Just as a tourist."

"So how come you told me you'd never been there?" Fisher asked.

"Did I?"

"Yeah."

"I was playing hooky from work. I'd called in sick."

"Man, you're a rotten liar." Fisher turned to Winston. "You take milk, don't you?"

"Sugar, too," said the patrolman.

"I didn't—you know, I faked that I was sick and I worried," said Edmunds. "I thought—"

"You thought I'd squeal you out?" said Fisher.

"I don't want to get fired," said Edmunds.

"Nice car," said Fisher. He pulled out a chair. "Did I say that already?"

"Uh, yeah. Thanks."

"How'd ya pay for it, James? Good loan deal from the bank?"

"Something like that."

"How come they didn't take a lien on it?" Fisher waited until Edmunds's eyes started to close. "James, you're going to have to stop lying here or I'm going to have to read you your rights. Sit down and let your tongue do what nature intended."

Edmunds reached to the nearby drawer. Fisher saw Winston starting to react, and put up his hand. Edmunds was only getting some spoons.

The coffee was done. Fisher filled three cups, passing them out one at a time.

"Who'd you talk to in New York?" he asked, sitting down.

"I . . ." James stopped talking.

"I'm sorry, James, but I can't hear you."

"This guy. I don't know his name."

"Would you recognize him if I showed you a picture?"

"Maybe. I—I don't know. I should—maybe I should talk to a lawyer."

"You need a lawyer?" asked Fisher. "The answer's that bad? What did you talk to him about?"

"Just—nothing, really."

"Well, if you didn't talk to him about nothing, then I guess you don't need a lawyer."

"They told me—the information they wanted was, it was nothing important," said James.

The cop started to say something. Fisher gave him a death stare and he shut up immediately.

Kids.

"I'm here about Kathy Feder's death," Fisher told Edmunds. "Murder."

"I don't know anything about that. Not a thing."

"You didn't hire anybody to kill her when you were in New York?"

"No! *No!* Kill her? Hire somebody. What the hell?" Edmunds nearly dropped the coffee cup. As it was, he splashed quite a bit of it onto the table.

"The guy you met hired you to spy for him, is that what you want to tell me?" asked Fisher.

"I . . . well, spying . . ."

Edmunds fell silent. Fisher took a sip of coffee, then another.

"Officer Winston might be right about needing a lawyer," said Fisher. "I mean, I could put you under arrest. I might put you under arrest. If I put you under arrest—would you have somebody you could call? A lawyer I mean. Or somebody who could recommend a lawyer."

Edmunds didn't answer.

"Could you call your mom or something?" Fisher asked.

"My family's in Wisconsin," Edmunds said weakly.

"What kind of cleaning detergent do you use?" asked Fisher.

"Huh?"

"To do the sink and stuff."

"I guess Comet."

Fisher nodded. "It's got an ammonia smell."

"How do you know?"

"I stuck my nose in the sink just now, filling the coffeepot." Fisher got up and went to the cabinet beneath the sink.

"Is it always Ajax?"

"Comet."

"Right. Is it always Comet?"

"Yeah, I guess."

"But never lemon."

Edmunds shrugged. "I'm not big on lemons."

"The guy who hired you—he gave you a name?"

No answer.

"Chinese guy, stands about five seven, eight? Weighs, I don't know—one forty, maybe. On the skinny side. Eats pretty well. Mighta taken you to a place in Chinatown he goes to a lot."

"It wasn't a Chinese guy at all. He was white."

"White?"

"We met at a diner. In Brooklyn."

"Brighton Beach?" asked Fisher.

Edmunds shrugged.

"Son of a bitch," said Fisher, pulling out his cell phone.

8

NEW MEXICO

Sandra and Sihar spoke little during the rest of the meal. The waitress came and cleared the table. Sihar asked for the check.

"We should have coffee," said Sandra.

"I don't know."

"We should have coffee," she insisted, touching his hand.

"Tea for me," he told the waitress.

"I think there's a possibility Terhoussen sabotaged our rocket," Sandra told him when she had left. "Or one of his people."

Sihar looked at her, so surprised he couldn't speak.

"The telemetry between the ground station and the satellite before launch. It was longer during the launch than during the simulation sessions."

"That's to be expected."

"No. There were two sets of encryptions, as if there was another message embedded in the standard set," said Sandra. "And he won't tell us what any of the telemetry is about."

"We wouldn't give him our code."

"We would if he asked, if it was relevant to our system, or its failure."

Sandra explained her theory of what had happened with the rocket, and how the telemetry could get past their own gateway. Parts of it seemed a little far-fetched to her as she spoke—not for technical reasons, but it just seemed unlikely, since it assumed evil motivations. But she pushed on, laying out her case, and by the time she was finished, she thought it had to be the truth.

Sihar listened in stunned silence, as if receiving the news that a close relative had died in an incredible accident.

"I don't know about this," he said finally. "We have no evidence of a pressure buildup."

"The explosion is the evidence."

"And then the values the instruments read—"

"Exactly the same as the last event."

"They should be the same."

"Similar, within tolerances. Not necessarily the same."

"I don't know."

"I can show you the simulations."

"I'm sure that the numbers will bear you out," he told her. "But it is not the simplest explanation. A burr in the pump or the line seems more logical."

"They were inspected and tested."

"True, but you and I both know those things, sometimes, the circumstances, even in the best conditions, flaws are inevitable. There are defects that do not show up. We often don't test for them. Take the space shuttle—"

"Phillip, you're not listening to me."

"I am."

The waitress approached. Sandra watched her set down the tray and carefully pour Sihar's tea. The woman seemed to sense her customers' tension— their companion had left in the middle of dinner, so how could she not? But she worked to appear oblivious, concentrating on getting the hot water to the precise level in the cup, pouring out Sandra's coffee so that there was room for milk and sugar.

Probably she was worried about her tip, Sandra thought. People who had had a difficult time over dinner were undoubtedly poor tippers.

"I think we need considerable proof to make such an allegation," said Sihar when they were alone. "This would be a crime. And what would be the motive?"

"His company is in financial trouble. With the explosion, he gets the insurance money. You see how he brushed it off?"

"I don't think he brushed it off. And he still needs the grant—he could have gotten that."

"This way he gets both," said Sandra.

"I think you misjudge him," said Sihar. "He's not concerned with money. He has his vision. You should understand this. You're not concerned with money."

"I wouldn't try to bankrupt another company."

"Oh, we're not bankrupt." Sihar took his teacup in both hands and blew gently on the surface. "We will survive."

"Would we survive another explosion?"

He took a sip, then put the cup down, spooning in more sugar before tasting the tea again.

"If what you say is true, and I do not believe it," Sihar added quickly, "but if what you say is true, and

Icarus were somehow responsible, if this was sabotage rather than a deficiency—"

"A *deficiency*?"

"A malfunction, then we would have nothing to worry about. There would be no need to sabotage us a second time."

"You think I missed something in the design?"

"Sandra, if I thought that, would I allow a launch to proceed?"

"You think that the inspection was bad."

"It was the preliminary finding. I'm not insulting you," said Sihar. "It would be my responsibility. We've strengthened the piping, all of it. There is no longer anything to worry about."

"Whenever you're ready," said the waitress, slipping the check onto the table.

Sihar tried to make conversation several times on the way back to the office, but Sandra said nothing.

"I am taking what you say very serious," declared Sihar as they neared the office, his grammar once more betraying his nervousness. "Very serious."

"Seriously," said Sandra.

Her correction silenced him. He drove her to her car in the parking garage. The area where the murder had occurred was still blocked off by orange cones and yellow crime scene tape, and Sandra had been forced to park on the fifth level, the very top of the garage.

"You are going home," Sihar said, pulling next to her car.

"Of course."

"I just didn't want you to feel that you have to work. You work so hard."

"Thank you, Phillip."

She opened the door and got out.

"I am very seriously thinking of this," he told her as she opened her car door. "Very seriously."

It was impossible not to think that he was patronizing her—impossible not to imagine that he would have treated a male employee, a male scientist, very differently.

But the result would still be the same, Sandra realized as she got into her car. The result would still be that the launch would go on, because Sihar felt he was obligated to proceed, and because he felt he had figured out what the real cause of the explosion was.

Her negligence.

Sandra rolled down the ramp, working her way out of the parking garage. The coffee had made her jittery.

A few hours before, she'd been ready to go home and go to sleep. Now she was wired. She needed to burn off some of the adrenaline, slow her mind down.

She drove out of the lot. It was late now, closing in on midnight.

She decided she'd drive a while. Drive and settle her mind as the road unwound in front of her.

Em waited until she had passed before starting his engine.

The Ford hummed to life. He put it into gear and pulled out onto the road, waiting until the intersection to turn on his lights. Then he started after her.

He would kill her tonight and be done with it. He wanted to get away, cut loose for a while. Maybe he would go to Mae Sai in Thailand, or maybe go across to Techilik in Burma. He could get women cheap there, and the action was good. He would need to be out of the States for a while anyway.

He could drink there, if he wanted.

Her taillights were ahead. She was driving slower than normal. Em took his foot off the gas pedal, slowing down.

Then he saw that she was going past the highway that led to her house. She was heading north, driving out into the stretch of open desert.

She was making it easy for him.

Sandra felt her mind starting to ease, her thoughts beginning to drift. There were old Indian ruins ahead, a pueblo she'd walked through a few times. She thought of them now, reminded herself of how to relax.

The night was clear, the moon not quite full but strong nonetheless. Sandra cranked down the window and felt the air streaming around her.

Not quite peace, but it would do.

Just as the tension slipped out of her neck, she noticed headlights in her mirror. The calmness she had felt depended on a feeling of isolation, and it started to evaporate.

She glanced at her speedometer. She was only doing forty, her speed reflecting her mood. She gave the car more gas, accelerating slowly. Then, impulsively, she pressed down harder. The Cayenne's motor roared. The acceleration pushed her back in the seat.

She could be alone if she wanted.

It took a moment before Em realized that she was accelerating quickly.

She was on to him.

He had to take her now.

He stepped harder on the gas.

Sandra felt a slight sensation of weightlessness as the car came up over a rise. It was still gaining speed, moving toward sixty, past sixty to seventy, to eighty.

The other car was staying with her.

She pushed hard on the gas pedal. The Cayenne was an SUV, but it was also a Porsche, and the turbocharged engine had more speed in her than practically any other engine on the road.

I shouldn't go this fast, Sandra realized as the speedometer topped a hundred. *It's dark. I'm being foolish.*

She took her foot off the gas and touched the brake. As she did, the wheels hit sand in the road, and she felt the rear end begin to slide to the left.

Em sketched a simple plan. He would drive alongside her, shoot her, disable her, then come back and finish her off. After that, he would be done.

Her car was fast; his was just a Ford rental. But eventually he would catch up.

The road straightened, he started to gain.

He was gaining, almost to her.

Then suddenly she was sliding off the road in a skid. As he went for the brake, she swerved back on to the road, back toward him.

The back end of the Cayenne struck the Ford and spun violently. Sandra tried turning the wheel but it didn't respond—the car was whirling in the sand, the tires unable to find any grip.

It stopped abruptly, energy gone. Gravity tugged one last time on Sandra's seat belt, underlining how foolish she'd been.

Dazed, Sandra reached for the window to lower it. The air was mixed with the smell of burnt rubber and exhaust. She thought she smelled gasoline. Panic gripped her in an instant. She pulled off the seat belt, pushed open the car door, and tumbled out, convinced the SUV was going to blow up. She lay on the ground, her brain at the center of a large shell that made the world around her sound like a hush.

The Ford fishtailed back and forth, swerving wildly. Em gingerly applied the brakes, easing toward a stop. He corrected his steering gently, trying not to overcorrect, which would just amplify the car's convulsions.

His speed dropped steadily.

Finish her, he thought.

Now back in control, he braked, then made a three-point turn in the middle of the highway. He could see the other car's lights, askew, off the road, in the distance.

Get up!

Sandra rose and looked at her car. The headlights were pointing toward the road. The left rear fender was bashed and crunched against the tire. The bumper was hanging off. The car was still running, but how would she drive it like this?

There was another car coming.

Sandra moved out to the road, her senses slowly returning to her.

Another car approached. She put up her hands to flag it down, waving. The car's headlights grew.

Something was wrong. It wasn't slowing—

The lights veered in her direction. Sandra ran two steps, throwing herself off the pavement as the car whipped by. The driver hit the brakes and began to turn around.

He's after me!

She flew to the car, pulled at the metal, threw herself in behind the wheel. Door still open, she stomped on the gas. The car jerked, the door slamming back, flying open then slamming closed next to her. There was a high-pitched screech behind her.

The wheel, rubbing against the fender.

She could smell rubber, something burning. The car wasn't right. It didn't move exactly straight. But she had to get away.

The other car closed in, came almost to her bumper. But the Cayenne continued to accelerate, her speed growing.

Go, she urged it.

The headlights started to drop back. Had she imagined all this? Was she crazy?

Someone was trying to kill her.

Terhoussen.

She saw the ruins ahead in the distance on her right. The car pulled to that side of the road, pushing.

"Keep going," she told it. "Go."

She kept her foot on the gas pedal, pushed all the way to the floor. She came to a rise and literally flew over it.

The rear of the SUV cracked as she landed. Something gave way and she started moving much faster. The road forked, one direction toward the ruins, the other due north.

Sandra killed the lights. *Faster, faster,* she told the car. *Faster.*

There was a bang. The car spun uncontrollably. The left rear tire had blown out.

9

AIRBORNE, EAST OF SANTA CLARA

"Bernie, I need you to do two things. Three things."

"Fish. Where the hell are you? You know what time it is?"

"Bernie, if you do these three things, I'll let you call me Fish. Number one, get yourself over to the Santa Clara police station and take custody of James Edmunds. Arrest him on espionage, jaywalking, and whatever else you can come up with. But be easy on him, because he's going to cooperate. Read him his rights, get him a smoke, that sort of shit."

"Espionage?"

"Number two, get a subpoena and sweep the Icarus building for bugs. Do it before they open. They may have another mole on the staff. I'd kind of count on it, actually."

"A subpoena? Where the hell am I going to get a judge at this hour? Let alone get the paperwork written. Plus—"

"Number three, I need a car to meet me at the airport in White Sands. I don't know if they do rentals there, but even if they do, they'll probably be closed.

I can jump a car if I have to, but then they'll probably put some sort of police bulletin out on me. So figure something out."

"Are you talking about White Sands, New Mexico? When?"

Fisher leaned forward and asked the sergeant how long it would take for the aircraft to reach White Sands. He told him it would be about half an hour.

"Half hour, forty-five minutes," said Fisher.

"Where are you, Fish?" asked Stendanopolis.

"Do those three things, and you can call me Fish. I may even buy you a coffee the next time I see you, though I wouldn't count on it."

10

NEW MEXICO

Sandra flew back and forth as the car spun, buffeted by the air bags as they exploded. Her face felt as if it were on fire. Her arms and legs were battered, her shins felt as if she'd been hit with a baseball bat.

In shock, she pulled open the door of the car and stepped out into the night.

Run!

Run!

Her legs didn't answer her brain. She was standing, her arms could move, but she seemed to have no control over the rest of her body.

The ruins were to her right, a quarter mile away. The moon turned the brown top a silvery yellow.

Run!

She leaned forward and began to walk toward them.

Em couldn't believe he had missed her.

And now he had lost her.

He backed off the gas, then took a deep breath, trying to clear his mind. His head was in a rush.

Damn New Mexico. Damn everything.

He'd left the locator device in the backseat, thinking he wouldn't need it. He pulled off the side of the road, then reached over the seat for the bag. It took nearly a minute to warm up, and by that time Em had already realized what it was going to tell him—he'd missed a fork in the road in the darkness.

He almost missed it again. The Ford's wheels barely held the pavement, squealing as he cranked the wheel to take the turn.

He glanced at the tracker on the seat. She was ahead, less than half a mile away.

His headlights caught the car, off the road.

She was almost to the ruins when she saw the headlights sweeping up behind her.

Sandra had to hide.

She'd been a fool to say anything to Terhoussen. But she was going to escape. All she had to do was last until morning. She'd hide in the old ruins.

Sandra tripped over a rock and fell into the scrubby grass. The car had stopped on the road behind her, near her car.

Go, she told herself. But she stayed on the ground, unable to move.

There was only one place she could have gone—the ruins of the Indian village out ahead.

Em doused the lights, then turned off the engine. Reaching up, he clicked off the interior light, then opened the door. He took his bag with him and went around to the trunk. He took his night glasses, and another magazine for the pistol. He left everything else in the bag, closing the trunk lid on top of it.

I could use some vodka right now.

That would be his reward. In Burma.

Sandra heard the car door close. She strained to see the vehicle, but all she could make out was a low lump of gray at the edge of the field near the road.

The first place someone would look for her was near the car. After that, they would think of the ruins. So she had to stay away from there, find a different place to hide.

Stay by the road. Maybe another car would come.

She began crawling, holding her breath, going south parallel to the road. After a few yards she stopped and listened.

He was walking out into the field. He was on her right, somewhere, but she couldn't see him.

Sandra flattened herself against the ground, willing him to move past quickly. She tried to soften her breath, push it into the dirt so it couldn't be heard. She sank against the ground, burrowing in.

Her phone!

Calling 9-1-1 in the desert wouldn't do anything. But she could call Andy, and he'd get help.

Once the killer was past her.

Something moved on his left, vanishing as Em turned toward it.

There was a row of scrub trees there, a shadowy

fence that cut off his view. There were bushes beyond them.

She must be hiding there.

Em went down on his haunches, slowly scanning the area. He knew something was there, but couldn't see what.

There was a time like this in Afghanistan. He'd had to be patient—very, very patient. And quiet. The man he was after had been wounded, and was out of bullets, though of course Em hadn't known that.

It was a matter of patience.

Em rose, gun ready, and began moving to his left, closing in on the trees stealthily.

There was another time, one when things didn't go as well. A pair of raghead bastards pulled an ambush on his unit. The bushes were a decoy—they came from behind him.

As Em started to turn around, one of the bushes leapt upward. He fired twice into it, then a third time, before realizing it was a deer.

As soon as she heard the shots, Sandra leapt to her feet and ran the final five yards to the road. She raced toward the cars, heart pounding.

Maybe he'd left the keys in his car, she thought. She ducked down, hands cupped against her face, looking through the window.

No such luck.

Quietly, she slipped back down to the ground and crawled to her car.

Where was her bag? It had been in the front with her. She didn't remember seeing it when she got out.

The door seemed to make an enormous amount of

noise when she opened it. She pulled it open and crawled inside. It was dark in the car. She felt around, didn't find her bag.

At any second, she expected to be pulled out. She could almost feel the hand gripping her.

Sandra backed out of the car, then slipped to the back. As she pulled the door open, the overhead light flashed on.

She froze.

Her purse was on the floor. She reached, grabbed it, pushed the door closed, and rolled backward toward the road.

The flash of light came from behind him, a small light magnified momentarily by the night glasses. By the time Em turned there was nothing.

Son of a bitch, she's back by the cars.

He turned and started to run, holding the goggles with one hand.

Vodka, he thought. *I will drink a liter of vodka.*

11

NEW MEXICO

Fisher made a show of buckling his seat belt as the Air Force jet dropped into its final approach to the White Sands airport, the engine noise increasing as the ground came up. The wheels bounced softly on the ground, and a long whistle announced that they had touched down. As the aircraft taxied toward the terminal area, Fisher took out his cell phone and started to call Bernie Stendanopolis to find out where to meet his car.

"Uh-uh," said the sergeant, wagging his finger.

"Hey, we're on the ground," said Fisher. "What's it going to mess up? Your coffeemaker?"

The sergeant frowned, but said nothing further as the phone came to life. It beeped. Fisher had missed a call.

He paged it up, assuming it was Bernie.

But it wasn't. It was Sandra Chester. She'd called just a few minutes ago, but hadn't left a message.

Fisher looked at the number, highlighted it, and pressed the button to dial.

Sandra's phone began to vibrate as she crawled through the ditch that ran on the far side of road's shoulder.

Sandra grabbed it before it rang. She didn't bother to look at the number.

"Help me," she whispered. "I'm along County Route A161, near the Indian ruins. Get the police."

She slapped the phone off, tucked it into her pocket, and continued moving along the road.

"State police don't have a patrol there, Fish," sputtered Stendanopolis. "You want to talk to them yourself?"

"Get the sheriff, then."

"I'm working on it. I gotta put you on hold."

"Call me back."

Fisher clicked the End Call button and bounded down the steps of the aircraft, running toward the terminal. A security guard came out from the door, unsure what was going on.

"You know where there are Indian ruins around here?" Fisher asked.

"Mister, this is New Mexico. There are Indian ruins every half mile. And by the way, it's Anasazi. It's polite to use the tribal name."

"How about Route A161? You know where that is?"

"Uh, what's that, a country route? Out beyond the missile range property, right?"

"How far?"

"Hour. Hour and a half." The guard shrugged. "Depends on how fast you drive."

"Shit," said Fisher. He started toward the rental counter at the other side of the hall. A single clerk was waiting there, sent by Stendanopolis.

"You must be Mr. Fisher," she said as he approached, holding out her hand. "I'm the manager, Dot Pierce. I was at home when Mr. Stendanopolis called. But I know how important this is and we're proud to serve the federal—"

"Those the keys?" asked Fisher, scooping them off the counter. "Where's the car? Out back?"

He started for the door.

"Wait, there's paperwork," shouted Pierce.

"Bernie'll get the paperwork."

The door closed behind Fisher before he could hear what else she had to say. Fisher sprinted toward the lot.

Just as he reached the row of cars, he heard a helicopter landing on the runway.

Fisher changed direction.

Em knew that she had gone back to the cars, but now she was gone, hiding again.

His head was pounding. The collar of his shirt was soaked in sweat.

You had to think like the enemy to survive. That was how he had gotten out of the ambush.

Where would he go, if he was a woman, scared, maybe hurt in a car crash? Dazed.

She'd start walking back to the base, looking for support. Another fire team would be watching.

Em got in his car, started it. The dirt was so loose he had trouble getting it back onto the shoulder. He drove down the road slowly, watching.

She was here somewhere, he knew it.

He drove a little farther, then stopped in the middle of the road and got out. The ragheads were very good at lying in the middle of terrain, this terrain, just watching, barely breathing.

He took the night glasses and began searching.

"I don't care who the hell you are, you gotta pay before you play," the helicopter pilot told Fisher. He held up his iPhone. "I need a credit card number. I key it into the phone, and the charge gets approved. Then you can fly."

Fisher, of course, was overdrawn on his own cards, and the Bureau's automated system would never approve the five-thousand-dollar charge the helicopter pilot wanted.

But to every problem there was a solution. Fisher reached into his pocket and took out the paper with the list of Hhou's charges.

"All right, here we go," he said. "Nine-eight-zero . . ." The pilot keyed the number into the app on his iPhone.

"I don't like the fact that you're not showing me a physical card," said the pilot.

"Do you honestly believe that a federal agent would be involved in credit card fraud?" said Fisher, strapping himself into the seat of the Bell JetRanger.

Sandra saw the car stop in the distance behind her. She waited until she heard the door open, then she scrambled from the ditch, running as fast as she could across the highway, back in the direction of the ruins. As she ran, the shell that had settled over her head melted away.

She heard something. A shot.

She fell to the ground.

Finally, Em had found her.

She was down, though he couldn't be sure if he'd hit her or not. It wasn't important, though. She'd be dead soon, either way.

He got back in the car, turned it around, and started down the road slowly.

I'm not in Afghanistan, he told himself. *She's not a raghead. Take it step by step; easy, easy. No mistakes.*

"Two places I can think that you're talking about," the helicopter pilot told Fisher, handing him the iPhone as they headed eastward toward County Route A161. "Which one do you want?"

Fisher squinted at the phone's screen. He could hardly even see the lines, let alone make a guess about how significant they might be.

"Take me to the ruins closest to Punchline Orbiters," he decided. "They're in a big corporate park about—"

"I know where they are," said the pilot. "Hang on."

Sandra heard the car coming for her.

Run!

She pushed herself to her feet and bolted toward the ruins. They were two hundred yards away, more, pale ghosts in the distance.

The car wheels squealed. The headlights spun around behind her and started to grow.

He was driving out after her.

The Ford got about twenty feet off the road before it started to bog down. He stopped, opened the door, and got out calmly.

She was forty yards away, in the lights.

"Don't make it hard on yourself!" he yelled.

Then he fired.

The shot disappeared in the darkness.

He fired again. She kept running.

Sandra couldn't stop. There was no way to stop.

The terrain slanted to her left, throwing her off balance. She stayed upright, arms out to help. Something smacked her right shoulder blade—a ricochet from a bullet that struck a rock behind her. She winced, but kept going. Then something stung her in the side. She folded to the ground, falling in a heap.

Finally.

Em held the gun down, walking slowly now, getting hold of himself as he tamped down the adrenaline.

Finally, he could get away, for a while at least.

Finally, he could have a drink. He could practically taste the vodka in his mouth.

He could hear a helicopter nearby, probably crossing south toward the Air Force base. He ignored it, continuing toward her.

Fisher's heart leapt as Sandra went down.

This is where you have to stay calm, he told himself. *Be Andy Fisher. Don't give a shit.*

But he did give more than a shit.

He had about Kathy, and that was the shame of it. He'd let her go, and that was the biggest mistake of his life. It was the one thing he should have fought for—the one time he shouldn't have hid behind his shell, behind the hard-ass he'd become, the bad-joke-making, chain-smoking federal agent who was too cynical, too sarcastic to be influenced by emotion.

But now he had to be Andy Fisher. Because either Sandra was already dead, and he'd failed again, or she was alive, and the only one who could save her was Andy Fisher—irreverent wise-ass who didn't give a shit for anyone.

She was moving on the ground, behind the rocks, where the assassin couldn't see her.

Be Fisher.

"Kill the lights," he told the pilot.

"I thought you wanted—"

"Just turn them off. I don't want him to see her."

"All right, mister, but—hey, what the hell are you doing?"

"Don't drop me," said Fisher, wrapping his hand around the seat restraint as he opened the door to the helicopter. "And don't slow down. Get in close. This PA thing works, right?"

Sandra heard the helicopter almost above her. But it was too late—she knew it was too late.

I'll face him, at least, she thought. *I'll make Ter-houssen kill me, face to face.*

The night suddenly lit as she turned over. He was standing a few feet from her, gun down.

It wasn't Terhoussen at all.

"You don't drop the gun, I shoot you where you stand!" yelled Fisher into the mike. "Drop the gun!"

The man stopped. Fisher guessed he couldn't see Sandra on the uneven terrain, though she was only a few yards away.

"Look, I know you're working for the Russians. You kill her, I got you on murder. Otherwise, it's just espionage. They'll trade you for some shit-ass code clerk in St. Petersburg. Don't be stupid."

Em stared at the rocks. The woman was there, some-where.

Dead, most likely; he'd seen her drop with his last shot.

But maybe not.

The helicopter was directly overhead, so close the wind from the blades threatened to knock him over.

He could shoot her. Get this right, at least.

What sense did it make?

What sense did anything make?

How many times had he cheated death in Afghani-stan? By all rights, he should be dead many times over.

It was the only thing that would stop his thirst.

He lifted the gun to his mouth, and in the same motion pulled the trigger.

12

NEW MEXICO

Fisher leapt from the helicopter and ran to Sandra.

"Hey!" he yelled. "Hey, you all right?"

"I don't know."

She was in shock. She was bleeding from the side. Fisher pulled her shirt away. Rock splinters had cut her, but not too deeply.

"I'm going to put you in the helicopter and have him take you to the hospital," said Fisher. "Can you deal with that?"

"The man with the gun—I thought it was Terhoussen."

"Nah," said Fisher.

"Did he hire him?"

"No, somebody else."

"Who?"

"To be honest, I was kind of hoping he would tell me," said Fisher.

Fisher had her sit up. Her face looked burned, and her hair and cheeks were covered with powder. The air bags in her car had exploded.

He lifted her into his arms.

"Where are we going?" she asked.

"You're going to the hospital," he said, picking his way over the swirling dirt to the chopper.

The pilot leaned over and pushed open the door. Fisher propped her into the seat.

"You got a towel?" Fisher asked the pilot. "Something hit her in the side."

"Got a sweater."

"Gimme."

Fisher wedged it in place.

"Let me ask you a question," Fisher said. "A heat source on the rocket—that could be a laser, right?"

"What?" said Sandra.

"To heat the side of your rocket. They could have used a laser."

"An external source?"

"Because the temperature wouldn't have to rise that much," said Fisher. "When it's under pressure. Charles's law. Mechanical Physics 101."

"Sure—"

"Go!" Fisher yelled to the pilot. He jumped back and slammed the door closed.

Fisher did know who had hired the assassin. Ultimately, at least. The problem was nailing him.

Fisher read the license plate on the rental car to a Bureau researcher back east, and within a few minutes he not only had information on the rental, but had the hotel where the assassin had been staying. The name he'd used was Mark Herat, and it was the same name on his phony Wisconsin driver's license.

He had other names on the other IDs in the false bottom of his leather overnight bag. He also had two passports, one American, one EU. And a diplomatic passport from the Czech Republic, sewed into the lining.

What he didn't have was anything connecting him to Konovalav.

By the time the sheriff's deputies arrived, it was past midnight. Fisher had already found out that Konovalav was booked on a flight arriving in Santa Fe the following afternoon—unless, of course, he somehow got word that his assassin had killed himself.

Fisher gave the sheriff's department some contact numbers, and told them that a backup agent was on the way. He didn't say how long the agent had estimated it would be before he arrived.

"The woman the helicopter took to the hospital—she needs to be protected," said Fisher. "And it would be great if this didn't hit the news media until some time after three in the afternoon tomorrow."

"You don't ask for much," said the deputy in charge.

"And I need somebody to run me down to the airport so I can pick up my rental car."

"That's all?"

"If you could tell me the best place to get a cup of coffee at this time of night, I'd be obliged."

Herat's hotel room was clean, without a suitcase or clothes. The night clerk didn't know anything about him. He'd seen him come in and out perhaps once, or so he claimed. Fisher asterisked the statement mentally when his description didn't match.

There was an Internet connection in the room, which meant the hotel would know where he surfed, but Fisher hadn't found a laptop. He needed permission from corporate to get the list, croaked the clerk. And they weren't open for another few hours.

The bartender remembered Herat, and her description matched.

"Sat there one night, right where you are, had a seltzer," she told Fisher. "Wouldn't touch a drink. He wanted one. I think he was testing himself."

"Reformed alcoholic?" Fisher asked.

"Maybe. But if he was really reformed, he wouldn't have come in here." She nodded at the television screen. "News program came on. He watched it pretty intently."

"What was it about?"

"War thing. Marines being ambushed in Afghanistan. It upset him."

"Afghanistan?"

"Yeah."

The Bureau didn't know Mark Herat. Some of his credit card accounts, however, paralleled a man identified by Interpol as Lopahin M. Janov, suspected of being a low-level Russian case agent. He had been implicated in two murders in Rome the year before, though no formal charges had been filed.

And he had served in Afghanistan, as a sergeant, under Konovalav. He'd been awarded several medals for bravery, and had saved a number of lives, including that of his commander.

Janov's accounts indicated he had been in New York two days before Kathy died. The Bureau would work on filling in the blanks, but Fisher already knew he was Kathy's killer.

Which didn't fill Fisher with the satisfaction he ought to feel. It filled him with nothing, an afterthought, the climax to a play that had ended hours before.

Fisher sat in the bar, waiting for more calls, sipping Jack Daniel's.

"I did remember something else," said the bartender. "He asked me where he could get a battery. Triple-A."

Fisher looked up into the bartender's eyes.

Hazel green. Nothing like Kathy's.

Or Sandra's for that matter. Sandra was pretty, in a scientific kind of way.

And a little standoffish to others, he thought. But that was like him—science was a shield.

"What kind of battery?" he asked.

"He needed them for a tape recorder. Not a tape recorder—it was like a little voice recorder. It was small."

"He showed it to you?"

"Yeah. It was smaller than an iPod. Black. I told him to try the machine in the lobby. That help you?"

"No," said Fisher, pushing his glass across the bar. "But refill this anyway."

The sheriff had left the vehicle at the scene, waiting for the FBI forensics team to go over it. Fisher didn't think he'd be so lucky as to find the recorder in the car, and he didn't.

He did find a matchbook for a bowling alley in the glove compartment. The matches were unused, and since they were under the rental paperwork, Fisher wasn't sure they even belonged to Janov.

"Help you?" asked the deputy watching the car.

"Nah," said Fisher. "What I need is a confession. Kinda hoping I might find one."

"That ever happen to you?"

"Not in this lifetime. But we live for our dreams."

Fisher decided to go back to the hotel and get some sleep. He was halfway there when his cell rang. The number was an FBI exchange. Fisher thought it was Festoon trying to deek him with an unusual number, but he decided to answer anyway—why not give the boss a thrill?

"Yeah?"

"Special Agent Fisher?" said a female voice.

"Last time I checked."

"I, uh—this is Cynthia Cheevers. I was calling regarding Lopahin Janov, alias Mark Herat. We, uh, found another credit card that seems to be associated with your subject and, uh, was used in your area."

Used only twice—once to rent a car, and another time to buy some miscellaneous items at a 7-Eleven.

"Triple-A batteries?" asked Fisher.

"No. It looks like maybe potato chips, coffee, a sandwich. Something like that."

"What about the car?" asked Fisher.

"Still out."

"Does it have a GPS locator system?"

"Yes," said Cheevers. "But it's going to take me a while to run down the proper people to have it activated. I may have to hand this off to the day shift."

"All right. Give me the plate and whatever other information you have on it," said Fisher. "And listen, you're at a computer, right?"

"Yes, sir."

"Can you get me directions to a bowling alley?"

"A specific bowling alley, or just any one?"

"A specific one," said Fisher, digging the match-book out of his pocket.

"Are you going bowling at this hour?"

"Of course," Fisher deadpanned. "There's nothing like knocking things down to get your mind working on a case."

Fisher found the rental car in the parking lot of the bowling alley. This wasn't particularly hard—it was sitting by itself in the corner of the lot, locked up and minding its own business. Nor was he terribly sur-prised: He figured the matchbook had been retained for a reason. Most likely the car was a backup vehicle, prepositioned in case something went wrong. The lot was only a few miles from the airport, and also hap-pened to be on one of the few bus routes in the area.

In theory, Fisher should have waited for a search warrant from the U.S. attorney's office. But he had never been one to go by theories, especially when he was carrying a pick and lock spring.

The car was empty; there wasn't so much as a speck of dust, let alone a matchbook or some other crumb to lead him to the clue.

Fisher leaned up against his rental and took out a cigarette, lit it, then stared at the dark horizon.

Would linking Konovalav to any of this make a difference in the end? The Russian would walk like Wan was going to. If he didn't spook first.

If it wasn't for Kathy, Fisher wouldn't care. An as-signment was a puzzle to be worked out. He'd play it to the end, let the U.S. attorney's office and the state worry about "justice."

But it was about Kathy, at least for him. He wouldn't even have been involved otherwise. Maybe no one would have. The Chinese and the Russians would have battled it out with a dirty American energy trader for the right to control the world's energy supplies for the next millennium.

Lovely.

But it was only love that had gotten him involved. Love. A four-letter word.

What would a defense attorney make of that?

Attorney: *Why did you first get involved in this case?*

Fisher: *Old girlfriend sent me an e-mail and I blew it off.*

Attorney: *Girlfriend?*

Fisher: *Love of my life.*

Attorney: *You? Capable of love?*

"Heh."

Fisher laughed at himself, and flicked away the cigarette.

He started to open his car from the passenger side, then realized the door was locked.

He'd left his keys in the car. It wasn't a problem, since the other door wasn't locked, but what if he had accidentally locked them in? Or lost them and was in a hurry.

Bigger problem for Janov. He wouldn't want to call the rental car company.

Where were the keys? He didn't have them with him.

Fisher went to Janov's car and got down on his hands and knees. There was a nearby streetlamp, but it didn't throw much light, and he had to run his hands under the fender to find what he was looking for.

Three metal boxes with magnets, all with spare keys. Including one that had BOWL imprinted on the nub.

Oh.

Oh!

In theory, Fisher could have picked the lock and then defeated the burglar alarm, getting into the bowling alley without anyone knowing.

But that would have been against the law.

Instead, he picked up a rock from the edge of the parking lot, and threw it through the window.

It took two full cigarettes for the police to arrive.

"Glad you guys could make it," Fisher said, holding up his Bureau credentials. "I think somebody might have tried to break in."

"What are you doing?" asked one of the cops.

"Besides responding to the alarm?"

"You heard the alarm?"

"I'd be pretty deaf not to hear it," said Fisher. He told them that he had checked around the building and didn't see anyone. "I thought we ought to check inside."

"Owner's on his way," said the cop. "He'll reset it. Then we'll have a look."

The owner was about fifty, unshaven and unremarkable, except for the large coffee he had in his hand. It had the dark, meaty stench of home-grown espresso roast. Fisher followed him inside with the others, savoring the aroma. After turning off the alarm, the owner started for the office.

"I found this outside," said Fisher, holding up

the key. "It might be related to the attempted burglary here."

"How do you figure that?" asked one of the cops.

Fisher rolled his eyes. "Because I found it outside."

"But what's the connection?"

"It was outside," said Fisher. He spotted the lockers at the side of the alley. "These lockers over here—anyone can rent?"

"Yes," said the owner.

"I still don't get the connection," said the cop, trailing behind.

Fisher found the locker.

"You know what? You better stand back," said Fisher. "It's very possible this is booby-trapped."

"Really?"

"Fortunately, I worked with a bomb squad when I was younger," said Fisher, pushing in the key. "Guy named Lefty. You know why he was called Lefty?"

The policeman moved back. Fisher opened the door. A voice recorder sat alone in the locker.

13

DALLAS-FORT WORTH AIRPORT, TEXAS

Gavril Konovalav had an hour between flights, which was easy in Dallas if the first plane wasn't more than a few minutes late. But with the plane running about twenty minutes late, Konovalav had to hustle to get over to Terminal B, which was on the opposite end of the airport from where he landed.

He hated taking the Skylink—the self-contained train that connected the airport's six terminals—but from past experience he knew it was the only way he'd make the connection. He trotted up the escalator just as the car arrived, lifting his wheeled bag over the threshold. There were only two other people in the car, and he ignored them as it trundled through the airport, the mechanical voice announcing each stop with the careful attention of an overcaffeinated nanny. Passengers got in, others out; finally they landed at B. Konovalav stepped out quickly, walking briskly down to the main level where the gates were, then threading through the crowd to get to the right terminal area.

Boarding had not yet begun. The plane to Santa Fe

was an Embraer commuter jet, with forty seats. Roughly thirty people were milling around the counter. None of them looked very happy.

"It's a reservation glitch," he heard one of the gate agents tell a customer. She was in her mid-twenties, with a face that would have been attractive had she not been so harried.

"You let that other guy on," said the would-be passenger.

"His seat was confirmed."

"So was mine."

"It's not in the computer at the moment."

"Look at this. It says confirmed."

"My supervisor is on the way," said the woman. "I know there's a hang-up. We'll get it straightened out."

Konovalav went up to the gate. "There's a problem with the plane?"

"No," said the attendant. "Some of the tickets are not going through at the moment. Some are. My supervisor is on the way. Some tickets are going through. If you want, I can check yours."

Konovalav handed it over. The machine beeped.

"Okay," said the woman, a little surprised. "You're in."

Konovalav took the ticket back and walked past the security guard at the gate. He could hear the other passengers grumbling behind him.

The Embraer seats were split two and one. Konovalav's seat was near the wing. He always tried to get one of the singles—he hated sitting next to anyone.

There was only one other passenger aboard, near the back of the plane, reading a newspaper.

Konovalav shook his head. The Americans were becoming as unreliable as the Russians.

"Guess we're the lucky ones," said Konovalav loudly. But the other man stayed behind his paper, unfriendly.

Konovalav stowed his bag, and took his seat. He took out a set of noise-canceling headphones but left them around his neck. Then he took out a book and started to read.

Fisher put down the paper and got up. He walked quickly down the aisle and slid into the seat across from Konovalav. He waited a second, giving Fred from the Santa Fe office time to slip out of the restroom in the back.

"Anything good?" asked Fisher.

Konovalav looked up from his book in shock.

"What's with the reservation computer?" Fisher asked. "Did you screw that up?"

"Me?" Konovalav slid his book into the seat pouch in front of him. "I'd rather suspect you of monkeying with it. It seems to be a habit of yours."

"What are those, Bose?" Fisher asked.

"Yes, they're Bose."

"They work?"

"To an extent."

"I've always thought about getting a pair, but I'm too cheap."

"Not surprising," said Konovalav.

Fisher leaned forward. "Do they serve coffee on this flight?"

"I believe they do."

"Is it any good?"

"Good is a relative term."

While they were talking, the door to the aircraft had been closed. The plane began moving backward from the gate.

"We're taking off?" said Konovalav.

"Looks like it." Fisher checked his watch. "A little early. Better than late, I guess."

"There's no one else on board," said Konovalav.

"You expecting someone?"

"A steward at least."

"I think this is a self-serve flight. You fly out here a lot, don't you?"

"I didn't realize that was a crime."

"I also notice that you went out to San Jose about— what was it, six months ago? Well, San Francisco. But you rented a car and drove over to San Jose. Not that I blame you. San Jose airport's kind of a boring place. No good coffee."

"What is it you're after, Fisher?"

"The idea of San Jose was to recruit the right person, right? Then once you had him, you didn't want to tie him to you, so he had to come to you. I'm guessing there's a cutout in there somewhere that I missed, but that's not really critical for now. Unless you're keeping score."

"I haven't a clue what you're talking about."

"Blowing up the rocket was actually easy, once you had the laser. It's very quick," said Fisher. "The explosion removed the evidence, as long as you knew exactly where to hit. Which, since you were able to get the plans from Icarus, was no sweat. The trick was hiding it. You needed someone on the inside. But Punchline is so small and loyal, and they're tight with their suppliers, so you had to get around that."

"I see," said Konovalav coldly.

"I thought your primary interest was Gazprom," said Fisher. "That's where I went wrong. I mean, I looked at you and the Chinese and I figured that you were after the same thing. The technology. The Chinese would try to buy it. You guys would try to copy it. Cultural differences."

Konovalav said nothing.

"But that wasn't what you were up to. Or at least not all of it. Your bosses are worried about Punchline. Their prices already undercut yours. You get a cut of the launch cost? I mean a fifty-million deal— ten percent is not bad change."

"I really don't know what you're talking about, Andy. Drinking before noon—even in Russia, we frown on that."

"Kathy Feder suspected that there was a spy in the office when she started comparing the bids, right? That's why she had those documents in a separate folder on her computer. And then she figured out that it was Edmunds, though I'm not sure exactly how that happened. She was pretty smart and Edmunds was pretty naive, so maybe she tricked him. He sent an alarm—I don't know yet if it was on that visit to New York, or through a cutout. I will find out, though. You can count on that." Fisher blew a smoke ring. "She did know he was spying, right? Or were you just being preemptive?"

"Katherine Feder I know. Or knew," said Konovalav. "But James Edmunds?"

"I thought he might actually have been involved in the murder or at least cleaning up her place. He's a bit of a neat freak. But he doesn't like lemons. So it wasn't him. I figure you must have gotten another professional to handle the apartment. They did a good job. Your money wasn't wasted."

"I have no idea what you're talking about."

"What about Sandra? Why did she get on the hit list?"

"Sandra?"

"Sandra Chester. Because you thought she figured out how you blew up the rocket? Or was it another competition thing—take her out, and Punchline withers. Her boss is a rocket scientist, but she's the real brains of the operation, isn't she?" Fisher reached into his pocket for the voice recorder. "Or maybe it was a little bit of both, huh?"

Fisher pushed the Play button. Em's voice sputtered from the small speaker.

"Was he a good soldier?" Fisher asked, snapping it off. "I assume he was at one point. Then probably he started drinking, right? No—it only happens that way in the movies. He always drank. Just for a while everyone was willing to look the other way."

"I don't know what you're talking about."

"Then he screwed up in Italy. Nobody saw him for a while. Let me guess—you rehabilitated him."

"I don't know a Janov."

"I guess you don't know what happened to him then," said Fisher. The plane was moving along the ramp, heading in the direction of the runway. "I got Janov. He was trying to kill Sandra Chester. Unfortunately, he killed himself rather than be arrested."

"I'll bet."

"Yeah, well, things like that are known to happen." Fisher held up the voice recorder, then slipped it on. Em's voice rasped from the tiny speaker. "But he left a pretty full record of things before he went."

"He's talking about Afghanistan," said Konovalav harshly. "He was talking about things we did. What we had to do, as soldiers. Your own army has been there. Ask them."

Fisher clicked it off.

"There's seventy-two hours of recording here," he said. "You want to sit through the whole thing?"

"You can't do anything to me."

"You mean, I can't arrest you?"

"You can't touch me. I'm a diplomat."

"Yeah. Everybody thinks that. Kind of a common misunderstanding."

"Where are we going?" Konovalav asked.

"Where would you like to go?"

"I have a ticket to Santa Fe."

"Well, we're heading in that direction."

"You're not going to shoot me, Fisher. You don't do those things in America. I don't believe you killed Janov, either."

"I didn't say I killed him. He killed himself."

"Where are we going?"

"You want a drink or something?" Fisher asked. "I can probably find something for you in the galley. You look pale."

Konovalav folded his arms in front of his chest.

"What do you figure it feels like to fall out of an airplane?" Fisher asked. "You ever wonder? You're in the emergency row. Door might open accidentally."

"You won't do that."

"Did I tell you that Kathy Feder was my girl-friend?"

Konovalav's head fell back against the seat.

"A lot of people think, hey, Andy Fisher. Who

would go out with him, right? He's such a hard-ass." Fisher paused for just a moment. "Kathy and I met each other in college. Strange how things happen. I was a dope, though. I didn't know what a good thing I had. Anyway, time passed. We got on with things. Then she sent me an e-mail the night she died. I didn't realize—well, let's just say I could have been there when Janov was, and I didn't go. So I kind of have that hanging over my head. It's almost like I want revenge."

"Maybe we can make a deal," muttered Konovalav.

"A deal? What kind of deal?"

"I could give a lot of information about our people here. A lot of information."

"Yeah." Fisher stared at the Russian's face. "I'm not interested in information, actually."

"I didn't kill her."

"You told Janov to kill her." Fisher held up the voice recorder. "I wouldn't have believed it, actually. I didn't. The translator went over it twice for me. I didn't take it well."

"I never thought you were an unreasonable man, Andy."

"Why kill Kathy?" asked Fisher.

Konovalav closed his eyes. "It was nothing personal. These things we do—they're never personal. You're the same way, I'm sure."

Konovalav's voice trailed off. His body seemed to have deflated. He'd given up.

"Pull yourself together," said Fisher. "Face it like a man."

The aircraft stopped at the edge of the ramp.

"Shoot me," said Konovalav suddenly. "I'd rather go like that."

"I'll bet."

"Shoot me." He turned toward Fisher. "You can say it was like Janov—I tried to resist when you went to arrest me."

It was tempting, extremely tempting.

"Shoot you because you ordered Kathy Feder to be killed? An eye for an eye?"

"Yes. An eye for an eye. I'm a murderer."

"Same with Sandra Chester?"

"Chester—the scientist? Absolutely. I ordered her killed."

Fisher rose, then reached into his pocket and turned off the other recorder.

"Cuff him," he told Fred, who'd moved up from the back. Then he walked to the cabin and rapped on the door. "We're done," he said. "Yeah, we're done."

14

SAN JOSE AIRPORT

The next day

Not that he didn't trust Stendanopolis, but . . . Fisher didn't trust Stendanopolis. So he substituted coffee for sleep and headed back to San Jose in the morning, hoping to use James Edmunds to tie more of the strings together.

Or any of them. It wasn't that Fisher wanted closure—closure in a case, he had learned, was like using a spoon to stir your coffee instead of a pen. It didn't actually change the chemistry, but it made people feel better about things.

No, Fisher still had a number of things he needed to prove, at least to himself. Konovalav's confession of murder wiped away any hope of diplomatic immunity for the Russian. But the way it looked now, at worst Wan and his right-hand minion Zhou would be recalled, free to return to China and make gazillions there. Loup's death made it easy for the Chinese to skate free. Fisher thought it possible that there would be some sort of evidence against the Chinese in the Russian spying operation; hence his desire to talk to Edmunds.

He got off the plane and walked through the gate door at San Jose, walking through the crowd of people anxiously waiting to board. Clearing the gate area, he realized someone had started to follow him. Before he had time to figure out who it was, the person closed the distance and cleared his throat.

"You're Fisher," said the man.

Fisher looked at the man without stopping. He had a several-day-old beard and sunglasses, along with an L.A. Dodgers baseball cap whose beak rode fairly low over his face.

"And you're who?"

"A friend. Come have a beer," he said, pointing to the small bar at the side of the main mall area.

"Kind of early," said Fisher.

"Never too early for a beer among friends."

Technically, it was, but somehow Fisher's new friend had managed not only to get the bar opened, but to have it serve a pair of beers.

Or at least that was what the waiter offered. Fisher got a coffee.

"How do you like it?" asked the waiter.

"Black. Extra sharp."

"Some good people vouch for you," said the man with the glasses.

"Amazing how many people you can fool," said Fisher.

The man smiled. He kept his head down, glasses on, cap low.

"You need evidence," said the man.

"On what?"

"Something that links Wan to the excitement in Yonkers the other day. Among other things."

"Which Wan?" said Fisher.

The man smiled, but shook his head. "I'm not a fool. Give me your cell phone."

"Why?"

"I don't want you calling anyone."

"Who would I call?"

"Anyone. Don't bother with TSA or the locals. They're not going to help you. Not today, anyway."

"You have a lot of pull."

"Just friends."

Fisher took the cell phone out and handed it over. The man opened the back and took out the battery, then gave it back.

"I can just get another battery."

"You should," said the man.

"How do you know I don't have a spare?"

"You're not the type. There's a self-storage place off 82 south of the city. This key fits a shed there."

He slid a key across the table.

"Am I going to need a bomb squad?" asked Fisher.

"There are a lot easier ways to kill you," said the man, getting up.

"You didn't finish your beer," said Fisher.

"Another time."

"Maybe you might want to," said Fisher. "Because you won't have one for a while."

The man smirked at him. Then turned around.

"You weren't really in the Rangers, were you? That's just something you say because it's impressive. From what I hear, you were a cook."

The man stopped.

"Why kill the kid?" continued Fisher. "Was it a screwup? Did your guy go too far?"

The man frowned, but said nothing.

"You shouldn't have let Loup make a wire transfer to your overseas account," said Fisher. "The IRS has those things nailed twelve ways to Saturday. It was a dumb mistake."

The man—Chris Freeman—started walking again.

"Wan wasn't particularly happy that you killed his people," added Fisher. "I'm glad you were able to pay him back."

Bernie Stendanopolis was waiting for Fisher in the no-parking zone out at the entrance to the terminal.

"He say anything when you arrested him?" Fisher asked.

"Not a word."

"You got the jerk he bribed to get in here, right?"

"On video. And he is singing like a canary."

"I love it when you dish clichés at me, Bernie," said Fisher. "What's with my boy Edmunds?"

"Edmunds is very cooperative. He admitted putting a USB key into the instrument panel when they visited New Mexico, but he claims he didn't know what he was really doing. I kinda believe him, actually. I think—"

"You know a storage place on Route 82, south of San Jose?"

"I guess there's one."

"Let's go find it," said Fisher, holding up the key.

"What's there?"

"I'm going to guess a bunch of evidence connecting Wan to the shooting at the Yonkers warehouse the other night," said Fisher. "Maybe some other stuff."

"Did Freeman give you that key?"

"If the key came from someone we just arrested, you might question whether it was admissible evidence in a case," said Fisher. "The question would be answered in the affirmative, eventually, but it would make a roomful of U.S. attorneys lose sleep for weeks. But if it was something I found on the table of an airport lounge when I was having an early morning beer, hey, what do you know?"

"I don't know anything," said Stendanopolis.

"I do believe you're starting to catch on, Bernie."

There was plenty of evidence in the storage unit, even more than what Wan had anonymously provided to Rolison implicating Freeman's operation in the attack on the nuclear plant. Credit card receipts that led to accounts with big cash withdrawals right before the attack on Loup's Yonkers headquarters. The rental receipt for the van used in the attack, as well as its gas. The address of a restaurant where a surveillance camera caught some of the perpetrators. Rap sheets on several of the shooters. Photos of Zhou meeting a week before with one of them. A trail of bills that showed that Wan personally had paid for some of their expenses. Telephone records for several phones Fisher didn't know existed.

And a tape that had Wan ordering the hit from his car a few minutes after visiting Zhou.

Some of the evidence, to Fisher's cynical eye, appeared, if not outright false, at least tainted. Others, the tape especially, would be of dubious value in a court case. But overall there was more than enough to identify and charge several of the men who'd been in Yonkers that night with second-degree murder, the highest charge allowed in New York State if the victim wasn't a policeman. Getting them to finger Zhou, and then getting Zhou to finger Wan, was up to Rolison.

Which, Fisher gathered, had been Freeman's aim. Pity he wasn't going to be in much of a position to enjoy his revenge. But maybe they'd share adjacent cells.

15

WHITE SANDS

A few days later

T. Parker Terhoussen raised his hands to his head as the rocket climbed from its launch pad. The ground rumbled and shook as it climbed. It began to spin, slowly, the rotation part of its control mechanism.

This one was going to make it. No one was standing in his way now. No more barriers.

He pushed his fingers against his temples. The rocket was becoming smaller.

Terhoussen glanced over at Sandra Chester, standing at the main monitoring panel. She had a serious look on her face, nodding to herself. That told him more than any instrument ever could. She was good, nearly as good in her field as he was in his.

Nearly. Her field was much more developed. His was still in its infant stages.

"See?" he yelled to her. "No problems. The risk was worth it!"

She stared intently ahead. Terhoussen smiled to himself. Within a few weeks, once they were pumping electricity, once the DOE was measuring it, everyone would appreciate his vision. Within a few years, with the country's energy needs completely met, they'd recognize his genius. They'd know that he'd done what had to be done.

"We're counting down to separation," said the controller calmly.

Something flickered to Terhoussen's right. He turned.

It was the annoying FBI agent, smoking again.

Terhoussen shook his head. The man was insufferable.

"Five, four, three, two, one," said the controller. "Separation . . . main stage is gone. We are exactly on schedule, all systems are green and at spec. Injection into orbit is on track for two fifty-three P.M. local time."

"A good launch," whispered Sihar, standing nearby.

"Yes," said Terhoussen. "A very good launch."

"Why wouldn't someone find you attractive?"

"I didn't say no one found me attractive," Fisher told Sandra Chester. "I said I don't have a girlfriend."

"Why not?"

Fisher looked across the wide expanse in front of them. The launch had gone perfectly. With her job for the day complete, Sandra had agreed to answer his last questions so he could satisfy Festoon and Stendanopolis, who had a million reports to fill out.

He'd also wanted to see the launch. Another incident would have meant he hadn't nailed all the facts.

Which happened, from time to time.

Fisher looked far into the distance. The mountains were zigzagged with red. White and brown stones were sprinkled into the slope, like the product of a crazy carnival paintwheel.

"So why don't you have a girlfriend?" asked Sandra again.

"Just lucky I guess. And you don't have a boyfriend. That's hard to believe."

"Most men are intimidated," said Sandra. Her side was bandaged, but it was hard to tell under her loose shirt. "It's been that way since college."

"That was a long time ago."

"Not so long," said Sandra. She smiled at him. "I understand why you became an FBI agent," she said. "You couldn't be dispassionate. A scientist has to be dispassionate."

Fisher laughed. "I thought it was because I was a cynical SOB."

"You're not really, though, are you?"

Fisher declined to answer the question.

"You're pretty good at it, aren't you?" said Sandra.

"Depends who you ask."

"So the Chinese were working with Loup to get the technology," said Sandra. "Loup owed them money but was trying to cut them out, because he wanted it for himself. Meanwhile, the Russians were trying to sabotage us. They wanted Icarus's business."

"They also wanted the technology," said Fisher. "Once they were launching the satellites, they'd be in a much better position to steal it. Or sabotage it. But Konovalav was going to get a piece of the launches, a commission."

"How much?"

"I'm not sure how much—he's come out with three different figures so far."

"More than a million."

"Oh, yeah. So maybe the Russian government really didn't know what he was doing."

"You believe that?"

"I'm pretty cynical," he reminded her.

She gave him a smirk. "That's just armor, Andy. I know you."

"No." Fisher tossed his cigarette to the ground.

"You're not going to leave that butt there, are you? It's littering."

"In the desert?"

"Yes. Which would you rather have clean? The desert or New York City?"

Fisher scooped it up.

"Do you still miss her?" Sandra asked.

"It was a long time ago," said Fisher.

Fisher found his thoughts wandering. He couldn't remember his last conversation with Kathy.

"Are you hungry?" Sandra asked suddenly. She grabbed his arm.

"Yeah. I could use some food."

"Killer chili okay?"

"I knew there was something I liked about you."

"Is that all?"

Fisher opened his mouth to say something sarcastic, then stopped.

"You know what?" he said instead. "It's not."

"No?"

"No." He reached for another cigarette.

"That's a disgusting habit, you know," said Sandra.

"Yeah, I know." He took out the pack, looked at it a moment, then slipped it back into his pocket.

"You don't have to stop smoking for me," she said quickly.

"Who said I was stopping?"

"But you're not going to smoke now?"

"I don't feel like it."

"Not at all?"

"A little." Fisher smiled. "But not so much. Your car or mine?"